Winter's Handmaiden
J.C. Wade

J.C. Wade Originals

Copyright © 2024 by J.C. Wade

All rights reserved.

No portion of this book may be reproduced in any form without written permission from the publisher or author, except as permitted by U.S. copyright law.

For my sisters, Melanie, Valarie, and Karina.
What a wonderful privilege it is to know and love you.

Contents

Prologue   1
Winter Wanes

1. Chapter One   7
   Discoveries

2. Chapter Two   18
   Turbulence

3. Chapter Three   22
   Under the Mountain

4. Chapter Four   33
   Winter Court

5. Chapter Five   42
   Goddess of War

6. Chapter Six   47
   Winter's Throne

7. Chapter Seven   52
   Leaving Oz

8. Chapter Eight   60
   Cailleach's Hammer

9. Chapter Nine   70
   Edge of the World

10.	Chapter Ten	81
	Murder in the Forecast	
11.	Chapter Eleven	90
	Morrigan's Well-Laid Plans	
12.	Chapter Twelve	94
	Bleeding Magic	
13.	Chapter Thirteen	99
	Hellhound	
14.	Chapter Fourteen	103
	The Path Less Taken	
15.	Chapter Fifteen	111
	In With the Dead	
16.	Chapter Sixteen	122
	Death's Door	
17.	Chapter Seventeen	131
	Dealing in Souls	
18.	Chapter Eighteen	144
	A Lesson on Morality	
19.	Chapter Nineteen	158
	A Benevolent God	
20.	Chapter Twenty	163
	Enter Sandman	
21.	Chapter Twenty-One	174
	Cloudy With a Chance of Feasting	
22.	Chapter Twenty-Two	182
	Twenty Questions	

23.	Chapter Twenty-Three The Deep	197
24.	Chapter Twenty-Four Between Worlds	204
25.	Chapter Twenty-Five Medicinals	210
26.	Chapter Twenty-Six A Friend	222
27.	Chapter Twenty-Seven Perfidy	229
28.	Chapter Twenty-Eight Painful Motivation	238
29.	Chapter Twenty-Nine Stay	242
30.	Chapter Thirty Doorways	253
31.	Chapter Thirty-One Brigid's Lamentation	270
32.	Chapter Thirty-Two A Greedy Choice	279
33.	Chapter Thirty-Three Soul Hunting	285
34.	Chapter Thirty-Four Old Wounds	302
35.	Chapter Thirty-Five Just Rewards	307

36.	Chapter Thirty-Six Verdicts	313
37.	Chapter Thirty-Seven A Council of Gods	319
38.	Chapter Thirty-Eight Confessions	325
39.	Chapter Thirty-Nine Hand Fasting	334
40.	Chapter Forty Spring Temple	349
41.	Chapter Forty-One A Fallen God	357
42.	Chapter Forty-Two Brigid's Blood	368
43.	Chapter Forty-Three Dagda	375
44.	Chapter Forty-Four Spring	381
Epilogue		389
Also by		392
About the author		395
Acknowledgements		396
Author Notes		398

Prologue

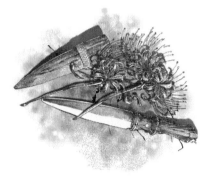

Winter Wanes

Deep under her mountain, Cailleach, goddess of winter, peered into the black pool of the mirrored lake. Shadowed, knobby stalactites above her reflected perfectly below, silent witnesses, leaning ever closer so they might catch a glimpse of the outside world.

No breeze stirred ripples to life upon the glassy surface; the silence that rang in her ears told the goddess that even the great cave she now resided in held its breath, waiting to learn what she might find.

Resting against her staff and breathing heavily from the long descent to the scrying pool, Cailleach shuffled forward until her muted reflection breached the lip of the pond. Wrinkled and white haired as she was now, with eyes no longer as sharp as they once were, still it came as a surprise just how frail she'd become in the long weeks since winter began.

In this state, she could not begrudge the moniker the mortals had given her. They called her a hag, a veiled, bent and ugly thing, reminiscent of the bleak existence they endured under her charge. She had many names, of course, and they varied as widely as the peoples upon the earth, but never before had she lived so fully up to the name as she did now.

Only months ago, she had been young and beautiful and as full and ripe with power as the enduring sun, but long weeks of tending to the duties of the winter season left her weakened. The time for the spring equinox had come and gone, and yet still she remained, withering away like a dried apple. The Goddess of Spring, called Brigid, had not yet come to lay her to rest as was her duty. She had not come to the ceremonial altar to perform the rites, to take her life's blood with the Blade of Somnolence. Overdue as Spring was, Cailleach could not wait much longer.

"I grow weary," she sighed to her companion, Durvan, one of the faithful dwarfs that populated her kingdom.

He made no reply and offered his lantern, the yellow light steady and bright even so far into the belly of the mountain where the very damp of the air clung to their skin, chilling them. The flame shone upon his dark, full beard, revealing the tight press of his lips. He could not hide his worry from her. His black, pupilless eyes spoke for him: she was dying. She'd never died before. It was a strange sensation, this withering of body and spirit.

At the end of each winter season, she'd grown weary of course, as all seasonal gods did. She, like all the seasonal gods, expected fatigue after employing so much of their power in their arts. She eagerly awaited her rest, impatient to pass into the usual deep sleep and wake young again, weeks later, fully refreshed. But Brigid had not come and so winter continued, raging on, pulling from Cailleach's dwindling energy. But Cailleach was not the only one growing weaker as the days passed. The human world suffered as well.

The mortals' cries for Brigid's return—for Spring's return—had so far been ignored. As the humans' winter stores had run light and their bellies burned with hunger, Cailleach's ability to control the elements faded, for just as she brought frost, snow, ice, and bitter wind, so too she kept living things in slumber. Plants and all manner of insects and animals were held in delicate balance by her hand. Without Brigid, the bitter winds Cailleach had brought forth and kept under tight rein would not go quietly as she, herself, so soon would. Winter would lay waste to all living things, humanity included.

"The stairs," she said in a voice like the wind. "I fear the stairs have stolen away my strength." With a soft motion, she bade Durvan light the remaining torches set into the sand surrounding the scrying pool and waited, watching with clouded eyes as the light within the cave grew.

Cailleach hobbled closer to the edge of the pool and used her staff to help lower herself onto the cool sand. With a subtle grunt of effort, she moved her staff from the edge of the water where it radiated cold, already forming a thin crust of ice.

Durvan was returning. She could sense his nearness, eager to remain at her side should she find need of him. Indeed, after her task was performed here, she would most assuredly need him to return to her rooms far above.

Peering more closely into the mirror pool, she narrowed her eyes, faded from purple to violet by the overexertion of her body. Cailleach stretched forth a quaking hand, gnarled and veinous, her fingers stiff and aching, and began the scrying spell, her rasping voice echoing in the chamber. The torch-lit surface of the pool rippled to life as though she'd tossed stones, not a spell into it.

"Show me Spring," she commanded. The reflections of the environment melted away, a swirl of color and indiscernible shapes morphing together to paint a picture. She saw the spring kingdom as it should be, the landscape budding with verdant life, streaming across the mirrored pond as if she viewed the scene from the eye of a bird.

Nests of hatchlings, newborn fawns, sprites and winged fairies of all colors and shapes flitted past her purview. Impatient, Cailleach waved a hand to wipe away the given images and said, "I wish to see the goddess. Show me Spring herself." The images dissolved in a sickening swirl of colors and reformed within seconds, shadows collecting to form a gloomy image.

Cailleach frowned, so discordant was this new image with the bright cheer of the previous scene. She stretched forward, squinting into the dim.

But it was not Brigid's form that appeared, rather that of a mountain hare, snowy white save for the tips of its black ears.

Cailleach took up her staff and stood upon shaky legs with a voluble popping of joints, her frown turning into a scowl. The hare was not in a burrow, or even on the heathland. No, it appeared to be in a cage. "Iron," she hissed with a small note of surprise, her weak eyes catching on the thinly wrought bars encircling the creature. "Someone has caught themselves quite the pet, it would seem."

Durvan approached, his head only just meeting her elbow, a furrow set deeply into his brow. "Is Spring known to take on such a form?"

In truth, Cailleach did not know with any certainty what form Brigid preferred to take when travelling between worlds or kingdoms. Though gods and goddesses, they were bound by rules. Laws constrained their lives as much as those of the mortal world. They were forbidden to enter another seasonal kingdom or into the human realm in their true forms with the exception of the feast days.

Feast days were the days of ceremony and of rites performed, when they would have to enter into each other's kingdoms to perform the rites associated with their authority and duties to keep the mortal world in harmony.

They managed ways around this rule, however. They could possess any living form and travel outside of their kingdom should they feel the need to. An animal or any other living creature could house their spirit for a time, leaving their body behind. Cailleach, for herself, often chose to possess birds, as she found them far faster and easy to control.

Durvan held his lantern aloft and craned his neck to better seen the pool.

"The scrying pool does not deceive," she said, motioning his light away. "Besides, when in use, the pool does not reflect our current environment. Your candle does not affect the state of those we are viewing."

Her eyes found the pool once more, where the image abruptly changed. Gone was the caged hare, replaced instead by an image of a woman, dressed most strangely. Cailleach, who could scry in every time and in any dimension, knew this woman to be far into the future of the human world. Why would the scrying pool show her this woman, so far removed from Brigid and herself, digging in the soil, her dark hair soaking up the sun?

She watched for a moment, waiting, but when nothing of import happened, Cailleach waved an irritated hand. "Show me Spring Court."

The refection of the woman crouched in a dirty hole dissolved, replaced with Brigid's throne room. A handful of tree imps, spry and twiggy, industriously scrubbed the colorful floor tiles on their hands and knees. Cailleach and Durvan both watched intently as a faun entered the scene, carrying a vase of joyous flowers, seemingly at ease.

"Her subjects do not appear troubled," offered Durvan needlessly.

"Mmmph," she grunted noncommittedly. Perhaps, in her weakness, the spell had gone awry somehow. "My power grows thin, Durvan." She had never before experienced such weakness, so pervasive and lasting as it was. Frailness pervaded her, even to her very bones. "Since my magic is failing here, I fear I must travel to the Spring Court to discern what has happened."

To his credit, Durvan did not scoff or ask how she planned to do such a thing. Instead he inclined his head, obedient, and offered himself. "I would go in your stead, my lady, and you give me the authority to speak for you."

The pool, without command, changed once more, returning to the woman living in the distant future of the mortal realm. Both goddess and vassal stared, speechless, at the strangeness of it all.

"Did ye say the right words?" asked Durvan skeptically. "Mayhap ye should end the spell and try again."

Cailleach shot him a quelling look. Duvan's mouth twisted sourly and he nodded, motioning for her to continue. That was as much an apology as she was likely to get.

Still, she did as he suggested and lifted her staff with some effort; the added use of the tool would help concentrate what power she still held. The spark of magic filled her nose. She could almost taste it, like spent ozone after a lightning strike. "Show me the Spring Goddess, Brigid."

The pool's dark surface rippled to life and coalesced into the image of the caged hare once more. Cailleach let her arm fall to her side, her staff nearly touching the surface of the pool. A thin sheen of ice formed there, the moist sand crusting underfoot.

The image shifted suddenly, reforming to the woman from the mortal world. Cailleach narrowed her eyes at the woman, now holding aloft the Blade of Somnolence. *Brigid's ritual blade.*

Chapter One

Discoveries

Maryn stood and stretched, her trowel and dustpan in hand, scowling as every muscle in her body protested. The dig site, not far from the historic thatched Blackhouse Arnol, proved remarkably interesting. The near-constant squatting position required of her for the past month, however, killed her back and legs. Unfortunately, careful excavation required meticulous work done through human touch.

Shaking her head to free her eyes of whisps of hair that had escaped her messy bun, she rubbed her itching nose with her forearm and surveyed the others around her, all as industrious as bees in a hive. Scott, the lead archaeologist, worked a scant six feet away, his dark arms dusted grey as he filled a basket with the Isle of Lewis' rocky soil to be sifted by one of the other members of their team.

The initial investigation of the old site began with the desire to find more artifacts related to the house, barn and byre, but to their surprise, they'd uncovered evidence of something yet to be identified only a hundred meters away, thanks to the modern technology of ground-penetrating radar.

"Do you think it could be Early Modern or . . . or Medieval?" asked Scott, unable to hide his enthusiasm as he filled his bucket. He referred to what was left of the foundation they'd uncovered, his brown eyes full of excitement—excitement she shared. Whatever they'd found had once been timbered, at least partially, evidenced by the small fragments of wood they found.

They'd first noticed the unusual landscape surrounding the dig, a series of sunken parallel grooves that ran a good distance from a nearby, inland lake. While some on her team thought them mere ruts from a long-forgotten conveyance, like the remains of peat farmers' wagons, Maryn believed differently.

She kept her opinion to herself, understanding that the less she shared, the less attention she'd garner from her coworkers. Secretly, she hoped the furrows indicated ancient earthworks, long eroded by the punishing rain and wind that perpetually bore down upon them from the Irish Sea. She sighed, imagining the potential lives from long ago, struggling to exist on the isle. She could almost imagine them.

The University of the Highlands and Islands Archaeology Institute had shown a keen interest in this particular site and, having come into some grant money—much in part to her own efforts—they'd jumped at the chance to advance their limited technological abilities and purchased the ground-penetrating radar technology. Seeing it in action, seeing all her hard work and effort come to fruition on the computer screen had been priceless.

The results from the GPR had appeared in bright lines and splotches, neon reds, blues and greens, outlining a rectangular rock foundation and something *more* that they could not decipher. The small, bright spots of color toward the southern wall sent her heart to racing. The size and shape hinted at a burial site deep in the ageless peat.

While she silently hoped for human remains, the likelihood was slim. Most likely they would find a stockpile of broken bits of pottery or refuse. Finding such a thing was still exciting, though. Archaeologists could learn a lot about people by going through their garbage.

"If not Saxon, then at least Norman," Scott suggested, pulling her from her thoughts.

"Perhaps," Maryn replied. "It's not a clay quarry in any case," she said with a wry smile, referring to an old joke they shared. She loved to tease him for his past exuberance in prematurely announcing his belief that a small quarry pit a construction company in Suffolk had unexpectantly unearthed had instead been a kitchen dump heap dating back to the eighteenth century.

Scott frowned at the neatly stacked stones he'd been unearthing. "It's not large enough to be a dwelling," he muttered to himself, "unless there's more that the GPR isn't seeing."

"Only time will tell." Maryn squinted at the overcast sky. It didn't look like rain, but the very air felt charged, as if an electrical storm brewed overhead. "Do you feel that?" she asked, picking up her trowel once more. "It feels like it wants to rain." She shivered in the cool breeze, pulling her jacket more tightly around herself. The weather had been strange for summer, uncommonly cold and blustery.

Scott glanced at the sky, shrugging. "I don't feel anything. What you're describing is most likely excitement." He wagged his full eyebrows at her as he dumped yet another trowelful of dirt into his bucket.

She huffed a laugh and squatted down, her tools near to hand. "Eager isn't even half of what I feel," she muttered. To be the first people to uncover this space for hundreds, if not thousands of years, made all the toil worth it. If finding precious historical artifacts came with the hefty price tag of a backache, Maryn didn't mind. A body? Even better.

So far they'd found little signs of life within the structure: bits of charcoal in the center, giving evidence to their belief that someone had lived in it, or at least used it for some task important enough to require a fire. A hearth could have lent warmth to the encompassing room, however small. Perhaps other rooms existed, which, after so much time, only the soil make up could identify. They already had several soil samples bagged and tagged, ready to bring back to Inverness.

Outside of the walls, one of her students had uncovered what looked like a long-buried rubbish heap, full of small-boned animals and some broken bits of pottery, well preserved in the boggy soil. They'd, all of them, smiled for days, uncomplaining over the difficult and often tedious work.

They threw themselves into their work after that, renewing their efforts, their delight growing as they uncovered more and more artifacts. Charcoal, slag, nails, and some tool fragments. Maryn forgot her aching back until the first few raindrops splattered on her skin in the early afternoon.

"Looks like you were right," said Scott, the regret he felt evident in his voice. He peered at the suddenly bleak sky, pregnant with incoming rain and sighed. "Let's get this covered quickly and call it a day."

Racing against nature, they worked together to cover their dig site with tarps and steaked them down from the rough winds that constantly blew from the sea. The sky darkened further still as the team quickly gathered their tools and trudged through the grassy field back to their cars, fifty meters away.

Scott held the box of artifacts they had procured under one arm, each piece nestled in its own neatly labeled plastic bag, the smile on his face contagious. "Let's meet for a drink at the pub tonight. I'm buying."

Spirits already high, the team eagerly agreed. "You joining us this time, Doctor Ferguson?" asked one of her students.

Maryn did not answer, distracted by Scott's hand on her elbow.

"Mare," he said, speaking as though he wished to impart a secret. "I'd like for you to be the one to take these into the lab on Friday. I'd like Deidre to get a confirmation on these and possible dates as soon as she can."

Maryn's smile froze on her face. While she didn't necessarily mind bringing the pieces they'd found to the lab, it was on the mainland, in Inverness, which would take her away from the action. They'd nearly gotten down to the level that would unearth whatever the GPR had picked up. "Do you think we'll uncover everything by Friday?" she asked, hoping her voice did not betray her disappointment.

"Look, I get it," Scott confided in low tones, his dark brow lifting, "but I don't want to entrust these artifacts with the less experienced on the team and I can't leave. I'm the lead. You'll be back here before you know it and I'll keep you informed on everything we find," he promised.

She blew out a breath and she looked back over her shoulder at the white tents covering the blue and brown tarpaulins hugging the ground. She swallowed her displeasure and agreed, just as the sky opened up. Sheets of rain pelted down upon them as they ran the remaining distance to their cars.

She would just have to work extra hard in the next two days. No way she was going to miss whatever the GPR had picked up.

Maryn awoke from a dream, sweating and panting, the images fading as quickly as water through her fingers. Falling? Or maybe she'd been in an enclosed space? She'd had an irrational fear of enclosed spaces ever since a cavern exploration had gone wrong when she'd been fourteen.

But even without recalling the images, she knew the dream had been unsettling. Silence filled the space of her rented room, not even the rain pattering upon the window offered comfort. Unable to go back to sleep, she flicked on the lamp which sat atop the small desk in her room and pulled the box of artifacts Scott had given her.

By the time the watery sun came up and everyone had had their coffee, she found herself back at Blackhouse Arnol, or close to it, the wind in her ears and the white-capped waves rushing and breaking against the rock-strewn beach. Gulls called from above, drifting in an upcurrent, mere shadows against an iron-clad sky.

The tents and tarps had shielded the dig site well. Only one corner where the wind had lifted a stake from the rocky soil had caused a minor issue, dampening the soil beneath into a mud puddle, but it could have been much worse.

Eager to get as much done as possible, Maryn skipped any conversation that precluded the day and set to work with her trowel and bucket. The resinous scent of wet earth filled her nose as she carefully scraped away layers of old peat and the occasional piece of bog iron.

She worked at the southern wall, close to where the GPR had spotted the anomaly. She reminded herself to go carefully, to not let her desire to reach the objects, whatever they were, cloud her better judgement. She must remain professional and rational. Haste and archaeology did not go hand in hand.

Still, she could not help her sense of urgency as she removed layers of earth, her well-earned aches and pains from so long in her current position forgotten. A current of anxious energy pervaded her so her hands shook by the time the edge of her trowel caught on something new. The monotonous scrape of metal changed, an alien sensation from the feel of the dense sponge of ancient peat she'd grown so accustomed to. With a soft exhalation, Maryn traded her trowel for her brush and pushed aside the crumbs of earth to reveal what looked like blackened but preserved leather.

Maryn stared at the spot for a heartbeat, forcing her hands to slow, her heart skipping as she held her breath. Not leather per say, but flesh and . . . dear God, was that hair? Her fingers faltered and she stared at what appeared to be the shell of a blackened ear.

Maryn forgot to breathe, her mind racing and her heart fluttering as she took in the improbable sight. She'd been right. *It was a body.*

Bogs excellently preserved human and animal life due to their low microbial counts. Like most living things, microbes needed oxygen, and without microbes, evidence of life remained unspoiled. She'd seen this firsthand, had examined Denmark's Tollund Man as a graduate student and had marveled at how well he'd been conserved. This person—this ear—looked just as perfectly preserved as the Tollund Man from 300 BC.

Maryn could hardly hold her brush. She stood on shaky legs and called to Scott from across the site, her voice strangely calm and so disproportionate to the riot of emotion welling within her. Again and again her gaze followed the curve of the ear protruding from the soil, just visible through dark hair sprouting from the ground.

"Yeah?" he asked from beside her and, at her silence, he followed her gaze. A hand gripped her elbow, a token of shared, unspoken emotion.

In the short space of quiet as Scott took in the marvel at their feet, Maryn finally found her breath. "We should take pictures," she suggested. The rational, professional, part of her brain still worked at least, even if the rest of her body seemed to have betrayed her. "We need to document this and . . . and call George at UHI."

"Right," he said, breathless himself. "I'll get the camera. You . . . you get the others on this as well."

And so, many hours later, with four of them working, they discovered that Maryn had found a woman—someone important made evident by the richness of her apparel and the adornment upon her preserved, woolen clothing. From what little they had exposed so far, shells and crystals embellished her cloak along the hem of her sleeve and along the edge of her hood in an intricate pattern. Even the woman's pointed shoes—laces still intact—indicated her wealth and importance.

She lay on her back, her hands folded neatly upon her middle, her head turned to the side as if she wished to gaze upon the sea.

"Viking?" asked Scott breathlessly at her ear, clearly as enthralled as Maryn. "A shield maiden?" he suggested, motioning with a blunt finger to the intricately crafted leather armor she wore.

Maryn leaned ever closer, careful to mind where she put her hands. The scalloped armor appeared mostly intact and unlike anything she'd seen before. They simply had nothing so well preserved to compare it to.

"She must be," muttered Maryn, absently. "Absolutely incredible."

Scott then called George, the dean of their college, who would get in touch with the proper channels. "We'll need to transport her back to the mainland and get x-rays and DNA samples and the like," Scott informed her needlessly, in an enthused, rich voice.

They continued staring down at the body as others set up portable light towers. Being late June, the sun did not set until after ten o'clock, but they'd set up a tent to shield their find from the elements.

Nodding absently, Maryn crouched near the woman as the space was flooded with artificial light, marveling at the clarity in her face. She had furrow lines between her brows, crow's feet at the corners of her eyes, and wide, high cheekbones set on either side of a hooked nose. She looked to Maryn as if she were merely painted in charcoal and if nudged, would awaken with blinking eyes from a long slumber to stand and dust the earth from her clothes.

"What's that?" asked Scott from beside her. He pointed at the woman's clasped hands, his eyes narrowed.

Maryn leaned closer. In the direct shine of the light, she caught a dull glimpse of something remarkably like bone, marbled and stained brown with time.

"I think she's holding something in her hands," she said, frowning slightly as she maneuvered herself for a better view. It was difficult to do so and not step on anything important, but when she moved beside the body and bent overtop her, Maryn got a clear view. "Jewelry perhaps? Some sort of religious talisman? I can see the edge of it just there."

Wordlessly, she held her hand out, like a doctor waiting for a nurse to supply a scalpel. "Thanks," she muttered as Scott supplied her with a stiff-bristled toothbrush. Carefully, she brushed away the earth packed around the woman's clasped hands to reveal her treasure. "It's...it looks like a blade," she said on a breath, resisting the urge to abandon all professional care and pry it free from the ground.

Blowing softly on the exposed edge, she could just make out a few carefully carved symbols tracing the length of the blade before it was swallowed up by the woman's loosely curled fingers.

She smiled up at Scott from her awkward position, one hand holding the toothbrush aloft. "It's a dagger of some kind. Ritualistic from the looks of it. I can get it out, I think."

With some patience, Maryn cleared away countless years of dirt from between perfectly preserved fingers, enabling the blade to fall free. Carefully, she lifted the point of the knife and found Scott's eager face once more. "Remarkable, isn't it? The first of its kind, I'd wager. I've never seen anything—"

A large clap of thunder drowned out her words, making Maryn jerk in surprise. The rumble reverberated through her very bones. Frantically, she looked down upon the woman's hands, worried her sudden movement had caused injury or broken the point of the blade she'd been pinching between thumb and forefinger.

Astonishingly and beyond all belief, Maryn had inadvertently pulled the entire artifact from the woman's body, intact. Maryn canted her head and studied it closely. Roughly eight inches in length and wide at the heel, the dagger was unexpectedly sharp, encrusted with filth, and surprisingly heavy. A slight smear of blood besmirched the central ridge, her finger smarting.

"Woah." Scott's breath stirred the hair near her ear. Maryn peered at the find, ignoring her cut. "I think," hazarded Scott, "I think this might be Pictish. Look at the haft," he all but whispered, his voice full of awe. Maryn's eyes traveled from the tip, just under her fingers, down the length of the artifact and saw what he meant.

Pictish symbols were easy to spot. They were stylistically simple yet realistic, indicating everyday objects and animals. And while they were intricate and beautiful, no one knew what the symbols actually meant.

The thunder rolled again, and a chill ran through Maryn's body as the wind picked up, stirring her hair at the nape of her neck. The tent above them shuddered and flapped violently as Scott held open a plastic bag.

"Strange weather," remarked Scott. "Looks like our fun is at an end for today," he said, sounding just as disappointed as she felt.

He barked out orders for tarpaulins to be brought. "Put this with the other things you're taking to Inverness tomorrow," he added offering her the artifact, now neatly enclosed in plastic. "Let's see what the lab can make of it."

Maryn stared at him. He still intended to make her leave the site? "Can't it wait?" she asked, raising her voice above the noise of hasty conversations and the sound of unfurled plastic.

Scott shook his head and motioned her to take a step back, his hands full of sheeting to cover the body. Together, he and Brandon shrouded the find, placing rocks on the corners to keep the wind from carrying the tarp away.

Maryn followed Scott to the other end of the enclosure as he shouted orders, her hands shaking. "This is my find just as much as it is yours," she said, a tremor in her voice. "You may be the lead, but I found the body. Let Brandon go, or Icle, and let me stay and see this through."

"Put those tools in the bucket and help with securing the site," commanded Scott to a rather slack-jawed grad student who had been staring out beyond the confines of the rock foundation at the gathering storm. Scott glanced Maryn's way, a look of regret in his brown eyes. "I know what you're saying, Mare, but I already told you: I can't leave and I won't trust this with anyone else. Besides, George will no doubt have the museum's conservators here in the next day or so."

He was right. Likely, as had been done to some of their other more interesting digs, the museum's senior conservator would come and take over.

They could do such a thing, being the source of much of the Institute of Archaeology's funding. She had a job because of them. Still, she could not help her disappointment. They would swoop in and take the body to London and she and Scott would barely be a footnote in their published journal.

"Call me once Diedre has the numbers," said Scott with finality.

Chapter Two

Turbulence

THE FLIGHT TO INVERNESS would not take long. A short, fifty-five-minute jaunt to the mainland, and she'd be back at her flat, just a short walk to the university. No matter how quick the trip, her mood soured. The cabin, far too small for comfort, didn't alleviate her temperament, nor did it help that she'd hardly slept (either from lingering disappointment or from her neighbor's snores reverberating through the thin wall of the B&B).

Either way, she'd had little rest and so by the time the small business jet's door closed, she ignored her laptop and book and pulled the bag containing the bone blade from her satchel. She squinted through the poor light in the cabin, thinking of what the rest of the team would find today. Another body? Maryn frowned, selfishly wanting nothing of the sort.

Maryn barely paid attention to the flight attendant as she instructed the small group of six passengers on safety. Maryn silently wished for some aspirin as the woman droned on, the weight of the object in the palm of her hand cool. Why did she long to hold the thing anyway? What more could she discover about it here, in the dim confines of economy seating? Not much.

She should stow it safely in the box with the other items they'd found, now resting in the overhead bin, but this piece, *her piece*, called to her. She ignored the desire to pull it out of the plastic bag, knowing she'd need stronger light to work out the intricately carved geometrical lines along the handle. Knowing that the lab offered the perfect environment consoled her. Once she got to the workroom, she'd clean it properly and then she'd be able to see the markings more clearly.

Maryn replaced the blade in her satchel as the plane taxied out to the runway and watched the asphalt speed by through the little oval window. Next came the familiar swoop of her stomach as the aircraft lifted and the runway fell away smoothly. Bunching up her jacket to use as a pillow, Maryn closed her eyes to the loud and reassuring hum of the dual engines, her satchel hugged close to her body, her arms crossed over the canvas.

"Are ye goin' home, dearie?" asked the passenger in the seat across the narrow aisle. Maryn opened one eye and surveyed her companion, an older woman with thinning blue hair. She dug around in her large purse and pulled out a brown paper bag, smiling as if she were sharing a secret.

The reading light above her glinted off her skull dully as the woman opened the bag and offered it to Maryn. "Have a biscuit, dearie. I made them special for my son, but I brought extra to share. Are ye married, then?" she asked, pausing in her ministrations to pin one sharp brown eye on Maryn.

At Maryn's negation to both, the woman smiled and returned her attention to her bag, pulling a rectangular piece of shortbread from the sack for herself. "My son is divorced these past three years. Geordie's his name. He's a good lad but he's in want of a woman. Men dinnae do well without a woman, ye ken," she said conspiratorially.

Maryn smiled weakly at the woman as she explained her intent to visit her son in the city for a week. She offered Maryn a second chance at a biscuit, speaking all the while. "My gran's recipe," she cajoled. "These've won the blue ribbon at the fair at least a dozen times in my lifetime."

Giving in, Maryn mumbled her thanks and took a buttery square. She never got a taste of the treat, however, for just then, a sudden pocket of turbulence rocked the plane. The bag of cookies fell from the woman's hands and scattered onto the aisle floor, breaking into countless pieces.

"Oh dear!" the woman cried as the lights flickered. The wind shear tossed them violently, their seatbelts the only thing keeping them from flying from their seats.

Maryn's fingers dug into the armrest, her jaw clenched tight as the plane bounced upward then dipped at frightening speed.

The seatbelt sign flickered above her head as the captain's voice cut in and out over the speaker.

"... apology—urbulence ... remain –ted...." Maryn's stomach lurched when the plane plunged once more. The baby in the back screamed, mixing with the worried cries of the other souls on the small craft.

Someone shouted a prayer. Lightning cracked outside her window and raised the hairs on her body. The sky had turned an inky purple so dark it appeared night, not noon.

The stewardess's face, now white to the lips, loomed briefly at her in the dim of the cabin before she, too, found her seat. She fumbled with her seatbelt, her manicured fingers shaking as she pulled the belt tightly across her hips. Seeing the woman's fear solidified Maryn's own. They were going to die.

The plane's nose dove toward the ground. Purses and backpacks rolled under seats and down the aisle. Oxygen masks fell from the ceiling, and she grasped hers quickly, pulling the elastic tightly to hold the yellow plastic to her mouth and nose. She helped the old woman as best she could across the aisle, who struggled to hold the thin elastic in her arthritic hands.

Lightning struck again and the engines died, creating an eerie vacuum of silence that seemed to press in on Maryn's ears. The plane tilted portside at an exaggerated angle, making the little accordion door separating them from the cockpit fall open.

Alarms blared, an incessant beeping that tripped as quickly as her heart. "Mayday, mayday," the pilot said. The entire vessel shuddered as if might tear apart; a queer sensation overcame Maryn then. Her fear suspended, replaced with clarity. Death by plane crash would be quick if not painless, and in the end, she would get to see Lolly and Pop again.

And Mum.

Some unknown source squeezed Maryn, forcing the air from her lungs. Blood dribbled from her nose, and the edges of her vision faded to grey. She closed her eyes, envisioning her grandparents who raised her, of their little cottage at the feet of the Trossach Mountains.

The plane jerked violently once more and she gripped the canvas bag in her arms all the tighter.

In that moment, seat B2, assigned to one Maryn Elizabeth Ferguson, was suddenly empty. The pilot negotiated the plane into a steep dive and, by some miracle, restarted the engines. The lights flickered back on as they regained power and leveled out from their freefall.

"We apologize for the disturbance," said the pilot over the PA system, sounding rather breathless himself. "We're returning to Benbecula. Please remain seated"

Passengers, still frazzled and frightened, clapped in joyous relief. No one remarked on the suddenly clear sky, bright and vibrant as the old woman asked, "But where has the lassie gone? She was just there."

Chapter Three

Under the Mountain

Maryn came to with a sudden jerk, her heart hammering in her chest. She blinked against the darkness. Her head ached, but not so severely that she couldn't focus her attention on more important matters.

The seatbelt strap across her hips had disappeared. In fact, Maryn realized that she lay upon her back, her hands neatly folded upon her breast as if she'd been carefully arranged by loving hands. That alarmed her. The sudden mental image of a body laid out for burial sent her heart leaping into her throat.

Desperate, her breath hitching, she flailed her hands outward, intent to push against her would-be coffin. Thankfully, her hands only found empty air, cool and stale. Forcing her grave fears aside, Maryn sat up, one hand going to the dull ache at her temple, the other clutching, much to her surprise, what felt like a blanket. She racked her brain, trying and failing to piece her timeline together. The last thing she remembered, she was hurdling toward the ground at an unthinkable speed, her very life held in the balance.

Stay calm. She forced her breathing to slow to a more natural rhythm. *It will do you no favors to lose your head.* Without a thought for the dark, her eyes moved unerringly to where her hand lay, fisted in the woven fabric underneath her, but she could not see it. Someone had placed her here, had seen to her well enough to give her that comfort, however small. But where was she?

Am I blind? Her heart lurched again, and she lifted her cold fingers to assess her face. She could feel no injury, but blindness could be a side effect of a head injury. But no, she probably wasn't blind, only in the dark. A very dense, wet dark that clung to her skin like clammy hands. She shivered and groped around her, feeling only the rough spun wool under her and cold stone at her back.

She frowned and placed both hands against the rough wall when a sound reached her: a clear rasp of skittering stone upon stone, as if an errant foot had toed it into motion. She froze, her eyes turned in the direction in which the clattering had come, her ears straining but all she could hear was the desperate pounding of her heart.

Mouth dry, Maryn shrank against the wall, her eyes darting uselessly in the inescapable blackness. "Wh—who's there?" she asked, the empty void swallowing her voice.

Whispers, low and unintelligible followed by the distinct step and drag of a foot catapulted her stomach into her throat. No horror film could top the sheer terror racing through her veins at that moment, her heart practically beating out of her chest. "W—who are you?" she demanded. The whispers faded into nothing before the room around her slowly blossomed to life.

The approaching light—a torch by the sound and flicker of it—gave her hints of her surroundings. She waited in a small chamber, no bigger than her studio apartment bedroom, but instead of plaster walls and second-hand furnishings surrounding her, granite encased her. The doorway opposite her opened into a dim hallway wall just beyond.

As the light grew nearer, it revealed that there was no door to her room at all, but a rough hole cut through stone, as if hands had carved the space within from the heart of a mountain.

Shimmering, orange light radiated from the torch as its owner finally reached her door, dazzling her eyes. Whomever arrived, his appearance did not invoke trust. He looked like an overgrown leprechaun who preferred seedy bars over rainbows.

"Na biodh eagal ort, a bhan-shagart," said the man, his voice full and rich. "Cha dean cron sam bith ort."

Maryn peered at him, trying to make out his features amid the sharp glow of the torch. Glittering eyes set under a broad forehead stared back. His wild, dark hair spilled from the crown of his head and covered his face with a full matching beard.

He stepped aside from the door, as if to make room for another person, and Maryn caught a glimpse of two broadaxes, honed and deadly, strapped to his back, the sharp points just visible at his hips. As he lifted the torch higher, Maryn's eyes fell upon a stooped, hooded creature suddenly filling the doorway.

The hairs along her arms prickled to life. Thoughts of trafficking raced through her mind. How had she gotten off the plane? Had she been drugged, somehow?

Breathy words escaped from the the newcomer, still framed in the doorway. Their gazes pinned Maryn in place, just like one of the bugs on display in the entomology department at the university. As the hooded figure moved more fully into the room, she realized that what she'd thought had been the drag and scrape of an injured foot was instead the grating of a knobby staff as it was drug forward, clutched tightly in an equally knotted hand.

The unsteady light from the torch cast a grotesque shadow onto the wall opposite, playing into her already intense fears.

"S—stay away," Maryn commanded. Despite her words, the shuffling feet and tortured breaths coming from the hooded figure continued toward her. Unable to escape, Maryn shrank further still into the rock wall behind her. Her mind raced, trying and failing to discern a way out. She could scream, but who would hear her?

Be still.

The whispered words caressed Maryn's mind, as soft as a summer breeze.

Eyes wide and her breaths stuck in her throat, Maryn watched helplessly as a gnarled hand, fingers curled into claws, stretched forth from the folds of the billowing fabric and pulled back the cowl covering the person's face.

Old was not an apt enough description. The woman looked like a witch fresh out of a Grimm fairy tale, the kind that ensnared lost children in the hopes of a tasty meal. Maryn cast her eyes about, eager to find something—anything—she might use as a weapon, but the room was void of anything save smooth granite walls.

Words blossomed to life once more within her mind: *Who are you? How is it you've come to have the Blade of Somnolence?*

Maryn stared, fear and confusion battling within her. "What's happening—who are you?"

The woman peered closer, leaning into Maryn's face, her strange, violet eye milky with cataracts. The other was squinted shut. *I am she who has called you through space and time. I am Cailleach, Goddess of Winter.* The woman stretched forth a hand and placed her cold fingers against Maryn's forehead, startling her.

A strange sensation passed through Maryn then, like a current of electricity, but cold and clinging. The feeling skulked through her skull and then, just as suddenly as the sensation had begun, it faded to nothing.

The hag let her hand fall away, staring into her eyes as if searching for something important.

"What have you done to me?" demanded Maryn. "Where am I?"

For the first time, the old woman used her mouth to speak: "I mean you no harm," she said in a voice like the wind. "I have opened your mind, so that you might understand me and all else while you tarry here."

Opened my mind? Maryn shook her head, her confusion growing. "Where am I?"

"You are in one of the realms of the High Fae. I have brought you through the pages of time to answer my queries. It was easier to pull you to me than to travel myself. As you can see, my days are numbered; I grow weaker by the hour."

Maryn gaped at the old woman, first taking in her haggard appearance and then that of the disgruntled dwarf. She'd grown up hearing all the lore and mythology associated with the Fae. Cailleach was, indeed, the goddess of the winter months. A hag and sometimes portrayed as a giantess. She was often pictured with her hammer and creel, breaking apart and building mountains as per her desire.

The hag's mouth curled up into a satisfied smile. "Yes, that's right," she said, apparently reading Maryn's mind. "I am she, the very one you recall. While I can take a variety of forms to suit my needs, this frail body you now see is what is left of my power. Time runs short, Daughter. Tell me, what do you know of Spring's absence?"

"I don't know anything about spring or…or fairy land," said Maryn, her eyes steady on the hag. "I don't know who you are or what you want with me. I can't help you."

Apparently, the little man holding the torch didn't like her answer. He shuffled forward, an angry scowl on his brightly lit face. His leather armor squeaked with each step as he drew nearer his mistress.

"Lies," he growled. "I saw ye with my ain eyes, holding Brigid's blade. Tell us, from whom did ye acquire it?"

Maryn's bewilderment only further irritated the dwarf, but the old hag, resting more heavily on her staff, squinted into Maryn's face with wonder rather than annoyance. "How very curious," muttered the old woman. Her gaze lingered on Maryn's features, a cold weight that erupted gooseflesh up Maryn's arms. "I think...yes, I think I see now. How marvelous. Truly marvelous."

Maryn's mind spun. She needed to get away from these people.

The hag straightened and waved a hand in an elegant manner for one so frail. A chair—if you could call it that—sprang from the very ground. Twisting vines of what appeared to be blackberry briars threaded and knotted together so tightly and so completely that its branches formed the legs, arms, seat and back of the chair. Last, a cushion appeared, the deep purple of an overripe plum.

Sitting with a soft groan, her staff laid haphazardly against the arm of her chair, the old woman withdrew from her voluminous cloak Maryn's canvas bag, which Maryn knew, held the artifact she'd been tasked to bring to Inverness.

"The scrying pool showed you in the very act of claiming Brigid's Blade of Somnolence. Durvan and I both witnessed you pull it from the earth after I asked it to show me my sister, Brigid. You cannot deny such, for I have it here, amongst your other possessions. Tell me, what do you know of the Goddess of Spring?"

"My name is Maryn Ferguson. I'm an archaeologist at UHI," she started, her eyes roving over the room, looking without success, for anything that might help her identify her location. "I know nothing of goddesses or this Brigid you speak of. I search out and study historical artifacts. I . . . The college is expecting me and will be searching for me once they realize I'm . . . I'm missing from the—" Maryn trailed off.

In the event of a plane crash, the authorities would likely assume her dead, her body lost, once it wasn't immediately found. Dread pooled in her stomach.

"How did you bring me here?" she demanded, her hands fisted on her thighs. "How did you get me out of the wreckage? Where are the others?"

The old woman's eyes glittered in the low light. "I see your fear, Daughter. Allow me to ease your mind. It was you, alone, that I pulled from the mortal world. No one from your time has been harmed." She turned slightly at the waist and indicated the blank, grey stone wall to Maryn's right. "I pulled you through that door."

With a mere poke of her staff, the granite wall melted away to be replaced by a curtain of stars, glittering and fathomless. Cailleach lazily swept the end of her favored implement through the silver pinpricks of light, making them sway. "This space is what we call The Other, a pathway in time."

The short man grumbled, chastising his mistress for wasting her strength, pulling Maryn's astonished gaze away from the impossible spectacle playing out before her very eyes. The room dimmed as the stars faded and the woman's attention returned in full force upon Maryn.

Maryn shook her head as if the motion could rearrange her current reality to one she understood.

"What do you want from me?" she asked, her fear changing shape. As terrible as abduction was, it was quite a different kind of terror to be confronted with such impossibilities. Her rational mind could not account for walls of light that danced and *sang*, for at the hag's touch, the light chimed. The sound passed through Maryn in waves, the very cells making up her body answering in kind, as if she'd been standing too close to a just-struck gong.

Opening the satchel, the witch withdrew the blade Maryn had found. It seemed to glow in the dim confines of the room, centered across Cailleach's open palm. "This tool," began the hag in a reverent tone, "is the key to my undoing and my rebirth." Lifting the relic, Cailleach drew an intricate knot of a triquetra in the space between them with the tip of the blade. The triangular figure with its three interlaced arcs shone silver-white, throbbing with life, just as the wall of stars had.

Maryn stared, dumbfounded and dared to draw closer, her nose scant centimeters from the hovering shape. It pulsated in time with her heartbeat, shimmering and vibrant. Tentative, she lifted a hand and dared to touch a glittering edge but pulled her hand back at the last second, her eyes going to the old woman's, as if to ask permission.

Cailleach inclined her head ever so slightly and Maryn, biting her bottom lip, reached out a finger once more. The touch and feel of the magical image reminded her of carbonation. A fizz of warm energy against her skin. She could not help her curiosity. "How did you do it?" she asked, running her hand through the middle of the triquetra. The shimmering light drifted like dandelion seeds on the wind, slow and aimless, only to reform once more, a tinkle of chimes sounding.

The hag said nothing and only stared, as if waiting for Maryn's brain to catch up and come to terms with her current reality. Maryn doubted her own senses. Yes, she saw and felt the—she grimaced inwardly even thinking the word—*magic*, but seeing wasn't always believing. A sudden memory popped into her head at that moment: her gran, her Lolly, fervently telling young Maryn that magic *was* real, if only she knew where to look.

How had she been brought to this place, alone and unhurt, with no memory of the plane's supposed crash? Where were the aftereffects of being drugged, if she had, indeed, been given something to render her unconscious for any length of time?

What's more, this hag, this self-proclaimed goddess, performed *acts* that no earthly, scientific means could explain away. *And yet*. And yet here she sat before Grumpy Dwarf and Winter herself, being convinced otherwise.

"My sisters and I are, each of us, maiden, then mother, then crone," said Cailleach, indicating the three parts of the image she'd drawn in the air. "Just as there is no clear beginning to our existence, there is no end. If I am to be reborn, I must first be laid to rest using this very blade. Without the performance of the rites, I will fade away, and bitter winter will rage on."

Cailleach's bad eye, a milky white in the shine from the hovering three-sided image, conveyed her sorrow. Maryn listened with the same careful consideration she had learned to use while studying in her undergrad years, searching out the questions that needed asking.

Licking dry lips, Maryn suspended disbelief for the time being, and asked, "For the sake of argument, let's say that the blade is the key to your slumber, or rest, or whatever it is you need, then why not use it on yourself? You have it now, so why not use it?"

"She cannae use it on herself," groused Grumpy Dwarf from the shadows. He'd taken up standing with one shoulder pressed against the wall, the torch now suspended from some unseen bracket. The sprouted blackberry throne and glittering picture show had engrossed her so thoroughly, she'd not paid him any mind. "Seasonal rites must be performed by gods," he explained, "and they must follow the course o' life. Spring follows winter, Imbolc follows Spring, and so forth."

"The ritual of *Alban Eilir* is performed with the sowing of seeds in the balance of day and night. Only once Spring's seeds are bathed in my life's blood, can the cycle continue. I must have Brigid. And soon."

Maryn pursed her lips. "But if the rite must be performed when night and day are equally balanced, on the equinox, I assume you mean—" She paused and waited for Cailleach's nod, then continued. "And, as you say, that day has come and gone, how do you know the ritual will still work?"

The dwarf pushed off the wall and came to his lady's side, his fathomless eyes resting on her withered face, a perfect picture of stoic determination. "The day matters less than the sowing of Spring's seeds in Winter's blood. When it happens, only then can the spring season begin. Enough idleness. Let us commence."

He turned to Maryn, his steely gaze unsettling her further, something she would have argued as an impossibility at this point. "If it's tae home ye wish tae go, Lady Ferguson, then first my mistress must be replenished. She cannae do such magic now; bringing ye here was bad enough." He huffed, indicating his disapproval of Cailleach's choice and leveled Maryn with a glare. "Find Brigid and restore her, only then will ye be sent back to yer own time."

Maryn's mind, which had faltered and stuttered at every turn as she'd tried to apply logic to this very insane turn of events, finally slipped into gear. "If I help you, you'll send me back home?" she asked the goddess.

Looking wearier than ever, Cailleach inclined her head. "I vow it."

Maryn took in a shaky breath, her grandmother's insistence that magic was real reverberating in her troubled mind. All the old fables, scores of fairy stories, of bedtime adventures told in her Lolly's enthusiastic voice. What if...what if Lolly's stories were true? She'd believed it once, as only a young hopeful could. Father Christmas, the Loch Ness Monster, leprechauns . . . all had been as real and immediate as the breath in her lungs.

But then life had ground it out of her, replacing awe and magic with logic. Fairy tales were just that, stories. *But all legends are borne of truth, Maryn*, she heard Lolly say.

Okay, what if the steady diet of fairy stories she'd been fed in her youth were, indeed, genuine? If so, Maryn knew what came next. As in all the stories, when there was a problem to be solved—some wickedness that must be stopped—a hero inevitably emerged. Some came willingly, others only with painful coercion.

Maryn grimaced. Perhaps she could circumnavigate all the unwanted soul-stretching if she embraced it all? Maryn had her doubts, but, above all, she wanted out of her granite prison. Something told her the first step involved acceptance.

She exhaled heavily through her nose, her mouth pressed into a thin line. "Where do we look first?"

A smile curled upon Cailleach's thin lips, her one violet eye sparking with approval. "You must travel into the spring kingdom and seek out Brigid's counselors. Her subjects are no doubt growing impatient for her to return to her body by now. Perhaps they know to where she traveled."

At Maryn's alarmed look, the dwarf explained, "All seasonal gods must remain in their domains, for that is where their power resides. They may travel in spirit, inhabiting animals and the like, but never in body, save for days of the rites." He looked at his mistress again, fear flashing so quickly across his features that Maryn wondered if she'd imagined it. "Would you not rather us to entreat Death, Mistress? It is he who can travel easily between realms. Perhaps...."

"No." Cailleach's sharp tone startled Maryn. "Do not venture into the underworld, Durvan. Not if you can help it. Arawn's kingdom holds too many dangers for a living mortal." With that she took her staff into her hand and said, "Come from this place. I wish for my evening meal." She looked skyward, to the craggy ceiling that quickly gave way to empty darkness and grimaced.

It was a long way up.

Chapter Four

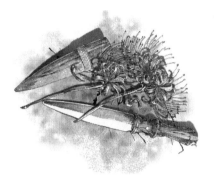

Winter Court

They'd made their way up the long staircase cut into the stone of the mountain, the steps worn in the center from centuries of use. Cailleach had been slow and had required support from her staff and servant, who dutifully went before her and helped steady her onto the next step. Now they were seated in a cavernous hall, a long table running the length of the room large enough to fit fifty people. The three of them sat at one end, Cailleach at the head of the table and Durvan across from Maryn.

Square pillars carved into the smooth granite walls drew her eye to the lofty ceiling. The columns, heavily decorated with etched runes and pictures depicting scenes Maryn could not begin to name, spanned at least thirty feet into the air. She itched to touch the images, to rub the carvings onto paper for preservation and for later, careful study.

Her gaze traced the long lines of the carved posts up to the shadowed, arched ceiling, where they artfully joined with their twins on the opposite side of the hall. The architecture reminded her of a gothic cathedral, save for the glaring absence of windows, seeing as how they were deep under Winter's fairy hill.

Maryn shied away from the uncomfortable reminder of sitting under so many tonnes of rock and earth with no clear exit, and instead focused on the dwarf across from her.

Durvan drank deeply from his goblet, a frosted bell of glass supported by more twining blackberry canes. The perfect picture of dwarf, he held his drink in one hand and a leg of some sort of large fowl fisted in the other.

Maryn eyed him, then Cailleach, warily. The hag, bent and deflated, appeared as no more than a rumpled lump of clothing to Maryn's right. She'd always imagined gods from the old stories as eternally beautiful, youthful and powerful, not as the shrunken shell of a witch, barely able to stay upright.

"It's rude to stare," grumbled the dwarf, replacing his goblet onto the black walnut tabletop with a suppressed burp.

"It's only...I thought gods couldn't die. When my Lolly—my grandmother—told me the old stories, I always imagined gods differently."

At Durvan's huff of distaste, heat rose into her cheeks.

Bristling, she said, "Well, doesn't being a god mean you're immortal?"

He finished chewing, his dark eyes glassy with candlelight, the furrow between his brows deepening. "All living things can *die*," he rebuked.

"The gods do not die as you mortals do," wheezed Cailleach, her good eye opening long enough to peer at her from within the depths of her cowl.

The goddess's long strands of silver hair cascaded from under the hood, bound in intervals with leather strips and decorated with small animal bones. Cailleach pulled herself upright, the hood falling back to reveal her face in the full light for the first time. Her skin was a light shade of *blue*, as if Maryn observed her from beneath glacial ice.

Lifting a goblet of red berry wine to her wrinkled lips, Cailleach drank deeply, leaving her mouth stained. "If Brigid does not preform the rights and usher in her season, I will fall into an endless slumber."

Maryn furrowed her brow. "Like a coma?"

"A stupor of consciousness," said Durvan, pulling her attention, "much like endless slumber without the hope of revival nor the reward of *Brù na Bòinne*. In time, she will diminish to nothing. Her essence will be absorbed into the world and Cailleach will be no more."

"*Brù na Bòinne?*" asked Maryn, feeling out of her depth. The name rang a bell, but she could not recall all the details from the fairy tales of her childhood. "I thought Annwn was the underworld."

Durvan gestured with his bone, clear of flesh now. "Annwn is for you and I, not for gods. They will go to dwell with Dagda, the All Father, in the halls of *Brù na Bòinne*."

"Death can come in many ways, I assure you," wheezed Cailleach, her wrinkled mouth barely moving. "I could die at another's hand—a god's hand specifically. In such a case, as with diminishing, my essence will return to the earth, absorbed into the ether." She paused as if caught hold in her own thoughts. With a slight shake, she added, "I could also choose to give up my charge to another and leave this plane of existence for *Brù na Bòinne*." She sniffed here and leveled Maryn with a wry smile. "I must admit that sounds tempting at the moment."

"Why not do it, then?" asked Maryn. If Cailleach could relinquish her godhood to another, and she could have eternal rest, wouldn't that give them all more time to solve the riddle of the missing goddess? "You could go to your eternal reward, as Durvan put it, and someone else could take over." *Someone younger.*

"Oh? And who might you suggest?" asked Cailleach, her eye glinting. "Who could do it? I have no daughters. I have no line for I have taken no man."

The last word was said with the slightest hint of disdain, making Maryn's mind erupt with questions. Could gods and goddesses bear children, then? Did gods and goddesses marry or was that solely a mortal custom? And if so, how often did such a thing happen? If they could not leave their ow kingdoms, how could the creation of children even occur?

Cailleach rubbed her temple, grimacing. *"Enough prattle.* Does your mind never rest?"

Maryn gaped at her. She hadn't voiced those questions out loud and yet Cailleach seemed to hear them. "You can read my mind?" She wasn't sure if she should feel amazed or violated.

Cailleach waved her question away. "Not as one reads a book. Your thoughts come to me as the ripples on a pond, a vibration of energy that carries with it your emotions. I can read your mind the same way you can read the weather. Your questions are as abundant as storm clouds."

Maryn stared at the god, her mind spinning with information, unable to order her own thoughts. *This is insane . . . a total nightmare.* But no dream could ever hold such visceral events and emotions. The gods were *real* and here she sat in one's hall. With a dwarf fairy, no less.

She still had questions, of course. Why not retire, so to speak? If death of a god differed from a human's passing, then what stopped Cailleach from ending it all? Clearly she'd been through the ringer. Perhaps the answer was as simple as she'd said, she wanted to pass on her rein to a child. Her own.

"Perhaps your curiosity might be more tolerable were I not so weary," Cailleach added in way of apology, pinching the bridge of her narrow nose. Her body appeared so frail, Maryn thought a stiff breeze could blow her to pieces and carry her away to the four corners of the earth.

Durvan straightened in his seat, as if calling the meeting to order. "When would you have us leave for Spring Court, my lady?"

"The way is not easy," said Cailleach after a heartbeat, her heavy gaze sweeping to Maryn, then her plate.

Of course it isn't. Maryn squirmed in her seat.

"T'would be best if you let the mortal rest. And eat." Cailleach sent a pointed look at her untouched plate of food.

Maryn couldn't recall much from the fairy stories her grandmother had told her, but a few things stood out: fairies couldn't lie, iron burned them, and humans should never eat or drink their fare, no matter how hungry one might feel.

"Won't eating your food bind me to you or something?" she asked. "Keep me here with you forever?"

Cailleach's mouth twitched into a crooked smile. "No, but it may refine your palate. Upon your return to the mortal realm, you may find your usual sustenance lacking." She frowned then, as though in thought, and added, "Take care outside of the mountain. While I have no wish to poison you, I cannot promise the same for other kingdoms."

Maryn eyed the roasted fowl and winter root vegetables on her plate. The beans on toast she'd eaten that morning seemed a very long way off, indeed. "It won't turn me into a toad or anything?" she asked, her gaze darting to Cailleach and back to the beets and parsnips.

Durvan snorted. "Toads dinnae do well in the cold, Lassie. Better for us were you kept as you are. Eat. We leave at first light."

The food, as promised, tasted as delicious as it looked. Maryn had to force herself not to lick her plate clean.

Soon after the meal Cailleach excused herself, helped by a strange creature Durvan called a Fomorian, an eerie creature straight from Maryn's childhood nightmares.

The Fomorian—Gorsh—had wide, yellow eyes, grey-green skin, and a loping gait like an orc or a goblin, but without the traditional loin cloth, black teeth and drooling mouth from her child's illustrated story book.

Before long Gorsh returned, waiting silently near Maryn's elbow.

"Yer meant tae follow her," advised Durvan, his speech slightly slurred from drink. "Go on, then."

Maryn blinked at him. "To where?" A vision of a pile of straw in a dank dungeon surfaced in her mind.

He scoffed and refilled his goblet, grumbling. Maryn heard the words "idling" and "human" before Gorsh spoke. "Hersself hass appointed a room for you. If you're finisshed, pleasse follow me."

Maryn couldn't help her stare. Durvan, at least, looked like something from her world. Gorsh terrified her. But she sounded normal. Well, except for the lingering, reptilian hiss on the 's' words. Maryn stood on shaky legs, unable to find her voice or her feet. She stumbled as she left her chair, eyeing the creature meant to escort her. She caught herself on the table, her face heating.

"Good night, Durvan," said Maryn with forced bravado. Grumpy she could handle, monster...not so much.

He barely registered her as he picked his teeth with the stiletto-style dagger he pulled from somewhere on his person.

Maryn swallowed her fear and followed Gorsh from the room, trailing slightly behind.

They walked through soaring halls, devoid of ornamentation. The only decoration were the carved pillars that lined the walls, lit by intermittent torchlight. Unless the black stain of soot marring the granite walls counted as décor.

When they turned a corner, a tabby mountain cat joined them, its fluff flouncing as it pranced to them from some hidden place. The feline rubbed against Gorsh's muscular, bowed legs, covered with what appeared to be deerskin breeches.

After several minutes of winding through dim corridors, passing heavy oaken doors and more dark passageways, the cat sat on its haunches next to a door the Fomorian gestured to. She bowed neatly at the waist, saying, "If you have need of anything, pleassse sssend Macha."

The cat—presumedly Macha—followed Maryn into her room, jumping soundlessly into a basket near the brazier where it immediately started bathing itself. Gorsh bowed again as Maryn, muttering her thanks, closed the door.

The room was lushly appointed with heavy, blocky furnishings, softened with pillows and cushions in misty greys and a delicate shade of lavender. Her bed, a monstrous four poster with dark grey velvet drapes called to her.

"You are the best thing I've seen all day," said Maryn, running a hand over the coverlet. It was as soft as silk.

The silence of the room pressed in on Maryn as she turned in a tight circle and took in her surroundings. Some clothes had been hung out for her, displayed on a privacy screen on the opposite side of the bed. Deftly taking a candle from the bedside, she drew closer to examine the articles of clothing.

A long, grey woolen skirt, heavy and full lay in wait, dangling toward the floor. Beside it she found a wide, brown leather belt, a billowing white shirt that would surely fall past her knees, grey woolen stockings, and a bodice the color of saffron, laced with a leather cord. Maryn fingered a bit of the skirt for a moment. It likely wouldn't do to wear her very modern human clothes in the fairy realm, which just happened to be perfect for rummaging around in the dirt in the middle of a mortal summer. Well, it hadn't *felt* like summer. At least now she understood the meaning behind the uncommonly cool weather they'd experienced.

On the floor a pair of leather boots abutted the screen. Someone had rubbed the boots with a shiny substance, probably fat. She lifted them and sniffed, wrinkling her nose. Fleece lined the interior, likely making them warm, but the soles were soft leather. She'd feel every pebble or stick she trod on. No, she'd better wear her own boots in favor of these.

As beautiful as the clothes were, they couldn't compare to the deep blue, fur-lined mantle draped over the corner of the screen. While the archaeologist part of her brain was busy cataloging the textiles and the skill required to make such fine garments, the long-buried girlish part of her relished their beauty.

As the candlelight moved over the folds of the cloak's fabric, the azure blue shimmered and changed, tricking her eye into believing that the cloak changed color. "What..." muttered Maryn, lifting the fabric to the side to see the light play upon the weave. Before her very eyes, the color shifted, twinkling as softly as rays from a silver moon, then changing back to blue, an iridescent current of color in all the hues of the deepest of oceans.

"A magic cloak." She laughed in the nearly empty room. She had a freaking *magic cloak*. "What does it do?" she asked the preening cat. It paused in its ministrations, its ears twitching, then promptly went back to bathing. Invisibility? A shield, as strong as armor? It could be anything. Maryn's fingers tingled with anticipation.

She lifted the heavy cloak from the screen and swung it over her shoulders, pulling up the deep hood to cover her head. She looked down at herself. Not invisibility, then. Still, it was warm and lined with pockets. She loved pockets. Maryn twirled, enjoying the feel of the swirling fabric around her ankles.

When she'd been a little girl, she'd spent countless hours daydreaming about such fanciful things as fairy lands filled with enchantments and magic but, as one does, she'd grown out of such childish whimsy, trading her imagination for academics and eventual friends. Now she only felt as though she was strapped into a steadily climbing rollercoaster, about to plummet over the edge, unable to stop the ride or get off.

She replaced the cloak, surprised she'd been taken in by a cloak of all things. Back home, her colleagues were likely going out of their minds with worry. How would the airline explain her disappearance? She'd have to ask Durvan.

Maryn observed the industrious Macha. "You wouldn't happen to have access to a hot shower, would you?"

Its yellow eyes surveyed her for a long moment before standing to stretch and yawn. With a twitch of a tail, it hopped off and slunk away, out of sight.

So much for Macha's help. Maryn catalogued everything from her satchel, her hands shaking as she lifted the blade into her hands once more. *Not just any blade. It belonged to Brigid, Goddess of Spring.*

Finished, she turned and found a steaming bowl of water, a smidge of soap and a cloth waiting for her on the sideboard. Macha sat primly beside it, blinking wide, golden eyes as if to say, "you're quite welcome."

Maryn, mouth open with awe, shook her head. "How did you—" She laughed. Stupid question to ask in the land of magic and fairies. "Thank you," said Maryn. "This is perfect."

She washed her face and neck and dry brushed her teeth, then changed into the neatly folded night rail left out for her on a bench behind the privacy screen. She fell into the bed, the feather mattress molding her body.

The oppressive dark just outside of the candle's halo loomed ever closer. Suddenly she was fourteen again, lost in the twisting labyrinth of Grand Caverns. She clenched her eyes shut, her hands fisted in the duvet. "You're not in a cave," she told herself. "You're . . . under a great mountain."

She opened her eyes and scanned the shadows, so reminiscent of damp, clinging air of her adolecent, living nightmare. Abandoned and lost, she'd huddled into herself, squatting into a ball at the edge of the path on which she'd been standing, too afraid to cry for help lest whatever she imagined was breathing in the dank gloom hear her and strike.

Despite having many years of emotional development since that experience, dark, enclosed spaces still affected her to near paralysis.

Maryn swallowed and called softly for Macha. Only when the subtle movement of the cat jumping onto the foot of her bed signaled it had joined her, did Maryn let out the shaky breath she held. "Thank you," she whispered.

She pulled the covers up to her chin and stared at the candle flame, afraid for the first time in a decade, to turn out the light.

Chapter Five

Goddess of War

"It didn't have to be this way," said Morrigan with a reproachful sigh. The goddess of war frowned at her captive, none other than Brigid, Goddess of Spring. Of course, Brigid wasn't *quite* herself. Morrigan stared through the iron bars of the cage at the vessel holding the goddess, a snowy-white hare, one glassy brown eye staring back at her. "All you had to do was agree to wait," she chastised.

They were alone in Morrigan's counsel room, a cavernous space with dark, sharp-angled furnishings, draped in velvet and furs. The cage holding Spring hostage sat upon the extensive table running down the center of the room, the many artful and well-loved weapons she'd employed over the centuries casting shadows about the room.

Morrigan wasn't asking too much. Spring, just like all the other seasonal gods, had more than their fair share of devoted worshipers. Every year, without fail, humans prayed to them and offered countless sacrifices to them. *Loved them*. Selfish, really, to keep so much devotion all to themselves.

"It's been an age since there's been a good war," she mused. "My subject's discontent grows by the day." She leveled a knowing look at the hare and said, "You know well what it means to rule. Postponing your season would have given great entertainment for my people and done nothing to harm your own. My subjects would have reveled in the spoils of combat for years to come. Insensitive of you, really, to ignore my plight."

Morrigan's home was substantial and extravagant, laden with bounties from the glories of past wars, but hers was a court of fickle-minded creatures, who were not content with idleness. Nor peace. Already there were whispers of rebellion amongst the ranks. She would not have unrest. She would not shirk her duty and ignore the needs of her people. She was their queen, after all, and a queen provided for her people's needs. If she did not, mutiny ensued.

When she'd asked Brigid to delay spring for a time—an easy thing, certainly, to induce an overlong winter—the vainglorious trollop had refused. An overlong winter would bring hunger, then desperation, then, finally conflict. Glorious battle. Humans were very predictable in that way.

What was a few weeks of Brigid's time compared to the centuries she'd already lived? Morrigan's subjects would be appeased, the human world would remember their forgotten goddess of war, and then Spring could commence with her duties, as usual.

But when Brigid refused, she'd left Morrigan with little to no choice but to take matters into her own hands. Of course she hadn't intended to capture the goddess, but Morrigan had never been a gracious loser. In her anger, she'd seized the goddess and brought her here, watching and waiting, as the human world grew more desperate by the day.

Her impulsive decision had been a mistake, not that she would admit such to Brigid. Her only thought had been of Brigid's selfishness, and she'd given no consideration to how the other seasonal gods might react. The other goddesses would notice—if they hadn't already—and *intervene*. Cailleach chief among them.

Morrigan clenched her jaw and glared at the twitching nose beyond the iron. What was she to do now, but to make the most of her exploits? A thought occurred to her then, a niggling remembrance that softened her grimace into a smile.

Gods had long memories. They had not forgot, she was sure, the disgrace Brigid had wrought among them. The scandal had been great enough to bind them to their own kingdoms, forever locked behind invisible boundaries. Long ago, before Brigid had taken a human lover, the gods could move among each other's kingdoms, cloaked in their own flesh.

Gods could take paramours, human or no, but the disgrace occurred when Brigid led her man to the Eternal Waters, which would gift him life everlasting. Such a scheme was forbidden—at least without permission from the All Father—and when they were caught, Spring's punishment was severe. Not only could she—and other seasonal gods—no longer travel to the other kingdoms in their bodies, save for feast days, but the son that grew within Brigid's body could not be hers.

The child was taken away at birth, given to her mortal father to raise. Brigid had been forced to watch from afar as her lover grew old and withered away to nothing, and her son blossomed to manhood never knowing his mother, or what he, himself, was.

Morrigan crooned for her crow, Feren. It lighted from its nearby perch with a sonorous cry, its green-black feathers shimmering in the light from the lancet window and landed upon her forearm. "She disgraced us all, My Sweet," she whispered to Feren. "Haps they will not resent my intervention, after all. Deep hurts can fester and grow with time. Of this we can hope."

Morrigan brushed a knuckle down Feren's breast, her eyes narrowed. The crow clicked its beak in answer, trilling hoarsely. "Yes, perhaps lofty Cailleach will appreciate me reminding Brigid of her sin. But we must be watchful, Dearest. Cailleach will be wishing for Spring's blade by now."

The rabbit turned in a circle, its ears brushing the iron bands, no doubt agitated. "If you had only agreed to help me," Morrigan chided, "you would have no need of punishment."

Turning her attention back to her bird, she said, "Go, and tell the others to canvas the skies. Bring me word of what you find."

Before long, Cailleach would take matters into her own hands. She would grow impatient, if not weary. A sudden realization slipped into Morrigan's mind, like a puzzle box's latch sliding, at last, into place. She gazed at the wall, unseeing, as her mind completed a half-formed thought.

Without Brigid, Winter would linger, weaken, and ultimately diminish. With Brigid locked away, she need only wait for the old hag's body to fail her. Cailleach would fall into a wakeless slumber, leaving Morrigan to rule. What did she need, aside from Cailleach's hammer and Brigid's blade? What was stopping her from being honored and worshiped by the human world? Only their lives.

And she held both in her grasp. *Almost.*

She had a portion of Spring, but getting her body wouldn't be too difficult. Not if she was careful.

A vision of herself ruling as both Winter and Spring goddess filled her mind's eye. She would be loved, her subjects revered. The power she would wield would demand worship. All she needed was Brigid's body and the ritual blade. Spring's temple, where the unmaking would need to take place, was the easiest part of her scheme.

She must contend with Summer and Autumn gods eventually, but they were wholly unconcerned with current seasonal events. They would not know of Morrigan's interference until it was far too late.

For now, there was no one to stop her, and when the time came for Summer to take her place upon the earth, she could deal with her then. Surely, with two relics of power—the Blade of Somnolence and Cailleach's hammer—no other god could displace her.

Her smile grew, her heart lifting in hope. Perhaps her impulsive choice to entrap Brigid had been for the best.

"I will be a most benevolent god," she told the white hare. "Pray, Brigid, where do you keep your blade?"

Chapter Six

Winter's Throne

CAILLEACH'S THRONE ROOM WAS dim and cool when Maryn entered it the next morning. At least a dozen animals surrounded the intricately carved stone slab upon which the goddess of winter sat. Macha the cat blinked solemnly from the goddess's lap, little paws folded demurely into a fluffy chest. Among other rodents, a half-dozen mice squeaked at Cailleach's feet; rabbits twitched their noses in Maryn's direction. A hedgehog waddled over Cailleach's slippered toes, spines undulating as it moved.

Maryn stopped short as she left the narrow passage that led into the chamber and blinked in the torchlight. Durvan narrowly escaped running into her. He huffed his displeasure and moved around her, standing as close as he could get to the throne. He didn't make it far.

Far more startling, a stag stood just to the left of her seat. Holly adorned in its proud antlers, giving the deer a festive air. To the right, a dark shadow moved—Maryn blinked rapidly to ensure she was seeing correctly—a great *bear* lifted its vast head. It raised its nose and sniffed, onyx eyes glittering.

All the breath seemed to have evacuated the space at the same time that Maryn's knees threatened to turn to water. Cailleach waved her forward with a pale hand. Her fingernails looked purple in the low light. "Come, Daughter. Do not fear me."

It's not you that I fear. Maryn's gaze swept over the menagerie of wild things in the room and bit her tongue. Unless Cailleach suddenly solved the riddle of the missing Brigid and had no further use for her, it was unlikely the goddess would be serving her pets Maryn Tartare for breakfast. Still, Maryn couldn't help her trepidation.

She moved closer, still giving the gathered group a berth of six or so feet. *Should she bow? Curtsey?*

She did neither, mostly because she didn't want to look like a complete idiot. More importantly, she didn't wish to take her eyes off the mammoth brown bear lumbering to its feet.

Cailleach's good eye roved over Maryn. "You find the clothes to your taste?"

Maryn looked down upon herself. With the shock of finding a small zoo in the room, she'd forgotten about the layers of clothes she'd donned. Her fingers sought out the heavy fabric of the cloak falling in folds from her shoulders. "They're very fine. Thank you."

"They'll keep you warm enough. Charmed, you see."

Maryn could only stare, her tongue as thick as her thoughts. Last night she'd fallen asleep to the hopeful thought that she'd wake to find this entire situation had simply been a bad dream. Instead, she'd been awakened by Macha's raspy tongue on her cheek in the pitch dark of a cold room. Gorsh came shortly thereafter to re-light the fire and help Maryn dress.

Maryn's disappointment quickly turned to apprehension. She hadn't been dreaming. Cailleach lived—for now—and required an impossible task in order for Maryn to even have a chance to return home. She had no idea how to solve this riddle of the missing Brigid. Somehow, she didn't think it would be as simple as walking to Spring Court—wherever that was—by following the proverbial breadcrumbs.

"I'll tell you how you'll accomplish the task of finding Brigid," said Cailleach, pulling Maryn from her thoughts. Her soft voice felt more like a threat to Maryn.

Cailleach lifted her arm half-way into the air, arthritic, clawed hand outstretched toward the stone ceiling. The sleeve of her sweeping, gauzy robes fell back, revealing the brown-grey body of an adder wrapped sinuously around a blue-hued arm.

Above Cailleach's hand, a dark smudge appeared, then grew. What started off as a charcoal blot no larger than Cailleach's fist, tripled in size, darkening and growing dense until—Maryn's mouth gaped—a hole appeared. A rent in the very fabric of the air.

Maryn's throat didn't want to work. The air grew heavy with static, making her hair stand on end. The snake's tongue tasted the electrified air as Cailleach reached into the space she'd created and pulled something—a weapon?—free.

Not a weapon. A hammer. Its handle was long, at least as long as her forearm, white as bone and carved with runic symbols. The hammer itself was two-sided, one end forming a blunt cudgel and the other shaped into a spike. The metal's tint glimmered green in the torchlight.

Is this—? It can't be Cailleach's hammer. A tool she used to make and break mountains. And, apparently, channel weather, for at that very moment, it started to snow.

Flurries of flakes fell from the stone ceiling, ignored by all. Well, all except Maryn, who stared wide-eyed at the dark expanse above her head.

"Give me your hand," said Cailleach.

Maryn obeyed, moving as if someone else occupied her body. The rodents at her feet made room for Maryn as she neared, retreating to the sides of the stone slab.

Cailleach took Maryn's wrist, forcing her palm up. An icy sensation crawled up her skin at the touch; goosebumps erupted up her arm despite the warmth and heaviness of her clothing. "Do you willingly accept this charge, Maryn Ferguson?"

Did she accept? She gazed at Cailleach's weary face, at her trembling fingers, bent and gnarled. She wanted to help the poor old woman. She really did. She also wanted to go home. "Y-yes, I accept," she said, hoping she wasn't making a huge mistake.

With the pointed end of the cudgel, the goddess drew a runic symbol on her hand, two parallel lines intersected by a third near the top. The lines burned orange, then gold, before disappearing into Maryn's skin.

"I bequeath to you the use of my hammer. May it serve you as it has served me, until it can be returned." Here she leveled Maryn with a look that clearly stated it *would* be returned. Or else.

The goddess drew another symbol into Maryn's hand, this one more intricate: a 'Z' shape with circles on each end. Maryn stared, her hand trembling in Cailleach's. "Join with my handmaiden," she commanded the hammer. "Serve her well."

Maryn stared at her palm for long seconds after Cailleach let go of her and the glittering runic symbol disappeared into her skin. She searched for something within herself, some change that had overtaken her like she'd read about in stories as a child. A vibration of energy, a wind that blew about her, or a light from above signaling that the magic had worked. Instead, Maryn felt...nothing.

Well, not nothing. The same trepidation she'd felt since her arrival still weighed her down. "Dan-ger, dan-ger" it said with each beat of her heart.

How was this hammer supposed to help her? Sure, as far as cool experiences went, wielding a goddess's magical gadget was as good as one could get. But what did Cailleach expect of her? To grind stone to dust? How would taking the hammer to some obscure mountain help her find Brigid? Not unless she was buried alive. The thought soured Maryn's stomach.

Cailleach offered Maryn the hammer, handle first. "Durvan will escort you to Brigid's court." Cailleach's mouth twitched into an almost-smile as Maryn's hand curled around the smooth handle. She held Maryn there, not relinquishing her tool just yet. "You needn't trouble yourself with such thoughts. You are far more capable than you believe and my totem will aid you as you will it."

Cailleach released her hold on the hammer, letting the full weight of the tool settle into Maryn's hand. It was heavy but well balanced. If worse came to worse, she supposed she could use it to defend herself. "Is this made of bone?"

"The femur of an old druid fiend." She leveled Maryn with a look. "Don't disappoint me and you'll not be used as a totem."

Maryn's nervous laugh died quickly. She wasn't kidding.

"Show that at the spring gate to gain entrance. They will know you speak for me."

Chapter Seven

Leaving Oz

Maryn followed Durvan through the hallways, down spiraling stairs, through hidden doors, and into the uncut, natural stone of a cavern. Maryn, kept pace with the dwarf, her senses on high alert as the grand, open hallways gave way to shrunken, twisted tunnels that required Maryn to duck her head and watch where she planted her feet.

There were no torches here, in the damp, close cave. Instead, a golden orb bobbed along, just over Durvan's head, shadows shrinking and fleeing before him, only to swallow Maryn up just behind.

Maryn muttered to herself, doing her best to keep abject fear from overtaking her. To say that small spaces scared her, especially caves, was an understatement. They terrified her.

After what felt like hours, her heart in her throat, Durvan led her into a slightly upward sloped, rock-strewn tunnel. The temperature plummeted with each step. Her hands shook with frayed nerves as they rounded a corner. Maryn's heart seemed to stop altogether, her breath arrested, as a terrifying sound filled the cavity.

The sound had most likely been present for some time as they'd traversed the narrowing, rocky terrain, but with her mind so focused on keeping up with Durvan and keeping herself from stumbling over the many rocks in their path, she hadn't heard it over her own tripping heartbeat.

It could not be ignored any longer. Maryn's feet stopped of their own accord. Rationally, she knew the sound was simply the cave *breathing*, where the wind and elements whistled over crevices, filling the space with an ungodly howl that drove panic through her veins.

Despite the scientific explanation for what made the sound, Maryn's steps faltered. Her heart pounded so fast that her chest hurt.

Again and again, she glanced behind to prove to herself that nothing followed her. Nothing save ominous dark pressed against her, but the vast emptiness at her back prodded her to walk faster, for Durvan, though still in sight, was too far away for her comfort.

"Don't leave me," she said, breathless. "I can't see well."

"'Tis only the weather," Durvan announced unnecessarily as she matched his stride. Embarrassment made her cheeks flame. She was a woman grown and yet old fears still gripped her and he could see them all.

Maryn affected an air of indifference. "Your little light makes the shadows grow. I can't see what's a real obstacle or just a ghost."

He grunted. "No need tae bristle up like a thistle. Ye needn't make excuses tae the likes o' me. Fear isnae shameful, Lassie. It's what you do despite it that matters."

Maryn had nothing to say to that. He likely wasn't trying to shame her, but the sting of embarrassment bit into her all the same. She walked in silence for several minutes until they came upon a narrow split in the ageless granite, much like a cat's pupil, white with the swirling snow beyond.

"Here is the doorway intae the North Mountain. Are ye ready?"

Was she ready to exit this terrifying death trap? Absolutely.

Durvan moved to a larger boulder at the side of the cavity and brought back two sets of long, delicate looking snowshoes. "Strap these on," he instructed, handing one set to Maryn with barely a glance. She watched how he put them on and copied him, tying the leather fasteners with a double knot. Never having used snowshoes, she'd likely spend more time falling than walking, but maybe falling off the mountain would be better in the end. She'd reach the bottom in record time, in any case.

Durvan retrieved mittens from his pack and wiggled into them. He gestured with his hairy chin to her, indicating that she should do the same. She did, also making sure her cloak covered her properly.

"Brace yerself." That was as much warning as she got.

She followed Durvan into the fissure of swirling light beyond and gasped.

The wind cut, stirring snow into the air and making it hard to see. "Can't she, you know, dial it back a bit?" shouted Maryn into the fray. Snow already gathered on Durvan's long beard and eyebrows, making him look like a disgruntled snowman.

"She cannae," he shouted back. "She's no' got the energy tae contain it."

That news didn't bode well. How far did they have to go, anyway? Cailleach said the journey would be difficult but Maryn hadn't asked for details. It didn't make matters any easier that she was also hauling a twenty-pound pack on her back.

Suddenly, the shelter of the cave didn't seem quite so foreboding.

"Come on," shouted Durvan, motioning her forward. "Let's no' stand here."

They stood on a high ridge, set halfway up a towering mountain peak. Snow obscured the top, but she could just make out the edge of the trail and empty air just beyond. She hugged the side of the mountain, staying clear away from the precipice, stepping high to accommodate her specialized footwear.

If this is the universe's way of telling me I need to work out more, message received. Her legs were going to be wrecked at the end of this.

An hour into their hike down the ridge of the great mountain, her breath was stolen for an altogether different reason. The blizzard, having dissipated into lazy, fat flakes at the lower altitude, allowed her to take in the landscape. Despite the cold, the majestic scene, washed in streams of sunlight that dared to break through the clouds, filled her with awe. Wind-swept slopes gave way to grey-black peaks, as if they trod on the ridge of a giant's fist, its knuckles exposed to the elements. Durvan paused on one such peak, sun-kissed and glittering.

He pointed down the face of the mountain far below, to a shadowed valley cradled at the feet of Cailleach's home. "That's where we're headed. To the wulver den."

That sounded ominous. "Wulver den?" Maryn cast her mind out. The term *wulver* sounded familiar but she couldn't quite place the mythology.

"Aye, great hulking wolves. Sentient...they're going to take us across yon expanse and beyond. At least I hope they do."

Maryn caught his shoulder with a mittened hand. "Wait, you *hope* they'll aid us?" she asked, her trepidation growing. "What happens if they don't? Do we become dinner?"

Durvan shrugged. "They're mostly nonviolent."

"*Mostly?*"

"Och, but yer a wee twitchy thing. Do ye wish tae walk the entire way? Leagues upon leagues?"

Maryn followed his gaze across the wide plain of shimmering snow, stretching unknown miles to another wide swath of trees across the valley. On the other side of the trees, the topography rose again to towering heights. It seemed impossibly far.

She swallowed heavily, her stomach in knots over their would-be escorts. "Is that where Spring's door is? In those trees?"

Durvan huffed a laugh. "If only it were so close." He shook his head, the crusted snow in his beard barely swaying despite the wind. "Spring's door is a week's journey away at least, through the southern pass. There." He indicated a dip between two peaks, partially obscured by clouds in the far distance.

The enormity of the task laid before them weighed heavily on Maryn. A week of travel? In this weather? Her legs would never make it. They'd abandon her and stay behind.

"A week at least?" Maryn grimaced. "What of my coworkers? My friends? Won't they be out of their minds with worry?"

Durvan hummed in his throat. "I 'spect they might at that." He shrugged his bulky shoulders, the wind in his beard. "But humans are fragile creatures. They disappear all the time, do they no'?"

This answer did nothing to alleviate her concerns. He was right, of course. People *did* disappear. Their faces peered at her on market bulletin boards or on the telly.

Once she made it home, how could she ever explain her absence? Maryn tugged on the end of her braid. She'd have to cross that bridge when she came to it. "And then what?" she asked, motioning to the distant mountain pass he'd indicated. "On the other side of the pass, what will we find? More snow?"

"Likely. Come now, best get moving. We want tae get into the valley before nightfall."

Maryn repressed a sigh and gathered herself mentally. She followed after the nimble fairy, carefully stepping where he trod. "I think I remember something about wulvers," she said to his back.

Wulvers, if she remembered correctly, were akin to werewolves in the sense that they *looked* like wolves, but they did not change from man to wolf at the full moon. Some stories suggested they sometimes took pity on human suffering by dropping food off at needy people's doors from time to time. But those were children's stories, and this was, absurdly enough, real life.

They'd be frightening to behold assuredly, especially as they would have to share the same space. No wild animal, no matter how calm it appeared, should be trusted. Supposing that luck was on their side, and it turned out that wulvers didn't hunt humans, they still might not want Durvan and herself in their space. Or maybe they did hunt humans? She couldn't trust her memory or fables.

"Is it true they leave fish for starving humans on their doorsteps?" She crossed cold, stiff fingers. Any creature that cared for the needy seemed less likely to eat her. An image surfaced from her old story book of an upright, gentleman wolf, wearing a plaid coat and hat, a fish folded in newspaper under his arm, standing on a stoop. Nope. No way she could trust the child's fable she'd been fed.

Durvan grunted. "I've heard tell o' them doing such from time to time."

"How many will we find down there?" she asked. Durvan wouldn't feed her to the wolves, of course, but she couldn't help her unease.

Durvan shrugged in answer, which did nothing for Maryn's nerves. For all she knew, the wulvers might be hungry enough to share *them* with their human neighbors.

She pulled the gifted cloak around her as they entered the shadow of the peak. Said cloak, though beautiful, served more than simple ornamentation. Cailleach's spell work repelled the wind far better than any modern winter wear she'd ever purchased, no matter how state-of-the-art or expensive.

Maryn's boots, however, were not to the same standard. She should have worn Cailleach's offered slippers. Snow encrusted and damp as hers were, her toes had turned to rocks and they'd only been walking for a few hours. And her hands! The fine bones in her fingers felt sharp under her skin.

Spring court was a week away at least! She suppressed a groan and stamped her feet, encouraging blood flow.

Durvan, for his part, seemed perfectly impervious to the cold. He seemed almost happy, in fact, smiling at her through the ceaseless wind. Or maybe it was a grimace, glinting at her through wind-tossed beard. His grumbling had lessened in any case, which suited her just fine.

After a long time, they descended Cailleach's treacherous mountain and found relative solace in the leafless trees. Durvan instructed her to remove her snowshoes and deposit them at the trail head." For the trek up," he informed her with far too much cheer.

The crunch of snow underfoot all but obscured any noise, so by the time the sun started to set, her ears had grown numb to sound.

"This way," instructed Durvan needlessly, like Maryn was likely to wander off, especially with the promise of wolves nearby.

He led her through an ice-encrusted copse of conifers, the bark glassy with frozen rain, the boughs drooping. Maryn's neck hurt with how often she whipped her head from side to side, ensuring they weren't caught unaware.

Several minutes later, Maryn, looking over her shoulder, walked right into a stationary Durvan.

"*Oof.* Sorry. Why have we stopped?" she asked.

He lifted his nose and sniffed. Maryn tentatively copied him but smelled nothing.

Durvan didn't respond, as usual, and walked on, the crunch of hardened snow filling the silence once more. After a dozen or so paces, he stopped again and held up a hand, forestalling her question. Head canted to the side as if listening hard, Durvan's eyes roved over the clearing, lingering on the spindled branches overhead. After a few beats, he shrugged off his apparent distrust of the goings on and waved her onward.

"What's wrong? What is it?" she asked him, her thumbs tucked under the straps of her pack, eyes roving.

"I thought there was something here."

"A wulver?"

"Not a wulver. Come on, the den is this way." He moved to the left, closer to the foot of the mountain.

Any relief she'd felt at having finally made it down the sloping goat's trail evaporated as they came upon a keyhole entrance on a rocky slope, just above head height. Someone, or something, frequented the trail in and out of said entrance, as evidenced by the discolored, packed snow.

Durvan stopped her at the bottom of the hill and cupped one gloved hand to his mouth. "'Lo the house!" he called.

A stretched, pregnant silence followed, making Maryn twitch. And then, a wulver emerged, *huge*, with its heavy winter coat, shining teeth, and long legs made for the hunt. It sniffed the air, no doubt getting a taste for the willing meal that just appeared upon its doorstep. How perfectly gracious of them to show up at dinner time.

Durvan bowed neatly, one hand thrown across his middle in a courtly fashion. Maryn didn't know what shocked her more, Durvan's manners or the fact that he attempted to communicate with a terrifying predator.

The creature stalked forward, its hungry eyes intent upon the dwarf as he straightened.

Chapter Eight

Cailleach's Hammer

Maryn was coiled, ready to run, her eyes darting between her escort and the terrifying wolf. A bone-chilling growl emanated from the beast. It reverberated in her chest, weakening her knees. As far as desirable deaths went, being eaten alive had to rank low on the list.

"Durvan," she hissed, taking a step backward. "I don't think—"

"Wheesht," chided Durvan. Maryn could only gape, her breath stolen.

"Greetings, *Mac a' mhadaidh-allaidh*. Herself has sent us below. Will ye no' permit us to rest in your care and share a meal?"

As it drew near, Maryn's amazement increased. Although the creature's grey and white coat could not disguise the fact that it had gone without its share of meals, Maryn didn't doubt it could easily overpower them both.

The beast stopped in front of Durvan, and after a beat, sat on its haunches. It sat most regally, its gaze shifting from Maryn to Durvan, who was already placing his burdens upon the ground, seemingly unconcerned.

Even seated, it was nearly as tall as Maryn, which didn't lend her any good feelings toward the animal. Still, Durvan's fearlessness lent her a portion of courage, however small.

The wolf grunted in the familiar way of dogs; its head canted to the side as it observed Durvan's movements.

"Aye, I thank ye," said the dwarf, to Maryn's bewilderment. "It's been a long day at that."

The wolf's answering reply consisted of an interrogative whine that Maryn—beyond all explanation—understood. At least to a degree. She *felt* its meaning more than she heard actual words, but it was a language all the same.

"Aye, you've got the right o' it." Durvan looked to the sky, in which clouds rapidly gathered. Then, as if in afterthought, he introduced Maryn to the majestic beast. "Forgive me, this is my charge, Lady Maryn of clan Ferguson."

Maryn smiled weakly as if that made perfect sense to her and tried not to hyperventilate.

The great wulver bowed its head in an unmistakable deferential gesture.

"Saxby's his name," informed Durvan. "Here," he said, tossing the wulver a piece of dried meat from his pack. "For your hospitality."

Saxby's wet nose inspected the offering, the weight of its stare finally leaving Maryn. The relief of his attention moving to the offered food brought instant relief. Even if the benign stories of wulvers held true, even the most stout-hearted person couldn't sit comfortably in its presence. Durvan notwithstanding.

"What news?" asked Durvan, offering Maryn a strip of jerky. She took it but did not eat it despite her hunger. Her eyes were only for the great wulver, now licking its formidable mouth clean.

Saxby deep groaned in his throat, which quickly turned to a soft growl, full of intonation and feeling. Maryn, thankfully spared mentally forming the wulver's noises into English by Durvan, listened with rapt attention. The dwarf asked more questions of the beast, which Saxby answered in the same growling, groaning form of communication.

All in all, Maryn gathered from their conversation that Saxby's efforts to feed himself along with his pack and any nearby villagers was proving increasingly difficult. The thick ice on the river prevented fishing, and any birds and rabbits left were few and far between. "We'll break up the ice for you come morning," promised Durvan.

Saxby showed his gratitude with a thump of his great, shaggy tail and then, without ceremony, he trotted back up to the den's entrance.

Durvan donned his pack and followed after, Maryn in his wake. Tarrying deep under Cailleach's mountain had been bad enough. Spending the night in a den full of wulvers tied Maryn's belly in knots. Still, she supposed sleeping in the den might be better than spending the night out in the elements.

The entrance to the den remained in darkness due to the ground sloping sharply downward. She paused on the threshold, squinting into the dim. The pinpricks of light—three sets of eyes—stared back at her. Maryn's breath hitched as her feet stalled.

Durvan, for his part, nodded his greetings to each of the other occupants in the small space. The eyes moved forward, coalescing into more great wolves, all with the same grey coat with intelligent eyes of varying colors.

One of the wolves, smaller than Saxby, stalked forward from where it sat at the back of the cave, nose twitching. Maryn rocked backward, ready to run, and realized just in time that the beast was interested in the jerky she still held in her hand. She'd forgotten all about it. Maryn readily offered it to the smaller wulver, her eyes no doubt as large as saucers. Its tail wagged happily as Durvan waved her in.

"Might as well get comfortable, Lassie. They willnae harm you. Come now," he said, removing his rolled furs from his pack.

Maryn sidestepped past the wulver sitting expectantly in front of her, doing her best not to look terrified. Couldn't some animals sense one's fear? Lord, she hoped not.

Maryn stood near Durvan, her back to the sharply sloping wall, so she had to bend awkwardly. The deeper she went into the cavity, the lower the ceiling. At least they were out of the wind.

Durvan, finished with laying his bedding out, summarily abandoned her, mumbling about gathering fuel for a fire.

In the silence that ensued, Maryn looked everywhere except at the wulvers; the weight of their stares rose the fine hairs along her arms. On the floor at the back of the cave lay an assortment of small animal bones and tufts of fur, obscured in shadow. Unfortunately, the dim prevented her from seeing if the wulver's residence contained human remains.

An age passed before Durvan returned, arms empty. "Nothing fit for burning," he announced. "Everything is covered in ice. We'll 'ave tae make do with huddling together."

She'd never been happier to see the fairy, despite the bad news of a fireless night, and busied herself with unrolling her own sleeping furs. The Fomorian had presented the roll, harvested from a great mountain sheep, to her that very morning—had it only been this morning? Heavy and slightly musty, Maryn prayed it would keep her warm. At this juncture, she was only relieved that it didn't belong to a wolf.

As they settled, the wulvers communicated, rumblings of not-quite-growls filling the space. Durvan dutifully translated.

She learned that there were a few scattered villages between their current location and their destination: Spring's doorway, at least a seven-day journey on foot in good weather. "Saxby warns that the villagers are growing desperate enough to eat their horses; we won't find much in the way of hospitality should we venture into a village."

Indeed. It sounded as if they had nothing left to share.

As the light failed, Maryn learned more about the wulvers. They lived here, in the borderlands between the human world and Winter Court. They helped to guard the hidden sheep's trail that led up the face of the mountain and, ultimately, the entrance to Cailleach's domain. Not only did they guard the trail, but they helped the humans in their plight where they could. Durvan, however, had use for them in another way.

"We will clear the river for you come morning, as I said," started Durvan, "but Herself has need tae deliver the lassie to Spring Court as soon as possible. Do ye think ye can take us through the southern pass?"

A deliberation between the wulvers followed. Maryn could feel the rumblings of their conversation in her chest. Durvan handed her a skin of magically enhanced wine, one which radiated warmth through her limbs for long hours, which she happily took, hoping it would help her sleep through the night. Anything to get through staying in a wolf den.

"When did we cross into the human world?" she asked Durvan after a yawn. Now that her bones had thawed a little, keeping her eyes open became increasingly difficult.

"As soon as we left the Fairy Dun," he explained. "When we exited the mouth of the cave, we entered the human world." He shrugged and amended, "Well, the borderlands between our worlds more like. Her temple is near, at the river, where it's easier for the humans to leave offerings."

Durvan then explained about the many doors into varying kingdoms. "Cailleach's kingdom lies in the north, amid the great mountains, but there is also a doorway hidden amid the sea wall. Each kingdom has doorways."

Likewise, there were portals into other kingdoms, scattered abroad. Once one entered the gateway, they would be transported to the fairy realm, thrust into a world of magic. Maryn tried to stay awake and listen, but Durvan's low voice lulled her eyes closed.

At some point she felt a shaggy body lay next to her, keeping her warm. She knew by its distinctly dog-like scent, and whether from the wine or her exhaustion, she couldn't muster concern, and promptly fell back asleep.

Startled awake by Durvan shaking her shoulder in the grey light of dawn, she blinked leaden eyelids and groaned. Hadn't she just closed her eyes?

"They've decided tae aid us in return for your help with the river."

"My aid?" she asked, stifling a yawn. What on earth could she do?

The wulvers were gone. Saxby paced beyond the mouth of his den, his huge feet carving a pathway in freshly fallen snow. Her entire body ached, her muscles protesting every movement, no matter how slight. "Get ye up, Lassie," encouraged Durvan. He handed her more enchanted wine and a strip of salted beef, which tasted faintly of blood. She grimaced as she chewed, but re-plaited her disheveled hair and saddled her pack upon her back.

"Saxby will show us the way to the river," he explained, and then they emerged from the cave's mouth, the bitter gusts of wind biting into her exposed flesh. Her cheeks stung, no doubt chapped, and her lip throbbed where it had cracked from the cold, but she kept her discomfort to herself. Durvan's nose glowed ruddy from the cold already, and Saxby's thick coat displayed droplets of ice. Critical sentiments would serve no purpose except to annoy the stoic dwarf leading her.

They must hurry along and pray they met no trouble on their long journey. Maryn followed the wulver, careful where she planted her feet. Durvan followed after, his occasional grunt as they clambered down the rocky slope from the cave reassuring Maryn that he still trailed close behind.

Maryn realized with no small amount of surprise, as her feet found the snow-dusted pathway at the base of the hill, that she felt quite safe, sandwiched between the wulver and the dwarf. She stopped for a moment and huffed a laugh, shaking her head. Never in a million years would she have believed she'd be in such circumstances. It bordered upon the ridiculous. Who would have thought she'd feel protected betwixt a werewolf and an axe-wielding dwarf?

None spoke as they traversed along the game trail. Maryn carefully ducked under low-hanging branches here and there, and pulled her cloak from a few clinging brambles, but all in all, the going was easy. The closely knitted trees and brush shielded them from the worst of the wind, creating an odd pocket of stillness. No birds fluttered in the bush. No rabbit tracks stamped the snow, adding to Maryn's concern for the world's delicate situation.

Eventually they exited the forest onto a rocky bank, dangerously piled with river stones and blanketed hollows perfect for ankle turning. Saxby led her well, however, and she made it to the iced river, overlaid with crusty snow.

Saxby nosed through the snow, huffing, then sat on his haunches twenty or so feet away.

"There's the lip of the river," translated Durvan. "Get Cailleach's hammer, aye, and break the ice."

Maryn obeyed, grateful to relieve the weight from her shoulders, if only for a short time. The short spike side of the hammer could be perfect for splitting rocks. Or ice, she wagered.

This time, as she held the hammer, something changed. A current of energy sparked to life as her fingers wrapped around the hammer's bone handle. *Strange.* Saxby whined and lurched forward a step, his eyes intent upon the glinting weapon as if he were a mere pup, eager to play.

"He wishes for Cailleach's blessing upon the burn. Say the words afore ye strike the ice."

Maryn turned to Durvan, her brow knitted. "What words?"

"Ye've command o'er Cailleach's hammer, do ye no'? Banish the ice, then and be done with it. Command that it no' reform, so Saxby and his pack can fish for their supper and for those round about."

Maryn glanced at Saxby, waiting patiently in the snow, then back to Durvan. "But I'm no goddess. How can I command anything, let alone ice not to form in *this* weather?"

Durvan's long suffering look showed his impatience. He gestured to the hammer in her hands. "Herself as gave ye use of the instrument as her handmaiden. Ye can feel its power, can ye no'?"

Maryn reflexively tightened her grip on the shaft of the hammer, searching with her senses for the current of energy she'd felt upon first picking it up. Yes, it was still there, a humming stream of *something* that laced through her veins, as if she were a conduit.

"That's right, Lassie," encouraged Durvan. She's given you rights and privileges to act in her name. You can access the hammer's magic. Only say the words and strike the frozen waters. Banish the snow and ice."

Say the words he'd commanded. What was she to say, exactly? Maryn licked dry lips and walked to Saxby, at the water's edge hidden below layers of frozen precipitation. She cleared her throat, feeling unsure, casting out her mind for anything that she might say.

Her first thought was of ancient Gaulish inscriptions in the *Book of Ballymote*. She'd read the book as a graduate student in the archives in the library basement. The text consisted of songs and other poetic speeches that made up bardic training in old Celtic cultures. Druid's spells, in other words. It was believed that ancient druids would have used hymns, chants and poems from the book to bless or curse. Incantations. *Magic*, in other words.

Of course back then she'd only been amazed at holding such an archaic treasure in her hands. She'd put no credence into the words at the time. And even now, she wanted to scoff at the idea of magic, but she couldn't. Here, with such strange companions and a goddesses magical instrument humming in her hands, she couldn't deny any of it. Magic—as ridiculously illogical as it sounded—was a reality.

She strained her memory, trying to recall even one of the verses she'd read from the *Book of Ballymote*, but her mind remained frustratingly blank. She was no singer, but she supposed simple words might do. Glancing over her shoulder at Durvan, her mind fumbled over what she might possibly say.

Ice don't come back? Abracadabra ice be gone? She snorted inwardly, knowing how absurd they would sound on her lips, how ridiculous she'd feel saying them.

Cailleach was known for her hammer and creel, known for the formation of peaks and the birth of valleys. The old stories told of the hag roaming the countryside, scattering rocks from her basket, tumbling towers of earth, and grinding some mountains to dust. Maryn considered these stories, coupling her knowledge of mythology to modern science.

If Cailleach's hammer could perform such magical feats, could Maryn crack the very crust of the earth? Could she form a fault line? Could the hammer in her hands form a vent from the earth's mantle to warm the water? The thought was more comforting to her than making up some half-forgotten druidic chant.

She cleared her throat, feeling exposed and unsure, and hefted the hammer over her shoulder. Heavy, it strained her muscles, but the tool was well balanced. "Open a vent." The wind snatched her words and carried it across the flat expanse of the river. *No good.*

She spoke again, louder this time. "Hammer," she started, "open the earth. Form a pathway to vent the mantle." This time the words held weight. Somehow, her words clung to her, to the weapon in her hands. Clouds gathered. The grey sky above rumbled and the hair on her body stood at attention. Static electricity hummed and sparked. The shaft of the hammer vibrated in her hands.

Just as she swung the hammer over her shoulder toward the ice, a scorching finger of brilliant lightning struck the head of the hammer from the gathered storm clouds. The spike of the hammer connected with the ice with a resounding *boom* that tossed Maryn to the ground.

Rumpled but miraculously unharmed, Maryn righted herself with the help of Durvan. Saxby barked and yipped, but she could not see him. The hood of her cloak obscured her vision.

The earth groaned; the ground quaked then stilled.

"That's done it," Durvan said, from what felt like a long way off, as if he was speaking from the end of a tunnel.

Maryn pushed the cloak from her head. The hammer's handle stuck out of the rapidly melting ice. Indeed, the snow surrounding the hammer turned from white to grey and spread as fast as spilled ink over a page. Her mouth fell open in shock.

Saxby hopped and lurched, barking merrily at the water's edge, which steamed slightly. "It worked?" she asked, surprise coloring her voice. It was impossible. Ridiculous. And yet Durvan had told her true. It *had* worked. She scrambled to her feet and rushed forward to grab the hammer from the riverbank lest it fall through and be lost.

Maryn peered at the hole Cailleach's hammer formed, to the black water below. The ice measured at least half a foot thick. There was no visible rent in the earth, nor any physical evidence of a vent as she'd commanded except for the fact that the ice was, indeed, melting.

The ice split between her feet, widening with a voluble crack. Maryn retreated back to the bank where Durvan waited, her chest heaving.

"That'll do. Best not linger too long," Durvan said.

She likely would get no more praise than that. She smiled at him all the same. "Proud, are you?"

He merely held her pack open for her. She deposited the hammer inside, feeling jittery and not a little amazed.

"Mmmph," he grunted. "Dinnae let it go to your head. The others are waiting at Cailleach's temple. We'll see how well ye employ it then." With that he turned and followed an exuberant Saxby back up the trail, leaving Maryn alone on the bank.

"What do you mean?" she called to their backs. "Great," she muttered to herself. She didn't think she wanted to use the hammer again. Even now her hair was stood on end. A restless sensation flowed through her limbs. She stared at her quaking hand. Would she have any lasting damage? *"Just great,"* she muttered, hastening to catch up. Then louder, "Seeing as I'm the *chosen one*, do you think you could at least slow down?"

"No," called Durvan from somewhere in the brush. "Come on!"

Chapter Nine

Edge of the World

T HE WINDING, BLUSTERY PATH to Cailleach's temple stole Maryn's breath.

Historically speaking, Cailleach's temple accurately depicted the time period—simple and easy to overlook if one didn't know what to look for—but after everything magical Maryn had witnessed, she expected something, well, *more*.

The temple proper was no more than a shallow cave; outside stood six large, rounded stones, covered in snow so that they merely looked like lumps of mashed potatoes. All four wulvers waited there, flanking a split in granite mountain wall, two on each side. As she neared, however, the air grew heavy, charged with some strange magic that prickled between her shoulder blades as if unseen eyes watched her.

No birds fluttered in the bush; no wind stirred the snow as she approached. The fine hairs on the back of her neck pricked to life as she entered the ring of stones, each about waist height. Curious, she pushed away the snow of the nearest stone and found faint etchings there.

"What do they say?" she asked Durvan, peering closely at the intricate lines and symbols. Swirls and zigzags, circles filled with pitted holes, crosses carved with interlacing spheres...it was all beautiful, but it meant nothing to her.

"Each stone tells a story of Cailleach. "These glyphs tell of how she holds all living things in repose, living yet dead, until spring comes to wake them."

Fascinating. Maryn wiped more snow away, exposing what might be a bear. "It's beautiful."

One of the wulvers spoke, a mewling sort of groan that pulled her attention.

"Come, they're eager to begin," said Durvan. He waited at her elbow and when she stood, gestured her forward.

"What am I to do?"

"Just go inside. The wulver will tell ye."

Completely out of her element, Maryn raised her brows, looking at him askance. Durvan, as ever, took no pity on her.

She passed the sentinels on either side of the cave's entrance, ducking under the lintel, marked with more symbols, finely dusted in snow.

On the floor of the short cave lived a pool of water that, despite the freezing temperature, remained liquified. Maryn inspected the roof above, looking for some source of water but found none. Clay jars—offerings—furs, arrows, knives, and other unidentifiable gifts left by praying mortals surrounded the pool. Just behind the puddle was an empty creel—a wide-mouthed basket woven from reeds.

She stared at it all. What did they expect of her? She turned and found four sets of canine eyes peering at her, blocking the exit.

"Er...."

One of the wulvers—Saxby, as he was the largest—padded forward. Maryn did her best to not recoil from him in the tight space. He nosed the basket, careful not to step in the puddle.

"You want me to use this?" she guessed. "And do what with it, exactly?" A ridiculous image materialized in her mind then of her using it gather snow to make a snowman.

"Dip the creel in Cailleach's lamentation, there," announced Durvan from outside.

Lamentation? Maryn bent and retrieved the surprisingly heavy basket, frowning. "There's no way this will hold water," she muttered.

Saxby pawed the ground as if impatient. She shrugged and maneuvered the edge of the creel through the shallow puddle, pulling water inside. When she righted it, however, no water seeped from the substantial holes lining the reeds. Maryn gaped in astonishment.

Saxby backed up, then and turned around, looking over his shoulder at her. Clearly she was meant to follow. She did, her interest growing.

Once outside, the sunlight dazzled her eyes and she had to blink several times to clear them. Durvan stood in the middle of the half-circle of stones waiting. "Set it here, Lassie, then retrieve the hammer." He indicated a spot in the approximate middle. Maryn obeyed, careful not to tip the basket and lose any of its contents.

She shrugged off her pack. "What does it mean? Her 'lamentation'?"

"Cailleach's tears on behalf of all living, from the very seat of her rule," said Durvan with reverence. "As a wise woman, she's lived tae a great age and 'as thus witnessed the eternal cycle o' life and death, which she, herself 'as endured countless times. Still, she mourns fer the loss o' each creature. Her lament for each fallen soul falls upon the floor of her mountain domain and trickles through the rocks to puddle here. Humans come to pay tribute, seek favor, and anoint themselves in the sacred waters."

Maryn, hammer in hand, stared at Durvan. What a beautiful sentiment. Cailleach didn't seem like the type to weep, but the story softened Maryn's heart all the same. "What am I to do?" she asked softly, lifting the hammer as if to present it to him.

He stepped back and pointed at a spot just beside the creel. "Awaken the earth, here, then empty the creel."

Maryn hefted the heavy implement in one hand, as if to test its weight. *Awaken the earth.* She frowned. Just how was she supposed to go about that? Maryn squeezed the bone handle, seeking and finding the tendril of something—magic—course up the length of the hammer and into her hand. It travelled further still up her arm, a quiet vibration of living energy.

She held the hammer over the spot Durvan had indicated. "Awake," she said, her voice hoarse. Nothing happened. She waited, breathless and was about to ask if she should have struck the ground when she recalled that she must pour out Cailleach's tears. Maryn fumbled with the hammer as she lifted the basket. She poured the water onto the ground, which immediately gave way, melting so that a small hole appeared in the ice-crusted snow.

The wulvers drew closer, as did Durvan, all peering into the three-inch hole Cailleach's lamentation had created.

To Maryn's utter shock, a tiny, curling tendril of green rose up through the center, then another, and another. There were dozens of them. They twisted together, like a beanstalk and darkened as they matured. Leaves and hairy little thorns sprang from the stalks. *Blackberry canes. Just like her throne.*

The canes groaned and creaked as they doubled, then tripled in size, bending and twining to form a strange shape. The wulvers barked and jumped, the smallest of them trotting up and down the length of the structure.

It only took a minute to form, but when it was done, the realization dawned on Maryn. "Why, it's a sled!"

"Aye," said Durvan, as if Maryn hadn't just preformed a miracle. "Let's get them hooked up to the gangline, then."

Maryn's understanding of sledding amounted to exactly zero, so she watched as the wulvers stood along what Durvan had called the "gangline," a long rope of twisted brambles, these free of thorns. To her amazement, vines had even formed around the shoulders and bellies of the beasts, like harnesses, and when they moved to stand in a line, the gangline *attached* itself to the harnesses.

There was a lot more to it, tuglines and necklines and an assortment of other terms Durvan insisted on her repeating, but she could barely wrap her mind around the fact that she'd performed magic. *Twice.* In the space of an hour.

"They're going to pull us," said Maryn stupidly. "These great, majestic, mythological beasts are going to pull us over *mountains*?"

Durvan paused in placing his pack into the sled to give her an exasperated look. "Aye, what did ye think I meant when I said they were going tae take us through this wilderness?"

"Well, I sort of forgot you said that," she admitted. "I was a little distracted by, you know, the fact that werewolves actually exist."

Durvan had already dismissed her. Maryn took in the flexible basket sled, set up off the ground. It looked lightweight and not at all reliable, but Durvan didn't seem the slightest bit worried.

"Are ye going tae drive or shall I?" he asked.

Maryn huffed a laugh. She would most definitely *not* be driving. "Er, you can. I'll just get us lost."

"It's settled, then. Climb in," he commanded, taking his place on the foot boards in the back. Maryn placed her pack in first and carefully climbed over the side of the blackberry basket, only to lose her balance and fall headfirst. The conveyance creaked ominously at her abrupt entrance but held. *Please don't fall apart and kill me.*

Maryn settled her back against the back of the basket, shaped to form a little seat for the rider. Even better, there were no thorns that pricked her. They seemed glaringly absent from anywhere they might need to touch. Once she was settled with her fur over her lap, Durvan commanded the wulvers start the journey.

"Walk on!" he called. The wulvers pulled, kicking up snow, their tails wagging. The runners slid over the snow and ice; it bumped here and there against hidden roots and stumps, but the going was, otherwise, smooth sailing.

No one will ever believe this. I don't even believe this.

Much later in the day, as Maryn grew sleepy, she spied a village. She desperately wanted to stop to satisfy her professional curiosity, but Durvan ignored her request.

From her seat, she spied at least a dozen circular dwellings with stone foundations only a few feet off the ground, indicating that the inhabitants had dug into the earth to create the majority of their living space. Doing so, living partially underground, kept the ambient temperature more manageable. *Very smart.*

Snow covered the steeply-pitched rooftops. Were they made of sod, timber, something else entirely? If only she could stop for a few minutes. So much had been lost to history.

As they skirted the edge of the village, a man—at least she thought it was a man—heavy with furs, raked through the snow so his goat might reach the hibernating grasses underneath. He lifted his head as they passed, dark eyes solemn, face haggard.

He was there and gone in a matter of seconds, obscured by the trees. She turned and watched the smoke from their dwellings disappear through the tress.

"Why won't you stop? We can give him food," Maryn shouted.

Durvan merely called for the wulvers to go faster. "The best help ye can give them is tae find Spring," he replied. His frothy beard, packed with pebbles of icy snow, gusted in the wind as he snapped the line in his hands.

Three days of travel, up steep passes and down hair-raising slopes, through steepled forests, and past more villages...three nights of sleeping between wolves and a snoring Durvan, three nights of endless stars and sagging northern lights, they finally came upon what seemed to Maryn as the very edge of Cailleach's world.

The towering, barren climes had gradually given way to gentler slopes, far less snowfall, and a wider variety of trees. The southern side of the mountain passes were as far as the wulvers could take them, as the sled could not easily navigate the fine dusting of snow that littered the ground.

At parting ways with the wolves, her heart squeezed. Despite the innate fear they inspired, she'd grown to appreciate not only their service in dragging them across countless miles, but their warmth.

There was something to be said in having her own pack of wild animals at her service. Nothing dared come upon them in the night. She'd likely not sleep so soundly again.

The sled's magical vines retreated from the wulver's backs even as the thornless canes wound about their great shoulders and chests withered and away and died. The vines fell to pieces, as brittle as ice. The sled, too, as if knowing it was no longer useful, fell apart so that it looked nothing more than a great, broken briar patch.

"Thank you for…for everything," said Maryn to the wulvers. Saxby bowed his great head, speaking in his way through whines and groans. Maryn didn't have to read minds or speak wulver to know was saying goodbye.

Misha, the smallest of the wulvers trotted forward and placed her fluffy head under Maryn's gloved hand. "I'll miss you most of all," whispered Maryn. "Thanks for keeping me warm every night." She stroked her grey and brown fur, amazed despite everything that she was touching a wild animal. Well, wild enough. Though intelligent creatures, wulvers were still animals.

"Report tae Herself that we've made it this far," said Durvan in his usual gruff manner.

Saxby whined as if to say, "You think I wouldn't?"

"Here," Durvan added, tossing them each a strip of dried meat. The wulvers greedily accepted his offering, their efforts in chewing the fare the only sound in the wood. They did better than Maryn, in any case. The jerky hurt her teeth.

Then, with a bark from their leader, the creatures turned tail and trotted back the way they'd come, unencumbered by a stout dwarf and a full-grown human. Without the beasts a sudden loneliness washed over Maryn.

Durvan handed Maryn her pack. *Back to business. It was time to walk.*

"You could have said thank you, you know," she said, searching without success for any sign of the departed wulvers through the trees. "They did bring us through the worst of the weather after all."

Durvan grunted and readjusted his axes. "Should servants o' Cailleach be praised for doing their duty?" he asked. The question was rhetorical but she couldn't help but answer.

Maryn frowned after him, following in his wake. "Servants or no, they did us a service."

Durvan grunted. "Fed 'em, didn't I?"

Maryn's stern expression softened slightly. Yes, that was as much gratitude and affection as Durvan was likely capable of showing.

Even so far south, the frozen, desolate landscape left her downhearted. Despite the many miles behind them, losing the wulvers, coupled with the weight of the unknown journey ahead, depressed her. She stared at what vegetation sprang from the smattering of snow, drooped and withered.

The sun, high and cold, could not cut through the bitter wind. Miraculously, a bird fluttered from a branch, a bright streak of life that instantly lifted her spirits. Life endured, even after such harshness. "Did you see it, Durvan?" she asked, her voice reverent.

He had. Squint lines around his eyes hinted that he smiled. "Aye. A wee redwing. A good sign, that. Haps things arenae so dire south o' the mountain passes as we first supposed."

Maryn could only hope. "Where to now?" asked Maryn. "Where will we sleep tonight?"

Durvan gestured with a thrust of his chin. "Across yon field we'll find an eastern road leading us tae the spring kingdom. If we step lively, we'll reach an inn by sundown."

An inn! A bed and a hot meal . . . maybe even a bath. Maryn's skin tingled with the prospect and quickened her stride. Druvan grunted at her enthusiasm.

They walked for hours, passing only one young boy in a field with a herd of goats. The sight lifted Maryn's spirits further. Something about the pastoral scene, in addition to the promised inn, ignited romantic thoughts in her mind of a cozy tavern and a genial innkeeper. He'd serve them hot stew and dark bread, seasoned heavily with rosemary and onions. They'd sit by the communal fire and listen to stories or even a bard.

When they finally came to the inn much later, all of Maryn's daydreams fell to pieces. The inn, nothing but a stable, sat in a windblown, open field. Nearby a croft, in no better state than their accommodations, lived the owner. Durvan paid him for their stay with a length of cloth and a jar of pickled eggs. Maryn frowned at the exchange. She'd rather keep the eggs and trade the jerky.

They shared the space with a small handful of other travelers, all of whom viewed Maryn and Durvan with distaste. No one spoke to them much less met their eye. Heaps of flea-infested straw served as their beds between stalls. Maryn's longing for a hot, sumptuous meal turned to ashes. Instead they ate their usual fare: salted meat—fish this time (oh joy!)—and charmed wine.

Maryn pressed her lips together as she took the fish from Durvan. She should be grateful for any sustenance, but she couldn't quite conjure the feeling, dreaming of take away from the Chinese restaurant near her flat. *Wontons and pork fried rice.* Her stomach growled.

"How much farther?" she asked, frowning at the "food" in her hand.

Durvan spoke around his bite. "If the weather holds, three days."

"Can we hire a horse and cart do you think? It would be faster."

"Och, aye. No doubt t'would be, Lassie, and who is it ye ken that has such a conveyance, or the time?" He shook his head, "Such a thing isnae so easily come by. The farmer here only has the one auld ox in the back stall, a pack of goats, and a handful of fowl."

Maryn's shoulders drooped. She handed her share of dinner back to Durvan. "I'm not hungry," she lied. She *was* hungry. Starving, in fact. But she couldn't bring herself to eat one more piece of salted *anything*.

Durvan shrugged as if to say "suit yourself." He handed her the wine skin, which she accepted. The wine would at least keep her warm if not make the hunger pangs go away.

"I'm going outside," she announced, "to, erm, take care of some business." She refused the communal pail set in one corner of the barn. Durvan gave her a look that clearly communicated for her not to go far, dally, nor cause him any trouble.

She ignored his look and wrapped her cloak more securely around her as she exited. While smelly, dirty, and decidedly not private, the stable, at least, provided warmth. Maryn's breath clouded before her as she walked around the corner to the long side of the structure.

Picking her way through the gloom, shapes of hand-held farming tools and what must have been a plow blade loomed at her in the dark. She couldn't relieve herself so close to the barn, but no trees lived in easy distance.

Maryn mentally collected herself and trudged through the dark towards the only line of bushes a good hundred paces away.

While she was in no way comfortable on this journey, she wasn't expressly miserable. Yes, she wanted to go home. She wanted a hot shower and clothes straight from the dryer. She'd do something questionable for a good cup of tea and her bed right about now, but, as an archaeologist she was also getting a first-hand education in all things *past*. She had landed in the latter part of the iron age, for heaven's sake. Would Durvan bring her far enough to see Hadrian's wall, assuming it was there?

A howl pierced the night, unlike any sound she'd ever heard before. Maryn froze in place, handfuls of skirts gripped in her fists as she stood from her crouch. *What was that?* She'd spent days with wulvers, had heard them howl and growl and even bicker with each other, but she'd never heard anything like that before. She tensed, the fine hairs on her body prickling with awareness. Whatever made that sound wasn't far away.

Maryn did not dally. She hastened back, her neck sore from constantly looking behind her to ensure she wasn't being stalked by some wild animal. The smell of the barn hit her as she entered: unwashed bodies and animal waste. She covered her nose and tiptoed over snoring men and women, all wrapped in cloaks and furs.

Durvan's lantern burned softly, a guiding light in the dark from where it hung on a nail on the far wall. He nodded to her as she came upon him. It endeared him to her slightly, to know that he wouldn't fall asleep until she had returned.

"Did you hear that animal outside? What was that?"

Durvan grunted and turned over in his furs. "Ye dinnae want tae know, Lassie. Rest now. We start out early."

When she went to unroll her bed furs, she found an apple, red and slightly withered, set atop her pack.

She smiled and lifted it to her nose, smelling the sweetness of the fruit. A rare thing so late in the season. "Thank you," she whispered, tucking into her cloak pocket.

Durvan, as ever, did not answer.

Chapter Ten

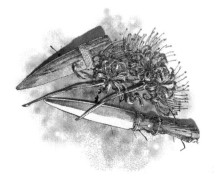

Murder in the Forecast

They walked for hours, trudging through snow-swept fields, through forests of towering beech and pine encrusted with diamond frost, across frozen lakes and endless meadows of broken, yellowed grain stalks. They stopped in a copse of evergreens at some point in the day when her feet slowed. She glanced at the high, cold sun overhead, by its position, midday.

Maryn gnawed on yet another salted beef strip while visions of a hot meal played across her mind. If she never saw another strip of jerky in her life, she could die happy.

"Whatever happened to the 'fairy food is so good, you'll be ruined for your own' business?"

Durvan actually smiled. At least she thought he did. His eyes crinkled and his beard twitched in any case. "I'm no cook," he offered as explanation. "We travel light and will often have to go without a fire."

"Will we have a fire tonight?" she asked hopefully. Her toes verged of numbness already, and they still had days of walking ahead of them. The thought of what was still to come made her chest tighten.

Durvan, not one for conversation, replied, "Perhaps."

She'd given up asking her many questions as they'd walked. The wind stole her words away just as quickly as they left her mouth, and she'd grown tired of shouting at his back. Everything hurt. Now, even at rest, Durvan evaded her questions.

"What does that mean?" she asked irritably.

Durvan's eyes found her own, pulled from where they'd been trained in the long-needled branches overhead. "It means I cannae say if it'll be safe for one. A fire draws unwanted attention."

Maryn looked across the field to the dark line of the forest beyond. Something about it made her wary, though she could decipher nothing unnatural from where they sat. She studied the black smudge of trees on the horizon, trying to discern from where her anxiousness came. Even from across the field she could see that the trunks were close, the branches ending in sharp angles like clawed hands. She shook her head, forcing her imagination away.

Durvan was up again, replacing his water skin in his bag. She groaned inwardly at how quick their rest had been and put her "food" into her pack without complaint. She made to stand onto her beleaguered feet, when he looked into the branches overhead once more, his head canted sharply upward.

"What is it? What do you see?"

He held up a hand—a shushing motion—his eyes narrowed on some hidden danger. "We're not alone," he confided, his voice low. "I think we're being followed."

When she opened her mouth to ask for details, he said, "Haud yer wheesht, Lassie, if ye ken what's good for you. Quickly noo," he said, motioning with a hand for her to hurry.

Maryn didn't have much to gather, but obeyed all the same. She shoved her water skin into her pack and hefted her burden upon her shoulders with less difficulty than she had when they'd first set out. Rather proud of her progress, she couldn't help her grin. They walked briskly up a slow rise, the iron-grey clouds kissing the horizon. A haze swathed the distant feet of the mountains, edged with black forest, at least a mile away.

Her sluggish and sore body complained after sitting but her joints slowly warmed to the exercise. "What did you see?" she asked, glancing back at the copse they'd abandoned. A single bird—a crow from the looks of it—lighted from one of the upper branches.

But no, not just one. Another joined the first, twin smudges against the clouds. As she watched, three more birds joined the others, their inharmonious *caws* sharp and discordant. Strange. Weren't crows more solitary birds? Did they flock like geese?

Durvan steadily climbed the small rise in the open field ahead, the crunch of straw-covered frost mounds loud underfoot. He slowed at the peak of the hill then stopped, his shoulders tense. More birds—six or eight, she couldn't count—flew towards them from the west.

Perhaps Durvan's unease fed her own, but her stomach soured. She couldn't say why the birds flocking toward them disturbed her, but when Durvan turned to her, his stoic visage uncertain, the unsettled feeling in the pit of her stomach intensified.

"What is it?"

"I didnae wish to, but I think we'll have to go in there," he said, nodding toward the hazy forest to the east. The very same woodland that seemed to warn her away. "We might be able to lose them in the Black Wood."

"Lose who? The birds?" she asked, searching the skies. The crows had gathered into a dark horde behind them, their screams sending a chill through her. No, not ordinary crows at all.

Durvan commenced walking at a quick clip, grumbling to himself, fumbling with something in his pocket. He withdrew a sling and a leather drawstring pouch. He did not slow even as he pulled the bag open with his teeth.

Maryn hastened to help. She took the bag from him and offered him a smooth, round river stone, about the size of the end of her thumb. Her hands shook as she palmed another and pulled the bag securely closed.

"Are they dangerous?" she asked, her throat dry.

"They're spies and unfriendly at that."

Maryn looked overhead. The swarm had doubled. They appeared to her as an angry swarm of bees. The caws and shrieks pierced through her, heightening her fear. Durvan paused long enough to place the stone in the center of his sling. He folded the soft leather around it, fisting the strings in his right hand. He swung the sling in a tight circle, the sound it might have created swallowed up by the birds.

He let loose and ran, not even waiting to see if it hit any of the incoming crows. She ran with him, the screams of the eerie flock growing louder, almost upon them. Maryn, with her longer legs, outpaced Durvan, but in her haste, she misjudged the uneven, furrowed soil, and tumbled as the toe of her boot caught on some unseen obstacle.

Pain burst through her shoulder and down her arm as she connected with the frozen earth. She ignored the pain. Durvan was pulling her to her feet, a fistful of her disarrayed cloak in his meaty hand.

The birds fell in a dizzying frenzy, a tornado of wings, sharp beaks and shredding talons. Pain sliced through her scalp as the birds yanked hair from her head. Talons scratched at her exposed skin. Eyes screwed shut, Maryn fumbled and staggered forward, her arms thrown over her head.

"Get ye gone, ye maggot infested curs!" Durvan shouted beside her. He waved his arms wildly, fighting off the biting, clawing horde. One of them caught hold of some part of his beard and pecked frenziedly at his eyes. His scream raised the flesh along her nape.

Durvan stumbled as he grasped the offending crow from his beard and crushed it in his hand. Maryn yanked on his leather armor, batting away the flapping wings and sharp claws with her free hand. Durvan's weight proved too much for her.

Desperate, Maryn dropped her pack and rooted into the central compartment, her hand searching for and finding the cool handle of Cailleach's hammer, ignoring the birds as they tore her cloak and her flesh. If Winter's hammer could open a vent in the earth, certainly it could make quick work of these pests.

She swung wildly, connecting with at least one crow. The flock swarmed around her, leaving Durvan. Maryn stammered, recalling that she had to use words, but she couldn't think. There was some disconnect between her brain and her tongue. She swung at the tornado of talons and wings, connecting satisfyingly with some of their fragile bodies. "Go!" she grunted. A mewling sound escaped her on her next swing. "Get! Leave us alone!"

While the hammer proved a useful weapon against the swarm, no lightning crackled above. Nothing supernatural happened at all. *How perfectly poetic.*

Durvan was on his feet now. He shouted at her to run, tugging on her cloak. She obeyed, her fist a vise around Cailliach's hammer. Durvan shouted, his voice a rasp. "Tae the black gates o' hell with ye! Dare ye enter *his* kingdom and ye'll no' see another day!"

Maryn, frantic, barely registered his words, having only the slightest bit of self-possession remaining. They sprinted, lungs burning, wings beating against their heads, hair parting from her scalp, the violent screams reverberating in her ears.

As soon as the shadows of the tall, straight pines fell upon them, the birds fled in a cacophony of wails, dispersing into the grey expanse of sky. Maryn fell to her knees just within the trees, her body shaking. "What *was* that?" she asked, glancing at her companion. Her breast rose and fell in quick succession, her lungs aching. He'd said they were spies, and perhaps they were, but *birds*?

Durvan's face had received the brunt of the attack; his left eyelid was swollen and bleeding, but he still had use of it. Her trembling fingers went to her own face, skimming its contours, slipping over trickles of blood that came from her hair line. She still held the hammer, her knuckles starkly white against the blue of her cloak. She touched a particularly sore patch near her temple and winced at the sting. Scratches crisscrossed her hand, as they did her face, but she was otherwise unharmed.

"I hate birds," spat Durvan. He swore emphatically, wiping blood from his face.

"Who would spy on us?" asked Maryn, her breath returning to something resembling normal.

He shook his head. "I cannae be certain. I can only say as who *might* have sent them. Whoever they belong to, now that they've see ye with yon hammer, they'll report back tae their master quick-like." His tone did not censure her, only state fact. Still, she felt the sting of error.

Maryn eyed the tool in question. "Hold on, I thought we just had to find Brigid. Now you think there's some plot against Cailleach?"

Breathing rapidly through his ruddy nose, he said, "What else could it be?"

"Should I not have used the hammer? I couldn't think of the words. I wanted the sky to open up and take them. I wanted lightning to kill them all, but I couldn't think of what to say."

Durvan grunted in agreement and pulled his bag from where it hung across his chest. After some rummaging, he pulled out a flask and a red handkerchief. "Words are important," he agreed. Dousing the rag with the spirits, he pressed the damp cloth to his face and winced.

"Why wouldn't they enter the trees?" She had to admit, she'd been uneasy about them herself, but that had been before a flock of murderous crows had beset them. She accepted the flask of spirits and applied it to her hands and face. "Ouch!" The cleansing stung something awful, but she meticulously applied it all the same. The last thing she needed was to get an infection in a world where antibiotics didn't exist.

Her heart slowed to something like normal, her shock lessening, but now the sores throbbed all over her body. She found a rather large gouge at her nape where a chuck of hair had been ripped away.

Durvan's eyes scoured the limbs above them, searching the sky. "I didnae wish tae come this way, but...." He shrugged here, indicating silently that under the circumstances, they hadn't had much of a choice. "This forest is the borderland between the human world and Annwn."

Maryn frowned in thought. "Isn't that the underworld? Death's domain?" At Durvan's nod she said, "But Cailleach said not to go there."

"Aye, I ken well enough what she said. I don't plan to enter his kingdom, mind, but if we travel along the border, we might avoid danger." His gaze lingered on the deeper portion of the woods where shadows clung heavily to rocks and stumps. To Maryn's mind, he looked unconvinced by his own argument. His uncertainty did not warm her.

The pines rose tall and slender. They swayed in the wind, branches creaking. Tiny mossy beards clung to the lower limbs of the trees nearest the field, twitching as the breeze pushed and pulled at them. Maryn's mind touched briefly on what dangers might lurk in this wood, which seemed oppressive at best, but shied away from the thought, unwilling to yield to further fears.

She swallowed the question of what might lurk here and focused on replacing Cailleach's hammer. When she finished, Durvan offered her the handkerchief, pointing out a line of drying blood trickling down her cheek from her temple that she'd missed in her own ablutions.

After they cleansed their cuts and drank some water, they set off, Durvan's gait hitching slightly with each step. He ignored her questions regarding his well-being and so she stopped asking, retreating once again into her mind.

Durvan said they traversed the borderlands of the underworld. What did that mean? Were there portals, like Cailleach's cave, that allowed one to enter the Fae realm dotted around Great Britain?

"Are there no villages near?" she asked, her voice small. Something about the forest seemed to command respect. Quiet.

Durvan must have felt it too because his answer was just as hushed. "There are no large villages near the borderlands. Most can sense the magic of the place, and when they cannae feel it, their beasts surely can."

She certainly felt something in the air, an ominous, oppressive feeling no doubt meant to keep people away.

They walked in silence, going slower as if they must tiptoe through the pines lest they attract some unseen menace. If she had a map, she'd ask Durvan to show her. Maybe she'd draw one for him if she ever got ink and paper. She searched her memory about the late iron age. "Are there armies here? Perhaps farther south?"

Durvan grunted, sidestepping a pinecone as long as her forearm. "There was an army that came. Built a wall, they did, but they left after some time."

Maryn's heart lurched. *A wall? Could he mean a Roman wall?*

Durvan continued. "They harassed the clans some, but they couldnae get a hold on them. Hard to conquer a people with no clear ruler, let alone no cities to occupy. The cold is what got them in the end. The invaders didnae last long. At least that's what I was told."

"You don't involve yourself with human concerns?" she asked, curious. "I thought humans prayed to the gods for help in such things."

"Mmmph," he said, sounding more like his surly self the deeper they penetrated the forest. The trees grew larger here, and the path narrowed to a single track, like a deer trail, which forced Maryn to walk behind. At least the canopy of trees kept out the snow, allowing only a fine dusting, the burnt orange of fallen pine straw peeking through the thin, white blanket.

The diminishing sunlight didn't bring comfort. Hollows and ravines pooled darkness, sending her imagination into overdrive. Talking helped some. She pulled her gaze away from these places and ignored the quickened cadence of her heart.

"Humans wouldnae pray to Cailleach during invasion. What need have they o' Winter in such a time? No, it'd be tae the goddess o' war, The Morrigan, they'd intreat. I only heard tell of the clan land's invasion through rumor."

"What sort of things do the humans pray to Cailleach for?"

After a thoughtful silence he answered, his tone reverent. "Cailleach is the land itself. My mistress shapes the crags and smooths the valleys. She is the very force of the elements and a guardian of all living things. Mortals pray to her to watch over their animals and beg rest for their land so that, come spring, it will be fruitful."

"You seem very loyal to her…to Cailleach. How long have you served her?"

Durvan motioned for them to take a branch of the trail that led to the north, which, she assumed, would keep them parallel to the farrowed field they'd left. "Two hundred years," he supplied. "My sire served Herself before me, and his father before him. My family has served the goddess for longer than your mortal mind can fathom, Lassie."

Maryn's mind boggled. *How old was Cailleach, anyway?*

"There's a dried riverbed up ahead a ways. We can sleep there tonight with a fire. The banked walls should keep the light hidden."

Maryn's hope for a restful sleep rekindled. "And maybe you can roast something fresh over said fire?" she asked, the wish evident in her voice.

Durvan mumbled something she could not hear and then, "We'll no' see any game if ye dinnae stop wagging that tongue o' yers."

Maryn smiled at his back. She knew she'd grow on him eventually.

Chapter Eleven

Morrigan's Well-Laid Plans

TORMID TRUDGED ALONG THE path to the goddess's shrine by heart. Well-traveled, even amid such poor weather, a deep rut had been carved into the snow and ice so that even a blind man could find it. Despite Brigid's apparent disregard for their suffering, the villagers continued to plead to her for relief. Though they had nothing more to give as a sacrifice—no more winter apples or portions of barley to lay upon her altar stone—still they trudged through the snow and bitter wind to offer all they had left: their tears.

They had left a boy there three days ago, wrapped in his winding sheet. It would be a long time yet before the ground softened enough to bury him properly, but he would keep in this weather.

Some thought leaving the poor lad upon Brigid's temple stone improper. Some said as how leaving a human child here would only anger her further. She would see it as censure, some said. Tormid didn't know what they'd done to anger the goddess in the first place, but he, as the clan leader, grew desperate. He wouldn't risk her wrath. He would retrieve the boy and bury him under the snow to keep any animals from him and until Brigid accepted their offerings and heard their prayers.

They had no food stores left, and only a scant few animals. The game had all left for warmer climes and the ice on the loch too thick to cut through. If spring did not come, and soon, they would have to resort to eating their horses. He grimaced as he walked the packed trail.

Climbing up the last of the little rise on which Brigid's altar stone lived, he found a man there. Tormid halted. The man, dressed in the white robes of a druid settled a basket upon the cluttered stone. He turned at Tormid's approach, his soft brown eyes curious.

"Who are you?" asked Tormid. No such creature had ever come near his village before.

"I am a friend," he answered cryptically. "I come at the behest of the Lady Morrigan, who desires above all the peace and welfare of her people." At Tormid's dubious look he hastened to add, "The Morrigan, at least, has the courtesy to hear and answer your prayers, does she not? I am come but where is Brigid?"

Where indeed? The Morrigan, a war-loving goddess, didn't much trouble herself with human concerns outside of a battlefield. What did she care about their suffering? But she had heard their pleas, apparently, and had sent someone.

"What manner of friend comes and doesn't give their name?" asked Tormid.

A soft smile played about the corners of the druid's mouth. Still young, he didn't have the body of a warrior, but that did not mean he wasn't dangerous. Everyone knew better than to trust one such as him. Magic wielders, they were, and as unpredictable as the weather.

The newcomer bowed neatly. "Very well. If you insist. I am called Ciaran," said the young man. His freckles stood starkly out upon his nose and cheekbones. His dark brown hair was cut tightly against his scalp.

Did he not feel the cold? Tormid, bundled up tight against the ever-blowing wind, shivered. Snow crusted his beard, yet this whelp didn't even wear a cloak.

"Now that we are friends," said Ciaran, "come and see what Lady Morrigan offers her people." Stepping slightly off to the side, he motioned to the basket, set near the dead boy's knees.

Curious, Tormid climbed the three stone steps and, giving a brief, sad look at the dead lad, removed the white cloth covering the man's offering. Tormid's mouth gaped at the bounty inside.

After an encouraging gesture from Ciaran, Tormid opened bags of oats and barley, crocks of honey, wineskins, and salted fish. "How—" Tormid shook his head, staring dumbfounded at the man, their supposed savior. "Where did ye come by all this?"

The druid's sad eyes fell upon the deceased boy. "The Morrigan is benevolent, is she not? I only regret that I am so late in coming. My brothers and sisters and I have been doing what we can to help other villages such as this. I will bring more when I can."

Tormid eyed the food, feeling a mix of relief and trepidation. "What does she want?" At the man's raised brow, he added, "The Morrigan. What does she want in exchange for the food?"

Ciaran looked upon him knowingly, nodding his understanding. "You are a wise man, who knows more of how the world is run than most. The Morrigan gives freely, but with this creel comes a warning. She has learned of a desperate plot against humankind."

Tormid stepped closer, eager to hear. "I knew something was amiss. It is unlike Brigid to ignore our prayers."

The druid lifted the large basket from the altar and handed it to Tormid. "Hear me, there is one among you, a mortal, that has stolen Cailleach's hammer," he said, both of them holding onto the basket. "It is she who now commands winter and holds Brigid hostage. If you see her, kill her, and take the hammer. It is humanity's only hope."

Tormid's fist flexed around the handle of the gift, his mind reeling. Someone had interfered with the seasonal gods? That would explain everything. No wonder that winter raged on and Brigid was powerless to relieve their suffering. The seasonal goddesses were at the mercy of another.

"She has the hag's hammer?"

The druid's eyes flashed. "Yes, and now she wields it against humankind. She must be stopped."

Tormid took the basket. "Yes, if we see her, we will kill her. Be assured of that."

Chapter Twelve

Bleeding Magic

Maryn rested well despite sleeping under an earthen overhang with her lumpy pack for a pillow. The fire had warmed her sore muscles into relaxation, and she'd slept like the dead—or as only the truly exhausted can. Durvan's kills—two grouse—and her foraged wild onions, made for a pleasant meal, further lightening her mood. A full belly, as Lolly used to say, served its own kind of magic. Anything tasted better than salted meat at this point.

Little snow remained along the ravine floor thanks to the many overhanging trees and rocky ledges jutting overhead. Sleeping saplings sprang from the ground, their branches catching onto her cloak as if wishing to hold her back.

They'd made good time this morning since entering the forest. They didn't have to plow through a foot of snow, at least; they only had to sidestep the occasional icy puddle or scramble over fallen debris. The trees shielded the worst of the weather and, even better, the ravine blocked the wind. Her poor cheeks and lips were so chapped it hurt to talk.

She compared this journey to the many fairy tales Lolly spoon fed her as a child. Many stories of the Fae stealing away humans centered around sickly children—Changelings—or greedy men wishing to catch a wandering horse near the water, only to find that once caught, they hadn't found a horse at all, but their untimely death.

Other stories described women being stolen by fairies, taken to be companions to otherworldly creatures in equally strange climes. And most importantly, a few stories of humans miraculously making their way back to the human world.

Was this borderland such a place? Could she, somehow, break free and return home? Durvan would stop her, she knew. Not that it mattered. She had no idea how to do it. Guilt pricked her conscience. Cailleach lay weak—dying. Not only Winter herself, but all living beings suffered under the raging, overlong season. Cailleach's words rang in her ears: *I've pulled you through time and space.*

"Durvan," asked Maryn, her voice raspy from disuse, "what year is it?"

"Eh?" he asked, turning his head to glance at her from over his shoulder. "Year?"

"Yes. When I was taken, it was far into the future. Anthropologically speaking, I think we're in the Pictish era, evidenced by the runes I've seen Under the Mountain and on Brigid's blade, but that doesn't tell me exactly *when* we are. The Pictish era spans six hundred years." She paused over something Durvan said the day before. "Yesterday you mentioned that an army had come and built a wall and harassed the clans. How long ago was that?"

Durvan hummed as he considered. "Och, I cannae say for certain. A hundred years? Five hundred?"

Maryn laughed. "There's a big difference between a hundred and five hundred. What you've described is the Roman occupation." She frowned. "At least I think it is."

"Och, but that concerned the humans, no' me. Ye cannae expect me tae ken all their squabbles and travails."

"Maybe they don't concern a dwarf, but they concern the gods, certainly."

Durvan grunted in response. "Aye, what of it?"

She watched Duvan's back as she followed closely behind, her mind working. "I've lived in Great Britain my entire life and I've never heard of a modern fairy tale. They all happened 'Once Upon a Time' or 'Long, long ago.' Does that mean that in my time, in my *present*, that the Fairy Realm doesn't even exist? Is that why I was pulled back to *this* time?"

Durvan huffed, sounding affronted. "Doesnae exist," he repeated, derisive. "Our realm always exists."

Maryn frowned in thought, silent for several beats. Maybe, because people in her time of science and logic didn't recognize seasonal gods, they chose to dwell in times when they were needed? Worshiped?

As a scientist, she could not reconcile with the thought that seasonal gods controlled the elements instead of the very precise tilt of the earth on its axis, ocean currents and other proven information. Some winters were more severe than others, which scientific methods could explain. But if what Cailleach said was true, then she, a goddess, controlled the severity of the season by her whims alone.

The weather at the dig site in her time had been unseasonably cool, even for a Scottish summer. Could the effects of Cailleach's weakness pervade all time periods? It hurt her head, trying to work it all out. The physics of time travel was way beyond her scope of imagination...and her pay grade. She pushed those dizzying thoughts away, unwilling to rehash Einstein's theory of relativity that she'd failed to wrap her mind around as an undergrad.

"Durvan, when you say we're on the borderlands, what does that mean, precisely? Are we presently in the human world?"

"We were in the human realm as soon as we left the throat of the North Mountain," he answered. "There are borderlands—buffers—surrounding doorways into our realms. We guard them and protect them using our magic and, if needed, our might, but it isnae often that a human stumbles upon a doorway. They prefer tae pray at shrines instead, away from the potential dangers that might bleed from the borderlands."

"Bleed?" asked Maryn from beside him. "Does magic often leak from doorways?"

"Magic?" He shrugged and rubbed a gloved finger under his nose. "Sometimes, magic. Sometimes creatures."

Maryn's stomach dropped. Surely he jested. She recalled, then, the terrifying howl that she'd heard at the inn. Maryn's imagination, a vivid, living thing since her childhood, had no trouble conjuring a disturbing image to match the sound.

Maryn pushed the thought away and, to distract herself, asked more questions of her escort. "Erm, Durvan," she started, trying to gauge his willingness to converse. He didn't sigh or grunt, which she took as invitation.

"I've wondered about something. If Cailleach pulled me through time and space, what does that mean for my time? I had a life, you know. A job...friends." *Sort of.* "Coworkers who will wonder what's happened to me."

"Aye, what of it?" he asked, nimbly hopping over a fallen log. Maryn had to scramble over the thing.

She pushed stray hairs from her eyes. Were Scott and Diedre, or her dig site companions Brandon and Icle, out of their minds with worry? "Is time passing for them while I'm here or is life suspended while I'm away?"

Durvan huffed a laugh, leveling her with a searching look, as if he couldn't quite gauge if she were joking. "Ye think time stands still for a single person? That you or I are so significant?" He shook his head. "No, life continues on, just as it does for you here."

His response saddened her. "But they'll be very concerned."

Durvan shrugged as if her concerns were trivial. "Aye, I 'spect they might at that, but this is imporant work you're doing."

She didn't know what to say to that. True crime and unsolved missing persons podcasts weren't popular for nothing. People disappeared all the time in unexplained ways. She recalled that poor old woman on the plane that had tried to share her biscuits with Maryn. Would people think the lady senile, claiming that Maryn blinked out of existence?

Evidence remained, notwithstanding. The flight record showed her name as a soul onboard. What would come of it? She'd just have to make sure she solved this mystery and returned home.

"Och, I thought as much," said Durvan, pulling her from her thoughts. He tapped the side of his nose, giving her a knowing look. "But dinnae ye fash. Find Brigid and Cailleach will put ye right back from where she plucked ye."

As much as she wanted to find Spring, a large part of her doubted their ability to do so. Days of travel and they were no closer in finding the missing goddess. Still, quitting was not an option. Maryn suppressed a sigh and reajusted the bag on her shoulders.

"One step at a time, Ferguson," she muttered to herself.

Chapter Thirteen

Hellhound

Hours later, still in the ravine and lost in her own thoughts on the absurdity of her current situation, the baying of some wild creature from above startled her. It sounded exactly like the sound she'd heard the other night.

Worse, the baying worried Durvan; the rhythmic ping of his axe blades as he walked slowed, then stopped altogether. The absence of the ringing metal created a vacuum of silence that pressed in on her ears.

Maryn studied Durvan's grave expression briefly before following his line of sight, somewhere beyond the escarpment. She didn't breathe as they both listened hard, waiting, but only the irregular patter of wet snow falling from the canopy of trees met their ears.

The gully they'd been traveling in for miles was an old, meandering riverbed. The twists and turns and jutting rocks made it impossible to see ahead of them or behind. The riverbank walls which had at first seemed such a blessing, now felt like a trap. *What now? Could they not go an entire day without something trying to kill them?*

Durvan shook his shaggy head, his beard swaying, and huffed sharply through his nose. "Keep moving. Quickly noo, Lassie."

He didn't need to tell her twice. An ominous feeling settled over her, making Maryn's already anxious condition worsen. After only a dozen or so steps, as if changing his mind, Durvan stopped in his tracks.

Shrugging off his pack, he removed one of the axes from his back. The blade of the weapon glinted dully in the weak sun, the opposite end formed into a deadly spike. "That's no wulver. Here," he said, thrusting the axe into her hands.

She staggered under the weight of the weapon. How did he carry two of them, plus a pack? "I can't use this," said Maryn, frantic. "I'll probably hurt myself before anything else."

Durvan leveled her with his usual no-nonsense glare. "Would ye rather face it empty handed, then?"

Ignoring his question, she instead asked, "What is it, if it's not a wulver?"

As if in answer, the air rang with a sharp, piercing bark, sounding much closer now. Maryn jumped, then stepped closer to Durvan. She gazed around the gully, feeling as if some many-toothed creature bore down on them, but her eyes met only the hills and valleys of boulders, rotting leaf mold, and skeletal twigs reaching for the sky. She tightened her hands upon the handle of her borrowed weapon. Maybe she could use the weapon after all.

"Come on," he growled. "We cannae stay here in this hole. We mun climb our way out afore it reaches us." He grabbed his pack and set off at a trot, not bothering to ensure Maryn followed. She did, of course, sparing a glance over her shoulder.

She hustled after the dwarf, her breath already coming fast, her heart pounding against her ribs. "What...is...it?" she panted after her guide. Carrying the heavy axe was taking its toll already. How could she possibly make it out of here with it in hand?

"Let's hope it's a wolf. And that there's only the one," answered Durvan cryptically.

Apparently spying a likely escape, he veered left where the packed soil gave way to a rocky outcropping. Thick tree roots led up to where a trunk jutted out of the rocks, caked with crusted snow. Maryn couldn't climb that. The rocks and roots ended a good six feet below the lip of the gully.

For such a short fairy, Durvan was surprisingly nimble, hopping and climbing up the rocks as if treading on steppingstones. Desperate, Maryn copied his movements, using the pointed end of the ax in the cervices of the rocks to aid her ascent. Durvan reached the tree amongst the rocks, he held out his hand. "Give me yer axe and I'll pull ye up."

Perched on the slippery surface, Maryn lifted the weapon, struggling to keep it steady. He grabbed it and heaved, pulling Maryn the last few feet up to where he stood just as an unearthly howl split the silence.

Durvan's teeth flashed amid his bristly beard as he said, "That's two."

Two what? What was he talking about?

"Quickly now," he urged. "We havenae much time. I'm going tae toss ye. Grab ontae anything ye can and run like hell to summat high. Climb a tree, or a rock, something ye can defend."

Maryn opened her mouth to protest, but nothing came out. She couldn't defend anything. She was a scientist, not a warrior. What was happening? Who, or what, must she defend against? Is that what "three" meant? Three of those somethings howling like wolves? Sweat broke out on her forehead and she trembled.

Duvan grabbed her elbow and shook her, his expression alarming her further. "If it's what I think it is, ye cannae let yer fear overtake ye. It's how *cù-sìth* trap their prey. Do as I say and ye'll live. Ye hear?" he demanded.

Maryn nodded quickly, trying twice to swallow. "I—I hear."

"Keep her head, lass," he affirmed sternly, then bent over, his fingers laced together to form a foothold.

He was asking quite a lot, but she obediently placed her right foot in his hands, the axe held in a death grip. Without warning, he tossed her upward with a mighty grunt. Maryn flew up the remaining distance to the lip of the small canyon. She thudded to the ground and dug the axe into the earth to cement herself. Her torso lay flat on the crusted snow while her legs dangled into the void.

She shimmied up and around, turning back to face Durvan, her hand outstretched. She wasn't nearly as strong as the dwarf, but she couldn't just leave him. He lifted his axe into the air, his stoic face peering up at her. Maryn's cold hands closed around the head of the axe, one hand on either side of the handle and held on for dear life.

She could not pull with any effectiveness, but Durvan didn't need her to. Using the wall of the gully for leverage, he walked up the side, his feet sending showers of earth to the ravine floor. When he reached the top of the axe and could climb no further, he lunged for a nearby tree trunk, wrapping his arms around its circumference.

"*Run*," he growled, his eyes peering into the middle distance.

Maryn didn't look; she didn't want to see. She took off, her feet slipping in the snow, her gaze pinned on a nearby boulder, backed by a prickly holly bush. Her breath came fast, a little mewling sound escaping her with each exhale. In her panic she forgot the weight of the weapon.

Stupid seasonal gods! She wanted to go home, where her only worry was paperwork and the occasional obligatory, disappointing blind date.

The swift footfalls of some four-legged creature gained on them as she reached her destination. She leapt with a cry, landing atop a lower rock. She scrambled up onto a higher ledge of granite, her lungs burning.

Move, move, move.

When she reached the top of the little bluff, she turned around, just as Durvan reached the mound. Beyond, a monster closed the distance, its powerful back legs coiling, preparing to strike.

Chapter Fourteen

The Path Less Taken

Muscles bunched and coiled under a mossy green coat. Maryn stared in horror at the creature. Black lips curled, revealing crowded, razor-like teeth gleaming with saliva. It's menacing growl reverberated through her body. She couldn't find her breath as Durvan raced for higher ground; the fierce line of his mouth pulled into a grimace.

"Dinnae show yer fear," he commanded through his teeth. "It can kill through sheer fright!"

Maryn tore her eyes away from the vicious animal, surely half as tall as she was, to help pull Durvan up the remaining distance. The jaws of the animal snapped, just missing his foot. If she thought it big, Durvan must think it giant. The thing surely overtook him in height.

Panting, Durvan nodded curtly in thanks and turned to face the beast just as it slid from the rocks, its massive jaws clamping on empty air. The beast's breath clouded the air as it coiled to jump again. Thankfully, it seemed to have some difficulty climbing completely onto the slick surface of their stronghold, its back feet unable to keep their footing.

"What is it?" Maryn asked, her heart tripping.

"First the crows and now this." He glowered down at the monster. "An underling of an enemy would be my guess. A *cù sìth*. I ken two such gods as favors the beasts. What they want with us, I cannae say."

"I might be going out on a limb here, but it seems to me that they want us dead," supplied Maryn, eyeing the leaping, clambering dog-like monster. Its staring eyes met her own green gaze and seemed to smile, exposing overlapping, needle-like teeth, perfect for tearing flesh from bone.

Immediately an image formed in her mind of it shaking her limp body ferociously, like a puppy might a toy, and she shuddered.

"Dinnae meet its eye," barked Durvan, giving her shoulder a firm nudge.

Her gaze broke from the creature at the rough contact and the terrifying image dissolved at once.

"Think of summat else," he advised, thrusting his weapon onto her. The weight of the two axes nearly toppled her; one slipped from her arms, the end knob of the handle barely missing her foot as it *thunked* against stone. She caught hold of the haft, preventing it from falling. Durvan fumbled in his pack. The snarls and growls emanating from the creature sent ripples of gooseflesh up her arms, the fine hairs standing on end.

Durvan withdrew a wicked looking knife, as crooked as a snake, narrowing into a deadly tip, replete with carved, golden runes and symbols. The blade itself appeared as green as oxidized copper.

"A spell-cast blade," he said, answering her unspoken question, "to combat such a beast."

She bobbed her head up and down as if this made perfect sense, her eyes wide. She clutched one of the battleaxes to her chest, the heel of the cutting edge pressing into her clavicle, her breaths shallow and fast. Durvan hefted the much smaller weapon in his right hand and growled, "Think of something . . . mirthful. Quickly, now."

Maryn mentally fumbled, tripping over her stupor of thought. Something mirthful. *Her cat, Frodo.* Yes, he'd been so cute and cuddly. He'd died when she was sixteen. She'd cried for a month after. *Not that memory.* Maryn discarded the sad remembrance and grasped onto the next. If only she could cover her ears to drown out the terrifying sounds. She couldn't *think*! *Pop, teaching her to drive. She'd driven the car into the ditch and dented the bumper. No. Her superior, Scott, getting locked in the port-a-loo at a dig site two years ago. He'd waited for over an hour in the reeking, heated confines of the plastic bathroom until someone had let him out. He'd worried that the stench would never leave his nose. The team had given him a wide berth for the rest of the day. They could smell him coming. She'd laughed every time she'd seen him for a month afterward.*

Remarkably, the monster faltered as it paced. It even seemed to shrink away a step, as if tripping, but then it resumed its ardent march in front of them, teeth bared, great shoulders rolling.

"Aye, that's it. Do it again."

Maryn swallowed heavily and cast out for anything light-hearted or humorous. She spoke out loud, her voice raised to hear herself over the racket. "Once, when Lolly was helping me complete a school project, she got up to get shears from the kitchen drawer. We-we'd been eating sweets and as she got up, she popped some in her mouth. Only it wasn't a sweet. It was her hearing aid. She'd forgotten she'd taken it out and was holding it in her hand. When pop came home, she told him the dog had done it." Maryn, her eyes screwed shut, could picture the memory perfectly. "He'd known it was her." Maryn's smile at the memory was more of a grimace, but the reminiscence was apparently enough.

Maryn opened her eyes to see Durvan leap from the topmost boulder on which they stood, straight for the monster, knife clutched in his fist. He fell atop the beast with an almighty shout. The *cù sìth* yelped, the sharp cry so at odds to its previous fearsome sounds.

They struggled soundlessly. Maryn forgot to breathe. The *cù sìth* righted itself, though it was limping, and clamped its jaws of Durvan's leg.

The dwarf screamed in pain. His cry raised the fine hairs along Maryn's nape. She was no warrior, no fighter. *What in the world could she do? How could she possibly help?*

Durvan fell, unable to keep his feet as the monster dragged him across the ground. Durvan cried out again and tried to right himself even as the demon dog thrashed its head side to side. Durvan flew like a rag doll onto the rocks.

Without thinking, Maryn sprang forward, barely registering the clatter of the fallen axes. Thankfully Durvan still held the wicked looking knife in his right hand. He grunted as Maryn pulled him farther upon the rocks by his cloak and beard, grimacing at the effort. *How much did he weigh, anyway?*

The *cù sìth* leapt for them both, soaring as if in slow motion onto the rocks. Maryn didn't even have time to scream, to think. Luckly, Durvan was ready. He lifted the blade as the monster landed, sinking it into its belly. The cù *sìth's* hot, reeking breath hit Maryn's face. Spittle sprayed. She tumbled backward as the force of its body fell fully upon them.

The sound of the monster's anguished, painful cry filled her head and made her skin prickle. Blood poured from its wound, spilling onto their legs and onto the rocks as it stumbled away. Black blood, thick and fetid.

The creature wasn't dead, but it didn't seem like it could do much other than tumble from the rocks and fumble a step or two before it fell. It did so twice before Durvan limped down the rocks, stoically ignoring his open wound, and approached from behind.

When Durvan brought the knife to the creature's massive neck, Maryn looked away. She should have covered her ears, too. The gurling mewl that escaped the creature would no doubt haunt her dreams. She shivered and dared to look as Durvan approached, the cloud of his breaths filling the air. He was covered in black sludge-like blood, his right pantleg shredded, the flesh beneath bleeding freely.

"It's done," he said unnecessarily as he slumped against a rock.

He looked done in, too. Her hands shook with the aftereffects of the tumult, her stomach queasy. She sucked in a lungful of air, forcing calm.

"Here, let me look at your injury."

Surprisingly, he did not argue. He sat heavily upon the lowest boulder, his feet dangling as he gulped air. Maryn sluffed off her pack and found her water skin. "Do you have any more alcohol?" she asked.

"No self-respecting dwarf would ever be without whiskey. In my bag. Side pocket," he added, gruff.

She cleared her throat and wiped at her face with her forearm before bending to rifle through his things. She found the flask quickly and handed it to him. He immediately self-medicated by taking two long pulls from the flask while she lifted his torn, fleece-lined pants. Thankfully they were thick, which Maryn thought saved him from worse injury. His wound didn't look nearly as bad as she'd anticipated. Scrapes were easy to clean; it was the two puncture marks in his muscled calf that worried her.

They sat in silence for a time, waiting for their limbs to quit their quaking. Durvan finally stood with a suppressed grunt of pain.

"Ye did well," he said, wiping his blade free of blood.

Her eyes, focused on the motionless monster, did not stray as she laughed. Humorless, it felt good to do so. The monster lay on its side, purple tongue protruding from a foaming mouth. Its shaggy green coat looked coarse, like an Irish wolfhound's hair. An accurate comparison, for this demon dog was just as tall, though with much more brawn. The hills and valleys of its powerful muscles bulged under its fur, and though now inert, they spoke to its might and stamina. They'd been lucky there had only been the o ne.

"Will there be more? You said 'that's two', before."

Durvan wiped sweat from his brow. "Those who hear a *cù sìth's* bark must reach safety before the third, or be overcome with terror tae the point o' death."

Maryn swallowed hard. "Why would the *cù sìth* enter the forest, but not the crows?" asked Maryn, forcing her eyes away from the gruesome scene.

Durvan replaced the dagger in his bag. "*Cù sìth* are harbingers of death. They belong to such a place—to Death himself—but there is one who captures and keeps them as pets. She uses them in times of war to spread dread and fear into the hearts of her enemies."

Maryn swallowed heavily. "Yes, I can see how effective they would be."

"The crows," he continued, his gaze sweeping over the trees, "were not borne of Death's kingdom. They daren't enter; their presence would be seen as an act o' war, as Arawn wouldnae look kindly on another being's spies snooping at his doorstep."

"Who? Whose crows? Who sent the *cù sìth* if it wasn't Death himself?" asked Maryn, her mind spinning.

Durvan pursed his lips and glanced her way. "I cannae be certain but...do ye ken the goddess o' war?"

Maryn scoffed softly. "Personally? No, I can't say that we've been properly introduced."

Durvan ignored her cheek. "The Morrigan," he said, "incites warriors to battle. Those who worship her often pray for bravery or for her to strike fear into their enemies." He stared at the unmoving creature he'd so skillfully dispatched, a furrow between his brows.

"So do you think that the goddess of war has some vendetta against us? And when her crows couldn't follow us here, she...she sent that *thing* instead?"

He shrugged. "Could be." He took back one of his axes. With no small amount of awe, Maryn watched his blood-speckled hands, sure and unshaking. How could he be so calm after such an ordeal? She was still trembling.

"I cannae understand why, though," he added.

Maryn had nothing to add as far as speculation went. "Will there be more?" she asked, sounding much braver than she felt.

"It's likely," he said with a frown. "When her pet doesnae return, she'll ken it was either taken by Arawn, or that we killed it."

We was a rather broad term, considering all she'd done was try not to melt into a puddle, his words cheered her all the same. "What now?" she asked, her eyes going to the ravine they'd exited. "Not back in there, I assume."

"We're going deeper intae the woods. Come now, make yerself ready. We shouldnae tarry. We haven't long before we lose the sunlight."

Maryn quickly obeyed, having no desire to spend the night out in these particular woods. She retrieved her borrowed axe with shaking fingers, her ears straining for the slightest sound that would indicate another stalking monster closed in on them. She could hear nothing save for the whoosh of wind through the piney treetops and her own heart in her ears.

Nervous to leave the relative safety of the outcropping and also unwilling to lag too far behind Durvan, she stumbled after him. Of course, he effortlessly navigated the descent off the granite boulders while she fumbled and slid on her back side at the steeper parts. Before long, her feet once more trod on the snow-dusted, pine needle-strewn forest floor, a lifeless monster at her feet. She eyed its huge paws, the black pads of its toes poking out through wiry green hair.

"Why green?" she asked, gripping the axe tightly lest it suddenly reanimate.

Durvan stared down at the creature, his face blank as if killing something with teeth larger than the length of his hand was routine. "Easier tae hide in wait, I suppose," he said with a slight shrug. "Ever seen a wee shepherding dog? They slink upon the ground, sae they dinnae frighten the sheep. They're patient, sheep dogs, waiting for the right time tae move. It's in the *cù sìth's* nature tae do the same, only this one—" he gestured with his axe "—has gone wild. I cannae see why Death would send the creature after us, and him not come along."

Maryn swallowed with some effort, her mouth gone dry. "Death uses these creatures to reap souls?"

Durvan turned away from the beast, and she followed, unwilling to stand there, alone, so close to his kill. "Arawn is a great hunter. He uses the hounds tae shepherd difficult souls. Those who dinnae wish tae enter the underworld. Those who would rather avoid his judgement."

Maryn glanced over her shoulder as Durvan led her deeper into the forest, their footfalls over loud to her ears. She could imagine what kind of soul would linger in the human world in order to avoid ultimate justice. Not a good one. "Is that where ghosts come from?" she asked, her voice hushed. "Hauntings?"

"Aye, sometimes. Come, Lassie. It's a long walk yet tae the door."

Maryn's next step faltered, and she had to catch herself. Her blood seeming to race, her body grown too warm. "What door?"

"Death's door," he said succinctly. "That way." He pointed into the appropriately dark forest behind their temporary battlement.

Maryn swallowed hard. Her chest hurt where her heart continuously beat a wild tattoo against her ribs. "Of course it is," she said, grimacing. She had no choice but to follow.

Chapter Fifteen

In With the Dead

The trek through the deepest part of the wood was mostly devoid of snow, the tree canopy above too dense to allow any through. Sunlight barely filtered through, casting deep shadows amongst the creaking trees. Maryn squinted continuously, wishing for a torch or her phone to help light the way.

They'd walked for hours. Maryn's feet ached and her stomach growled. They'd had to backtrack once, Durvan having lost his way, which didn't help matters. The sun hung low in the sky by the time they came upon a small clearing absent of birdsong or a stirring breeze, however small. The dark clearing held only a stone cross centered between two towering trees. Heavily etched Pictish symbols covered the stone cross.

"Here," grunted Durvan in his usual brusque manner. He pulled off his pack and rummaged around briefly, while Maryn took in her surroundings. The dark, oppressive forest had not changed since they'd first entered, the long shadows feeding into her fears. Every hollow potentially housed some grotesque creature intent on taking their lives. Without thought, she took a step closer to her escort.

"You're quite sure we're safe here?" she asked, starting at the creak of a branch overhead.

"Aye, as safe as a mortal can be," he replied, still digging through his bag. "But it's no' the forest that ye should be concerned o'er, aye?"

His response failed to ignite any warm feelings in her. Maryn stilled as he drew out the same wicked-looking knife he'd used on the *cù sìth*.

Mouth gone dry, Maryn struggled to get her words out. "Wh—what is that for?"

"Death's door requires a sacrifice," he started, gripping the weapon firmly in one beefy fist. His unsettling black eyes found her own. "You must pay the toll, Lassie, and ye wish tae enter into such a place as Annwn and keep your soul."

Maryn stared at the blade and took a step back. "A sacrifice?" She sounded breathless even to her own ears.

Here Durvan smoothed his tangled beard with his free hand, his tone grave, "Whatever you surrender must cost you something, and it must be given using the proper words else your offering will be for naught."

Fear gripped her. She had nowhere to run. "Didn't Cailleach say not to go this way?"

Durvan's uneasy look told her he didn't like going this way either. "Aye, but I cannae see how we can get tae Spring Court with yon beasts afoot."

Maryn flexed her fingers, unsure of what to do or say. She couldn't very well insist they travel as they had been. They'd barely escaped death a mere hour ago. She trusted Durvan, but now he demanded a sacrifice from her?

Did he expect her to choose her least favorite finger for him to cut off as payment? "What sort of sacrifice?" she asked, her mouth gone dry. She looked about her, as if an alternative plan would suddenly sprout from the snow-dusted forest floor.

He stood and slung his pack over his shoulder, motioning toward the cross. "The kind of sacrifice befitting the god o' death." He stalked forward, leaving Maryn rooted to the spot, her hands gone clammy. She couldn't do this. Cailleach asked far too much of her.

Durvan paused at the stone, the two about the same height, and beckoned her forward with an impatient wave of the dagger. "It's you as must make the sacrifice, Mortal. Come. *Closer*," he said with a slight huff when she moved forward only a step.

Maryn gritted her teeth and obeyed, taking the necessary steps to the foot of the cross; her fingers curled into her palms. Durvan nodded firmly and bade her kneel before the cross, to which she refused.

Letting out a string of impolite grumblings, Durvan said, "It's a sacrifice o' summat ye hold dear, ye great bampot, no' yer life. Ye could offer a host of things, but I'd wager that its yer pride that Arawn wants."

"The god of death wants *pride*?"

Durvan cast her a look that told her just how thin his patience waned. "Ye'll have tae trust me," he said, his works brooking no argument. "Arawn is no' only the guardian of lost souls, he is the assessor by which all departed are judged. All dead must stand before his court in their time and be assessed. A great lover o' virtuous and courageous deeds, Arawn. It would be just the sort of thing he'd want, yer pride."

Maryn frowned. She wasn't a prideful person. And even if she could somehow sacrifice something so intangible, how could that require her to be on her knees with a wicked-sharp blade held far too close for comfort?

"Yer hair, I think," he said, assessing her. She felt rather than saw his eyes roving over her form. Her hand went unerringly to the object of his desire.

"My hair?" she squeaked. Sacrificing her hair was vastly better than giving up a finger (or more), but still she faltered. She'd cut her own hair with kitchen scissors as an adolescent, and the outcome had been nothing short of horrific.

"Aye, ye see," said Durvan knowingly. "Yer as riddled with pride as a fish is with worms. Stop yer havering," he commanded, though she'd made no further protest. "Unwind yer plait lest I lose hold o' my patience altogether and take everything I can grab hold of."

Scowling, Maryn fumbled with her knotted hair, tugging on the elastic tie holding her braid in a bun at the base of her skull. Her dark plait fell down her back. Her breath hitched. Her eyes stung. Performing a ritual against her will, even if it was only her hair, to enter the Kingdom of the Dead unsettled her.

She'd been kidnapped, dragged through time and space, attacked by a murder of crows, had slept with wolves and narrowly escaped the *cù sìth* . . . she'd been forced on this ridiculous journey with a surly tour guide, her feet hurt, she desperately needed a shower, and *this* was her breaking point?

She knelt at the base of the cross, so distraught that even her professional curiosity failed her. In any other circumstance, she would have loved to study the ancient artifact before her. Her hands shook; she pressed them into her middle, doing her best to keep calm. Just hair. Insignificant, really, in the grand scheme of things. And yet it somehow gained her passage into a land full of . . . of dead people.

"Say the words after me," instructed Durvan, not one bit sympathetic. In one fist he held her plait and in the other, the crooked blade.

"Not so high," groused Maryn, as the cold metal brushed the nape of her neck. "Move the blade down some at least, would you?"

He expelled a huff of annoyance and moved the blade a few inches further down the long rope of her hair. "I beseech thee, Master of Annwn, Unmaker. Accept this, my offering, in place of my soul, and allow entrance into thy kingdom."

Lips numb, Maryn copied his words, fumbling once or twice. Durvan was patiently repeated the parts she forgot and then, with a swift jerk, her hair parted ways from her skull. Her hand flew to what remained of her hair, assessing. It fell in a jagged, asymmetrical cloud well above her shoulders.

Durvan laid her offering upon an arm of the cross, where it unfurled from its plait, dark strands drooping over the edge. She held her breath, waiting for some miraculous change to the forest but nothing happened. Disappointment welled within her. *She lost her hair for nothing?*

"I'm not cutting anything else off, so you can forget asking."

Durvan ignored her and replaced the dagger, the perfect picture of calm. And then, just as sudden as a clap of thunder, the earth opened up at their feet, reminiscent of a grave. They tumbled head over foot into the dark. Maryn couldn't even scream. Her breath left her, snatched from her lungs. Dirt rained down on them, the roots of trees clung to them as they fell into what most assuredly must be the center of the earth.

But no, somehow, they righted, and their descent slowed gradually until they came to a gentle stop. Her feet touched soft earth and only then did she dare open her eyes. She found herself standing on a springy, moss-covered patch of ground, her head dizzy as if she'd had too much wine.

As she gasped for breath, her hands shaking, she took in her surroundings as well as she could in the dim. Absurdly, impossibly, they stood under the great canopy of a weeping willow tree, the soft glow of some light source beyond the leafy branches dully illuminating the space within.

At their feet were dozens of mushrooms of the most terrific colors and sizes; electric blues, brilliant, fiery oranges, and emerald caps rose from the decaying forest floor, the pungent scent of rotting wood filling her senses. And amid these brilliant mushrooms hovered what appeared to be hundreds of blue fireflies.

She gaped at the beauty of it and bent closer to see.

"I wouldnae touch the little buggers if I were you," advised Durvan gruffly.

Maryn snatched her hand back from a nearby glowing orb. "Why? What is it?"

Sparing her a glance, he moved forward, scattering more lights. They retreated from under the mushrooms, taking to the air and further lighting the confines of the space under the willow branches, giving the entire scene an unearthly glow. Maryn scoffed at herself. Of course it was unearthly. They'd just arrived in the underworld.

"They're sometimes called Luring Lights by mortals. Or will-o-the-wisps. Tricksy blighters in any case. Dinnae pay them any mind, lest they lure ye down dark paths."

Maryn, having grown up in Scotland, knew all too well the mythology associated with the little lights. "I thought they were supposed to be the spirits of the dead," said Maryn, moving closer to Durvan.

"Aye," he said, pulling back a curtain of dangling branches separating them from the outside world. Light poured into the space, making the wisps retreat to their hiding places as quick as a flash. Maryn shielded her eyes against the contrasting light. "Ye've got the right o' it. Dead fairies they are. They werenae trustworthy in life, nor are they in death, and so they are punished to live out their existence as lesser beings."

Maryn forgot her next question as her eyes adjusted. Annwn—the underworld—did not meet her expectations. Visions of fiery lakes, sulfidic fumes, and many-toothed creatures lurking around every dark corner had filled her mind. She stopped in her tracks, speechless.

"But it's... beautiful," she said finally, turning on the spot to take it all in. The sweeping, verdant landscape, like a summer meadow, invited her in. The sun lingered low on the horizon, casting vivid pinks and oranges across the sky in a stunning display of color. In the far distance to the right sea sparkled, the gulls riding high on an unfelt wind.

To the left trees dotted grassy fields, and straight ahead, where Durvan already headed, she could just make out the black spires of a great castle peeking out above a rise.

"What did ye expect?" asked Durvan over his shoulder, stalking off across the grassy field. Maryn rushed to catch up, her eyes roving to take it all in.

"Well," started Maryn, "caves full of bats and stinking fumes, for one. Damp and rot." She shrugged, following a colorful bird as it startled from a branch by their passing. "You know, the stuff of nightmares."

"Och, aye, there's plenty o' creatures 'ere as would curdle yer wame quick enough, but ye'll no' see them, nor the holes they hide in. It's only the souls of those who've lived lesser lives as would be banished to such places."

"Lesser lives?" asked Maryn, ducking as an overlarge insect buzzed her head.

Durvan made a noise of assent in his throat. "As I said. Just like the will-o-the-wisps ye saw at the doorway, there are some as have lived their lives poorly and so they are relegated tae an existence befitting their choices."

"Like being sentenced to their own personal hell," surmised Maryn succinctly.

Durvan did not spare her even a glance as he said, "Haps fer one such as you it would seem hellish. But for them, they wouldnae wish tae live as you do. In life they craved dark places and committed even darker deeds. Death does not change who we are and so too, in death, they are placed where they would be most comfortable."

The god of the underworld certainly seemed far more understanding and merciful than she'd assumed. The hill grew steeper; the dark, foreboding spires she'd first spied upon exiting the weeping willow gate hidden by the knoll. "That doesn't seem like much of a punishment, living where souls are most comfortable."

"No?" asked Durvan, his heavy brows raised. "Living surrounded by others ye cannae trust nor love doesnae sound just to you?"

"I suppose you're right," conceded Maryn, panting as she climbed the last part of the rise. Thrusting a gullible or naïve spirit in with such spirits would be one thing, but spending eternity with others just like you—or worse—would grow old rather quickly. There probably wasn't much "eternal rest" going on in such a community, if she could call it that.

Maryn could not help her gasp as the castle came into full view. Standing at the top of the grassy hilltop, she gaped, her gaze sweeping hungrily over the vista. The castle was magnificent, with its many turrets, towers, and mullioned windows reflecting the sunset, reminiscent of the kinds of castles depicted in Dracula movies. The image should have inspired fear, but Maryn could only see the beauty in it. Even the grounds were like something out of a dream.

A river ran in front of the building, spanned by an arched, white stone bridge. Plants clung to the path's supports, like some great sea monster intent on taking its revenge. On one side of the castle lived a well-manicured hedge maze, its walls on the furthest side obscured by mist. In the waning sunlight, Maryn watched as flickering lights appeared within some portions of the maze, as someone—or something—roamed within.

As they drew closer, Maryn saw that the castle was adorned with a variety of statues, depicting mythological beings both beautiful and grotesque, beings that had terrified her as a child. Situated atop the ornate stone gate stiles, for instance, stood alarming likenesses of Dullahan: headless riders on black horses, their heads tucked neatly under their arms, their staring eyes seeming to follow their progress as she and Durvan drew closer.

They trudged onward, Maryn stumbling a time or two due to her inability to keep focused on her feet. She could do with about five more sets of eyes. As they neared the gate, the bubble of curious awe living within her breast died. On either side of the creaking gate, standing atop a stony wall, waited the Dullahan she'd spied from afar.

Maryn could not help but shiver as she passed the iron bars; the weight of the riders' gazes bored into her back. Their feet crunched loudly as they followed the road that led across the bridge. Maryn resisted the urge to look behind her, so great was the sensation of eyes upon her, but she was too frightened to look.

Not until they'd moved most of the way across the great stone bridge did she realize that the statues ahead of them were actually *living beings*. The two people—if she could call them that—situated at the end crossing were draped in flowing gowns that seemed to lift on an invisible breeze their piercing eyes striking fear into Maryn.

Unable to resist any longer, she glanced back at the Dullahan statues. They *had* moved, angling themselves so as to view Maryn and Durvan's progress down the road. Maryn's heart leaped into her throat, and she fought down a gasp. In their free hands, the Dullahan held unfurled whips, as if ready to strike them should they venture back their way. Maryn knew well enough from stories that it was not just any whip, but a human spine. She whirled away from them, her breath uneven.

Instinctively taking a step closer to Durvan, Maryn tried twice to swallow before she could speak. "What are they?" she whispered, indicating the two beings directly blocking their path.

"Banshees," he answered succinctly, not sounding worried in the least. "Portents and guardians of the deceased."

His unconcerned attitude lent her a small measure of courage as they came to the head of the bridge, but it sputtered and died as the first of the beings spoke.

"Who comes?" Her voice, breathy and melancholy, filled Maryn with a nameless sorrow so that she suddenly felt like weeping. The beings towered over them, their pale blue eyes piercing through flesh and bone to her very soul. If only she could hide, shrink away where their penetrating stares could not reach her..

"Annwn has no place for the living," the other warned. "Depart."

Maryn couldn't find her voice, but she was saved from answering as Durvan stepped forward and bowed neatly. "Here arrives Winter's Handmaiden, come to commune with Arawn, God of Death."

Both sets of eyes left Durvan; the full weight of their milky gazes falling upon Maryn. Her knees turned to water, nearly buckling.

"This mortal claims to be Winter's steward?" one of them asked, her breathy voice doubtful.

Thinking quickly, Maryn shrugged off her pack and removed Cailleach's hammer, its green sheen sparking even in the shadow of the keep. "I am Winter's Handmaiden, come to speak on her behalf to the—to the god of death."

The banshees eyed the hammer in Maryn's hands, their long, dark hair floating in a phantom wind. After several heartbeats of silence, the specters moved aside, saying in unison, "Welcome to Annwn, Handmaiden of Cailleach, Goddess of Winter."

"Be warned," the one on the right added, her soulless eyes boring into her, "Your living spirit is bright and attracts many eyes. Guard her well, Master Durvan."

Maryn could not move away fast enough from the bridge's guardians. Her hands tightened on the hammer. Would Cailleach frown on Maryn using her tool against beings from another kingdom? She would if she had to, regardless of who it might upset.

Durvan was silent as they walked along the oyster shell path toward a long, sweeping staircase. Maryn's heart beat loud in her ears. It thumped wildly in her chest, her mind reeling. She didn't know what to expect inside Death's home. Almost everything about the underworld had challenged her expectations thus far.

"What's he like? Arawn?" she asked. "Big and scary? Dark cloak and wicked sharp scythe?" Her nervous laugh at the end of her sentence drew Durvan's curious eye.

"Much like that," he answered. "Save for the scythe. Arawn is a hunter and a warrior, so it is a bow and sword that he carries." He added then, almost as an afterthought, "Some that have displeased him have had his dogs set upon them. Do take heed no' tae offend, lest he have reason to release his hounds on you."

Maryn's stomach dropped somewhere to the vicinity of her knees. She'd already met one of his hounds today and had no desire to meet another. Ever.

Maryn stopped in her tracks, her gaze taking in the imposing height of the building. Great fires winked into existence upon the parapets and along the walkways as the sun's light faded, casting the grey stone a dull, flickering orange. The sight only seemed to add to the ominous feel of the place. How had she ever thought it beautiful? Now it only seemed terrifyingly ominous.

Maryn desperately wanted to tell Durvan she'd changed her mind, but she kept her feet. Not only did want to avoid the creatures she'd met, but she wanted to go *home*. To her quiet life of books and history. Getting there could only be achieved by helping Cailleach find Brigid.

She forced courage, squashing her fears deeper into the recesses of her brain. She and Durvan would march through Death's doors and . . . and beg for assistance. Assistance from the Grim Reaper. *What could possibly go wrong?*

"I'll try not to offend," she muttered, her blood gone cold.

"Come," commanded Durvan. "The sun in nearly set. Let us greet our host before the feast is laid."

Chapter Sixteen

Death's Door

Two formidable men, their dark hair slicked back and shining in the torchlight, threw open the steel-studded doors at their approach. They eyed the newcomers with benign curiosity but did not stop them nor ask them questions, much to Maryn's relief. She stared at their black eyes, alight with reflected, flickering light, and suppressed a shudder. There was no white to their eyes at all, only the reflective dark reminiscent of a shark.

After Maryn and Durvan passed the sentinels, the two men closed the doors behind them with a resounding thud that felt all too final to Maryn. She tightened her grip around the hammer, the thin strips of leather wrapped around it smooth under her touch. She took a steading breath, trying without success to calm her racing heart. The man on their right motioned them forward, indicating that she and Durvan were to escort themselves to the little sitting area not far away.

The entrance of the castle was high ceilinged and gothic themed, the towering walls and stained glass somewhat like Notre Dame with its tall pillars and ornate buttresses. Durvan led her to the indicated parlor offset from the foyer on the right, the chairs high-backed and ornately carved with grotesque faces, pulled into terrifying, toothy smiles.

"What were they?" hissed Maryn, canting her head toward the front doors. The sentinels there did not put off human vibes in the least. "Vampires?" she whispered nervously. She was only half joking and held her breath as she waited for Durvan's response.

Durvan, who was seated beside her on a hard bench, gave her a sideways look. "Eh?"

"You know, blood suckers." She lifted her bent fore and middle fingers of one hand in illustration of fangs. "Prey on women who leave their balcony doors unlocked. Supposed to dislike garlic."

Shaking his head, Durvan said, with no small amount of disgust, "Arawn wouldnae allow the likes o' *abhartach* within these walls. No, those folk are selkies . . . souls as were lost at sea, come to Annwn to rest. *Abhartach*, indeed."

She rifled mentally through her memories, trying to place where she'd heard the term before. In the ringing silence she recalled a book centered on Irish folklore that she'd checked out from the school library as a child.

The drawings alone had terrified her, but the lore hadn't been any better. The *abhartach*, a cruel master who'd mistreated his people, fell by their hands. Having killed their lord, the people buried him three times—due to minor inconvenience of him escaping the confines of his grave to torture and *feed* off of the population he'd cruelly mistreated in life. In the end, a druid advised a more lasting solution. He was ultimately buried upside down to prevent his rising again.

She replayed Durvan's words. *Arawn wouldnae allow the likes o' abhartach within these walls.*

Maryn stared at the side of his ruddy face. What was worse, knowing that a version of vampiric undead *existed* or that they were so horrific that not even the god of death would allow them near him? She decided not to ask where they might live.

In an effort to distract her mind, she took in their surroundings. The ceiling arched grandly overhead, and wood paneled walls gave way to stone at window height. An array of game trophies one might find in a hunting lodge decorated the area. While there was little in the way of art, the space oozed comfort and grandeur. She might even find it charming were she not so frightened. A rich rug in deep red covered the wide-planked floor. Her gaze traced the interlocking, geometric designs along the border as they waited.

They didn't have to wait long. All too soon, another selkie, this one female, her tightly fitted leathers squeaking with the slightest movement, made her way down the hallway toward them. Her long hair shone just as black as the door sentinels, her skin so pale she could pass for a ghost. With a start, Maryn realized the woman *was* dead. Maybe not a ghost in the common sense, but certainly not alive.

She stopped before them, her black eyes settling on Maryn with a cold weight that made her want to squirm. After several heartbeats, the selkie said, "Welcome Durvan, son of Horgan, most noble of dwarves."

She looked at Maryn again, her silky tone a mismatch for her cold expression. "Dare you make a claim on Winter's hammer, Mortal?"

Maryn looked to her lap where she clutched Cailleach's treasure in her icy fingers. Maryn found her voice. "The goddess has asked me to aid her. She ... Cailleach is too weak to come herself and so has sent me to investigate the source of her troubles. We...we come into Annwn under duress."

"We seek asylum from the god of this world," provided Durvan, "and passage to Spring Court."

If the words surprised the woman, she didn't show it. Her gaze lingered on the hammer, then on Maryn's face, her mouth tight with disapproval. "What business does Cailleach have across our great waters?"

Maryn's grip tightened reflexively on the hammer, calling upon practiced confidence, borne from countless hours as a graduate student and then as a professor. She'd stood on shaking knees under the piercing gaze of students and various acumen with twice her experience. The trick was to act like she had all the answers. If they got even a whiff of her uncertainty, they'd eat her alive. This guard of Annwn, surely, was no different.

"Cailleach's business is her own," Maryn said with forced confidence. "We seek an audience with the god of death."

The black eyes of the selkie sparked with displeasure. "What is your name?"

"Doctor Maryn Ferguson," she answered automatically. She wished her words back. Wasn't there some rule that names had power? She'd probably just given the woman the key to her unmaking. Lord, she watched too many movies.

Shapely black eyebrows rose. "From whence do you hale, Doctor Maryn Ferguson?"

Durvan interrupted. "She is sent by my mistress and bares her totem. This alone proves our efficacy. Does the Court of Death no longer honor old ties?"

The selkie's eyes narrowed at his tone. The blood drained from Maryn's face. Was this the reason Cailleach specifically said not to come here? And while they'd had a very bad day, practically forcing Durvan to turn to the god of death, Maryn had to wonder which was worse: what roamed the forest or the monsters they currently faced.

Clearly, the court did not welcome them if this is how they were treated. And this was only a servant. How would the god of death deal with them?

"Come then," said the selkie icily. "The judgement is nearly finished. If you wish to speak with him, you will give your message in the hall when he is finished."

Maryn followed Durvan's lead, doing her best to look confident, staring at the selkie's ribbon of onyx hair sway as she walked.

The long hallway rebounded with their collective footfalls. Maryn's gaze to swept the walls and peered through darkened windows. Even Durvan seemed nervous, stroking his beard repeatedly as if to refresh himself. What must she look like? Or smell like? Certainly not presentable, especially to an unwelcoming god.

The selkie brought them to an arched, twin door, framed by two pedestal sconces. The flames within grew as they neared, as if sensing their presence, dispelling shadows into the furthest corners of the broad hallway. Maryn hungrily took in the ornate door, which was white save for an embossed silhouette of a tree. Its golden branches perfectly mimicked the roots below, and under the roots was a sun—or a moon, perhaps—the fire reflected in the gold.

Their escort rapped upon one of the doors with a fist, and the doors opened in sequence, revealing a glittering hall beyond.

Maryn blinked against the dazzling light that fell over them.

The rectangular room measured at least sixty feet long with a high, trussed ceiling that drew the eye. Fat, dripping candles set in tall candelabras spanned every ten feet or so, on either side of towering stained glass. These windows covered the opposite wall from where they stood.

Her attention caught on an image in the last frame of glass of what looked to be a man—a father, perhaps—cradling a limp body, his head lifted to the sky. The colorful glass angled sharply into almost jagged pieces. Maryn stared at the look of utter agony on the man's face, his mouth open in an unheard wail. Her chest tightened. Why would anyone memorialize such an image in glass?

A crowd of people stood to their left—about fifteen to twenty—silent and staring, dressed in a wide array of styles and extravagance. Some wore nothing but soiled breeches and overlarge shirts—one man barefoot, while others flaunted clothing as fine as any medieval king might own: fur cloaks, kempt hair, clean faces, colorful tunics and long surcoats that fell to their pointed shoes.

She took in their clothing, wishing she could examine the make and quality of their garments. Historical study only went so far. What small examples academics had at their disposal were, of course, motheaten, moldy and incomplete. Depictions in art helped modern understanding, but still left a lot of questions.

As Maryn stared from afar, one body shifted from the back, exposing a misshapen arm, grey in color, its elbow joint like a knot in a rope. Another entity, whom she had first assumed to be a child, was clearly *not*. It removed its red cap with spidery hands, wringing it as one might draw water from a rag.

Maryn pulled her gaze away from the crowd and took in the figure to their right. She could not help the gasp that escaped her when her eyes fell upon the creature. It sat upon a bone-white throne, tall and straight. Its billowing robes seemed to evaporate before her very eyes, as if it were made of smoke from smothered fire. The grey of the cloak, cascading from wide shoulders, never dissipated, despite the curling vapors.

Worse yet, its head appeared to be a deer skull, substantial antlers outstretched, set atop a thickly corded neck. The long over-robe resembling a medieval cotte—a deep red, like blood, with black symbols stitched vertically down its chest. Deerskin trousers peeked from beneath the robe, ending somewhere inside black calf-high boots.

She and Durvan had clearly interrupted something, for before this strange creature—who could only be the god of death—stood a small fairy, brown and as wrinkled as a shriveled grape. It wore a brown mantle over a dirty, white tunic and boots made from . . . red felt? It bowed its head as if showing reverence, but its twiggy hands balled into fists.

What had the selkie said? Something about the judgement being nearly finished. Maryn glanced back at the gathered sprits, presumably freshly assessed.

"You feel I have judged you unfairly, Bwbach?" asked Death, his deep voice soft and impartial. "It is true you were once a brownie, but your choices have twisted your soul and made you into a new creature. A brownie no longer, but a boggart."

"*I'm a brownie*," he insisted, his reedy voice raised. "It's the maid that angered me so. Worked for years, I did. Threshed the barn full of corn in a single night. Dashed the cream in the churn, too. And what thanks did I get?" he asked with no small amount of bitterness. "Her betters pass on and there's no more benevolence tae be had for poor Bwbach. Not a thread given. No sark, no hose. No milk left for me. Turned the cat on me, she did. That foul creature!" he wailed.

The god of death listened silently to the brownie's speech, unmoving save for the whisps of smoke snaking from his cloak. After a beat, Death said, "There are many households who would welcome the service given of a brownie. Why choose such violence against the maid? Your corruption has damaged more than just yourself."

The brownie bowed his head and cried, sobbing into his hands. "I was angry," he admitted. "Cut me deep, she did. Bwbach was good to his family."

Gauging Death's feeling toward the fairy was impossible, what with the vacant stare from blank eye sockets, , but his body language appeared composed, as if not easily riled. He'd no doubt heard every possible excuse to every wrong choice since time began.

"Your misdeeds resulted in the maid's dismissal," continued Death solemnly. "Without a place, she and her child suffer." He paused, his head canting to one side for a beat. "I fear it will not be long before we receive the babe into Annwn."

The brownie's twiggy fingers delved into his scant, curling hair and howled. "I meant the babe nae harm!" He shook his head, his overlarge ears flapping. "I only wished the maid tae get a taste for her ain treatment. Turned me oot in the cold! No food for Bwbach!"

"Yes," said Death, his tone remorseful. "Choices have many unwanted consequences. That does not make us immune to them."

The brownie sobbed all the harder, mumbling. Maryn thought she heard the word "cat" again but couldn't be sure.

After a long silence, broken only by the sniffling of the brownie, Death said, "This is my decision." He stood, exposing his throne.

Maryn gaped. It looked to her to be made from bleached bones: tapered long bones along the legs and arms of the chair, rounded scapula angled like wings near the top, knobby vertebrae artfully arranged in a beatific pattern. Hundreds of them knit expertly together to form his judgement seat. Hopefully they weren't human.

Arawn moved toward the fairy, which looked into the deer skull with equal measurements of avidity and trepidation. Indeed, Maryn seemed to hold her breath at the awaited judgement. "For your malfeasance against the maid, and all those who suffered indirectly, you are hereby sentenced to serve her family for three generations. You may not dwell nor rest here, in Annwn, until you've fulfilled your duty. Only then, can you reenter the Black Gate and find true rest."

The brownie-turned-boggart fell to his knees, a knobby fist raised. "Three generations?" he cried. "Isn't fair. No, no. Too long...too many cats."

Maryn's heart squeezed. Poor little thing.

"You will endeavor to help the maid as she finds a new place. You will provide for them, she and the child, and you will learn to stave your temper. If you wish to reside in Annwn peaceably, you will do as I have ruled."

The fairy sniffed. "And i-if I dinnae wish tae go back?"

Maryn barely breathed as she watched the scene. Death knelt before the weeping fairy and, with a voice laced with regret, he said, "You will have no place. You will find no rest, and after the three generations have passed and your penance goes unfulfilled, you will be bound to live with those who have chosen similar paths, away from your family." Silence rang through the hall. "The choice is yours to make, however."

Maryn recalled then the little will-o'-the-whisps she'd seen under the tree. It seemed to her a steep price to pay for the brownie's vindictive choices. How often had she said or done something out of anger. Then again, Death had said the child would soon die. Death, apparently, took the business of dying very serious indeed.

A pregnant pause, and then the fairy said, "I-I will s-serve the maid and her child, as you've ruled."

Death took the fairy's hand and lifted him to his feet. "Very well. Sit with us and dine, and then on the morrow you will be escorted to your place. Serve well, fair one."

The fairy, shoulders quaking, slunk back to the group of other departed souls. She watched him go, a mix of emotions whirling in her chest. When she looked back at the god of death, a jolt of fear pierced through her. Those black, empty eyes were settled squarely onto her and Durvan.

Chapter Seventeen

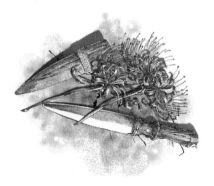

Dealing in Souls

Dealing in Souls

"Bow before the Unmaker, Mortal," hissed the selkie from behind her. Maryn had been so busy openly staring at the spectacle—*god*, she corrected—that she'd apparently failed to show the proper amount of respect.

"*Seriously, Durvan?*" whispered Maryn out of the corner of her mouth, seeing her companion on one knee. *He could have clued me in.*

She dropped to one knee and bowed her head, her angular hair falling over her face like blinders. Footfalls, soft but audible in the vastness of the room, approached. His shadow fell over her. Boots appeared in her line of sight, and she stared at them, her skin prickling. His gaze pressed on her like a weight, as if he could read her very soul with only a glance.

He probably can. Unease unfurled in her belly. Would he, the judge of souls, find her wanting?

"Durvan of the North Kingdom, son of Horgan," announced the selkie, "and his charge."

"Rise," Death said, the deep baritone of his voice rebounding in the room.

Maryn stood, as did Durvan, but she kept her eyes downcast lest she offend him. *That wouldn't bode well for my eventual eternal rest.* He walked around them in a circle, as if taking in every aspect of them, carefully assessing. When he'd completed the circle, he drew very close to Maryn. She shivered, and, unable to help herself, dared to look up into the hollow eye sockets of the deer skull. The uncertain feelings that had been fluttering somewhere around her middle intensified.

Arawn lifted his hands to the skull and removed it from his shoulders. Not his head, then, but a mask. Relief flowed through her, turning her knees to water. The god of death was not a monster, not a strange amalgamation of man and beast, but a man in truth. A god, yes, but still a man.

Knowing that her mother and grandparents didn't live in a realm ruled by a faceless beast comforted some recessed part of her heart. And after viewing the brownie's judgement, she knew Arawn had judged her departed family fairly. She could sense it as clearly as she could feel the sun upon her skin at the height of summer. Intimidating though he may be, his even-handed justice spoke volumes.

The selkie that escorted them appeared and took the skull from him. Arawn studied her with golden-hued eyes set over a long, straight nose. His wide mouth turned into a speculative frown, his dark eyebrows testifying to his curiosity.

A long-fingered hand stretched toward her, open-palmed. "Give me your hand, *Bearer of Neach-Gluasad Talmhainn.*"

Earth Mover, he'd said. Maryn's gaze darted to the hammer in the left hand. In her trepidation and nervous condition, she'd forgotten she even held it.

She hesitated to comply, eyeing his outstretched arm. Touching him would be unwise, and equally dangerous, defying him.

A small smile tugged at his long mouth, as if he could read her very thoughts and found them amusing. "I promise to give it back," he supplied, one dark eyebrow arched.

Maryn reluctantly gave him her right hand, biting her bottom lip. Her left hand clenched around the hammer on instinct, her only defense in such a place. The image of her clubbing Death on the head nearly choked her. She'd never been the victim of hysteria-driven madness before, but this seemed a likely moment to push her over the edge.

His touch ignited her blood. Her heart pounded in her ears and her skin...her skin *tingled*. Her very soul strained against bone and muscle, eager to answer to him. *To obey*. Startled, she jerked her hand away from him, her eyes wide. Her skin itched where her blood rose to the surface. "What—"

He leaned forward intimately, his scent enveloping her. She winced, both afraid and amazed at her reaction to him. "My apologies. It's not often I receive living guests. I have gained two and twenty souls this night, Little Mortal. I'm *tired*. I vow not to reap your soul. Not yet."

Shocked, she found his eyes. *Was he teasing her?* Was that a spark of amusement in his gaze? He still held his hand open for her in invitation, a small smile curving one side of his mouth. It did not mock, but it certainly didn't calm her either.

Inhaling, she gathered the dregs of her courage. *Could she refuse a god?* It didn't seem like the time to try and so she offered him her hand again, prepared this time for the strange sensation of his touch. His hand was curiously warm. She hadn't noticed before. Strange that death would feel so *normal*. As normal as could be expected from a reaper of souls, save for the tingling that ran up her arm that sent her heart skittering.

She frowned at their contact. How could this be? Everyone here—the recently judged, the selkies, Death himself—they were all *substantial*. They appeared as any human—not as an apparition. Could she touch the brownie? Or the others? Maybe only the god of death had a body? Was *he* dead?

Her internal questions died as the furrow in Arawn's brown deepened. She had little experience with palm reading, a parlor trick meant to pray on the desperate, but this was Death. No parlor tricks here.

Flushed and overwarm, Maryn held still, resisting the desire to pull her hand away. She studied him, just as thoroughly has he studied her. His hair was long and dark—nearly black. It fell in a wave to his shoulders. A circlet of fine bones was set upon his head, likely belonging to a bird. His cloak was more substantial up close, less like rising heat vapors from sun-seared asphalt. Still, the cloth, to Maryn's eyes, seemed to move. Grey smoke slithered over the surface, like swirls of gas trapped in a vial.

Some part of her brain warned her that she was staring, that she should not be so bold in her appraisal of him, but she couldn't help herself. He had the keeping of all departed souls; her family was here, somewhere, in this vast kingdom. He'd judged them and given them a place of rest. He was also nothing like she'd expected.

She stared at their connection, wondering at how her blood seemed to vibrate, as if the very make up of her body—every cell—awaited his command. Was this how he reaped souls, through mere touch? He traced the lines upon her palm with a gentle forefinger, the question in his eyes growing. A wrinkle appeared between his brows and his strange, otherworldly eyes narrowed onto her face before letting go of their connection.

"Welcome, Maryn, daughter of Maeve, Handmaiden of Winter." She flexed her fingers, trying to erase the curious sensation his touch elicited. What was he looking for in her palm? Her past or her future?

Death turned his attention to Durvan. "And you, master dwarf."

Durvan bowed in an expert fashion so discordant to his usual rough manners.

"What brings you to my court, and in such a circumstance? It is unlike Cailleach to permit anyone access to her hammer, let alone allow a mortal to wield it."

"My Lord, Unmaker, we come with urgent news from my mistress. We beg for an audience."

"Then please sup with us before the sentences are carried out."

With a wave of a hand the room changed. The throne disappeared, replaced by a long table, replete with platters piled with food and glinting, silver goblets full of wine.

Sentencing? Maryn frowned inwardly. Allowing others to witness sentencing felt unkind to her; she wouldn't appreciate strangers gawking at her while she was carted off to who knew where. Then again, she'd observed the judgement of the brownie. Perhaps that was part of the ceremony, being openly judged in front of your peers, much like it was done in the human world.

Maryn followed Durvan toward the table, her eyes sweeping the elaborate meal thereon. Platters of fish, legs of mutton, a variety of fowl, all glistening with gravy, nestled amongst arrays of vegetables. Her stomach growled audibly, making her cheeks pinken. Finally, something other than salted, dried meat! But even as she salivated, she questioned the purpose of the meal. Why would the dead need to eat? *A nice gesture, to be sure, but*—her thoughts trailed off as a servant appeared at her side.

The servant, reminiscent of the brownie recently judged, looked taller and less like a gnarled tree root, but still held that otherworldly appearance that took her aback. His toothy grin was similar to a jack-o-lantern's. He moved to take her bag, his thin hands dark against the woven strap and she jerked it back on reflex.

The jack-o-lantern bowed, solemn. "May I take your things, Handmaiden?

"N-no. I've got it," she assured.

The creature looked just as startled as she felt. "Wouldn't you rather me take your things, Handmaiden? I'll put them in a room for you. Others are preparing one now, even as we speak."

Maryn looked to Durvan for instruction, but he was deep in conversation with Arawn. She hesitated. This was her responsibility. The hammer and the blade. She didn't feel right about letting her bag out of her sight. "Thank you," she said, "but no. I'd rather hold onto it myself."

"What of your cloak? Do you wish to keep it with you as well?"

Maryn considered then shook her head. She removed her bag, placing the hammer within, and let him take her cloak, noticing with some embarrassment how soiled it was.

The creature bowed and clutched the smokey, soiled article to his narrow chest, his spidery fingers dark against the sapphire blue fabric. "Needn't fuss. Needn't worry," he said good naturedly. "I will take great care in the keeping of your things."

Maryn watched him disappear through the doors, the weight of the bag heavy in her hand, before joining Durvan near the head of the table.

Death—Arawn—stood there. He pulled out a chair adjacent to his own as she approached, gesturing for Maryn to sit. She did, feeling out of place and uncertain, her bag on her lap. If he or Durvan thought it strange for her to have it at the table, they made no mention of it. She couldn't see Durvan's bag, nor his pickaxes, and considered that maybe it would have been safe for her to give the fairy her bag after all.

Durvan took a seat across from her. Arawn stood at the head table, drawing all eyes. "Welcome subjects, friends," he added, nodding slightly to his only living guests. "Annwn is a place of eternal rest. Let us sup together before you depart to your respective destinations."

A cacophony of noise filled the hall as benches scraped away from the table and the gathered guests sat. A hum of conversation filled the room. Maryn could not help her stares as the spirits commenced eating. How did they eat without a body and, just as important, *why?* Why eat without a body?

Durvan's foot swung out and knocked into her shin. Her squeak of surprise and wince at the contact couldn't be helped. He gestured none too discreetly in their host's direction with a jerk of his head. She rubbed her leg and shot Durvan a glare before giving her attention to the god.

She'd been so busy staring at the dead filling their plates, drinking and eating, she hadn't even heard him speak. "Sorry," she said, her face warming uncomfortably. "I suppose I'm a bit distracted."

"Not at all," said Arawn who looked rather bemused. He considered her for a moment, as if he were trying to make up his mind, then leaned toward her. He lowered his voice. "The answer to your question, Little Mortal, lies in the essence of a soul. My subjects eat and sleep and do all manner of activities not because they *must*, but because they *can*. I do not need this fare," he said, motioning with a hand to his plate of fish with white sauce and truffles, "but I eat, because I *enjoy* it. Here the departed have substance. Not a body of flesh, as you do, but they can feel and touch, weep and laugh, and most of all, *remember*. Food brought them pleasure in their first life. They remember that and it still brings them joy."

Little mortal? The term made her feel like a child. *Then again, I probably seem infantile to a being as old as Death, comparatively speaking.*

Maryn pushed her thoughts aside and took in the faces of the dead around her, some solemn, others joyful. Where would their sentences take them after dinner?

"Of course they have substance now," he continued conversationally, "but if they venture beyond the confines of Annwn, their souls diminish and they lose their corporal form. Some, so much so, that they cannot even be seen by mortal eyes."

Maryn blinked at him. Was that where ghosts came from? "So I would not see them outside of Annwn? They'd be invisible to me?"

Arawn's strange eyes searched her own for the barest of seconds, as if reading some hidden part of her. It made her feel exposed though she could not say why. It made her feel as if she didn't know herself at all. An uncomfortable feeling, that.

"It is the same for all the living, though some can sense the dead and even glimpse them from time to time."

"We appreciate your aid," said Durvan, with a subtle clearing of his throat, bringing them back round to the point at hand.

Arawn's mouth twitched, his eyes sparking with suppressed amusement. "Thank you, master dwarf, for reminding us of your purpose in coming here." He turned to Maryn, his golden eyes falling to her hand where she clutched a weighty, two-pronged fork. "Your guide tells me that you've had quite the adventure since being plucked from your home. You must be famished. Please eat."

Plucked was an apt term. "Since being kidnapped, you mean?" she asked, though without venom. She huffed a soft laugh and piled roasted potatoes onto her plate.

"We gods don't like to use such accurate terms," he said, his eyes smiling. "Let's call your presence here a . . . *scenic detour.*"

Maryn couldn't help smiling back. Who knew Death had jokes? She relaxed slightly, despite everything weighing on her. While she and Durvan hadn't made it to Spring Court, they were relatively safe, and Arawn seemed keen to help them out. But how much did he know? What had Durvan told him?

"I've got to find the missing Brigid," she supplied, her eyes roving over the other fare.

"So Durvan says. While my servants gather information in the Spring Court, you are most welcome to bide here and enjoy the comforts of Annwn. You will be safe." He paused and frowned. "So long as you stay within the boundaries, of course."

Maryn, in the middle of lifting her cup to her mouth, paused and found his startling eyes once more. Ignoring the strange quivering in her middle, she said, "I don't have time to wait. Cailleach is . . . she's dying." How absurd she must sound to him, telling the god of the underworld about how she was in a race against death itself. Against *him*, rather.

Arawn frowned and looked at Durvan. "You said she was weak. You didn't say she was diminishing."

Durvan grunted, his eyes darting around the table as if he didn't appreciate the audience. "She grows weaker by the day," he whispered. "I fear she will succumb to oblivion soon."

Sleep didn't sound so bad to Maryn. "Why can't sleep be its own reward? She's tired, isn't she? I imagine sleep sounds rather enticing at this point."

A sadness touched Arawn's eyes. "It might seem that way to a mortal, with a limited view of eternity, but we were not made for endless slumber; we are meant to live. I will visit her and lend her what strength I may."

A servant appeared and offered Maryn a plate of what looked like quiche. Her mouth watered as the servant added a wedge to her plate. She'd always assumed that death was nothing more than an everlasting sleep. Continuing on seemed rather exhausting to her. "I think I'd rather sleep," she said, recalling the brownie's judgement. "I can't imagine living a full life only to find that I can't just *rest* at the end of it."

Arawn's answering smile wasn't pitying, but still it made her feel small, like a child once more.

"Annwn is a place of rest, of course, but it is also a place of justice. Those who come here can accept their judgement as is and live out eternity in the place best suited to them as they are, or they can choose to go back, if necessary, and fix things they aren't proud of. It's an opportunity for justice to be meted out . . . and a mercy for them. Many choose to return, so that they can rest peaceably, with their minds at ease and their hearts knitted."

Maryn grew silent, trying and failing to wrap her mind around the concepts of eternity. Would she be able to live forever happily, knowing she could have resolved painful moments in her life? She pictured Jacob Marley in *A Christmas Carol*, moaning a warning about the eternal chains that bound him. No spirits here had chains. Then again, she'd seen so little of the place.

Where would she be placed? Or Cailleach? If the winter goddess died.... Maryn's stomach lurched.

If Cailleach dies, how will I get home? Despite her concern for Winter and the suffering human world, she wanted to go home to her simple life of studying the past, to her bed, to her cat. She spared a quick, fervent prayer that her neighbor, Mrs. Angus, would see to his care.

Despite her quiet existence, her work fulfilled and defined her, so much so that solitude didn't affect her negatively. Attending natural science museums as a child with her mother had solidified her resolve to study the past. She'd dedicated her life to it, to making her mum proud.

Such devotion came at a cost, though. Reflecting on her relationships, so far removed from the human realm, made her wish she'd spent less time working. Any conversations she had revolved around archaeology. With students or colleagues.

She'd only had one serious college boyfriend. Collin's infidelity had debilitated her for a time, but her work had saved her in the end. She'd thrown herself into school after that and told herself to be glad for one less distraction. She vowed to never waste another minute on idiots like him. Maybe spending all her time and efforts in her field had limited her....

Maryn grimaced. She understood what Arawn meant. Going back to the living realm could be a mercy.

"If Cailleach dies—diminishes, I mean—how will I return to my time?" she asked.

Durvan and Arawn's conversation halted as they both looked at her. Durvan didn't appear to appreciate the suggestion that his mistress might die. He huffed, scowling, and took a drink from his goblet. Arawn, however, lifted a brow. "Does your scholar's mind ever rest?"

Maryn's mouth fell open in a most unbecoming fashion. *How could he possibly follow scattered, unfinished ideas in my head while holding a conversation with Durvan?*

His brow rose higher. "First, I can, and do, follow thoughts because it is part of my job. The mantle of being the Unmaker," he said waving his fork in a way she took to encompass all of eternity. "Second, I can't *read* them, only sense them, but you already know that. Your face gives most of what you're thinking away more than the storm in there." He gestured at her forehead and sat back, expectant.

His easy interpretation of her innermost thoughts should have alarmed her. Perhaps she would feel the proper concern tomorrow, after a good night's rest, but now, she could only conjure interest. Strangely, Arawn's ability to sense her most private thoughts didn't feel like an invasion, but rather . . . recognition. More like he saw the worst parts of her, and still accepted her, warts and all.

He turned to Durvan, letting her process her thoughts, no doubt. "I'll send out an envoy first thing in the morning. You're welcome to accompany them rather than rest here, if you prefer," he offered, "but you needn't worry over your mistress. I will not let her collapse into oblivion."

Durvan looked mightily relieved, the rigid line of his shoulders softening. "I thank ye, Unmaker. Ye have my favor, as meager as it may be. Should ye require my axe, ye need only ask."

Arawn accepted Durvan's noble offer with the proper amount of gravity it deserved. He lifted his glass and drank, sealing their fellowship. "I will see to Cailleach's suffering while you solve the issue of Brigid's disappearance."

Why would a powerful god such as he not step in and help solve the mystery himself? Clearly it affected him, if not just through his hounds being stolen away and used for nefarious purposes. She didn't dare ask. He might take her questions as impertinent. He was, after all, giving them passage across his vast sea to Spring's back door and lending Cailleach strength. Perhaps he could give no more than that.

"How long will such a journey take? Across the sea, I mean," Maryn said. *Please be quick.* They'd already wasted so much time on foot.

"Not long. A day," he said, his stare like a weight, making her want to fidget.

Choosing boldness, Maryn asked, "Can't you send me home? In the event that Cailleach cannot," she added, sparing a glance at Durvan.

Arawn sat back, his elbows resting on the arms of his chair, his long-fingered hands folded over his middle. "I'm not in the habit of keeping other gods' promises. It's souls I deal in, not flesh, after all. If you had left your body behind and had ventured into Annwn for your eternal rest, then, yes, I could technically—" he flicked two fingers here, emphasizing his words "—send you home to reunite with your mortal body." He shrugged and added, "That is, if not too much time as passed. You wouldn't thank me for sending you back to your body after a certain point."

Maryn grimaced, images of zombie movies playing in her head.

"But you have entered into my kingdom whole and very much *alive*." He paused, a look of consideration entering his gold eyes. "Unless whomever is after you has their way," he said, deadpan. She had to look at his face to discern if he was trying to be funny. He wasn't. Maryn swallowed hard, her appetite waning.

"Brigid could potentially send you home, if Cailleach cannot," he added, his brow slightly furrowed in thought.

Maryn fiddled with her cup. "Who is it, do you think, that wants to harm us? Durvan suspects the goddess of war."

Arawn pursed his lips. "Morrigan is not best known for her temperance." He shrugged, looking thoughtful. "Of course, she could simply be bored, but I doubt it. Do be careful, won't you? It's not wise to go about, brandishing powerful totems, especially as a mortal."

Maryn's uneasiness flared to life. "Whomever is after us, their spies saw me with the hammer," she supplied. "Durvan seemed to think that maybe she might be interested in claiming it."

Arawn's thoughtful frown deepened. "And you hold both goddesses' relics, do you not?" At Maryn's nod, he added, "I can't see what the goddess of war would want with Brigid. She has her own court to tend to, nor would she wish the wrath of her sisters, I would think."

"What about you?" asked Maryn, thinking that if he could read her thoughts, she might as well voice them. "If someone did take Brigid hostage, wouldn't you feel the need to involve yourself?"

Durvan groaned, a wide hand sliding over his grimacing face. "The Unmaker deals in lost souls, Lassie," he growled. "No' in the machinations o' fickle goddesses."

Maryn hesitated. *Had she said something offensive?*

Arawn sat forward. "Be at ease," he said, though she wasn't sure to whom he spoke, her or Durvan. "The dwarf is right," he continued. "Gods do not insert themselves into other courts. Not unless they want to start a war. If another god breaks a law—which we have no proof of as yet—and it affects our subjects, then we have leave to confront or even war against them. But, as it is—" He shrugged.

"So we need proof." Maryn sighed, exhaustion overwhelming her.

"We thank you for the escort across the waters," said Durvan, terse. He gave Maryn a meaningful look that she took to mean she'd overstepped. She looked at her plate, the food gone cold, the gravy congealed. "We will be careful," said Durvan.

No amount of preparation or care could keep them from harm with an unknown power on their heels, but she kept that to herself.

Chapter Eighteen

A Lesson on Morality

Soon after dinner, all manner of servants entered, banshees, selkies, a smattering of brownies, and one startling creature Durvan told her was a *fear gorta*. It resembled an emaciated human, haggard and bent, with dark, sad eyes, ringed in purple. Clothes hung from its bony, bent frame, its stringy hair limp. Without any meat to it, she couldn't tell if the spirit was male or female. Looking at the poor soul stirred something within Maryn's breast. Was there no solace to be found for such a creature, even after death?

These servants acted as escorts, taking the freshly judged souls to their respective places. Some souls, apparently unhappy with their judgements, who previously sat sullen and quiet through the feast, now filled the air with their wails. Some begged Arawn, beseeching him on their knees, hands clasped together. He took his time with them. He did not appear annoyed or even impatient. One by one, the souls left of their own accord, escort at hand.

She couldn't tear her gaze from the interaction. At some point she clamped her gaping jaw shut. How could he pass judgements and carry out sentences for countless souls over and over again and still retain his compassion, or even his enthusiasm? Did he do this every night? She would have long ago grown numb to their cries. Even now, as angry tears or fearful supplications filled her ears, she wanted to run away to some quiet place where their tears did not trouble her. Her heart ached. How could he live this way?

To distract herself, she walked to the tall windows, each painted in a spectacular, detailed scene. The first depicted a vast battlefield, replete with broken pikes, shields, and swords. Corpses littered the back and middle ground in a gruesome display of spilt blood and broken limbs. In the foreground stood a man in leather and furs, a hard look in his eyes, bloodied sword in hand. As Maryn stared into his black, pitiless gaze, a shiver ran up her spine. Whomever this man was, he did not project an aura of mercy. At his feet lay a smattering of coins, glinting silver and bronze.

Maryn moved on, her interest piqued. The next towering window showed a beggar on his knees, thin and weak, at the mercy of a group of glowering faces. The beggar's clothes, much the same as those worn by the man in first image, hung loosely from his now frail body. None of the gathered crowd in the middle ground showed this needy man any mercy. But no, at the edge of the group a man held out a loaf of bread, round and full, but his visage did not show pity. He looked almost skeptical, as if he did not trust the man on his knees.

Maryn frowned and moved to the next image. In the foreground, a weeping woman holding a child in her arms knelt amongst long stalks of wheat or grass. Just beyond her, smoke rose toward a blue sky, and, further on, orange flames devoured the field. Each of the images depicted was terrible-. *Did these depict the seven deadly sins?* Maryn counted the windows. Only five.

She wrapped her arms around herself and moved to the next image, the wails from one judged soul rising gooseflesh on her arms. This window showed an execution. Angry, shadowed figures watched from the background, forming a semicircle around three men in the middle ground.

The accused knelt, his face contorted in anger, a sword held to the back of his neck by the man on the right. On the left side stood another man, his hand staying the falling blade. Maryn leaned closer, looking at the man stopping the executioner. He looked—Maryn glanced back at the first two images to compare—yes, he looked like the same man in all three images. The clothes remained the same; only his eyes had changed. They'd lightened from black to the rich amber tone of honey.

Maryn took the few steps required to stand before the final image depicting the same subject holding a limp child in his arms. Perhaps the emotive situation playing out behind her was getting to her . . . maybe nerves and exhaustion played a part, and that's why the image moved her so. Either way, the man's anguished face turned to the sky, his mouth opened mid wail, brought tears to her eyes.

She had never lost a child, but she had lost close family members. She closed her eyes against the emotions that welled up in her. If she was honest with herself, she still suffered the pain of losing her family. Maryn's world consisted of friendly acquaintances having no real lasting ties. Had she subconsciously kept her colleagues at an arms distance on purpose?

The room had gone silent at some point. She took a deep breath and opened her eyes to find that she wasn't alone. Arawn hovered beside her, as silent as the grave, his gaze on the image before them. Strange, but her usual compulsion to fill the silence did not overwhelm her as it sometimes did back home. How could she feel comfortable standing next to a god, her very heart written on her sleeve?

"It's so...painfully beautiful," she murmured after a time, her voice reverent.

Arawn said nothing for a beat, his eyebrows drawn together. He glanced her way. "There aren't many who would find beauty in such a scene."

"Oh, I don't know," she said fairly. "I think anyone who's had the burden of living after such a loss understands."

Arawn turned his full attention onto her then. She had to lift her chin to look into his eyes. "Burden of living," he parroted. "Interesting choice of words. What would you say if I told you that this man...this subject you see here so artfully illustrated, is burdened still, even in death?"

But the afterlife was supposed to be a reprieve, wasn't it? "You mean to say that these windows are more than a story on morality? These things really happened?"

"Does it matter?" he asked. "What if I told you that this man deserves his suffering?"

Maryn looked back at the previous windows. "I see no crime so severe as to require eternal suffering. There has to be some respite for him, no matter how he chose to live his life."

"So says the woman who finds beauty in this man's torment." His words were not unkind, only curious, as if Maryn were a puzzle he wanted to solve. "Let me tell you this story," he said, motioning for her to return to the first pane. She moved with him, ignoring her weariness.

"Long ago," he began, his eyes skimming over the gruesome image with no apparent emotion, "there lived a selfish man. He had no real cause to be, save that his family was poor and often went without. He wanted more for his family, and for himself, so when he came of age, he set out to make a name for himself. He found his fortune in the strength of his sword arm."

Typical, as all stories of woe went, the boy grew hard as life's cruelties beset him. Tender feelings gave way to unchecked cruelty, and eventually, a black heart.

"He became a great warrior though practiced brutality, killing anyone for coin, uncaring who he might hurt, or if their deaths were justified. For years he hunted people, salted fields, burned crops, ravaged the weak. For *money*," said Arawn, his tone full of censure. "At first he shared his earnings with his family, but as corruption festered in his breast, he soon forgot whom he'd loved. And after a time, he couldn't even love himself."

Ah. Maryn looked to the second image of the same man now wasted away, begging for food. "Until he was cut down…made low by some circumstance and had to rely on pity from the same people he harmed. Is that right?" she asked.

Arawn's eyes shone with some unknown emotion. "Something like that." He gestured toward the last window. "Knowing what kind of life he lived, knowing his atrocities, some would say that his anguish is deserved. Hearing this, I would ask, do you still find beauty here?"

Maryn considered each image, her thoughts slippery with fatigue. On one hand, the mercenary's destruction had affected not only others, but himself. Was that penance enough for his crimes? The images certainly hinted that he'd learned his lesson, but would those he injured feel the same? She couldn't say. "I'm glad I'm not the judge," she answered honestly. She shook her head, pity for each presented subject filling her heart. Who could say what degree of suffering constituted penance? Certainly not her.

Arawn stared at her for a long second, his thoughts hidden.

"Is that why these are here? To remind you of your role as judge?" she asked.

A look of sadness washed over Arawn. "The story is a carefully honed reminder of learned compassion, humility, and forgiveness."

Maryn wet her dry lips. "Then yes," she answered. "Yes, I still think it's beautiful." At Arawn's curious look she continued. "If studying the past has taught me anything, it's that people evolve. There has never been a people on earth who haven't had to overcome obstacles, whether they be geographical or genetic or cultural." She paused, her fingers finding the strap of her bag. "We, each of us, are born into chaos. Is it any wonder that the turbulent seasons in our lives would eventually give way to maturation? To the evolution of self?"

"You're very perceptive for one so young."

Maryn smiled at his words, though she found no humor in them. Maryn had experienced enough heartache to last two lifetimes, and this past week hadn't helped any. She'd probably go grey by the end of this adventure. "Life has a way of teaching us the hard lessons. Plus, I've had a lot of therapy." She shrugged, her small laugh sounding more like an exhale.

Arawn returned her smile and moved to the middle window. He pushed upon the glass, the image of the accused man splitting in half, to reveal a wide balcony. *A door.*

He ushered her out with a hand. She'd never seen so many stars. She looked for familiar constellations but could not find them.

"You're in another dimension, so these stars will be quite different than what you're used to seeing."

Maryn glanced at him sideways.

His face was upturned, as hers had been, to the velvety night sky, pierced with light. "As I said at dinner, one doesn't need to be a god to see the curiosity written so plainly upon your face."

She was probably being rather transparent, but she was also physically and emotionally exhausted. She walked forward to the edge of the balcony, which overlooked the maze she'd seen from afar. Blue flame sconces lit the border of the labyrinth, and a mist lay heavy on the ground, obscuring the path.

"Your curiosity is to be expected," he said to her back. "I welcome questions, but first, I wanted to lay down some important guidelines while you're here in Annwn."

Maryn consented, though it was strange he wished to have this discussion. She and Durvan weren't staying long. They'd depart come morning.

"First you must realize how anomalistic hosting a living mortal is for us here in Annwn. The spirits will be drawn to your vitality. You are like a living ember in the dark."

"The dead in the hall didn't seem interested in me," she offered.

Arawn agreed. "No, they wouldn't be. They had enough going on not to take any real notice of you. Others, though, won't be so preoccupied." He ran a long finger over his chin and leveled her with a stare. "If someone approaches you with a task—asks something of you—you mustn't agree."

Maryn took in a careful breath, alarm bells going off in her head. "What could they possibly want from *me*?" She recalled the Dullahan flanking the front gates and swallowed hard. She read in a folklore book about the headless creatures using their trusty spinal whip to remove the eyes from onlookers. She shuddered despite herself.

It didn't matter if a person was eight or twenty-eight. Some things were just downright terrifying. And now that she'd learned they actually existed.... Maryn took a step away from the balcony edge, her feet finding the halo of light from the open door.

"Not all the dead are at rest," said Arawn. Maryn ran her hands over her arms, suddenly chilled.

He continued. "Some feel they have unfinished business. The worry is, that when they discover a living being here on the estate, they might have it in their mind to *attach* themselves to you."

Maryn didn't even try to hide her feelings; her face pulled into a grimace of abject horror.

"Yes, quite right. It's an uncomfortable business, possession." He adopted a cool air, waving a hand as if to erase his words. "But, I daresay, if you take care to stay in the keep, you should be quite safe from such spirits. Those who tarry within the walls have purpose to the running of this kingdom. The rest—" he gestured to the black expanse beyond the balcony railing "—are another matter entirely."

Don't agree to help any dead people. Got it. The last thing she needed was to be bombarded with more supernatural quests.

"Do you have any questions?"

Did she have questions? Her mind was *full* to bursting with them. Where to start?

She cleared her throat and swept a pointed finger overhead. "You said we're in another dimension. Which one, and how does it fit together with the human world? Durvan said we were in your borderlands up above, but was that still a part of the human world? Or do the borderlands exist in your dimension?"

"Let's start with the first questions you put to me." He didn't laugh at her rapid-fire questions, for which she was grateful. "This dimension doesn't 'fit' together with the human world, as you said, in any way, save for the doorways that connect us together. We are wholly separate and distinct from the human realm, but where the doorways exist, there is some overlap."

Maryn thought of a Venn Diagram, separate spheres that connected and existed outside each other save for one overlapping portion in the middle. Separate spheres and yet not.

"The borderlands are, indeed, in the human realm," he continued, "but the veil that separates our worlds is weaker at these points. It's in these regions that our magic bleeds into your world. Sometimes humans get glimpses of us in these overlapping boundaries."

Maryn's mind spun. Anthropologically, she could see how, perhaps, all the world's religious cultures—both extinct and those still in existence—might have been created based on what occurred in these "thin spots" between the worlds. Did the ancient Maya, for instance, worship their polytheistic gods from what emerged from the borderlands in their part of the world? Were temples and altars built upon these doorways, beseeching whatever powerful being lived beyond?

"My Lolly believed in magic," she said. "She told me all the old stories."

She might be able to see her grandparents again, here in this place! A thrill shot through her. Her heartbeat tripped as she did an about face and met his knowing gaze. "My mother," she said, her eyes wide. "I haven't seen her since I was seven. Can I see her? And my grandparents?"

Arawn, his eyes suddenly distant, shook his head. "Gods are bound by laws, just as humans are. One day you will see them again, but not here. And not now."

The line of her shoulders sagged, the little bubble of hope that had emerged within her rupturing in a nebula of disappointment.

"It's not for cruelty's sake, but kindness," he said gently. "As I say, I am bound by laws, Little Mortal. But imagine, if you would, seeing them again as you are, falling into their arms and feeling the full force of their love and affection for you. You would never wish to leave."

When she opened her mouth to protest, he said, "No, Maryn. It's not your time."

Maryn turned her face away, so he would not see her sorrow. Somewhere in the recesses of her foggy brain, she whispered to herself that she needed to get ahold of herself. She was far too tired for such a conversation; it was making her weepy.

She changed the subject. "We're leaving tomorrow for the Spring Court," she said, her voice thick, "but Cailleach saw Brigid in a hare's body. If Brigid isn't *really* there, what should I be asking her subjects? What should I be looking for? If they knew where she'd gone, surely, they'd be out looking for her already. What can I possibly glean from them that could help us find her?"

Arawn's shrewd eyes showed his admiration. "Cailleach was right to choose you for this task."

Maryn surreptitiously wiped her misted eyes, a sudden surge of irritation overcoming her. Right for the task? She wasn't good for anything in his realm. She was a talented researcher. She could churn out journal articles about archeologic methods and theories in her sleep. She could run a field school for undergrads without batting an eye, but *this*? Nowhere on her resume did it read, "Adept at tracking down an absconded god."

"You're wrong," she said. "She chose me because I was unlucky enough to be holding Spring's blade when she happened to look in time."

Arawn lifted one dark brow. "Come now," he said, looking down his long nose at her, "you're far too intelligent of a person to believe your own lies. You're exactly the right person for this task."

Maryn sniffed and looked away, her inadequacies filling her mind.

"Despite your discriminating, rationally educated mind, you're not so rigid in your thinking that you discount the remarkably peculiar circumstances in which you find yourself. *You believe*, which is astonishing, in and of itself, seeing as how you live in a time where the supernatural is seen as perverse. Something the ignorant use to explain away life's troubles.

"Did you know that some who die refuse to believe it? They wander, aimless, or even insist that they're *not dead*, despite all the evidence to the contrary. I must go into the human realm and hunt them down. I have to ensnare them, lest they spend the whole of the afterlife as ridiculous *ghosts*." He shook his head, as if just thinking about it exasperated him.

He eyed her, askance. "And yet, here you are, educated, rational, and secure in your modern ideals, thrust into the *bizarre*, and you march forward. You trek across a frozen wasteland, followed by spies, make further sacrifice—as if you haven't sacrificed enough—to gain entrance to a place contrary to mortal existence, and still you stand here, plotting how to solve the riddle Cailleach thrust into your hands. You don't find that remarkable? I certainly do."

Maryn couldn't help her watery huff of laughter. Arawn lifted a hand in the air, fingers toward the sky, where a cloud formed just inside his fingers. The haze grew denser, then solid. With a neat snap of material, he flicked the newly formed handkerchief from the sky and presented it to her.

She took it hesitantly and wiped her eyes and nose. It was as soft as a cloud and smelled slightly of rain. "Th—thank you."

"Not at all," he said, dismissive.

No wonder he was the god of death. He had an uncanny way of helping people process their feelings. Of *seeing* their true selves. Her emotions were bouncing all over the place and now she was crying. Under normal circumstances, she'd turn away in shame, but with him, she felt completely accepted. He could see her so plainly, better than she saw herself, apparently, and it wouldn't matter if she railed or cried, or spat curses. *He's good at his job.*

"Speaking of sacrifices. Can I have my hair back?"

Arawn's affronted scoff pulled her gaze. One large hand clutched his heart. "You would demand a gift, freely given, returned? That hardly seems sporting."

"Not a gift," she said pointedly. "A sacrifice."

The weight of his gaze fell over her features, lingering on her neck, her shoulders. "As lovely as your long hair surely was, I cannot give it back. Magic doesn't work that way." He looked back to the stars. "Besides, you're as lovely as ever."

Ignoring the compliment, Maryn straightened and took a steadying breath. "Okay, so let's say, for the sake of argument, that I'm the 'chosen one' for this task." She used quotation marks to emphasize the dubious nature of such a claim. "Let's say I walk into Spring Court and ask all the questions I just asked you. They're probably just as clueless as we are, or Cailleach would have heard from them by now. What am I supposed to do then?" She frowned in thought and stared at nothing.

After a beat she continued. "There's more to this. Brigid is captured. Cailleach saw her in a cage. We know nothing of who might have captured her, and, what's worse, you can't intervene because," she shrugged, "such a crime doesn't involve you or your subjects. Yet." She leveled him with a look that she hoped communicated how ridiculous she found this notion. "Cailleach is dying, Maybe Brigid, too, and that doesn't concern you?"

Arawn considered her, his lips pursed. "Gods do not fall under my jurisdiction. They do not come to Annwn to rest. They go to the All Father, for they are of his making."

"Semantics," she replied. "It's still death, isn't it? What of their subjects? They fall under your jurisdiction. And the humans. They're suffering in this endless winter as well."

"A fair question, to be sure, but many souls come to me each season. Winter is especially difficult for humans. How shall I differentiate the death of souls this season to years past? I can see no difference and I see every passing."

Maryn gaped at him. *Every passing.* How did he have time for anything at all? No wonder he wasn't coming with them to Spring. His schedule was full. For eternity.

"If it is The Morrigan who captured Brigid, why would she be interested in the first place?"

"Or be interested in you. Don't forget the crows and the hellhound." He turned toward Maryn fully then, his brow furrowed. "I've known Lady Morrigan for some time. The goddess of war is . . . flighty." He waved his hand as if shooing a fly. "Impulsive. Rash, though she may be at times, she's not witless. It's not like her to capture a god. While the crow spies could have belonged to any god, the *cù sìth* are another story. They belong to *me*, yet that hound Durvan dispatched wasn't sent by me."

"Let's say for the sake of argument," began Maryn, "that she's guilty. If she's as impulsive as you say, and she did capture Brigid, why not just kill her? Why hold Spring captive?"

Arawn lifted his eating knife, the light glinting along its edge. "She could not kill her without a ritual blade. Maybe she doesn't have access to one or, perhaps, she is merely waiting."

Morrigan wanted a blade? Perhaps Brigid's ritual blade, now neatly encased in her bag so inconspicuously placed upon her shoulders? *Is that what Morrigan was after?* But how would she know Maryn had it? She couldn't.

"Why wait?" asked Maryn, meeting Arawn's eye.

He opened his arms. "Perhaps she doesn't wish for Brigid's soul to tell on her."

They both fell silent.

"You're tired," he said after long seconds, his baritone thrumming through her. "Forgive me, for keeping you up so late. Allow me to escort you to your room. I'm afraid my usual servants for such tasks are otherwise engaged. You'll have to make do with me."

He motioned her toward the double doors that they'd exited. The warm glow from within the hall spilled out onto the neatly laid stone of the balcony, a halo of illumination that faded at his feet. She stared at the spot, fixated mentally on her mother and her grandparents. "Are they happy?" she asked.

Arawn knew of whom she spoke, if the understanding, albeit sad smile he gave her was any indication. "Yes, Maryn."

She fell into step with him and said nothing as he escorted her through the great hall and up a flight of stairs near the entrance. Not until he stopped at a heavy, oaken door did he speak. "At their judgements," he said, sounding reflective, "their thoughts were of you." His voice was soft and low and seemed to play in her blood. She met his strange, gold eyes and struggled to think of what she might say.

Her mum had been so sick; so frail. What she would be like now? Would she still be a shell of a person Maryn recalled, like that creature in the great hall? Now was as good a time as any to ask. "I saw . . . I saw a soul down below that looked, well, *starved*. When I last saw my mum, she didn't look much better, and I just wanted to ask—I just wanted to know if—"

"You want to know if she's been restored."

Maryn blinked rapidly, staring at her feet. Lord she was tired. *She was turning into a watering pot!*

"The creature you saw below is not human. She is a race of fairy. Her kind often enter the human realm to warn of oncoming famine. Do not trouble yourself. Your mother is well and whole, and, as I said, quite content."

Unable to speak, she simply reached out and grasped his hand, a silent "thank you," and opened the door.

At the last minute, just before shutting the barrier, she turned. He stared at the hand she'd squeezed. Touching him had been an impulse. Why had she thought she could just touch a god, for heaven's sake? She wanted to apologize for overstepping but held her tongue, thinking speaking about it would only embarrass them both.

Arawn bowed smartly. "Sleep well. I'll have someone escort you to the docks in the morning."

Chapter Nineteen

A Benevolent God

Maryn's appointed room was much like the one she'd had under the North Mountain. It was grand and richly furnished, with the glaring difference being noticeably above ground. The most ethereal, gauzy curtain she'd ever seen overlaid the bank of floor to ceiling windows on the opposite wall. The moonlight spilled onto the floor in a puddle of gold through one of the open draperies.

Dozens of flickering candles gave the room a very festive ambiance; a smoored fire glowed sleepily from the hearth, as slow and steady as her breathing. The whole room, with its soft cream sofa and matching coverlet on the bed, offset in rich crimson and dark green accents, looked like something out of a Christmas catalogue, sans decorated fir tree and stockings hung out for Father Christmas.

Best of all, though, a steaming copper tub sat upon a sheepskin rug near the fire. Maryn nearly groaned with anticipation and hastened to the ivory and gold accented privacy screen on the opposite side of the bed to undress.

Maryn found her cloak there, carefully hung upon a peg as well as a white night gown, as soft as well-worn cotton. She started to undress, first removing her bag from her shoulder, which she hung under her cloak. The weight now released from her tired shoulders, Maryn felt at least a stone lighter and three inches taller.

She hastily disrobed and sank into the water, a sigh on her lips. Hot enough to be almost uncomfortable, the bath was perfect. She found soap and cloth on a little rack on the edge of the tub and scrubbed. And scrubbed. The scent of jasmine perfumed the air and her skin.

Maryn had been dirtier—it was the nature of field work—but she'd never *felt* so soiled. Sweat and a bone deep fatigue, coupled with frayed nerves had left her begrimed in more than one sense.

By the time she'd washed her hair twice and scrubbed her body pink, the water turned a dingy grey and too cool to linger in for much longer. Maryn eagerly toweled dry and dressed in the provided night gown. Eyes and limbs heavy, she blew out the candles and climbed into the sleigh bed, oddly unconcerned for a mortal in the land of the dead.

The Morrigan's favored human servants, the druids, gathered in her council room, their heavy robes obscuring their fragile, human frames. She filled her lungs with the stench of their unwashed bodies, relishing it. She'd smelled much worse from the fields of battle, where blood poured, and bowels spilled, but still.... Theirs was the odor of dedicated disciples.

Her crow, Feren, cawed loudly from the back of her chair, interrupting one of the druid priestesses. Her comments had offered little. Morrigan lifted a hand, forestalling the woman as she opened her mouth to speak.

Each of the thirteen humans set before he waited, silent, in their places around the circular table, eyes downcast. They'd each spoken in turn, regaling Morrigan of the progress they'd made planting the seed of her benevolence to the scattered clans.

Their soft, plaintive voices echoed off the white, plastered walls of the room. Though covered in heraldry, shields, swords, spears, and other testaments to her skill and dedication to the human cause, Morrigan suddenly found the sight uninspired and inadequate.

Nothing was nobler than solving hostilities through the art of war. The spilling of blood is exact and final. No greater sacrifice could be made. War exhilarated her but now that her new plan was well underway.... How she'd ever thought it enough? Cailleach's majestic halls, the twisting labyrinths of ore-laden passageways, and Brigid's glittering halls called to her. She would have them both, and their servants' doting.

Only one druid had yet to speak. Morrigan turned to her right and gestured for him to start. A long, sinewy male with hair the color of freshly turned earth, he wore roves the color of dull iron. He looked young, save for the lines around his soft brown eyes, set in a freckled face. He sat straighter in his chair at being acknowledged and bowed his head in deference.

"Tell me, what news do you bring your mistress? Ensure your words are constructive to our purpose."

"Ciaran, Your Grace," he said, as if she cared to know his name. Morrigan's eyelids fluttered with the effort to hold her tongue.

"I've just come from south of the wall," he said, his voice breathy and thin, "where the clans have joined together to better share their resources. Their stores have nearly run out and most of their livestock slaughtered.

Some of the clans eagerly accepted your gifts, whereas others—" He inhaled slowly through his long nose. "Others would not take what was offered, claiming they would not anger Cailleach or Brigid."

Some humans would resist change. Soon, it would not matter. The choice would be made for them, but still, inciting anger or fear would work against her cause. She wanted her transition to becoming both Spring and Winter to be as graceful as possible, something she was unaccustomed to. Subtlety held a certain beauty, she was learning, though it wasn't in her nature to embody such a virtue. Earning the human's trust would take time. The populace must *warm* to her.

Morrigan tapped her fingers upon the stone table. "Hmm. Yes. And did you inform them of Cailleach's usurper? Were they willing to protect themselves from this upstart?"

Cairan bowed his head. "Those who accepted your gifts promised to retrieve Cailleach's hammer for you, should they find the human among them."

Morrigan took a deep breath, her eyes roving over the priests and priestesses. "There is something else," she said carefully. Feren fluttered onto the table where she stroked his long, sleek feathers, the soft trill coming from him as sweet as any song. She feigned concern. "This human usurper that's absconded away with Cailleach's hammer has also hidden away Brigid."

Morrigan let the weight of her words settle before adding, "It is my obligation to offer what protection I can to the Spring Court against further damage in this delicate time, until their mistress is found. A select few of you will go to *Alban Eiler* and act as my emissaries. Brigid's subjects are no doubt sick with worry."

Morrigan hid her smile at their widened eyes and looks of shocked concern. "You will go," she said, pointing to the druid, Ciaran, and two others. She favored them for their dedication and for their skill in weaving spells. "For your loyalty, I will imbue you with further magic. Go, cast your spells upon the gates of *Alban Eiler*. Protect Spring's subjects against the evil plan afoot.

Live amongst her courtiers and ensure they do not allow Brigid's capor into their midst."

The chosen few bowed their heads, some smug, others concerned, all ignorant to her lies.

Chapter Twenty

Enter Sandman

MARYN AWOKE FROM SLEEP, yanked from tranquility into sudden awareness. She'd been dreaming of her childhood home. Her grandmother had been industriously pulling carrots from the kale yard while she caught ladybugs amongst the chamomile blossoms.

Maryn blinked in the darkness, the pleasant dream and the feelings it evoked, ripped away and replaced by an oppressive sensation. Goose flesh erupted upon her arms. What had awoken her?

Maryn sat up and looked around her room, alight with the slanting, reflected light of the full moon. The skeleton key still rested on her bedside table, just as she'd left it. Nothing seemed amiss. Her eyes swept across the carpeted floor to the cavernous fireplace, empty save for stray beams of moonlight.

But then, in her periphery, the gauzy curtains framing the many-paneled French doors blew softly in an unfelt wind. Her view onto the balcony was limited to only that small sliver between door and jamb and so she could discern no threat, but something within her told her to be wary.

Her heart, which had seemed to stop for one terrifying, suspended moment at the sight of the open door, thudded painfully back to life. Maryn clutched at her bedclothes, her mouth gone dry, as she stared at the gap the open door had created.

Those had been closed. Granted she hadn't checked them before tumbling into bed, but she would have noticed if one had been left open. Wouldn't she have?

After waiting an indeterminable amount of time straining her eyes and ears, and finding nothing out of place, she braved looking under the bed (just in case) and padded across the floor. A sudden gust of wind must have pushed the doors apart.

Never one for forced bravery, she felt rather proud of herself as her hand closed upon the painted porcelain knob. Just as she began to push the door closed, a soft musical sound reached her ears. Someone beyond the confines of her balcony hummed a jaunty tune. She opened the door wider and peered out, looking left and right, before taking soundless steps to the edge of the railing.

The moon's vivid light revealed a woman below who was, indeed, humming. Stranger still, Maryn *knew* the tune. One of their childhood favorites: a ridiculous song about a man who wore a kilt instead of trousers, causing an uproar amongst his townsfolk. Her gran would change the lyrics slightly to include Maryn in the story, much to her delight. Had the tune invaded her sleep and spurred the lovely dream she'd had of Lolly?

Lolly. Remembering her warm eyes and soft body, her musical laughter and cheeky sense of humor filled Maryn with deep longing. Her heart stuttered, leaving it bruised.

Maryn stared at the back of the woman amongst the neat hedgerows below. Her calico print dress of light blue, her dark brown hair set in neat rows of rollers, and the apron bow tied at the small of her back stirred a nameless emotion within her breast. She looked an awful lot like Lolly before she'd died.

"Let the wind blow high, let the wind blow low, through the streets, in my kilt I'll go. All the Lassies say 'hello.' Maryn where's yer troosers?"

Maryn's breath caught in her throat. Had she heard correctly? Had the woman said "Maryn"?

Fingers gripping the stony banister, Maryn listened harder, unwilling to look away for the slightest moment.

"She's just come down from her bedroom fair. She's ready for school but what have we here? All the lads will shout, 'Ave a care! Maryn where's your troosers?" The woman paused in her work, humming once more, as she clipped another flower from its stem and placed it in the basket at her feet.

Maryn. She'd said her name. She was sure of it. The world suddenly clouded as Maryn's eyes misted with tears. She was here. Her gran. Her Lolly. The god of death had said Maryn couldn't seek out her dead relatives, but he'd said nothing about *them* finding *her*.

Maryn had to try twice to find her voice, but took up where Lolly had left off, silent tears tracing her cheeks. "To wear the kilt is my delight. It is not wrong; I know it's right. The highlanders would get a fright, seeing Gran in her trousers."

Her grandmother turned halfway, surprise evident on her cheery face. "Losh, is that you, Mare?" She turned fully, allowing Maryn to see her completely.

A sound halfway between a laugh and a sob bubbled out of Maryn. Her beloved grandmother was just as Maryn remembered: round cheeked, smiling eyes, her bird applique apron stretched over her ample bosom. Her house slippers, a dingy pink, completed the ensemble.

Gran threw open her arms, motioning for Maryn to come. "Och, my sweet Lassie. How I've longed for you, dearie. Come doon tae me quickly, my darlin' and let me look at you proper."

"I'll be right there," Maryn assured, and turned on her heel. Slipping her feet into her unlaced boots, she fumbled with the ties and rushed for the door. Flustered as she was, she'd forgotten that it was locked and ran into it, smacking her nose.

She swore softly but the pain and her blurred vision couldn't deflate her elation. Maryn fumbled with the key. Finally, hands shaking, she pushed the door open and raced down the dim corridors, only missing a turn once.

No one impeded her noisome exit, and before long, she left from a secondary door and raced as fast as she dared down the oyster shell walkway in the direction of her balcony. She turned the corner of the building, her heart hammering in her chest, and then slowed to a stop.

No one stood near her balcony. "Gran?" she called.

Maryn searched the area, her heaving breaths slowing as she stood amongst the fragrant flowers. Maybe she'd gotten turned around. Maybe she'd taken the wrong exit. Maybe that wasn't her balcony up above after all. Maryn frowned into the hedge, spotting a few fallen jasmine blossoms that Lolly had been cutting. "Lolly? Where are you?"

Maryn went to the hedge, her footfalls loud in the crushed shells, and picked up a fallen stem. She hadn't dreamed it. Lolly had been here only a minute ago. Revolving in a tight circle, Maryn called again, and this time, a faint reply reached her.

Turning sharply toward the sound, Maryn peered at the distant corner of the building, some fifty feet away. There, just outside the shadow of the castle, stood her grandmother. Lolly's white apron glowed softly in the moonlight like a specter. "Wait," Maryn called, lifting the billowing fabric of her nightgown. She hastened forward, gravel crunching.

Her grandmother waved cheerily and cupped her hand to her mouth. Maryn slowed so she could hear her. "I'm off to get yer grandda! Come along, dearie!"

Maryn lifted a hand, calling for her grandmother to wait, but Lolly turned around the corner of the building. Why wouldn't she wait? Maryn wanted to see where they lived. *How* they lived. Was her mother there, too?

Maryn's hasty steps turned into a jog, then a run. She turned the corner just as her grandmother's retreating form entered the hedge maze. Maryn's lungs burned by the time she reached the pathway leading into the seven-foot-high hedge. She faltered for only a breath, but at the faint outline of her grandmother's fulgent calico dress disappearing at a bend in the path, Maryn plowed forward.

Was this maze some sort of doorway, like a magical combination lock? Two turns left, two turns right, straight ahead, success?

"Wait for me!" she cried, waving a hand. "Lolly!" She followed the path her grandmother had taken, a ninety-degree left-hand turn. The path ahead lay straight and dim, but the darkness couldn't hide the form of her grandmother at the end of the row.

She redoubled her efforts to catch up, taking the right-hand turn her grandmother had disappeared behind, making a mental note. Turn left, then right....

The path darkened here, further inside the maze so finding her grandmother was impossible. Maryn slowed, following the path despite the warning that grew within her. "Gran—" started Maryn, but her words died on her lips when she turned the next corner—her only choice—and met with a T. Which way?

"Gran!" called Maryn. "Wh—Wait! Where did you go?"

Maryn bounced on her toes, searching the ground for any sign that Lolly had passed this way. Over the sound of Maryn's breath and her tripping heartbeat, the sharp crack of a twig snapped just behind her. Maryn whipped around but nothing was there. Just hedge and shadow.

Fear, sharp and immediate, spurred her on. She took the right-hand path at random, her eyes roving, her breath quick. She didn't feel like calling out now. She glanced over her shoulder several times before coming to a dead end. Maryn turned around, slowing her pace as she doubled back. Adrenaline made her stomach queasy.

Maryn crept to the T once more, willing her heart to slow. She stood still, not exposing herself to the path where the twig had snapped. She took a deep breath. *Don't be silly. Probably just a deer taking a turn in a terrifying maze.* She'd seen enough horror films to know better. And hadn't Arawn just warned her not to leave the castle?

Maryn forced herself to lean forward, to peek around the corner of the hedge. Nothing. A laugh—more like a shaky exhale—passed her lips. Maybe she'd imagined it.

"There ye are, my wee darlin'," her grandmother said from right behind her. Maryn whipped around so fast she got a crick in her neck.

Lolly stood before her, a strange smile on her face. "I've waited so long tae see ye, Mare," she said.

Maryn didn't go to her. Something was off, though Maryn couldn't put her finger on it. Gran's eyes glittered darkly and the timbre of her voice didn't quite match what Maryn remembered.

Fear dampened Maryn's excitement at seeing Loly again. With it came clarity: the real Lolly would never lead her on such a terrifying chase.

Maryn gripped her elbows, her gaze darting from shadow to shadow, wishing for Durvan—wishing for her grandmother in truth—and took a few tentative steps backward. She had no idea how far she'd gone into the maze, but the distance felt suddenly impossible to span. She was trapped.

To her horror, Lolly's face fell away like melting wax, exposing a face from her nightmares. It stretched and grew, morphing into a humanoid shape made of shadow and vapor. Empty, black eye sockets, no nose, and an impossibly wide mouth full of needle-like teeth leered down at her.

A scream lodged in Maryn's throat and she turned to flee, only to be met with another toothy shadow. Shapeless, save for the suggestion of a head and long arms, its twig-like fingers, long and pointed reached for her.

Blacker than the night, dense, and yet seemingly without substance, the shadow people had her trapped. They descended upon her faster than she could draw breath. Their spiderlike hands groped at her, scratching her, and filling her with cold dread.

Her body trembled as the immediate world around her melted away. The feel of the earth under her and the too-close hedge vanished, replaced with bright fluorescent light.

Maryn's worst memories assaulted her, filling her mind so fully that it was as though she experienced them again for the first time.

She was suddenly five again, small and scared as she stood in her mother's hospital room. Beeping monitors and astringent fumes assailed her senses. Frail and wan, lay her dying mother, tubes sprouting from her wasted body.

A blue cap embellished with little crocheted daisies and a bulbous bumble bee covered her mother's bald head. Lolly had made it for her, allowing Maryn to pick out the colors of yarn. Her mum's fragile body hadn't moved from this spot for ages. Her sunken eyes dull, her colorless lips trembling with the attempt at a brave smile only frightened Maryn further.

A hopeless longing filled Maryn's young heart. Where was the woman who'd carried Maryn on her back to bed, helped look for caterpillars in the garden, and raced her to the street corner on the way to school?

The longing cut into Maryn, making her knees wobble and her chest ache. She stood at the end of the bed, staring at the dying husk that was her mother. It hurt. Everything hurt these days. She could not carry the sensation. Her little body could not contain it.

She covered her mouth with her hand, forcing away a sob. What would happen to her when her mother died? Where would she live? Who would love her as thoroughly and as relentlessly?

Maryn didn't understand this illness, but she knew enough. Her mother was barely living—alive enough only to feel the constant pain of existence. It wasn't fair. What had either of them ever done to deserve *this*?

"Lovey," croaked her mother, her eyes heavy with medication.

Maryn drew closer, relieved she still lived, even with a half-life. She was desperate for even the smallest portions of her mum. "When are you coming home?" Maryn asked.

The colors in the room swam together, spinning and changing shape. The hospital bed, endless tubes, and incessant beeping disappeared. Maryn was suddenly at Middlevale Preparatory School, a new student in a new, uncomfortable life. Arriving in the middle of the school year was difficult enough, but for an orphan who had lost her smile, it proved sheer misery. Worse yet, she sounded different, having spent all of her years on the other side of the country. She was an outsider even to herself.

Her mother had died over seven months ago, and yet Maryn's tears would not stop. She could not keep them away, no matter how valiantly she tried. And tears, to her utter misfortune, fueled a playground bully's fire.

"Not even your mother liked you. I'd die too, if I had a daughter like you," gibed Sarah McDowel, her freckled face alight with menace. Her gaggle of friends laughed, peals as sharp as broken glass in Maryn's ears.

She ran, the cacophony of playground laughter surrounding her. She had nowhere to go. Nowhere to hide. The staff did not allow students into the building until after their break, and so she pushed her way through the space between the rubbish skips outside of the dining hall, the only place she seemed to fit. The only place she would not have to see or be seen. The smell overpowered her, but she had no other option. Maybe "Rubbish Bin Rat" would prove less painful than "Orphan."

Maryn's view of the red dumpster dimmed, the sickly-sweet aroma of rotting food fading away, replaced by the stale, damp air of Grand Caverns. The ceiling of this part of the cavern hung low but wide, with large stalagmites and stalactites spiking from the floor and roof like the teeth of some great beast ready to devour her.

She stood alone and uncertain, left behind by her classmates and her friends. Friends she'd gained after her grandparents had spent their life savings enrolling her in private school.

At first, nothing but her own breathing punctuated the stagnant air and the shushing of her pleated skirt as she adjusted her weight from foot to foot. The damp cave kept puddles; they littered the brick pathway, adding to the wet atmosphere.

Brushing her anxiety away, Maryn hurried from the room, carefully following the narrow string of lights tacked to the wall. The distant sound of voices led her to the next chamber, but the path diverged into two here, one up and one down. She strained her ears but the acoustics of the room made it impossible to know which way to choose with any certainty.

Unwilling to linger for too long, she chose a path at random, her quickening steps slipping on a turn. After several unnerving minutes, Maryn stopped when she entered another expansive room, gloomy and cluttered with hulking, shadowed rock formations. She forced her eyes away from the shadows, unwilling to let her mind make ghoulish figures where none lived.

She held her breath, listening hard for her missing classmates, for any sign that she was not the only person wandering the passageways.

Heavy silence pressed in on her. Across the room, metal stairs descended further into the depths of the earth. She approached warily, the sensation of being watched shivering up her spine as she passed column and stalagmite, replete with clinging shadows.

Don't be ridiculous, as if she could browbeat her slippery thoughts into behaving. *There's nothing in here but salamanders.*

She peered down the winding steps, forcing bravery, stretching on her toes as if that could help lengthen her gaze. The light failed halfway down the staircase, giving way to darkness. Maryn furrowed her brow. Surely if her class had come down these steps, she would have heard it. Dozens of shoes on metal grates would cause a great deal of noise.

What about the other pathway, the one she'd hastily discarded? Biting her lip, Maryn retreated and made her way back past the looming, hidden devils. Supposedly, feigned courage repelled things that went bump in the night. Maryn hummed the whole way back, glancing over her shoulder so often her neck started to hurt.

The other path turned out just as fruitless, however, sharpening Maryn's concern into barely contained terror. Lost and alone, with no clear way out, Maryn's eyes stung. Without exit signs, the caverns were an endless maze.

Her current pathway led to yet another corridor, varying pathways branching out like arteries in three different directions. *If you stay put, someone will find you.*

Turning in a tight circle, Maryn eyed the narrow, dimly lit pathways, recalling the large sign posted outside the entrance: "Stay with your group. Areas do not remain continuously lit." She crouched against a railing separating her from a slick rock, comforted by having a flat bit of wall behind her. At least nothing could grab her from behind. She wrapped her arms around herself, as the cool air seeped into her bones.

The absolute silence in the cave made any shuffling from her feet overly loud to her ears. Lord, she hoped they'd find her soon. She hadn't walked through this space with her class, had she?

Suddenly, in the far distance, a metallic bang echoed dully through the passageways, and then, without warning, the small bulbs illuminating the pathways blinked out.

She stared, wide eyed, into the oppressive dark, breathing ragged, mouth dry. The very air seemed to carry weight, as if it pressed in on her, making it harder to breathe. It clung to her skin, fixed itself to her lungs as she inhaled, the dark claiming her in every oxygenated cell coursing through her system.

Was that the sloughing of a robe, a whisper of movement from somewhere within the dark? Or maybe the sound came from some disembodied ghoul, come to feast on her blood. What better place for a vampire to live? No sunlight to harm them, a perfect eighteen degrees year-round, and countless tourists to single out and prey upon. Authorities would likely never find her body in such a maze.

Tensed tightly, her body trembling, Maryn swept her useless eyes in every direction. She didn't feel like humming now.

Waiting for her eyes to adjust turned out just as futile as her attempt to locate her class. She'd never seen such absolute darkness. She couldn't even see her hand in front of her face. The same sound came again—someone, something, breathing, only it wasn't coming from her. She held the sticky air within herself, her gaze darting about the space.

Her digital watch chimed the lunch hour. She jerked in alarm at the shrill sound and cringed at the nimbus of blue light illuminating her immediate vicinity. It would know right where she was now. The light dazzled her eyes, the imprint of the numbers on her watch face burned into her retinas for several seconds.

In her terror, Maryn shrank further into herself, tears filling her eyes. She tried to quiet her pitiful sniveling, her breaths that came too fast, but she could not.

They'd left. Abandoned her. She imagined her schoolmates getting off the bus back home, their parents waiting for them. They'd go home to a warm meal and a dry bed. Lolly and Pop would be there, waiting, but Maryn would be hours away, maybe dead from fright or something's dinner. Rocking, she bit her knuckle, her body as tense as drawn bowstring.

Then, out of the darkness, a distinctive sound made her breath hitch—footsteps, growing closer. Was it her teacher? A Grand Caverns employee come in search of her? A soft yellow light bobbed toward her, like a torch held in someone's hand.

Relief uncoiled in her belly, warm and immediate. She hastily wiped her cheeks and eyes, and stood on shaking legs, but as the figure drew closer, she recoiled, the metal handrail biting into her back. It was a man—she supposed it was a man—tall and hulking. In one hand, he held aloft a soft yellow orb radiating light. Not a torch, but a ball of fire.

Chapter Twenty-One

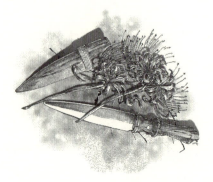

Cloudy With a Chance of Feasting

Shadows gathered under his eyes and in the hallows of his cheeks, wide brow and high cheekbones illuminated brightly. His lips were pulled into a severe line, his eyes radiating anger. His cloak seemed stitched from darkness itself. It coiled and whorled where it met the ground, like fog rolling across a meadow, like churning thunderclouds rallying for devastation.

She froze in fear, dizzy with panic and adrenaline. He drew close; a scream knotted in her throat. Maryn scrambled to the side, but it was useless. He had her in seconds, a long arm reaching for her. He did not clap a violent hand upon her, however, or snarl in her ear with a promise of pain. Indeed, the anger she'd seen in his eyes was gone, replaced with soft concern.

At her hasty retreat, the gentle hand under her elbow fell away. He made no protest as she pulled from him, looking about their surroundings as if they puzzled him. Maryn dared to look at the man again. He wasn't a monster after all. She expelled a shuddering breath, exhaling some of her anxiety. He seemed familiar to her, but she could not say how she knew him.

"Where are we?" he asked, the rich baritone of his voice rumbling through her. The orb of light left his hand where it drifted toward the ceiling between them, sharpening shadows into knives. The presence of the light should have lessened her fears, but it didn't. How was it made? Who or what was he?

If nothing else, the light would give her a forewarning of any further attempts to touch her. Not that she would get far if she tried to run.

Maryn stared, taking him in. He didn't seem like a monster, but he was clearly not a teacher or cavern employee. His clothes came out of a fairy tale, like a king or a magician, with high black boots polished to a sheen, a long dark tunic embellished with silver embroidery, and a lengthy dagger sheathed at the hip. About his shoulders swirled a cloak that seemed made from smoke itself. Smoke and secrets, for it seemed to whisper over the ground as he moved.

She forced her mind away from his appearance and replayed his words. *Where are we?* But didn't he live here? Wasn't this his... lair? Twice she tried to answer, before she found her voice. "Y—you don't live here?"

The droll turn of his lips as he surveyed their whereabouts told her otherwise. "No," he said wryly, touching the slick surface of the wall. He rubbed his fingers together as if testing the water's viscosity. "How old are you here?" he asked. "Twelve? Thirteen?"

Maryn shook her head, confused at his question. What did he mean, How old was she *here*? Still, she answered him. "I-I'm fourteen."

He canted his head to the side, surveying her with some amusement, and drew in a long breath through his very straight nose. A pinprick of light reflected in his dark eyes. "And what is it, exactly, that frightens you so? The dark?" he asked, "or being lost?"

Maryn's eyes found the shadows, darting from the corners of her vision back to the strange man. "It's what I *can't* see." She licked the dryness from her lips and added, "What lurks just beyond." Saying it out loud—acknowledging her fear—lent her a modicum of courage. She uncoiled from herself, letting her arms fall from where they'd been wrapped around her torso, and met his eyes. "Wh—who are you?"

He appraised her and pointedly ignored her question. "You shouldn't fear what lives beyond the curtain of darkness. Whatever abides in gloom should be afraid of *you*."

Maryn shifted under the intensity of his gaze. She had the uncomfortable feeling that he could peer into her very soul. "Dark creatures fear the light," he continued, gesturing a hand at their present surroundings. "Shine, Maryn, and they will have no power over you."

Maryn thought he sounded very much like one of the fortunes she'd read from a cookie. *A man cannot be comfortable without his own* approval or some such stereotyped nonsense. Wait, he'd used her name. She stiffened. How did he know her?

"Who are you?" she asked again.

"I'm not the monster lurking in dark corners," he said, divining her thoughts. "The monsters here are feeding on your fears. You musn't give them the opportunity."

Her teachers would tell her there was no such thing as monsters, which is what she'd *wanted* to hear. Her stomach dropped.

"So there *is* something here? A . . . something that wants me?"

He shook his head, a pitying look touching his features for the briefest of seconds. "No, Maryn."

Relief shot through her.

"*Not 'a' monster*," he continued. "There are three, in fact."

Maryn recoiled, her eyes skittering over shadows, peering into pitch-dark crevices. She couldn't see any monsters, couldn't even hear them. But as she inspected the dark corners of the cave, shapes emerged. Dark, slinking shapes that slithered over the uneven floor. They were vaguely humanoid, but *wrong*, with impossibly long limbs and twiggy fingers like spiders.

One pounced on her, as lithe and speedy as a cat, but she did not feel the weight of a blow. Instead, Maryn's vision of the cave and the strange man disappeared; blinked out and replaced with more haunting memories. They raced through her mind, like the furious turn of pages in a book.

Her mother's graveside service, sunny and warm, so contrary to her feelings. Her Pop falling in the yard, a hand clamped to his chest, his face beaded with sweat. Her cries for him to get up, her frantic screams for Lolly to come help.

Lolly's hand losing strength in Maryn's, her eyes closing on a sigh. Her first serious boyfriend at university, Collin, breaking her heart. It hurt, being left.

Abandoned.

The whole of her life was filled with people leaving. She was alone. Unloved. She had no one in her life save a revolving door of students and coworkers. Her whole body ached with the force of the memories. "Stop," she said, gasping. "Make it stop. *Please.*"

Hands touched her. Warm and gentle. Her blood stirred, raced in her veins. Her breathing came fast and then a sob broke free from her clenched jaw.

Next, a man's voice in her ear, insistent: "It should come from you. You must banish them."

She shook her head and sobbed. "Everyone I've loved has left me."

"Tell me something good," the voice prodded. "Tell me about Pop."

Maryn shook her head, trying to focus on the man's face. She peered at him as if through a tarnished mirror. *Pop?* Icy, clawed fingers wrapped possessively around her neck even as cold breath fanned her face. "Stop," she begged, crying outright. She lifted her hands defensively, trying to push away the sensation but nothing was there. Everything was so dark.

"Shine, Maryn," insisted the voice. "Tell me about Pop."

Maryn stammered; her throat tight, "P-Pop? He... he was my grandda." Talking seemed to get easier as she forced the words out. "H-He had a heart attack when I was seventeen. He missed my graduation, but I . . . I knew he was p-proud." She swallowed hard, feeling the icy grip around her throat weaken.

Maryn paused. Though bleary-eyed, she could make out the feet of the man that had come to her in the cave. She frowned into the dim. None of this made any sense.

How was she here, in Grand Caverns at fourteen, and yet could recall Pop's heart attack? And beyond. Lolly's and Collin's memories were far removed from secondary school. She had memories to span nearly thirty years of life. Good and bad.

At her realization, the fingers of fear that had laced around her slipped free with a hiss. The shadows that had caught hold of her darted back into the gloom beyond the man's floating light.

Not just any man. *Arawn*. She righted herself, wide-eyed, and watched in amazement as the walls of the hated cave flickered, showing her a glimpse of maze, before solidifying once more into Grand Caverns. She wiped her tears away and took Arawn's offered hand, allowing him to help her stand. Immediately her skin tingled where he touched her.

"Pop had the best laugh," she started, staring at the stone walls surrounding them. "It was contagious." One time Lolly sneezed so thoroughly that she'd lost her false teeth. They'd shot from her mouth onto her dinner plate and splashed in the gravy. Pop had laughed so hard he'd had tears in his eyes. She'd laughed too.

The walls of the cavern dimmed, flickered, then returned, though not as they should have been. Insubstantial and partially transparent—a ruse. She understood what Arawn meant now, about shining. Whatever had attacked her, *wanted* her scared. He'd said they feasted on her fears. She mustn't give them access.

Maryn squeezed his large, warm hand. "Mum gave the best gifts. She once tried her hand at knitting and took on the substantial occupation of making me a jumper for Christmas. It was awful," she said, the knot in her chest loosening. "I have a picture of me wearing it. It was striped pink and brown in intervals with an appliqué reindeer sewn in the middle of the chest." The walls of the cave melted away completely at her watery smile.

The maze reappeared, dark and close with the radiance of the moon hindered by the tall hedge, but the shadow creatures had gone. Gone with nary a sound, just as swiftly as they'd come.

She let go of Arawn's hand, her breaths coming fast. "What were they?"

"Puka." He gestured toward the path in a sort of "shall we" gesture.

"Shape shifters. Was it your mother they impersonated to lure you away?"

She fell into step beside him and shook her head. "My grandmother. Lolly."

They walked for some time in silence. Her hands trembled despite herself. You're safe now, because of Arawn.

"Thank you for coming for me," she said. "How did you know I was out here?"

He grunted, his boot sending a stone skipping into the hedgerow. "Your exit wasn't exactly covert. I'm glad to see you've tied your laces at least, even if you forgot your cloak."

Maryn's face heated, embarrassed that she'd rushed headlong into danger with nary a thought for her safety. She shivered, either from recent events or from the chilly night air.

"When I say, 'stay within the walls,' what is it you actually hear?" he asked, casting her a significant look.

Maryn shrugged uncomfortably and opened her mouth, prepared to explain, but he spoke first.

"I tell you there are dangers in Annwn that you have no defenses against. I tell you stay within the keep and to stay away from errant souls and still, you take it upon yourself to scamper about my kingdom at will. In the middle of the night, no less."

She had the good grace to appear contrite. She slowed and touched his wrist. "I'm sorry for abandoning the keep and . . . and ignoring your warnings. It's just that," she shrugged. "Seeing Lolly—"

His eyeline fell to where her hand touched his wrist, and his censure tuned to something else, something quiet and contemplative. He glanced her way, the hard line of his mouth softening. "I can well understand your desire to see her, but as I said before: now is not the time."

Maryn fidgeted, twisting a loose thread from her sleeve around her index finger. The pukas had made it abundantly clear why she shouldn't leave the estate. They'd shown her, too, how terrible it would be, ripped away from her family once again. Her heart had leapt with joy at seeing the puka Lolly. And now, despite knowing that it had been a trick, Maryn's heart ached in places she thought long healed.

Seeing her real family and having to say goodbye once more would surely break her heart in two. As it was now, she felt weighed down with longing.

"You did well, fighting off the pukas. Facing your fears is never easy."

Maryn rubbed the back of her neck. Had she done well? She could only conjure images of her cringing, weeping younger self. She gritted her teeth against the flush of embarrassment sweeping through her.

"Facing one's fears seems to be a reoccurring theme here in the underworld," she said, her voice barely audible over their footfalls. "First the rogue hell hound and now the pukas." She reached out a hand, brushing the soft foliage of the surrounding yew trees. "Both bested with happy memories. Why is that?"

In answer the conjured a fairy light grew in its brilliance. Their surroundings fell into sharp relief, the hue of the magicked sphere touching upon each feathery sprig in the nearby hedges. "Darkness cannot stand against your brilliance, Little Mortal. It flees, just as this light dispels the night from around us. You hold all the power you need to fight your demons."

If that was true, why didn't Maryn feel triumph ring through her? Why did she fight the urge to weep instead?

"I think it has to do with the fact that fear has a way of shackling us," he said, contemplative. "It binds us so we can't move forward. A hard lesson to learn."

Oh, how well she knew it! She'd shaped her entire adult life around fear, hadn't she? Work replaced any real relationships she might have, removing potential hurts. And now, thanks to those fetters, she lived alone, her life filled with fleeting distractions.

"What would have happened if you hadn't come? Would they have killed me?"

Arawn shook his head, the light exaggerating the hollows of his cheeks and the severe line of his mouth. "They can't kill you, Maryn, but they might make you wish for death. They—" he waved a hand in a tight circle as he searched for the right word "—attach themselves to souls to feed. The more trauma in their life, the better the feast."

She shivered, and not from the cold. They made their way along the noisome path, their footfalls crunching loud in the crushed shells. Her eyes found the banshees off to the left, guarding the bridge. They floated there in the moonlight, a bright, terrifying spot in an otherwise bleak landscape. She'd never been happier than to set foot upon the stone steps leading into the keep. Would she ever stop being afraid?

Chapter Twenty-Two

Twenty Questions

Maryn awoke abruptly from a knock at her door. Light streamed through cracks in the curtains, and sat upright, appalled that she'd slept so late. She scrambled out of bed, hair a tangled mess, and hurried for the door.

"C-coming," she croaked. She scrambled for the key set atop the nightstand and fit it in the lock. She paused, Arawn had warned her about errant souls asking things of her, but the people in the castle were safe, right?

"Who is it?" she asked, just in case.

A pause, then a muffled, "Its only me, Arawn."

Only Arawn. The god of death at her door. Maryn pulled in a breath to calm her nerves, and hastily finger combed her hair. She winced as her hands caught on a particularly large bramble, then gave it up.

She turned the key and opened the door. Arawn, gentlemanly enough not to comment on her appearance, bowed neatly. "Good afternoon, Lady Maryn."

Lady? "Erm, just Maryn is fine." Her left hand gripped the door handle. She lifted her chin, hoping that she didn't look as awkward as she felt. "Look, I'm sorry I slept so late."

Arawn lifted a forestalling hand. "No need to apologize. I've delayed your departure until the morning." He paused, his hand going to the door frame, peering at a knot in the wood.

Is he as uncomfortable as I am?

"I came to ask...that is, I wanted to bring you to the docks, to acquaint you with your escorts for tomorrow before you cross The Deep. Would you like that?" He seemed different from last night. Less familiar somehow. Stiff and formal.

Maryn shrugged one shoulder. "Er . . . sure. Just let me get dressed."

Arawn's hand fell away from the door frame. His features softened. Was he relieved? But that couldn't be right. What reason could the god of death possible have to be nervous around her?

As if on cue, in the stretched silence that settled around them, her stomach growled, long and loud.

"I'll have some food brought up for you and a change of clothes," he said with a soft smile.

Maryn blushed, glancing at herself. She'd been so worried about her hair, she'd answered the door without putting on her robe. Her insides squirmed. "Er, thanks." Now would be the perfect time for the floor to swallow her whole.

"No hurry," he added, and then he turned and departed without so much as a goodbye. His muffled footsteps died away, and still Maryn stared at the opposite wall of the hallway. "Well, that was weird."

Why would Death come to her door instead of sending a servant? She shut the door, her brow furrowed in confusion. Last night's tub had magically gone from the rug. A fire suddenly sprang to life in the grate, startling her. She warmed her hands while she waited, realizing that her bed had made itself, the covers neatly smooth and her pillows plumped. She could get used to magic.

A servant did not deliver the food and the change of clothing. A tray appeared magically, full of fruit and cheese and slices of warm ham. A cup of—Maryn sniffed it—Anji Bai Cha finished the ensemble. How did he know she liked this tea? That he knew such small details about her after only just meeting her both alarmed and amazed her.

Had he read all those things in her palm or was there more to it?

Next to the tray waited neatly folded clothes. First, a shirt and trousers, the former a dark blue, embroidered with silver thread around the cuffs and hemline, much like the night sky, studded with stars. The latter, the buff of a newborn fawn.

While Cailleach's gifts were lovely, cumbersome skirts took second place to trousers. She ran a hand down the suede-like material of the leggings. Next to the pile sat an ivory comb, a pair of woolen socks—black—and a belt made to accommodate a knife. She lifted the comb, running a finger over the teeth.

He'd thought of everything, and he'd left her alone to see to herself, knowing she wouldn't wish for a servant to attend to her. She smiled and set the comb aside, picking up her fort to eat before her breakfast got cold.

An hour later, sated, brushed—both teeth and hair—and dressed in Arawn's offerings, Maryn was ready. The trousers stretched and moved with her easily but also kept her warm. She belted the bone knife into its sheath, set over her tunic. Beautiful and dangerous all at once, like one of his selkies, Maryn felt prepared for anything, even if she didn't have armor. Maryn double-checked her bag, ensuring the hammer still lay within. She'd leave in here and lock the door behind her as she left.

She slipped the key into her pocket and tried the handle. Satisfied, she met Arawn at the bottom of the stairs. Without his cloak, he exposed more of his physic. His broad shoulders, heavily muscled, tapered down to narrow hips, where a belt, much like hers, boasted a long dagger. His high boots, polished to a sheen, ended just below his knees. Maryn swallowed and looked away. Hopefully, he hadn't caught her staring. If he had, he didn't tease her about it. *Thank the stars.*

"Ready?" he asked, unnecessarily. *She was here, wasn't she?* He made for the front of the castle, pulling on black leather gloves.

She fell in step beside him, searching for something to say. She flexed her fingers in an effort to dispel some of her nervous energy. Getting a private tour of the docks, escorted by the god of the underworld, didn't happen every day.

"Is Durvan joining us?" she asked, breaking the silence. She looked about as if he'd spring from a shadow.

"He's currently with my armorer, seeing to his weapons."

"Ah." She'd counted on the dwarf accompanying them. Her stomach squirmed. "Well, thanks for the clothes."

He looked her up and down. "They suit you. I'm glad you like them."

"They're perfect." And they were. They fit her like a glove. How did he know her size? *More magic?*

The sentries on either side of the heavy front doors opened the way for them. They saluted Arawn with a fist to their hearts, saying nothing, eyes straight ahead. She and Arawn descended the steps, the afternoon sun bright overhead. The banshee sentinels hovered at the bridge with the hated Dullahan farther afield.

Arawn, apparently sensing her fear, said, "You're a guest here; you've no need to fear them."

Maryn laughed on an exhale. "Don't I?"

Arawn's gaze lingered on the banshees, their strange eyes following them as they walked along the path. "They're not meant to be frightening. They perform an important service for the dying."

"They reap souls, too?" asked Maryn.

"No," said Arawn, shaking his head. "They foretell death . . . prepare the soul and its family for what is to come."

"How is that helpful?" she asked.

Arawn shrugged. "Sometimes families are separated, especially in times of conflict and war. Wouldn't you, as a mother, wish to know that a beloved son or daughter would soon cross over instead of just never seeing them again . . . never knowing what happened to them?"

What a terrible situation. Still she had to admit that never knowing what happened to a child just might be worse than living in the unknown. "I suppose you're right." They passed by the floating banshees, who moved aside to let them pass. Their strange gazes bore into her back as she and Arawn crossed the bridge.

"And the Dullahan?" she asked, gesturing toward the frightening aspects of the headless horsemen atop the walls. They flanked the road, their torsos turned toward them. One of the horses knickered and shook its shining mane, then grew still again, like a statue.

Maryn took an unconscious step closer to Arawn. "You can't tell me they're not terrifying."

Arawn's private smile was not directed at her, but at the creatures set as sentinels on either side of the great, black gate. He almost seemed *proud*. "Well, yes," he conceded, "but they're meant to be. They make up the cavalry in my army."

Maryn gaped at him. "You have an *army*?"

He shrugged. "Of course I do. We all do. Gods, I mean. We haven't always been at peace with one another."

Maryn gaped, her mind reeling. "When was the last war?"

Arawn waved a hand in dismissal. "Oh, some time ago. It's been an age, long before my time. Still, I keep them trained and ready."

They drew even with the great gate. She stood so close to Arawn, that her elbow bumped his arm. She should move away but couldn't bring herself to do so. The closest Dullahan held a grotesque head in the crook of its arm. The skin, white and mottled with rot in places, stretched tight across bone. The eyes were worst of all. Its gaze appeared made of flame, glowing bright orange even in full sun. She couldn't help shivering and looked away.

The gate squealed open, the grating of metal so loud that Maryn winced.

Arawn, seemingly at ease, led her through the curling iron gateway. Maryn couldn't get away fast enough and did not breathe easily until they passed out of sight from the monstrous creatures. Arawn led her up a slope in the opposite direction from which she and Durvan had come, when they'd first arrived in Annwn.

"Better?" he asked, sparing her a glance. "I'm sorry they frightened you."

Maryn shrugged and stepped over a broken branch littering the pathway. A stiff breeze pushed and pulled at her tunic and hair as she huffed up the hill. Arawn walked beside her with his hands behind his back as if the steep incline didn't affect him.

"Are you quite sure you can't go with us?" she asked. "To spring, I mean."

He shook his head. "I'm afraid not."

She paused, catching her breath. "But you could go, right? If you had the time. You aren't limited like the seasonal gods, are you? Durvan says you can travel to any kingdom so you can perform your duty of gathering souls."

"I can enter any kingdom, including the human world. Because humans are frail and their lives so brief, I wouldn't be able to rule Annwn with any real efficiency if I didn't delegate soul gathering duties to others from time to time." He paused, looking over his shoulder at his castle. "But I can never leave for long. I must rule *here*, in Annwn."

"When will you go to Cailleach to lend her strength?"

His gaze brushed against hers as he answered. "Tomorrow, while you're crossing The Deep."

What other types of duties does the god of death have? How might he go about lending strength to Cailleach?

She didn't ask, distracted by the view from the bluff. Vast and silver with sunlight, waves crashed upon the rocky beach, so reminiscent of the Hebrides on which she'd spent much of her life. Seals sunned themselves on exposed boulders, their brown and grey speckled bodies stark against the verdant tangles of seaweed clinging to every surface.

"How lovely," Maryn said between breaths.

Arawn, whose gaze had been cast far into the distance, found her own, his golden irises tinted with the slightest touch of green. She had to force herself to hold his penetrating gaze. She felt exposed once more, like he could see clear into her soul.

He wasn't just a ruler of a vast and beautiful kingdom; he was also Judge. Assessor. What about her own soul? What did he see and did he find her wanting? She gulped, too terrified of the answer to ask.

He broke the contact, his face a mask.

Maryn watched the side of his face as he gazed at the sea. His strong jaw, prominent cheekbones, and chiseled lips were as perfect as one of Michelangelo's statues. Tall and graceful, elegantly built and beautifully articulate, he was the picture of a god. But there was something more. Some unspoken melancholy she sensed in him tugged at her heartstrings.

She looked away, afraid he'd catch her staring.

Far below, a pier thrust out from the left side of a juttying rock formation. A sleek vessel secured in place with ropes to pilings completed the long, robust dock. Her eyes widened at the sight. The ship, narrow-bellied, sat high in the water, reminiscent of Viking ships portrayed in drawings and in museums.

Her gaze lingered on the figureheads on both ends, where the long planks converged to a high point. They would depict some sort of mythological creature. She smiled to herself. Not mythological. *Real.*

"Dragon or mermaid?" she asked, pointing to the boat.

"Ah," said Arawn, following her line of sight. "I'll take you down so you can see for yourself. I'll introduce you to my captain, as she'll be escorting you and Durvan across the sea tomorrow." He indicated that they follow an adjacent path in the windblown grass to their left.

Tucking a stray hair behind her ear, Maryn fell into step beside him. He would not be on the ship with her tomorrow. Anxiety bubbled up within her. After his recusing her from the pukas in the maze, she felt *safe* with him, as if she was a child, and he a responsible adult who would "take matters from here."

Durvan kept you safe enough.

Despite her nerves upon first waking up and finding him at her door, Arawn comforted her. Maybe his frankness, or his ability to *see* into the heart of a person and not make them feel uncomfortable, soothed her. Somehow, he felt to her as a friend should, accepting her despite knowing the least-attractive parts about her.

Maryn frowned inwardly. Was she so desperately lonely that she imagined some sort of rapport—friendship—with Death? She pushed hair from her eyes. When she made it back home, she'd say *yes* more. Yes to drinks after work with coworkers. Yes to girls' nights at the cinema. Yes to a life outside of work.

How can I possibly return to a normal life after something like this?

Maryn pushed those thoughts aside. "Can you go in your true form to other kingdoms, then? In your body I mean, or do you have to project your spirit outward, as with Cailleach and Brigid?"

"Are you collecting information for one of your scholarly journals, or are you merely curious?"

Had she overstepped her bounds? But no, he smiled at her. He was teasing her. She shrugged, hiding her answering grin. "It's in my nature to seek answers. I'm a scientist, after all."

The corner of Arawn's mouth twitched higher. Perhaps he, too, saw how incongruous human, scientific logic was in a world amongst fairies and gods.

They walked under a windswept oak, its branches twisted and gnarled. "Yes, I can travel in my own body. But it's my selkies," he said, motioning toward the jagged coastline, "that do most of my soul gathering. They are swift in the water and, upon reaching the human world, can shed their skin. It's comforting for your kind to be met by one of their own at the time of their unmaking." He paused, the wind lifting his hair, exposing his temples.

"Unmaking," Maryn repeated. Interesting term. "Your servant called you the Unmaker."

He rubbed the back of his neck. "I have many names."

"Which do you prefer?" asked Maryn, unable to hold her tongue. Her face warmed with a blush. Was it rude to ask a god such personal questions?

His startling gold eyes met hers and her breath stilled. "Arawn," he said simply. "That is the name my mother gave me."

Before Maryn could ask about the parentage of gods, he continued, "Despite my selkies doing much of my soul gathering, I am burdened with knowing the last breath each living creature expels. I do gather souls on occasion, especially when said spirit needs coaxing."

Maryn raised her eyebrows, surprised Death needed to entice anyone into this beautiful kingdom. Then again, they—like her—might not understand just how idyllic Annwn truly was. "Tell me about the doors of the Fae kingdoms," Maryn said. "When we fell into Annwn, we travelled underground, but—" she gestured with a hand at the vast sky and sea before them "—we're clearly not inside the earth."

"No," Arawn agreed. "The human world and the Fae world are separate, only connected through doorways here and there. As I said, there is another doorway into the human world across the sea. It opens very near Spring's doorway. In the human world, there would be markers—stones usually—indicating entry points."

"How many doors are there?" asked Maryn.

Arawn smiled in answer. "There are many doors. Especially for me."

It made sense that a reaper of souls would need lots of doorways. Who or what might have met those of her loved ones that had passed on? Arwan himself, or a servant? She hoped their journey into the afterlife had been peaceful; she'd always believed her mother was happier released from the frailties and pains of her body. She'd been in such intense pain for so long, Maryn couldn't remember a time when her mother had been healthy.

And then there was her Lolly, who'd mourned the passing of her husband for nearly ten years before she, herself, had died. As sad and difficult as Lolly's death had been for her, a part of Maryn had found solace in the belief that her gran's suffering had ended. Knowing now that they lived on, brought her comfort.

Arawn abruptly stopped walking, his gaze like a weight. "You don't fear me." He hadn't phrased his words as a question, but the shape of one hovered behind the words.

She pursed her lips, her brow furrowed a she stopped beside him. "Should I?"

The wind stole his huffed laughter. His mouth twisted into a wry smile. "Most living mortals fear me, but not you. Why is that?"

She licked dry lips. She met his gaze evenly, a strange sensation crawling across her skin. "Maybe it's because I've seen the mercy in death." She shrugged. "Perhaps for others, who've had different experiences, they might not feel the same."

Children taken too young, for instance, or families of murdered souls would feel quite the opposite. But for Maryn, who made a living studying the past, of keeping it alive, death didn't seem so terrible. Though difficult and painful for those left behind, death was merely an unavoidable consequence of birth.

"For me," she said, looking over the beauty set before them, "seeing Annwn only confirms my viewpoint. Yours is a necessary service. Resting here for all eternity after a life of struggle and isolation seems pretty good to me."

Of course, most people wouldn't welcome death, regardless of what they thought would meet them on the other side. Empty nothingness or a kingdom rich in color and life, death was a mercy.

Arawn gave her a pensive look. "Some souls agree with you. Some come willingly and, if they approve of my judgements, are content. But, as you saw last night, not all souls are at peace. They cannot deny their acts and mistakes, but neither are they always so quick to accept my judgement. Some despise themselves—and me—for a time before they find peace."

Maryn pressed her lips tightly together, the sound of wailing from Death's courtroom echoing in her mind. Poor things. Strange that, when faced with an afterlife, souls remained the same people they'd been while alive. "How long until most come to terms with the life they lived?"

Arawn looked to the sea, his gaze upon the distant horizon. "It largely depends on their willingness to see themselves as they truly are. For most, it comes quickly, but for some . . . some can't let go of what was, and search, always, for who they can blame or what wrongs befell them while living. It's not easy to grow and change after death."

Much like living. They commenced their walk. Maryn's hair flew about her in a sudden gust of wind. Clearly, being a good person didn't get any easier after death. And his was the difficult task of helping souls through life's trauma to find ultimate peace. If they let him, that was. Maybe it was something in his voice, or in the tightness of his features that hinted at the burden he shouldered, but Maryn felt suddenly sad for him.

"What about you?" she asked him. "Who helps you find peace?" She cringed inwardly at Arawn's answering frown. "I'm sorry. I shouldn't have." Arawn didn't answer her, and no wonder. What right did she have to ask such personal questions. She hastily changed the subject. "What's that?" she asked, pointing toward a distant ship, a mere spot against the skyline where the sea met atmosphere.

He followed her finger out to the glittering surface of The Deep. "That, Little Mortal, is what we call 'a boat.'"

She relaxed at his joke. The laugh that escaped her sounded more like a snort. Arawn's lips twitched as her face flamed.

As the trail veered downward toward the beach, Maryn watching for ankle-twisting rocks on the steep slope, she said, "After all my studies of mythological gods, I'm surprised that you're . . . well, so ordinary. You're a far more sympathetic and genuine than I imagined."

Arawn lifted a brow. "Oh? Well, we gods are much like people in that way, with varying personalities and experiences that have shaped us. But I've got quite a lot to be going on with. Death being the process that it is, my duties aren't what one would call glamourous. In fact, I can't even take holidays."

"But how is that fair?" Maryn asked, indignant on his behalf. She wasn't a god, of course, but even she needed a reprieve from her responsibilities. "The seasonal gods get to rest. Why not you?"

Arawn paused, thinking, as they navigated a switchback in the trail. "There *is* rest, but not as you might think. There's no delegated season for death. How could there be? Who do you suppose would take over for me during my absence? No, my rest will come when my time as the god of Annwn is over . . . if I relinquish it to another."

Maryn slowed and leveled him with a questioning look. Cailleach said something similar, citing her lack of children as a reason to carry on. "Do you have a family? Children who can take over for you?"

Arawn offered his hand as they came upon a steep decline, where smooth boulders turned to jagged, broken steps. "Children to keep up the family business, you mean?" he asked, amusement coloring his tone.

Maryn took his offered hand without thought, forgetting the strange way his touch called her blood. As soon as her skin made contact with his, it rushed toward him, leaving her flushed.

She missed her next step and fell into him. At the contact, something tugged her middle, as if a fisher's knot were stitched to her very soul. The line tugged sharply as she fell into him, then receded just as quickly as it had appeared. For a dead man, he was perfectly solid. *Was he dead?* She wasn't sure.

She wanted to ask about it but did not, an unaccountable shyness overcoming her. Somehow, asking about why he affected her soul—her blood so readily—seemed obvious. Yet something about the rush of intimacy at each brush of contact defied words, like a schoolgirl experiencing her first crush all over again. That line of thinking alarmed her, and so she pushed it away, burying it deep.

Maryn turned her head to hide her heated cheeks. "Well, all I'm saying is, if I had the world at my feet, I'd take a vacation from time to time."

Arawn's teeth flashed white as he grinned. They continued along the path, and after a short distance, he resumed their conversation. Talking together, pickup up the exchanged as old friends might do, warmed her.

"To answer your question," he said. "I have no progeny. I've never taken a queen."

Maryn frowned at her feet, careful not to repeat her earlier clumsiness. She remained quiet for a long while, the only sound coming from their footfalls on the path. She knew better than to ask about a god's love life.

The wind picked up, bringing with it the smell of saltwater. "If you could take a break from all this," she said with a wave meant to encompass the entirety of Annwn, "what would you do? Sleep?" she asked with a hint of a smile.

Arawn drew in a long breath, not meeting her eyes. He shrugged one shoulder in an offhand way. "I don't know," he mused. "I haven't given it any serious thought."

Maryn raised a brow. How could he not think about it? Most people she knew lived holiday to holiday, counting down the days when they could unwind for longer than a weekend. "Come on, there has to be something," she prodded. "People you'd like to catch up with. Places you'd like to see?"

Arawn didn't answer right away. Finally, he said, "There is no place I *can't* go now. If I wanted to travel to the farthest reaches of the globe, I could—and do. No, I suppose it's people I would care to visit. Time spent together without the burden of responsibility or the separation my station imposes."

Burden of separation. The words struck a chord with her, making her heart squeeze a little. He was surrounded by souls—subjects—but no one to commune with? No one to laugh with?

Every person who'd ever truly loved Maryn had gone. They were here, somewhere in the beautiful dimension, and she had no access to them despite her nearness. Was he just as isolated? Surrounded by souls, yet alone all the same?

If only she could change that for him. An impossible a task for a mortal human to help a god, surely. Still Arawn deserved happiness.

Maryn eyed the line of his broad shoulders ahead. "You said the selkies help you with gathering souls. Is there not someone who could shoulder more of your responsibilities? Couldn't you delegate some of your other tasks to someone else so you could take the time to visit those you care for?" *So you could, I don't know, relax.*

"Such as?" he asked, pausing to help her over an eroded area in the trail. "The souls here are my subjects and it's my duty to see that they have eternal rest."

"And it wouldn't be restful if you gave them godly duties," Maryn finished for him. How lonely he must be. Moreso than herself. She had coworkers at least.

"Yes. Exactly." He shot her a reassuring smile, as if he knew her line of thinking and wanted to prove her wrong. "And I have distractions from time to time. You being the latest."

Maryn had no answer to this. A distraction once a decade? A century? How terribly sad. She cleared her throat. "So tell me about what I should expect once we cross your sea." They were nearly to the beach now, the steep incline giving way to pebbles and coarse tufts of grass. Sun-dried water plants that had been washed ashore littered the beach in neat, organized rows where the tidal waves had left them.

"You should be careful to avoid people, I think. Starving humans are often desperate, and we do not know what all is afoot. Whomever is behind Brigid's capture could know your intent. Spring's borderlands may be dangerous."

Maryn was more worried about monsters. What else might she and Durvan be up against?

"I cannot spare my selkies for long. Durvan will see you safe. Follow him as you have, and all will be well."

Maryn frowned. "And if we're attacked by some beast?"

He shrugged. "You did well enough before. Just avoid their pointier bits, hmm?"

Maryn scoffed, her mouth turning up with a reluctant twitch. "Is that your way of lightening the mood?"

Arawn glanced at her sideways. "Is it working?"

"Not in the least."

Chapter Twenty-Three

The Deep

THE NEXT DAY MARYN and Durvan, weighed down with additional food and water in the packs, boarded the ship. Arawn waited on the pier for them to pass, speaking softly to his selkie captain. He nodded as she and Durvan passed him, a silent goodbye written in his eyes.

Maryn returned the gesture, feeling a sort of hollowness pervade her breast. The next time she saw Arawn, she'd be dead. How odd. She looked forward to that day, whenever it happened. She'd be glad to see him again.

Durvan, looking green already, crossed the gangplank and sidled into a space at the prow of the ship.

For a fairy that preferred living in the heart of a mountain, the depths of the sky above, mirrored below in black sea, might prove too much for him. Still, imagining any scenario where Durvan wasn't in complete control proved impossible. She frowned after him as she stepped onto the boat. She didn't fancy Durvan's sick all over her shoes.

Eager to continue their search for Brigid. The end of her journey dangled just out of reach. Soon, though, they'd arrive at Spring's kingdom and get to the bottom of Brigid's disappearance.

Home—her tiny flat, the quiet nights spent alone, the kitchen table covered in articles, maps, essays, and other work-related paraphernalia. Work *was* her life. It consumed every part of her day and bled into her nights. Well, she had her houseplants and her cat, Darcy. He needed her. Sort of.

As with all felines, Darcy didn't really need her. More like she needed *him*. He had probably already safely holed himself away in a neighbor's apartment, having escaped through the little door she'd installed in her living room window. He liked to come and go, using the fire escape to reach the rooftop.

As wonderfully exciting, if albeit terrifying, this adventure had been, Maryn longed for home. Who covered her classes? The grant application she'd started had been left unfinished. If she didn't get back soon, she'd miss the deadline. Scott would have to cover her lessons, and with his busy schedule, she worried about how he would accomplish it all. She sighed as she crossed the wooded planks of the ship to where Durvan sat, his cloak pulled tightly around him as if striving for sleep. She settled beside him, glancing at his wrapped body.

As busy as work kept her, she still wanted more for herself. When she got home, she'd just have to take the initiative and make necessary changes. Maybe she'd even date more. After Collin, she'd never really allowed for the possibility of romantic relationships, being too preoccupied with professional commitments.

"Set free," hollered a selkie from the dock. He tossed a coil of rope to a companion standing in the ship not far from Maryn. No sails, not even a mast, nor any oars occupied the boat. A wide wheel, however, manned by the intimidating lady selkie she'd met their first night in Annwn, waited near the back of the vessel.

"Make way," shouted the captain.

Only four sailors, including the captain, manned the ship. They likely did not need more hands without sails to work. The ship moved under her feet, a quiet vibration not unlike riding in a car. The dock slipped away, the ship effortlessly gliding through the still, black waters of The Deep.

A stiff breeze brought on by the forward motion of the boat filled Maryn's nostrils with the scents of fish, rotting seaweed, and some other cloying odor she could not name. The captain barked an order at a deckhand as Maryn stood to better view the long neck of the dragon ship. It rose sharply into the air, ending with a grotesque carving of the figurehead, a forked, crooked tongue tasting the air. Who knew grindylows were so terrifying?

"Are you well?" she asked the dwarf. He opened one bleary eye, peering at her much like a pirate, and grunted his reply. "I'll be better once we're off this bloody ship," he muttered.

Maryn took the few steps required to look over the side, examining the water. The shallowness of the hull brought the side of the boat to only knee height at the center.

"Mind you don't get too close," warned a shipmate from behind. She turned and met his unsettling, black gaze. Would she ever get used to their strange eyes? How could anyone in the human world mistake them for a mortal? "One little bump from an errant wave and—" He made a regretful click with his tongue, shaking his head.

Maryn frowned and peered into the water, seeing nothing but a black expanse of smooth glass save for a rippled wave from where the ship cut a path. "Why?" she asked, her voice holding all the gravity of a frightened child being told a ghost story. "What happens if I fall in?" She could swim. Quite well, in fact, but something told her that the selkie wasn't concerned about her swimming ability.

"The Deep is the home of the damned," he said ominously. "Believe me, they'd like nothin' more than to get you in their bony grasp." Maryn's expression must have shown her alarm because the sailor's grin widened.

"Och, aye, Lassie. Fall in there," he said, motioning with the coiled rope to the vast sea, "and they'll swarm to you like flies tae honey."

Gooseflesh pebbled to life along her arms. "Why would they want me?" she asked, sure her soft voice betrayed her fear.

He gazed into the water; his mouth twisted as he considered his words. "There are some that lived such terrible lives, that there is no place for them *but* The Deep. Here they have one purpose." He paused, his eyes boring into her. "Did you know Annwn is an isle? No? It's large enough, with mountains and valleys and all of the needful things we souls require, but an island still. No one gets in or out without permission."

"And these souls," she hedged. "They ensure Annwn cannot be breached?"

"That's the right of it," said the selkie, tapping his nose. His slick, black hair shone in the sun, glinting blue. "Arawn might've given his blessing for your crossing in and out of his kingdom, but those that reside in The Deep, they only know one thing." He drew in a long breath, his gaze returning to the black surface of the water. "They hungered for blood when they lived, and they hunger for it even now. They're never sated. They never stop."

Maryn's mouth had gone dry. She wrapped her arms around herself, suddenly cold, and took a careful step back.

"So mind where you step and keep away from the edge," warned the selkie. "We'll reach the other side by morning."

Maryn resettled herself near Durvan. The underworld was certainly vast with a myriad of souls living in it. How did Arawn manage it all? Her respect for him grew.

The selkie deposited the coil of rope onto a peg just inside the prow at her feet.

"Sir," she asked, uncertain how to address such a creature.

The selkie scoffed and looked down at her. "Call me Brem. I ain't no sir."

"Brem," she repeated. "Nice to meet you. I'm Maryn."

He sucked his teeth and said, "I ken fine who you are."

Right. Of course he does. "Well, Brem, I'm curious about your kind. Can you travel the seas without a ship? Arawn told me how he delegates some of his soul gathering to those like you. I imagined that you would swim across, to the various doorways, not sail. Are the damned souls that infest the waters interested in selkies, too?"

"*Lord* Arawn," he said, giving her a significant look, "appoints a select number of us to help in the reaping, and we *do* swim in these waters. It's you and yon dwarf that require the ship."

She grimaced internally at her impropriety. "And do you often help *reap* souls for Lord Arawn?"

"Aye," he said, staring at her with some expectation. "When it's asked of me."

"Where do you keep your . . . well, your seal skin?"

"Now that's a highly personal question for two souls of such small acquaintance," he said with a sly smile and a wink. "I might tell ye, were we tae share a pint or two."

"Leave the lassie be," grumbled Durvan from his cloak. "She's not for you."

The selkie laughed and walked away, the little charmer. Clearly, selkies could lure unsuspecting mortals out of their bodies, for Brem *was* charming, black eyes notwithstanding. Warm, quick witted, and attentive, he seemed just the sort of man a lonely villager would befriend.

Maryn sat near Durvan, her back resting against the high wall. She glanced at his immobile form, glad for the information that it would only take a day to reach the opposite shore. "Arawn warned me that whoever is behind Brigid's capture might be watching the Spring borderlands and the selkies cannot be spared for long," she said. "Could—could you train me on how to defend myself? I don't want to be a hinderance to myself or to you."

Durvan lifted his head from where it rested against the prow and considered her for a long moment from under the fold of his hood. "Mmph. I suppose it would be best to take this time tae teach ye tae use a blade." He sat straighter and grimaced, his face losing what color it had. "On second thought," he muttered, "let's 'ave Brem show you a thing or two."

Brem needed little convincing, and so in no time at all, Maryn found herself standing mid deck, Brem opposite her. "It's your feet that we must start with. A narrow stance makes it easy to topple you. See," he said, pushing one of her shoulders. She stumbled backward, barely keeping her feet. Thankfully he didn't push her so hard that she fell into the side of the boat and toppled in. "Widen your stance and it'll be harder to push you around."

Maryn obeyed, moving her feet apart. "Like this?"

He pushed her again and her shoulder rolled back instead of her losing her balance altogether. "Aye, like that. Now, the next step is the blade. What have ye got?"

Maryn lifted a hand to show him a short knife Durvan had lent her, one he'd pulled from his boot. She wasn't about to use Brigid's blade. She'd returned it to her bag, where it resided next to Cailleach's hammer.

Durvan's given blade was about five inches long, fixed, and double edged, coming to a sharp point. Brem inspected it, eyes narrowed, then showed her how to hold it. He wrapped her fingers around the grip, instructing her to point it up, toward the sky.

"Keep your body behind your knife," he said, moving her hand from her side to her middle. "You're small, which is good for defense, but you can make your body smaller by shrugging your shoulders or ducking your head. Good," he praised. "Never turn your back on your attacker. Keep your knife between you."

Maryn followed his cues, most of which included the proper height to hold the blade. "Don't extend your arm out so far," he chided. Before long others joined, offering their own bits of advice as Brem pretended to attack her. Maryn attacked too tentatively, too slowly, she failed to roll away from strikes, and left her face undefended. In short, she was rubbish at using a knife.

"Nonsense," said Brem when she voiced her lament. "You're a novice is all. Keep practicing."

Maryn kept at it for a while longer. Brem even switched with another would-be attacker, a woman called Reitha. She fought even better than Brem, or maybe Maryn was just getting worse.

Some time later, completely fatigued, she found her spot near Durvan. "You might as well take this," she said, handing him back his knife.

He refused it with a shake of his head. "Ye cannae expect to improve without it. Keep it. Use it. I've got others."

She didn't argue and placed it into one of the many pockets her cloak boasted. "What's the spring doorway like? Should I expect to sacrifice something else?"

Durvan's eyes were closed, his face wan. "We cannae enter by ourselves. The door intae the Spring Court is a mirrored lake, guarded by a water horse. Ye mun climb upon its back and it'll bring ye through the gate."

"A water horse," she repeated. She couldn't say why it astonished her. She'd seen all manner of creatures from the fairy stories. Fables said this creature lured greedy souls into capturing the ethereal being, but once they mounted its back, it would return to its watery home and drown its victims.

"Aye, show the hammer and all will be well."

Maryn certainly hoped so. She didn't much fancy dying today.

Chapter Twenty-Four

Between Worlds

"Prepare mooring!" shouted the captain, startling Maryn from an uneasy doze.

She rubbed her bleary eyes and staggered to her feet, unsteady from the perpetual rocking of the boat. The dawn's glittering rays stretched across the sky in vibrant shades of purple. Footfalls pounded on the planks as sailors rushed to dock the boat alongside the awaiting pier.

The journey across The Deep had left her cheeks chapped with wind and her hair wild. Durvan had slept the whole of the trip and missed her nearly vomiting over the side from the relentless waves that rocked them. *Lucky him.* She'd gotten little sleep, pressed against the curved prow. Durvan's snores hadn't helped any, either.

She helped him to stand, noticing his movements matched hers for stiffness. "Walking should help," she offered.

Durvan grunted a reply, his gaze fixed hungrily on the shoreline.

This side of The Deep did not disappoint. The rocky beach, littered with massive boulders, gave way to towering cedars that dotted the hillside.

Fog clung to their branches, misting the air. Giant ferns, certainly as tall as Durvan, kissed their feet.

Maryn followed Durvan off the ship and onto the dock, eyeing a fat frog set atop a breeched boulder, emerging from the water's edge.

She and Durvan didn't wait long. The crew set off with them, their feet silent on the spongy trail. No one spoke as they entered the aged forest. The only sound came from the errant twitter of a bird or the drip of water pattering on a fern leaf.

Surprisingly, Durvan's stiff movements did not soften as they wound their way through the ancient forest. Only a few miles inland, the selkies stopped and made their farewells, intent to return to their duties or rest in Annwn. The captain imparted detailed instructions on how to leave Annwn and enter the borderlands. Maryn repeated them to herself quietly, ticking off the details on her fingers.

Continuing on without the selkies concerned Maryn. A shadow of worry grew in her mind. She didn't doubt Durvan's abilities to see her safely to Spring, but she'd found safety and support here, in the underworld. Leaving Annwn felt, well, dangerous.

"Spring's mirrored lake is only a day away," said Durvan. "If we make good time, we'll arrive tomorrow afternoon."

The selkies were lost to her now. She could no longer see them through the trees. She pressed her lips together and readjusted her pack. "I'm glad I have you, Durvan."

He huffed through his nose. The rising color on his ears told her she'd embarrassed him.

They walked for a long time, slowing as the trail steepened. On the other side of a ridge, they found the stream the selkie captain had indicated.

"We mun only follow this stream, here," Durvan explained, his voice rough with disuse. "The door intae the human world is set in yon trees."

Maryn followed his line of sight, grateful the walk wasn't too much farther. The downhill slope gradually leveled out, and soon after, Maryn found the desired animal trail that led from the water into the conifers. Durvan followed behind silently, save for the rhythmic ping of Durvan's axe blades with each step.

The easy trail quickly changed, the upward degree of the slope sharpening so that Maryn's breathing grew loud in her ears. She almost missed the change in Durvan's pace. The regular sound of his axes grew uneven, and when she looked over her shoulder, she found that the distance between them had not only increased, but Durvan's awkward steps had grown progressively labored. He limped heavily now, favoring his right leg.

"Are you all right?" asked Maryn, alarmed.

Durvan shot her a glare that clearly communicated what he thought of her question. "I'm hale enough. I'll bide. Dinnae stop."

Maryn waited until Durvan closed the distance between them, her concern growing. Sweat peppered his brow and he looked as pale as a sheet. She let him pass, noticing how he would not meet her eye; she followed after, watching his unsteady gait.

He was far slower than she was used to. Even with his shorter legs, he often outpaced her. Now, she had to slow to a stroll to keep from overtaking him. "Are you quite sure—"

"Mind ye keep yer nose in ye own parritch, Lassie," he growled, pushing himself harder. His limp increased as they crested the hill.

Maryn scowled at his back. "What's wrong with your leg?" A week ago, she would have kept her tongue, chastised by his curt manner. While harping on him in his current mood would get her nowhere, Maryn's concern for him outweighed any desire he might have for silence.

"There," he said, pointing to a great yew tree ahead of them on the trail.

She followed the indicated direction with her eyes, her mouth falling open. The base of the tree had to be at least seven meters in girth. This yew looked nothing like the carefully manicured hedges that lined Arwan's maze, tall and slender.

The ribbed trunk rose from the forest floor, the thick branches reaching for the sky beginning to curve back toward the ground about fifteen to twenty feet up, as if the poor old tree was too tired to hold its arms up for much longer. The roots of the tree poked up from the ground intermittently. The branches and roots looked to Maryn like a great tangle of thread, knotted and confused and impossible to untangle.

"*This* is the door?" she asked, approaching with caution. She peered through one of the looping roots, much like a thread not tugged tightly against the fabric of the earth. "Am I to offer another sacrifice?" She peered at her left hand. "My fingernails could stand being cut. Is that a sufficient enough payment?"

Durvan must have felt terrible indeed, not to make disparaging comments about her suggestion. He wiped his brow with a forearm, his breath coming short.

She watched, silent, as he leaned against a root, balancing on his left leg. "The captain said no sacrifice must be made to leave Annwn. You must only make one to reenter. State your business. The yew will do the rest."

Maryn took a careful path around the entirety of the tree, studying the trunk. Yews were strange in that they were not a single, smooth body rising from the forest floor. Instead, it looked as if hundreds of smaller trees grew together, melded into one. "Is there a . . . front?" She refrained from asking if it had a face. She didn't want to know. All too easily, Maryn conjured an image of the trunk splitting open to form a grotesque mouth and eyes.

Durvan shrugged. "The selkies didnae say. Just—" He waved a hand in a "get on with it" gesture.

Maryn pursed her lips, pushing aside her concern for the dwarf. The best option, as far as she could gather, was to get him to Spring Court. They would know how to help him, surely. Most likely too proud to seek assistance from Arawn, Durvan suffered in silence. She'd get him help for him in Brigid's court, whether he liked it or not.

She returned her attention to the tree. Cailleach said words held importance, but what should she say? Would the door somehow find her wanting and deny her exit? There was only one way to find out. She cleared her throat, careful not to step on any of the yew's roots and gazed up into the tangle of branches overhead.

"I'd like to leave Annwn, please," she said. Her tentative voice seemed to hang in the air. She waited, breathless, for several heart beats. Nothing happened.

"No' like that," grumbled Durvan. In the shadow of the canopy, he looked even paler. "State yer business. Tell the door who ye are with some authority. Ye must mean it."

Maryn bit back her snarky retort and tried again: "I am . . . I'm Winter's Handmaiden, tasked with entering Spring Court. Arawn has given me leave to cross his borders. Allow us to pass. Please," she added, lest the doorway to think her rude.

This time the branches began to sway as if disturbed by the wind, but Maryn felt no such breeze under the canopy. A few brittle needles still stubbornly holding on, fell from trembling limbs. The ground beneath her feet rumbled and quaked as one of the more substantial roots pulled itself from the ground.

The middle portion of the root that had been exposed to the elements rose into the air. Maryn hastily backed away, nearly tripping over a moldering stump, but managed to catch herself. Dirt crumbled from the rising tuber as it rose up, up, forming an arched passageway. Portions of the root remained underground, so that the doorway imitated a jump rope held on the upswing.

Maryn, eyes wide, side stepped closer to get a better view of the newly formed door. From the side view, she had only seen the present forest, thick and close, but standing before the door, she looked out to an altogether different scene. Golden sunlight shone in from the opening, painting the dim, snowy forest floor in brilliant shades, limning everything in a soft yellow light.

The topography differed greatly from Annwn's seaside forest. On the other side of the portal, the borderlands into the human world looked like something from a Christmas card. A long, sloping meadow ringed with sugar-frosted conifers. The snow sparkled like diamonds in the sunlight.

"That's brilliant," she said, awed. Magic tingled through the air; hair rose along her arms. Would she ever get used to it?

Durvan moved through first, trying and failing to hide his limp. He'd picked up a sturdy stick while waiting for her to open the portal but it didn't seem to help him much.

Maryn followed after him, a warm tingling sensation washing over her as she stepped over the threshold, into the human world.

"Any idea where to go now?"

Durvan grunted and pointed to the right—downhill, thankfully. Maryn turned around, peering into the tear in the fabric between worlds, a dark smudge of forest suspended in midair.

Chapter Twenty-Five

Medicinals

D<small>URVAN'S INJURY WORRIED</small> M<small>ARYN</small>. Badly.

Maryn lifted the fur covering his leg and grimaced. She'd assumed he'd be as impervious to damage as the mountain he lived under, but clearly, she'd been wrong. Apparently, the liberal dousing of whiskey after the *cù sìth's* attack hadn't been good enough to stave off infection.

They'd trekked down the heavily drifted hillside into the dense evergreens, where the snow lessened considerably. Blocked from the worst of the wind and precipitation by the thick boughs, the snow measured low enough to see fallen logs and stones.

She'd helped Durvan to a substantial boulder a good distance into the copse, against which he'd promptly slumped. He wouldn't take food, not that she could blame him, but she'd coaxed a little water down him, at least.

Her worry had intensified when his "rest" had turned to fitful slumber. She'd helped him to lay down and covered him with his fur, her pack nestled under his head. She'd tried her hand at healing magic, using Cailleach's hammer, but it either hadn't worked or healing took time. She hoped for the latter.

She fussed with the fur laid over his trembling body. "Why didn't you have this seen to in Annwn?" she asked, eyeing the purple, inflamed puncture site on his calf. It oozed a fetid, green substance that made Maryn's stomach turn. Bodily fluids didn't usually bother her, but this terrified her. If she were home, she'd take him straight to hospital. Here, though, she had no such luxury.

He shrugged groggily, his eyes glassy with fever. "It didnae bother me o'er much at the time."

She scoffed in response. "Well, it's bothering you now, I'd wager." She replaced the fur covering his legs and sat back on her heels. It was a testament to how poorly he felt that he allowed her to inspect his wound at all.

She frowned down at his sleepy form, not really cross with him, only worried. She glanced at the sky, gauging the light. "I'll . . . I'll make us a fire."

At least she hoped she would. She'd seen Durvan light a fire with a snap of his fingers. If only it could be so easy for her. But she wouldn't get far without fuel.

Durvan's response came by way of snores.

A long time later, wind whistled through the pitiful structure she'd erected, the boughs shielding them unable to protect them completely. It had taken her well over an hour to cut low-hanging branches from conifers and another hour at least to lean them against the large rocky outcropping she and Durvan rested against.

By some miracle, she'd started a fire. Nothing so miraculous as calling down lightning from the blue sky, but still an accomplishment. Using Durvan's knife, she'd curled off bits of dead branches for tinder, and then, with flint, a lot of determination, and a little swearing, Maryn proudly produced sparks.

Now that a fire crackled, worry quickly overtook Maryn. She knew basic first aid, but without supplies, little could be done for Durvan. She rummaged in his bag for whiskey. *It couldn't hurt to douse his leg once more with it.*

He didn't even flinch when she drenched his injury.

Panic threatened to overtake Maryn. She had to do something. They couldn't just sit here. No one from Spring Court expected them, which meant no deployed search parties. The selkies wouldn't come for them. They sailed for Annwn and Arawn assumed them well on their way to Brigid's court.

No one was coming.

Maryn gathered more sticks as her mind raced. Durvan likely wouldn't wake without medical intervention. Dwarfs were supposed to be hardy folk, but even fairies had their limits. What would happen if he didn't wake in the morning, or even the next? Their food stores wouldn't last long without what he supplemented in hunting. And what of the cold? Hypothermia was just as likely a death scenario as starvation once their enchanted wine ran out.

Some creatures in the forest would no doubt welcome the chance to gnaw on their bones. She shuddered. If another hell hound happened upon them, what then? She couldn't defend herself, much less Durvan. The thought made her ill.

She couldn't linger here, sitting by a fire and rationing their supply of food, waiting for a miracle. Durvan needed serious help. Leaving him terrified her, but the thought of him dying was even worse. How could she possibly get on without him? Or Cailleach, if she survived.

She deposited her bundle of sticks without ceremony outside of the shelter, her heart's cadence increasing. Surely some clans lived here about. Durvan had said as much, but how to find them?

Maybe if she climbed to a high point—like up a mountain or to the top of a tree—she could get a better vantage. Perhaps she could find clues: smoke from fires, structures, penned animals . . . something denoting someone besides themselves lived in this wasteland.

Arawn had said the trek to Spring from the water's edge would take two days travel on foot. Brigid's court would be the best place to go; they would have the ability to heal him, surely. Hopefully Durvan *had* two days.

Now she'd have to face the gate-keeping water horse alone. Maryn's hollow stomach dropped.

There. The decision had been made. But how could she possibly make it happen? She had no compass, and her sense of direction wasn't stellar, but she could follow the landmarks the selkies had discussed on the ship. Spring's doorway was due west, in a grove of birch saplings. She would find it by trailing the mouth of the river she and Durvan had been following.

Maryn added more fuel to the fire and stared at Durvan's motionless form, her worry growing. "I'm going to get help," she told him. He made no sign that he'd heard her. He barely seemed to breathe, in fact. "I'm going to start a fire outside of the shelter to give you some warmth for as long as it can while I'm gone." She swallowed, looking about her, at the grey sky overhead. "Hopefully, I'll find a village nearby that can lend us some aid." She licked dry lips and swallowed her fears. "I've got the stream as guide, at least, and—" She trailed off.

Would the landmark be enough?

Maryn took off her pack and retrieved Brigid's bone ritual knife. It was easier to wield than the hammer and would likely grant her entrance into Spring just as easily. In fact, it might prove more useful in that regard. She placed the blade she'd borrowed from Durvan into his loosely curled fingers. *Just in case.*

"I'm taking the hammer with me," she informed him. "I'd be quicker without it, but—" She trailed off with a shrug and made a little pillow out of her bag for him and placed it under his head. His fever raged on. "There's food in my satchel and water here." She placed the canteen near his limp hand. "I'll hurry," she promised, her throat tight. "Don't die, Durvan. Please don't die."

Hours later, hoping Durvan's stubborn nature would sustain him, Maryn found what she was looking for. Tendrils of smoke rose into the air through the trees as she crested a ridgeline.

The dense forest gave way to a sloping hillock, open and drifted with snow. Across the quaint glen, in a thicket of old growth trees, Maryn spotted what looked like a stone wall. From so far away, she couldn't be sure, but the smoke was a good sign.

She hesitated. Both Arawn and Durvan had warned her about staying away from starving villagers. Desperate people often turned to violence. Being mauled for her meager rations didn't interest her one bit. If she left her bag here, hidden, she could retrieve it on her way back to Durvan—medicine in tow.

Maryn backtracked a short distance, to a half-rotted stump she'd passed, and slipped off her bag. Teeth gritted, she clasped Cailleach's totem tightly through the canvas, considering. *Do I bring the hammer or leave it here?* She could use it as a weapon if worse came to worst, but she couldn't wield it with any real amount of skill. When she'd fought off the crows, the weighty totem's inertia had wanted to pull her along with it.

She was far more comfortable with a knife, anyway. She'd left Durvan's short dagger with him at the shelter, but she had Brigid's blade. She bit her lip, unsure.

I'll be right back. An hour, tops. Maryn expelled a breath and whispered, "Don't go anywhere," and shoved her satchel into the hollow.

She walked around the stump, viewing it from different perspectives, to ensure no part of it could be seen, and walked away before she could change her mind.

Filled with equal parts hope and trepidation, she left the security of the dense forest and trudged down the hill and out into the open. Time seemed to stretch as she battled the foot-deep snow of the meadow. The wind pushed against her, snatching the hood from her head. Maryn hunkered, her shoulders rising to her ears as she pushed herself faster.

A dog barked, making her heart lurch into her throat. She faltered, searching the treeline ahead for any danger. She didn't mind dogs, but this one didn't sound friendly. Maryn's hand found the bone knife in her cloak pocket, her fingers squeezing tight as she waited. A medium-sized dog trotted from the trees and spotted her about twenty yards away. It barked frantically but did not approach. Yet.

"Hey, puppy," she crooned, her nerves jumping. "Sweet puppy. You don't want to eat me, do you?"

It growled; its hackles raised. Maryn swore inwardly and pulled the knife from her cloak, just in case.

A man's distant voice called from the trees, a shout of indistinguishable words, just as jarring to Maryn as the dog's barking. Grisly images from true crime tv surfaced in her mind. *Statistics show that most murders occur by someone you know, a husband or wife, for instance. Not a random stranger you startle out in the open.* But modern crime measurements offered no solace.

The dog's continued barking pulled the man right to her. He emerged from the thicket after mere moments. He discovered her immediately. Even from so distant a span, she saw mistake how he narrowed his. He called the dog off, adding, "She willnae harm you unless I command it."

How nice. Let's be sure not to upset him, then, shall we?

From what Maryn could see under the thick wolf's pelt covering his shoulders, he'd been outside for some time. Ice clung to the hem of his grey cloak, the bottom third of which turned dark with moisture. The long brown cotte he wore fell to his shins, exposing wooly boots, strapped to his feet with leather cord.

"My companion is hurt," she called back. "I come looking for help."

The man remained silent for a moment, an errant, mittened hand stroking his dog's head.

"Come on, then. You can tell Froda."

Maryn released the breath she'd held hostage in her lungs. Was Froda a healer of sorts? She had only one way to find out. Maryn dared to move forward; her hand still clasped around Brigid's dagger. She would take no chances.

The ground sloped gently, but Maryn's breath still came short as she approached the pair. Her entire body hummed with awareness.

"What's wrong with your friend?" asked the man. His brown eyes took her in, touching her head, lingering on the blade, and ultimately falling to her feet.

"He was bitten by a wild dog," she explained. "The wound festers, and he has a fever."

The man's narrowed gaze fell behind her to the woods. Was he looking for some hidden threat? Apparently satisfied Maryn came alone, he said, "I am Tormid. Froda makes medicine. I'll take you to her."

Relief swept through Maryn. She could have collapsed in gratitude but if this trip had taught her anything, her troubles were far from over. Even if she'd found a village that could help Durvan, they still needed to get back to him. She prayed he'd make it. And herself. Exhaustion pulled at her limbs.

"I'm Maryn." The wind nearly stole her words away.

Tormid's eyes lingered on her face, his brows knitted together as if she were a puzzle he intended to solve. After an awkward moment of his staring, he turned abruptly and called to his dog.

Maryn followed in Tormid's footsteps, carefully placing her boots into the wells he created in the drifts. They walked up the steep incline. Maryn slipped once and Tormid helped her up with a hand under her arm.

"Easy, lass. The village isnae far. Keep yer feet."

"Th-thanks," she muttered, readjusting her hood so she could see.

"That's an interesting blade you've got," he said.

Maryn went very still, then forced her feet to move. She shrugged. "It was my father's," she lied.

Tormid did not comment. They passed the rock wall she'd spied from across the meadow, a waist high barrier made of stacked fieldstone, neatly fitted together. Tormid helped her over, then his dog, before hopping over it himself in a fluid motion.

They walked along a snow-packed trail, through spindly trees, past a stone altar littered with objects Maryn did not have the time or capacity to identify, and, after several long minutes, ambled into the village.

Maryn paused at the first of the circular structures, the walls made of waddle and daub. Heavy stones, strung together with cord, held down the roofs to keep the thatch from blowing away. Snow partially covered the structures, most of it likely having melted away from the fires within. Smoke rose from a central vent in the peak of the rooftops. The doors, set inward, connected with the interior wall, the which created a sort of covered entryway for the inhabitants.

Tormid looked over his shoulder at her, as though to make sure she still followed. "This way," he prodded, motioning her forward, through the interspersed line of circular buildings.

In the center of the village sat two long houses of similar construction. No people lingered about that she could see, though she did spy a cat and another dog.

Maryn's heart tripped in her chest. A Pictish village, complete with long and round houses? The stuff of her nerdy dreams.

"Where are all your people?" asked Maryn, her eyes roving.

"Most of the men are hunting, but the women are here, tending to what animals we have left. In the byres." He motioned to the closest long house. Maryn followed, committing everything to memory. The longhouses ran at least eighty feet long and about eight feet high.

He approached the closest long house and knocked his boots against a driven post.

"The animals live in the long houses, then? What sort do you keep?"

He looked at her like she was daft. "Same as most, I would think." He pushed the door open for her on leather hinges and ducked inside.

The smell of animal waste filled her senses in the dim confines of the building. She removed her hood, squinting as her eyes adjusted. Directly in front of her was a sizeable paddock, mostly empty. Feathers littered the earthen, straw-strewn floor. A half dozen rather skinny chickens scratched and pecked, looking for food.

A fire in the center of the building lit the space, warming the manure-scented air. Maryn refrained from covering her nose with her hand and instead opted to breathe through her mouth. Around the fire sat a dozen women and children, all hands industriously occupied.

An iron pot hung suspended over the coals. A young lad stirred the contents with a wooden ladle, black with smoke and char. A dozen pairs of eyes found them as Tormid shrugged the fur off his shoulders and draped it on a peg near the door, where other animal skins hung. They looked like deflated wolves and foxes set in a row, eyeless and sad.

Maryn followed behind Tormid, vastly curious yet accountably shy. Her eyes skittered over every aspect of the living quarters. Three empty animal pens lined the long wall, evidenced by the straw and manure covering the ground. A lengthy bench set into the wall on the opposite side of the structure held sleeping people, covered in colorful blue and saffron yellow blankets and silver furs. Maryn itched to investigate. *Were they wool or made from flax? How did these people go about the weaving process? How did they make their dye and how was it set in the fabric?*

The weight of their stares kept Maryn rooted at Tormid's side. He greeted those gathered and bent to press his forehead against an older woman who removed stitches from what looked to Maryn like a slipper. She pulled at the threads; her arthritic hands purple with veins.

"Froda," he said, indicating Maryn. "I bring a lassie in need of your talents. I found her as I was checking traps."

Maryn stared rudely. The Romans named the people of this time "Pictii", which in Latin translates to "painted ones." Anthropologists could not prove this to be definitively true, but Maryn now could. The old woman's hands weren't covered in blueish veins, but tattoos. Her face also bore symbols, swirls and angles across her cheekbones. *What did they mean?*

"You bring me another mouth to feed instead of game, Tormid?" The woman's rheumy gaze travelled from Tormid to Maryn. "I had hopes that we would have more to eat than boiled leather." With that, she handed a piece of slipper she'd carefully deconstructed to the boy at the pot, who took it and added it to the steaming water.

Maryn's heart hurt for these people. They were starving. They had only a few animals left, most likely saved for their milk and what eggs they produced. If only she had some way of helping, some food to give, but she had only a pocket of jerky and a near-empty wineskin. She would gladly give it, but there were more mouths here than she had food for.

"I don't need food," supplied Maryn. "Only medicine."

Froda squinted at Maryn, as if trying to discern her ailment.

"It's not for me, but for my escort. My friend," she amended. While Durvan would probably not describe her in such a way, they'd been through far too much to *not* be friends. And now that he was sick—possibly dying—a kinship for the old grouch gripped her.

"What ails this friend of yours?"

"Bitten by a . . . by a wild dog."

The old woman's feathery brows rose. "Is that so?" She looked in a pointed way at Maryn's dog-less hands, as if she should have brought it with her. Maryn supposed that these hungry villagers might be desperate enough to eat a dog, but not a *cù sìth*. No one could ever be that desperate.

"The dog wasn't . . . It was sick."

The woman's focus sharpened on Maryn's face, suddenly interested. "Where was he bitten, this friend, and does the wound weep?"

Maryn took a step closer. "It bit him here," she said, touching her own calf. "And yes, it does weep. It's infected."

The old woman stared at her, no indication of understanding in her eyes. Perhaps they didn't have a word for infection? Maryn tried again. "He's hot to the touch and delirious. H-he can't walk."

Froda lifted a finger, silently asking for assistance. Tormid moved to help her up, lifting her by her elbow. "I'll need my things," said Froda to no one in particular. She shuffled forward then stopped, gazing up at Tormid. "You might think to ask that druid for some of his magic." Here her eyes cut to Maryn in a marked way. "It sounds like this might be serious."

Maryn worked to keep her face neutral. *Druids? Magic?* She hoped actual medicine would be involved. Of course, in this primitive time, antibiotics would seem magical. *Sick? Here, drink this potion.*

An image flashed in her mind then, of Cailleach opening a portal in the bowels of her mountain, of conjuring a throne of blackberries to rest upon. Maryn *heard* the stars that night. And then, had not only witnessed magic, but she'd also performed it herself. With Cailleach's hammer.

Medicine or magic, if it saved Durvan, Maryn didn't care what it was called.

"Thank you for your help. What can I do?"

Froda leaned heavily on Tormid's arm. "You'll take my medicine to your friend tomorrow. Tormid will help you."

Tomorrow? Maryn's hopes deflated. She shook her head. "Can't we leave now?"

Froda's gaze swept up her frame, from toes to crown. "The sun will set soon, and the hunters will return with the twilight. Now we rest and prepare for the morning."

Maryn, crestfallen, nodded. The dark could be dangerous, she'd learned. Nocturnal creatures prowled after sunset, and with poor light, she could easily turn an ankle or break a leg in a fall. She'd also hate to get turned around. What if it snowed? Yes, *what if it snowed?*

She couldn't leave Durvan alone all night. The fire had surely burned to nothing but embers by now. Maybe she could get the medicine and go back on her own. These strangers wouldn't insist an outsider stay overnight. It was not like they had much hospitality to share, after all.

Chapter Twenty-Six

A Friend

Tormid covered the woman with a heavy blanket at the door, draping it over her silver hair. Maryn itched to touch the covering, staring at the weave. Wool, most likely dyed with woad, just like the old woman's tattoos.

Tormid opened the door, ushering in a gust of frigid wind. Maryn shivered and drew her cloak tighter. Her hand ached, and she looked down to see she still clutched the bone knife, her fierce grip causing the pain. She towed the knife in her pocket. Had she breeched some unknown social convention, carrying a weapon around? She probably had, if the lingering looks Tormid and Froda gave each other were any indication.

They made their way across the packed snow to one of the surrounding huts. A dog barked, then another, a chorus of alarm.

"That'll be the men coming home," said Froda as way of explanation. "I'll take care of the lassie, Tormid. You go see about the priest, aye?"

Tormid's beard twitched in the wind, but Maryn thought he looked displeased, or at least reluctant, in the way his lips pressed together. He bowed his head and opened the door for them. The door itself was composed of long sticks woven together and hung with leather hinges. Frozen, cracked mud clung to the crevices between the spindly limbs.

"In ye get," prodded Froda.

Maryn hesitated then pushed herself into the dark, enclosed space. Arawn told her not too long ago that creatures in the dark should fear her, not the other way around, but Maryn couldn't quite conjure the much-needed confidence. It wasn't pukas that made her nervous here, but strangers.

People could be monsters, too, especially those in desperate situations. She didn't like being alone, holed away in this hut. Some part of her brain told her that this situation should be avoided, but she couldn't leave empty handed, either.

She slipped her hand into her pocket, her fingers finding the bone handle knife with ease. She turned in a tight circle, taking in the space. Despite the dim confines of the room, light from the throbbing, orange embers, allowed Maryn to see a ring of stones set in the middle of the circular room. Shadows of familiar shapes pulsated into view. The legs of a table, the back of a chair, a pot, a basket. So much she saw, and then the door shut, taking the majority of the light with it.

Maryn forced her breathing to slow. Her hand tightened around the knife. Maryn didn't want to hurt anyone, of course, but if they attacked her, she'd have no choice. *Stop it. Froda is helping.*

The old woman shuffled around the room anticlockwise, grunting as she lifted something. Maryn followed her dark figure, turning in a way so as not to give her back to the woman. Froda placed two split logs on the embers, sending sparks flying. Maryn stared at the woman's eyes, sunken in two bruised sockets in the low light, before she blinked the image away.

She was being stupid, imaging Froda intended to harm her. Maryn, flushed and overheated, removed her hood as the old woman lit tallow candles with a piece of straw she'd plucked from a basket. Light helped. The homely space, packed with the basic accoutrements of living, eased her further. A suspended cord ran the length of the room overhead, from which an assortment of dried plants hung.

Medicine.

Froda swung an arm holding an iron pot over the rekindled flames. "Grab me that, would you?" she asked, pointing to a branch of some nameless weed overhead. "And that one," she added, gesturing to a wilted sprig of brown *something* hanging near the wall.

Maryn did as instructed, careful not to snag the dried branches on anything and scatter leaves. She stood awkwardly, herbs in hand, as the woman rooted through a reed basket set atop a trunk.

"That's fine garb ye've got, Lassie," said Froda, glancing at Maryn's exposed tunic and trousers from between the opening in her cloak. "Havenae seen such fine garment in these parts before."

Maryn pressed her lips together, hoping her eyes did not betray her fear. She would wager that the villagers could barter quite a lot with Arawn's finely stitched gift. All they need do is tear it from her body. The silver thread alone was worth more than her life.

She hadn't thought twice about changing back into her more cumbersome skirts.

"Where did ye come by such fine garb?"

The god of the underworld gave it to me. I stole it—found it. I bought it. Maryn chose not to answer—couldn't think of any possible answer that would satisfy the woman and not bring more suspicion upon herself. Instead, she changed the subject.

"Do you live here alone? It's quite nice." Maryn looked about the room. No clear weapons lurked amongst the clutter of life, save for an iron poker laid atop the flat stones of the fire ring. She strained her memory. Had Froda left the small knife in the longhouse or had she hidden it away on her person? Maryn took a step toward the door, her nerves frayed.

Froda's long stare unnerved her further. An icy chill ran up Maryn's spine. "Not until recently," answered Froda after a beat. "I lost my daughter and grandchild two months past."

Maryn let out a shaky breath. "From the . . . the overlong winter?"

Froda, having found what she'd been looking for in the basket stood, her eyes surveying Maryn intently. She held something in her hands, cupped so Maryn could not see it. "Not the winter, though it's been hard enough. She died in her childbed, soon after she delivered her dead son."

"I'm so sorry," said Maryn automatically. "That must have been terrible for you."

Froda moved to the iron pot and tossed in whatever she'd been rootling for. Apparently, she saw the question in Maryn's eyes because she gestured to the steaming water. "Sheep's knucklebones. They'll tell us whether yer friend will live or die."

She motioned for the herbs Maryn held and then broke the stems three times, crumpling them over the mouth of the pot. She picked up the iron poker. Maryn tensed. Froda lifted a grey brow, casting a curious look at Maryn, and stirred the contents three times, anticlockwise. After this, she leaned forward and spat right into the water.

"Come on, your turn," said Froda, waving Maryn forward with some impatience.

"You want me to . . . spit. In the *medicine*?"

Froda, shot Maryn a dubious look, as if she couldn't believe Maryn would ask such a stupid question.

All of Maryn's hopes for Durvan's recovery shattered in one fell swoop. What had she thought? She'd fallen into the Middle Ages, after all, and while they had herbal remedies, the people of this time had no concept of germs or the importance of cleanliness.

"Ye wished for a potion tae heal yer friend, did ye no'?"

Maryn wanted to cry. How could she have been so stupid? She shouldn't have come here. She should have gone straight for Spring. Maybe she still could. She took a steadying breath and threw caution to the wind. The luxury of time had gone long ago.

"I heard that somewhere nearby is a loch, guarded by a water horse."

If Froda wasn't suspicious before, she certainly was now. All the color drained from her face. Her rheumy gaze darted to the door then back. "What of it?"

Maryn shrugged. Her fingers flexed around the smooth handle of the bone blade. Alarm bells blared in her head. She needed to leave. But first, she needed to know where she could find the spring gate.

"Is it far? I need to get there." Then, hoping to ease Froda's suspicions, added, "I'm told there is magic there that could heal my friend. Herbs to collect. Th-the water weeds are especially...." Maryn trailed off at Froda's cold look.

"Outsiders do not go there, nor speak of that sacred place." Her eyes narrowed. "Who told you of Brigid's temple? What business do ye have in coming here, really?"

"I . . . I didn't know there was a temple there," she stammered. Maryn took a step toward the door. Froda followed, picking up the iron poker. "It's as I said, my friend is sick. He needs help."

Froda's lip curled. "What's this friend's name?"

Maryn stammered. "H-his name is Durvan. He's down the valley, waiting for me. For help."

"Where'd ye get yon knife stowed away in yer pocket?" demanded Froda. For someone so old and frail, Froda could certainly move when motivated. She took three threatening steps toward Maryn, circling around the fire, and raised the rod as if to strike.

Maryn didn't linger. She turned and hastened for the door, fumbling with the wooden peg that held the door closed for the barest of seconds, then sprinted into the fading sunlight. Dogs barked, a shadowed gathering of men in the center of the village turned their heads in her direction, their faces dark.

Maryn darted to the right, between two huts, her arms pumping, her breath puffing from her in grey clouds. With each mewling exhale, Maryn's fears compounded. She barely heard the old woman shout as she entered the shadowed forest. Branches whipped against her face, pulled on her cloak.

What did they suspect of her? Where had she gone wrong? A man shouted. He didn't sound close. A cacophony of baying filled the air. Maryn ran faster. She ducked under a branch, barely missing being closelined. She tripped over a root and tumbled forward. Pain shot through her shoulder. She cried out, tears springing to her eyes.

Rough hands grasped her shoulders and turned her over. She thrashed and kicked, her hand fumbling for her pocket, for her only defense.

"Easy. Be still," said the man.

She clocked him with a fist, right against the side of his head. Maryn's hand throbbed with pain.

"Och!" He pulled his hands away, holding them up in the universal gesture of nonviolence. "Hurry, they're coming. This way. Hurry now," he said, taking a few steps away from her.

Maryn rolled onto her knees, breathing hard, and glared at the man. She'd never seen him before, of course, but why should she trust him?

He was dressed in a long grey cotte. His hood had fallen away, exposing his youthful face. A shout pierced the air. The villagers were gaining on her. The man held out a hand for her, shaking it in a way to urge her to accept his help.

As soon as her hand clamped onto his, he pulled her roughly to her feet. "This way," he said, leading her deeper into the woods. "We can lose the hounds in the water."

She followed after him, hand in hand, her heart in her throat. Twice he saved her from falling and hurting herself further. Her shoulder radiated pain, her lungs burned, her face stung after catching so many twigs in the face.

They made it to the water in a matter of moments, but it felt like an eternity to Maryn. Frigid water filled her boots as they plunged in, but she ignored the cold, pushing her body harder, forcing her tired legs through the shin-deep river.

The sound of their frantic breaths faded away in the commotion in the water. Surely, the dogs would hear them. Surely, they would be upon them at any moment. They did not slow and followed the river upstream as it wound around trees and hills. The baying of the hounds lessened, and with each fading bark, Maryn's heart slowed infinitesimally.

Full on dark shrouded the woods now, but on occasion, a stray moonbeam broke through the canopy. Her apparent savior slowed, then helped her to exit the water.

"I think we've lost them," he said unnecessarily.

Maryn peered into the dark, looking about them to ensure no one followed, she could barely make out the man's face, let alone anyone hiding in the wood. "W-who are you?" she asked, folding her arms around her shivering body. Her teeth chattered. She was wet through, her cloak heavy with river water. She could barely feel her feet.

He wiped a forearm across his nose, sniffing. "A friend. You can call me Ciaran."

Chapter Twenty-Seven

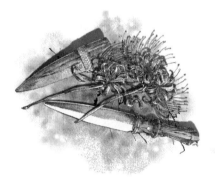

Perfidy

Ciaran was about her age, she'd wager. Tall enough to be an adult, at least. Children did not venture from the safety of the village alone, after dark. She thought she'd spied a smattering of freckles across his cheeks and brown eyes before the sun had fully set. He wore clothes like a monk but would any such person exist so far north during this time?

"What's your name?" he asked.

"M—Maryn," she chattered.

Silence and then, "We need to keep moving to get warm. We can't stay out here all night."

Maryn heartily agreed but had nothing to offer in the way of warmth aside from a nearly empty skin of charmed wine. She didn't know where to go or how to build a fire from nothing. She had little food, no change of clothes. She was at the mercy of this man, whomever he was. It terrified her despite her relief.

"Do you live nearby?" he asked.

It was bizarre, conversing with a faceless stranger. Maryn—near to hysterics—almost laughed at the absurdity of her circumstances but clamped down hard on the impulse. The last thing she needed was this stranger to think she'd gone round the twist.

She shook her head, forgetting that he couldn't see her. "No," she said, her voice croaking. "I'm travelling with a friend, but he got hurt. I wandered into the village, looking for help but—" she trailed off. She didn't feel like going into the particulars, nor did she trust this man, who appeared from seemingly nowhere not far from the village.

"Are you f-from the village?"

"No," answered Ciaran. "I'm travelling through to the spring temple. I'm a priest of Brigid."

Maryn nearly fell into him when she stood from the rock she'd been resting against. He was going to the temple? He was a priest? *A druid.* Her mouth dry, Maryn tried twice to swallow. "Is the temple near?"

"A few miles," he said. "Where is this companion of yours? What ails him?"

Maryn's breath stilled in her lungs. *What should I do?* An image of Durvan's purple leg, festering puncture sites, and fluttering eyelids spurred her on. She had to trust this man. She had little choice in the matter, despite her dislike of the situation.

"A bite from a wild dog. He's unwell and can't walk." She turned around in the dark, hopelessly lost. "I'm afraid I've lost my bearings. I came from—" She furrowed her brow, her brain fuzzy with fatigue. "I followed the water downstream. There was a meadow and then village wall...."

She held her breath, knowing her "directions" were a long shot.

The sound of gravel underfoot, the sluffing of snow as he moved filled her ears. The shadow of him turned upriver. "Very well," he said. "There's a wee cave I know of, but let's rest here a bit before we backtrack. I'd rather not come across whomever chased you."

Maryn agreed and chuffed her hands. She wriggled her toes in her boots, her body rigid with cold. "Why d-did you help me?" she asked.

He did not speak right away. Maybe he was preoccupied with her abysmal directions, or maybe he didn't know the answer. After a beat, he said, "I saw a maiden in fear for her life."

Maybe, but did he come from the village?

Maryn pressed her lips tightly together, her gaze darting around them. Perhaps she'd spent too much time in surly Durvan's company and had adopted his pessimistic outlook, but Maryn didn't trust Ciaran's answer.

Time slowed as they waited, ensuring her pursuers had lost their trail. As she shifted her weight and chattered, Maryn fretted over Durvan. How could she find him in the dark?

Ciaran called her closer. "I think it's safe enough now for this." He whispered into his hands. A blue flame appeared in his cupped fingers, dazzling her eyes.

Magic.

"How—"

"I'm gifted power by the gods for my service to them. Here," he said, gesturing for her to take the flame. "It will not burn you but keep it close and cover it with your other hand to hide the light. We don't know who might still be in the wood."

Maryn stared, mesmerized, as Ciaran dumped the ball of fire into her hand. The blue orb licked flames onto her skin but, as he said, it did not harm her. Warmth radiated from the pulsing light. She wished she had two more to stuff down her boots.

"This way," he instructed, moving downriver, thankfully on dry land. "We'll rest a bit there and then we'll find your friend."

Maryn reluctantly agreed. While eager to return to Durvan, if she hid a bit longer, maybe the villagers would lose interest.

Her feet squelched with each step as she followed closely behind, keeping her eye on the hem of his robe. They stopped several times as they picked their way through the dense foliage, stopping to unstick their clothing from clinging vines, jump across eroded portions of the riverbank, and, most importantly, listen for stalking villagers.

Against all odds, they arrived at Ciaran's cave without incident. Maryn had no idea to where he led her, save that it was in the general direction from which she'd come. Their shelter turned out to be less of a cave and more like an empty space between three large boulders. Some ancient glacier had deposited them, no doubt, the soil underneath removed by human hands or from the elements. Maryn collapsed gratefully against the side of a cold rock, her heart tripping, her toes throbbing.

Despite the close quarters—with just enough space for two people and a small fire—Maryn had never been happier to rest. Evidence of hunters or some other occupants littered the ground, charcoal bits of a spent fire.

Ciaran immediately set about gathering fuel for the fire. Maryn waited alone as the wind whistled between the rocks, shivering. He returned shortly, appearing at the mouth of their shelter laden with sticks. She suppressed a yawn and moved to help him arrange them, letting her blue flame slip from her fingers into the would-be fire.

It went out almost immediately.

"Afraid that won't work," he said, a smile in his voice. The druid rubbed his hands together over the wood, creating friction. Orange sparks fell from his hands, much like the spatter from welding. "It only lives as long as your energy fuels it."

Against all odds, the damp wood ignited and, before long, a smoky, struggling fire licked to life.

"It needs my energy?" she asked. "But I don't know any magic."

Ciaran smiled again, as if her questions amused him, as if she were a mere child, asking where the sun goes at night. "Energy is all around us, in the air, the earth, in you and me. Even though energy is present in the very air we breathe, it is scattered. Unorganized. In us, however, the energy can be channeled more easily."

Maryn leaned closer, warming her hands over the flames. *Did that mean that anyone could do magic?*

"How did you learn to harness magical energy, then?" she asked.

Ciaran shrugged and added another stick to the fire. "I gave my life to the gods."

In the light of the flames Ciaran's features came into sharp focus. His dark brown hair and eyes absorbed the orange glow of the fire; his freckled cheeks and nose stood out starkly against fair skin. Wrinkles fanned out around his eyes as if he spent most of his time squinting into the sun.

Maryn thought of her title, "Winter's Handmaiden." She'd performed magic using Cailleach's hammer, but barely, and then only with the goddess's totem in hand. She certainly couldn't create fire from her bare hands. Curious, she asked, "Do these gods you align yourself with give you artifacts? Something tangible that gives you power?"

Ciaran's dark eyes, near black in the firelight, met her own. "I'm given knowledge," he said. "Totems are for the gods alone." He held her gaze for a stretched moment of silence before Maryn looked away.

"You're sure we'll be quite safe here?" asked Maryn.

He seemed to consider this for a moment, looking over his shoulder into the oppressive night. "We'll take turns keeping watch. Best take off your boots and stockings and warm your toes. The fire won't last long without more fuel. I'll go gather more, but first—" He gestured to her in cloak. "Do you have any food in there?"

"Oh, erm, a little." Maryn's wet clothes clung to her skin so she felt like she was trapped in a paper bag. She pulled out damp jerky, wrapped the handkerchief Arawn had conjured for her. "Not very appetizing at this point, I'm afraid."

Another pocket held a near-empty flask of charmed wine. She nearly groaned in relief, anticipating it warming her aching digits. She hesitated. She really ought to share with Ciaran. He'd saved her, after all, and was just as wet through. And as a druid practicing magic, she doubted he'd be frightened of Cailleach's magic punch.

"How long do you think we'll need to stay? I'm concerned for my friend." *And for the stashed hammer.*

She took a few mouthfuls, her belly warming instantly, and sighed. Soon the warmth would spread to her extremities and, perhaps then, she'd be able to loosen the ties of her boots. Now, her fingers fumbled uselessly.

He eyed the jerky dispassionately. "Er, not long. Is that all you brought?"

"Traveling light," she said, offering him the wine.

He declined. "I'll, uh, I'll have some later. I should really go and get some fuel for the fire. Try and relax," he said, and then he left.

Maryn shrugged and corked the wine. Considering present circumstances, she regretted leaving all the furs with Durvan, but she hadn't felt right about taking any warmth from him. Besides, she hadn't planned on being out all night, nor taking a dip in the river.

The wine warmed her fingers, but her toes still ached. She flexed them in her boots, her socks sodden. She grimaced. If only she'd brought the hammer with her. She'd give anything for a hot spring right about now.

The sharp crack of a stick breaking a ways off pulled Maryn from her thoughts. She sat up straighter and squinted into the dark. *Probably just Ciaran.* It really wasn't very kind of her to sit here idle whilst her savior hunted for wood. With snow blanketing the ground, he'd probably resorted to breaking branches off trees.

The small light the fire afforded made seeing into the dark all the more difficult from where she sat. Alone, cold, and virtually blind to the world around her, Maryn's anxiety grew. She couldn't even see the spindly alders a few feet from the shelter with the firelight. Maryn left her pack and crawled out, careful to keep her trailing cloak out of the struggling fire. Moving her body would do her good in any case.

She peered into the inky dark just outside of the entrance, listening hard but heard nothing. With no idea in which direction her companion travelled, Maryn set about searching her surroundings for anything that might burn.

She tramped through the snow, their previous footsteps turned to inky shadows in the dim moonlight. *Was that a voice or only her imagination?* Twice more she stopped, straining her ears. The crunch of snow muffled any other sound in the forest, making it impossible to locate potential danger while walking.

She scanned the forest ahead and behind, following the stream that had brought her to the village. It couldn't be far. Thinking of the little settlement brought Maryn up short. Froda. She'd sent Tormid to fetch a priest. She'd wanted him to use magic on Durvan.

Was Ciaran that priest? Maryn held her breath, her stomach in knots. It seemed mightily convenient now that she wasn't being chased down like a rabbit, for the druid to appear out of the blue when the villagers had mentioned one themselves.

Uneasiness roiled through Maryn. She swore under her breath and moved faster through the trees, away from the shelter. She patted herself down, relief washing over her as she found Brigid's blade still in her cloak pocket.

She moved as stealthily as she could, then belatedly realized that anyone looking for her need only follow her footsteps in the snow. What could she do? She didn't trust Ciaran. She couldn't stay, nor could she simply wander in the dark of the wood.

She thought of Arawn, how he conjured a fairy light with such ease, how he calmed her. He'd make short work of her sodden clothes, no doubt. *Oh, Arawn, where are you when a girl needs you?*

Her heart beat heavily in her chest, echoing in her head. Tired and overwrought, near to panic and doing her best to stave off hysteria, she kept moving. *Get the hammer and find Durvan.*

Voices. They came again, carried on the breeze. Torchlight flared to life over the crest of the hill behind her. Five? Six? Maryn ran.

Twigs caught her cloak and scraped her face. She ducked under limbs and tumbled down steep slopes. Her breaths came in wheezing gasps. Her lungs burned with cold. She tasted blood at the back of her throat. Shouts followed her, far too close.

Run, she told herself. *Run, run, run.*

Maryn fumbled and loped, her over-taxed body fighting her the whole way. She burst into a clearing minutes later and found Ciaran there, waiting, as if he'd known she'd come this way all along.

"Y-you," she wheezed. "Why the pretense of helping me?" she asked, trying to rein in her frantic breaths.

"Give me the hammer," he said, friendly tone abandoned. "I know you've got it."

Maryn scowled. How had she thought his freckles made him look so innocent? *Idiot.*

"It's not in your pack so it must be on you. Give it over and I won't hurt you."

Hammer? How did he know she— The answer came quickly: the spying crows that had attacked she and Durvan in the borderlands of Annwn. They'd seen her with the hammer. She'd used it on them—or tried to with little effect.

"It was you," she said, her voice a rasp. "You sent the crows."

"Not my spies. They belong to my new mistress."

Men's voices called from behind. They couldn't be far. She glanced over her shoulder to judge. The glow of their torches would tell her.

Ciaran tackled her. She hit the ground hard and with a full-grown man plowing into her middle, she lost her breath. Maryn scrambled to shove him off, her mouth working like a fish. She couldn't move him. She couldn't breathe.

Ciaran's hands roamed her body, no doubt searching for the hammer. When he came up empty handed, he scrambled off of her. He jerked her by the collar of her cloak, easily hauling her to her feet. Maryn fell into him, still gasping for breath. A trickle of air made its way past her raw throat. She sucked it in. More came. More.

Torchlight illuminated the ground, casting long, sharp shadows.

"I'll ask you once more," said Ciaran. "Where is the hammer?"

Chapter Twenty-Eight

Painful Motivation

"I HAVE NO HAMMER," she said. That much was true. It currently rested in her pack, stashed in a rotted stump.

Snow began to fall in flitting, tiny flakes. They dusted Ciaran's hair, some clinging to his eyebrows. The villagers arrived. Rough hands grasped her elbows. She twisted and fought against her captors, kicking and bucking, but it did no good.

"I find it highly distasteful, hurting a woman," said Ciaran.

Maryn, chest heaving, took in the men around her—at least the ones she could see. Bearded faces, glittering, dark eyes, angry furrows in brows. "Then let me go," she said, venom lacing her tone.

Fat chance. Ciaran's hands patted her down and found Brigid's blade in her pocket. At first, she thought he might not understand just what he'd pulled from her cloak, but his double take dashed any hopes she held in that regard.

Eyes wide, Ciaran held the Blade of Somnolence up in the torchlight.

His shock fell away, replaced with anger. His flinty eyes cut to her; his mouth turned down in a furious scowl. "How did you come by this blade?" His icy tone drew the men closer. They pressed in, looking at what the druid held.

Maryn's bowels turned to water. Terror seized her. She could tell them everything, of course, and they would probably kill her anyway. She thought of Cailleach, withered to nothing, and of Brigid, trapped by this monster—or whomever he served. All of Cailleach's hopes—and in relation, the world's hopes—were squarely pinned on Maryn. And she'd failed.

She'd been so close. Spring's doorway was only a few miles away.

You've not failed entirely, a voice seemed to say. *They may get the blade, but so long as you don't talk, they won't get the hammer.*

Maryn bit her tongue. Perhaps Durvan would survive. He was made of tough stock, after all. If they killed her, her soul would go to Annwn; she could tell Arawn to go get Durvan....

The druid brought the edge of the bone blade close to her face in threat. "A cut for every lie, I think," he hissed. Spittle hit her face.

The flakes fell in earnest now, fat clumps too heavy to flutter to the earth. They dropped in earnest, like tears. Cailleach's frozen tears. *I'm sorry.*

"I thought you found it distasteful to hurt a woman," she said, her breath coming fast. Her lungs burned with cold. Her feet were numb, and her chest ached from the incessant pounding of her heart.

"Yes, but in this case, I fear that I must." He took a deep breath, as if to calm himself—or to gather his nerve—and met her eye. "I am bound by duty to this world and that of the otherworld, after all. Now, tell me. Where is the hammer and how did this totem fall into your hands? We druids have been in the Spring Court for some time now. No one has spoken of its whereabouts or its disappearance."

Maryn didn't answer. Ciaran narrowed his eyes and pulled the sharp edge of the ritual knife across her cheek; a mere flick of the wrist. He cut her just under her left eye. She jerked at the violence. Hands gripped her, pinned her to the spot. Pain blossomed to life. She sucked in a sharp breath as warm blood streaked down her face and neck.

One cut. *One*, and she lost all her resolve. She couldn't do this. She wasn't a soldier, trained against interrogations. She couldn't keep silent, but she *could* lie.

"Where is the hammer?" asked Ciaran again. His gaze held steady on the blade, watching as her blood glistened black in the flickering torchlight.

"Stolen," she said on a sob. "Please, it was stolen from me."

Ciaran's eyes narrowed on her face. "Who stole it?"

"I . . . I don't know. In the night, while I was sleeping."

Ciaran's scowl deepened.

"I swear," she said. "My friend and I slept in a barn with others. We awoke early and set off. It wasn't until later that I noticed it was gone. We went back, of course, but...but it was too late."

"Could be lying," said one of her captors. He held her right arm in a vise-like grip, his breath heavy in her hair. "How do we know she isn't lying?"

Ciaran pursed his lips, looking uncertain. "Pain is motivation enough, I should think." The blade lifted to her right eye. She sucked in an involuntary gasp. The pain would be worse this time, knowing what to expect. She shrank away but kept her eyes fixed upon the weapon.

Tears and snowflakes obscured her vision, lingering on her lashes. "The blade . . . the blade," she said, licking her lips. She tasted copper. "I didn't steal it. It was given to me," she said. Her mind reeled for something Ciaran would accept. "My friend paid a hefty price for it. I-I don't know who stole it from Spring. They didn't give their name . . . they wouldn't show us their face. Th-they were dressed like you."

The knife hovered close to her cheek. "*Liar*," he hissed. "A member of our order would never—" His words died, his mind working behind his eyes.

She'd struck a chord. Hope blossomed in her chest.

"A man or woman?" he demanded. "Tell me!"

Maryn whimpered, wincing away from the hovering blade. "A—a woman." If he distrusted anyone, it would be someone different than himself.

Ciaran swore, rotating the blade in his fist, and plunged it into her chest.

Chapter Twenty-Nine

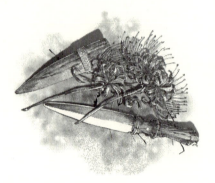

Stay

Maryn coughed, spurting blood, her eyes wide. Pain burned in her chest. At her involuntary gasp, the very corners of her vision dimmed. Her hands became suddenly free. She fell into the snow, staring at the fat flakes. Footsteps and voices faded away as her fingers fumbled over her chest, to where her blood poured from her, so very near her heart.

He missed, she thought, half delirious. He'd missed her heart. Despite his poor aim, it tripped and fluttered in its breached cage.

Voices around her argued but she barely registered them, snatches of words struggled to the surface through her shock and pain.

"—don't know where she hid Brigid's spirit!"

"... Hasty."

"*She still lives.*"

She moved to cover the wound, to use whatever strength she had left to staunch the bleeding, but she could barely move for the pain. Warm blood soaked her tunic and heated her perpetually cold hands. A face loomed over her then, and she redoubled her efforts to focus. Was it the villagers, eager to finish her off?

Pain lanced through her at the slightest breath, but *not* breathing didn't help either. Her vision dimmed further, her breath choking from her with an agonizing gasp as her lungs begged for air.

"What did I say about keeping away from people and pointy objects?"

The rebuking voice helped her double vision to coalesce into Death's face as he stared down at her, his mouth pulled into an angry frown.

Arawn.

Relief surged through her. But how had he known she needed him?

"A-about t-time you came," she said. Her body spasmed, sending a cascade of pain across her breast.

His gaze traveled to her chest, and a flash of something like panic entered his eyes.

Maryn coughed, and an agonizing tremor rocketed through her. Spots flashed in her vision for a moment, her breath stuttering. She realized then that Arawn would only be here for one thing. He'd told her once, that he was burdened with knowing the last breath each mortal took. *How many did she have left?*

The thought of dying didn't seem as upsetting as she'd first imagined. In fact, the promise that the pain would soon end brought immediate comfort. And then there was the added promise of Annwn. Quite soon she'd see her *real* Lolly and Pop. And her mother. Involuntary tears gathered in the corners of her eyes and trickled into her ears. It would be over soon. The pain would end.

"Stay," said Arawn. She might have laughed if she had the ability. Where could she go?

He left her side. She felt his absence keenly, as if his nearness had stirred her soul, and now it resettled itself, bracing for agony. Distant shouts. The ground reverberated with retreating feet. Maryn counted the seconds between breaths, trying to delay the next need to fill her lungs.

She held off as long as she could, careful to let air in slowly. She screwed her eyes shut, her hands clenched. She felt Arawn return in the way her blood or her soul—she wasn't sure which—responded. Whichever part of her his nearness affected, a lightness returned, as if champagne coursed through her veins instead of blood.

"It hurts," she whispered, her lips barely moving. She opened her eyes and found his concerned face. "I h-hid the h-hammer. You need—" She couldn't finish, the pain overwhelming her.

He bared his teeth in a grimace, a flash of white in her failing vision before his face blurred into obscurity. She wished she could see his eyes. They were so strange and beautiful. Her breaths wheezed from her, shallow and quick, each a stab of pain. "Please, Arawn" she slurred. "Make it stop."

Arawn's face loomed into focus again, but he didn't reassure her that all would soon be well, that he'd take her pain. He didn't call her from her body or even touch her.

"Your left lung is punctured," he informed her. "It's filling with blood. He missed your heart, thankfully, but there's quite a lot of damage."

She fumbled drunkenly, her fingers searching out Arawn's large hand. She barely discerned his warmth. Dully, she registered the wetness of her bodice, of a trickle of warm fluid tracing her sides to pool at her back.

"Arawn," she tried. Her mouth moved but no sound formed on her lips. *Look at me.*

He spoke but his words came out muffled, confused, like they'd been submerged underwater.

She closed her eyes. Her breathing slowed. The sharp pain ebbed to a dull ache. Snow stirred around her. Someone called her name.

"It . . . it doesn't hurt so much now," she wheezed, and then, just as easy as falling asleep, Maryn died.

She stood outside of her body, relieved. Happy. How wonderful to be free from the pain.

"No," growled Arawn, from where he knelt next to her body, his attention focused on her spirit form. "I told you to stay."

Stay? It was far too late for that. She could hardly have stopped the momentum of her spirit peeling away from her ruined body. Maryn snorted. He must be joking. Death didn't stop people from passing; he carried away their souls. Eternal rest sounded very good to Maryn right then. Her smile faded, however, as she took in his stony expression. *He's serious.*

She stared down at what had housed her spirit for the last twenty-eight years and frowned. The gory sight should have frightened or saddened her. It was *her* body, after all, but she could only feel relief.

The men that had surrounded her were now gone, the woods still and empty.

Maryn ignored Arawn's surly manner and ran a hand down her spirit form. She was solid, yet *not*. She understood now what Arawn meant about spirit bodies only being a type and shadow of physical forms. Maryn had substance but she was also fluid and unencumbered so that, in retrospect, her physical body seemed as clumsy and as inefficient as walking in too large shoes.

Next to her broken, still body, little flowers bloomed on the forest floor. Delicate white and yellow daisies sprang from bloodied snow. She hadn't seen any flowers on her journey until now, and no wonder, with how the last two days had gone. Spring's door must be very close indeed, if there were blossoms to be trod on.

Arawn stood and glowered down at her as if she'd committed some great offense. His look brought her up short.

"No, Maryn. It's not your time. You have to go back."

Maryn shrank away from him, afraid he might force her. "What do you mean? I can't just *go back.*"

For one, she didn't know how, and for another, she'd clearly vacated the premises for a reason. Maryn had never wished for death—not really—but now that it had happened, she wasn't keen to return to life.

"You will," he all but growled and abruptly turned to kneel at her body's side. He tore open her tunic, exposing her wound, a dark pucker of flesh, shining with blood. She realized then how well she could see.

Despite the dark, Arwan, herself, and the woods were perfectly clear. She moved closer. "What are you doing?"

"I'm going to fix you."

"You said you didn't deal in flesh," she reminded him. His reaction confused and frustrated her. The last thing she wanted was to experience that excruciating pain again. "In case you haven't noticed, I've had a really bad day. I don't fancy going back to *that*."

"Oh, so you do hear me when I speak," he said in an infuriatingly pointed manner, his irritated gaze pinning her to the spot for one long second. "Are you hurt elsewhere?"

She frowned in response and crossed her arms. "No," she spat. "He cut my face and then stabbed me in short order."

She moved closer despite herself and peered over his shoulder. She could hear him muttering. "I told her to stay hidden. I told her to not trust *anyone*."

He placed his hand over the weeping wound. Maryn might have flushed at the intimate contact, but she wasn't even sure if the dead *could* blush. Still, she felt something akin to embarrassment as she surveyed him. A blue light radiated from under Arawn's palm.

"Why are you doing this?"

"As I said, it's not your time."

"But—" Maryn's question was forgotten as she noticed more flowers sprouting from the ground. Green shoots uncurled from the bloody snow as if in a forward time lapse, growing taller, forming leaves, then buds. Crocus, anemones, hyacinths, and daisies bloomed in full color before her eyes. "What's happening? Are you doing this?" she asked, awed.

Arawn didn't answer. He pulled his hand away, exposing her wound. The gaping wreck of her chest had closed. Blood still soaked her clothes, of course, but beneath the rent in her tunic, her flesh had knit back together, pink with new skin. She probably wouldn't even have a scar.

Healing her made no sense. Why would Death *remake* her? "Aren't you supposed to sweep me back to Annwn or something, to live the rest of my days in peace?"

"You're not going to Annwn. At least not as a soul," he responded. He wiped his thumb over her wounded cheek, erasing the cut as easily as erasing a line in the snow. He stood and turned to her spirit form, lifting a hand as if to touch her. Maryn backed away.

"I don't want to go back in there."

Arawn let his hand fall, his mouth turned into a long-suffering frown. "I'm not taking your soul to Annwn. I've healed your body. It can sustain life. You just need to—"

"Why don't you want me?" she blurted. "Am I unworthy of Annwn? Is that it?"

He shook his head as if to dislodge a pesky fly. "Don't be ridiculous. Everyone has a place in Annwn."

His words wounded her. Ridiculous, was she?

"Everyone except me, it seems. Why, Arawn? Is it because of Brigid? You want me to go back into a ruined body so I can find her? Is that it?" Her voice quavered as her temper grew. "Well, I've decided that I've had quite enough of having my choices made for me. I never asked for this impossible task in the first place and now you're bullying me back into it all. No, Arawn. Take me to Annwn. Take me to Lolly and Pop and my m-mum." Her voice fully broke at the end.

Tears fell freely from her eyes, pearlescent and not quite wet. She wiped them away, her fingers coming away with only a whisper of tears. They shone wetly enough on her fingers, yet they remained dry.

He stood very close. His smell and warmth suffused her. His apparent anger left, replaced with something akin to pity. It shamed her. The tenderness in his eyes made a spot in her chest—right where her heart should be—ache.

"Maryn," he said, his voice gentle. "Dearest Maryn." He lifted a hand to her face as if to caress her but stopped short. "You *are* worthy of Annwn. Of so much more. Never doubt that." He licked his lips, looking suddenly unsure.

His gaze traveled to her broken body, to the flowers that littered the snowy forest floor, then back. "You must return because there *is no one else*. You took up this burden, as heavy as it is, and now you must finish it. Look," he said, gesturing to the flowers sprouting around her body. "You are linked to Brigid both by blade and by blood."

"I—I don't understand." She hated how her voice quavered.

"I sensed it in you the night you came to the keep. I read your life in your palm. Do you remember?" At her nod he continued. "I can . . . smell it on you, like a field of wildflowers. Heady and—" He broke off, swallowing his words and looked away as if embarrassed. "Not just anyone would have been able to pull Brigid's blade from her temple, no matter how long dead she laid."

"But . . . what are you saying?"

"I'm saying that I didn't do this." Again, he motioned to the bed of flowers surrounding her body. "Your blood raised these blossoms. You, Maryn, are a descendant of Brigid."

Maryn's stomach dropped and her mouth gaped open. "What? How is that even possible? She's a goddess. I'm *human*," she said, pointing to her very dead body.

Arawn leveled her with a long-suffering stare. "Do you really need me to tell you about procreation, Maryn? Brigid took a human lover long ago. You're a distant product of said affair."

Maryn stared at him, waiting for the punchline. It didn't come. He was in earnest. It was dizzying to consider. It didn't make sense. "Okay," she hedged, "but I've never *bled flowers* before, Arawn. Why now?"

He exhaled through his very straight nose. "I can't be sure, but I think that the longer you tarry in a god's realm, the more your innate magic awakens. Perhaps using Cailleach's hammer awoke it in you. Perhaps being cut by Brigid's blade did the job." He rubbed his forehead. "It's a long story. I promise to explain everything to you, but we shouldn't stay here." He frowned down at her prone form, his brows creased.

Maryn tried to order her mind. She was a descendant of the spring goddess. He said she had magic. What could she do aside from bleed daisies? Could she create sparks from her hands like Ciaran? If she stayed dead, would she ever find out? She bit her lip, her curiosity piqued despite herself.

"You have to go back," Arawn explained, "because your death stoppers your potential, damns Cailleach, abandons Brigid, and leaves the human world in shambles. Not just in this time, but in all times, Maryn. Time to you is linear, but to gods, every time in what you call 'history' happens simultaneously."

Maryn's mind fumbled for distant remembrances of physics classes in her undergrad. "Einstein was right," she said, awed. It was incredible. Impossible. And yet . . . and yet Arawn's words rang true. The universe was not made up of three dimensions—up/down, left/right, forward/backward—but of *four*. The latter being a time dimension.

"So, life is happening all at once? Every period of history from the creation of the world to the death of the sun . . . it's all *now*?" Puzzling it out made her head hurt.

Arawn smiled at her amazement. "More or less," he said with a shrug. "And there will be time to reflect on it all, but right now, there are more pressing matters."

More pressing than the realization of the theory of relativity?

"I would take you to Annwn to rest if I could, Maryn," said Arawn, "but don't you see? By starting out on this path, you've surrendered yourself to its completion."

Truth rang in his words. Although she'd been plucked from her time against her will, she'd taken up the task. She'd agreed. She'd used Cailleach's hammer to open the earth, she'd fought through cold and monsters. She'd even died for the cause. She thought then of her own time, of the unnaturally cold summer they were having. Einstein had been right and Cailleach's winter was pervading every fold of time.

"Will it hurt?" she asked, her voice soft. She glanced at her body, her spirit hands folded into fists. She'd never considered herself a coward, but apparently the promise of pain was enough to prove her wrong.

His gaze softened. "You'll only be weak. Tired. I'll bring you back to Annwn to recover. Alive."

"Why not Spring? We're so close."

Arawn's lips pressed together briefly before he shook his head. "After what's just happened, I can't promise you safety there. I can in Annwn, however." He ran a hand through his hair, his gaze distant. "I should have just gone myself," he admitted. "I should have put everything on hold and gone into Spring Court and asked your questions for you. If I'd done that, you wouldn't be in this situation."

"It's all right." She relaxed her clenched hands. "How were you to know? Besides, getting to Spring Court wasn't your job, it was mine. Just as you said." And, from what she'd gathered, dropping everything to help a hapless mortal travers kingdoms wasn't so easy for Death.

Maryn swallowed hard and lifted her chin, forcing bravery. "Okay," she said, glad that her voice didn't waver. "If you say it . . . it won't hurt, I'll go back. I'll do as you ask. On one condition," she added, a finger raised.

His mouth quirked. "What's that?"

"You'll teach me how to heal wounds like you just did for me. Durvan's leg is—*Durvan!*" How could she have failed to tell Arawn about her companion? "He's hurt, and I'm not sure where he is, exactly; that's why I'm here, alone." She explained everything then, the words falling from her like water from a carafe, a tumbling cascade of desperate chatter. "And we have to go back for the hammer!"

"I know," he said, placing hands on her shoulders to still her. "I *know*. A selkie went to retrieve him. He's alive," he added at Maryn's worried expression. "He's in good hands."

"You knew? But why didn't you come sooner?"

Arawn cast her an apologetic look. "I didn't know until you were stabbed. I sensed your ultimate passing. I saw you in my mirror and wondered why you were alone. I found him shortly thereafter and came immediately. I'm sorry I couldn't have prevented this. It's not strictly allowed, anyway, stopping souls from committing wrong."

Maryn thought of all the hate crimes and terrible atrocities carried out by humans every day. "Why can't gods stop people from hurting others?"

His shoulders lifted in an apologetic shrug. "If choice was removed from you, how could you be fairly judged at your death?" He took a breath. "Maryn we need to go. Please," he gestured to her body. "The choice is yours. What will it be?"

She stood at her feet, staring at herself. She looked so small. Frail. "What do I do?"

"Lie down," he instructed. "You'll fall into yourself quite easily, but it won't feel right. Not until I knit you back together."

"How will you do that?" she asked, sitting down. Her spirit form sank into her middle, legs aligned. "Knit me back together, I mean."

"Well," he said, circling her. "It's quite simple. I will *make* you instead of *unmake*. I will breathe life into you, Maryn. Lie down, if you please." He flexed his hands. Maybe she wasn't the only one with unsettled nerves.

Lying in her body felt as unpleasant as refitting a hand into a wet glove. Cold, clinging, and uncomfortable.

He knelt beside her, looming over her, a hand on each side of her arms to support himself. He stared at her mouth. If she had breath to hold, she most assuredly would be holding it now. It felt awfully intimate, this *making*.

"Live," he whispered, just before his mouth settled over hers.

The sensation was curious, like a kiss, but distinctly different. As his breath passed her lips, a weight settled in her chest then rapidly spread outward toward her limbs, like a cascade of bath water. Her spirit form solidified as it connected to her remains, clinging and heavy. Her heart lurched into action, her blood barreling through her veins. She gasped for breath as her eyes flew open.

She stared into Awan's golden gaze, felt the weight of his calloused hand at the base of her throat. His thumb caressed her clavicle for the barest of seconds as he moved two fingers to her pulse point. "Welcome back," he said, his voice low. "Now, let's got get your bag."

Chapter Thirty

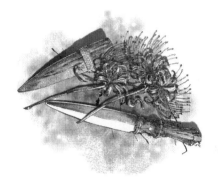

Doorways

It turns out that dying takes a lot out of a person.

Arawn pulled away, leaving Maryn flushed and weak. She tried to move, to sit up, but lacked the strength. "I don't think I can stand." Her limbs felt heavy, as if encased in concrete, and her chest, where the wound had been, felt bruised. Filling her lungs strained the newly made flesh there. Even her heart ached. She took shallower breaths, wishing for sleep.

"Nor walk, I'd wager."

Maryn tried to move and failed. She grimaced and shook her head.

"I suspected as much." His narrowed gaze gave her pause. She knew the look etched on his features: absorbed, curious. She'd seen it countless times as an archaeologist held a new discovery in their grasp.

"You've never done this before have you?" She tried to force her eyelids to stay open, but they dragged at her like lead weights. "I'm your first remaking."

He looked slightly uncomfortable, his eyes unable to meet her own. "The mechanics are basically the same. I had no doubt," he assured, waving a flippant hand.

Maryn scoffed, barely an exhale.

"Where did you hide the hammer?" he asked, looking about them as if he'd spot it amid the branches of trees or spy the handle poking free of the snow.

"There's a stump, on a rise outside of the village."

He held out his hand, palm up. "May I?"

When she didn't respond, he sighed and took her hand in his. He peered into it, much like he'd done the first time she'd met him.

"What do you see?" she asked, her curiosity piqued.

The long line of his mouth relaxed as his eyes darted to her face. "You're aware that I can read souls, can you not? Do you have a head injury you didn't tell me about?"

She rolled her eyes. "I mean, can you see where I stashed the hammer?"

"Hold on, I'm looking," he murmured.

She waited, watching as his index finger traced the lines along her palm.

Long seconds passed where Arawn's brow furrowed then relaxed. At one point he closed his eyes, his mouth pressing into an angry frown.

"What's wrong?" she breathed.

He sniffed sharply and opened his eyes, his pupils blown wide. "I'm of a mind to visit this priest who killed you."

"Y-you saw all that? In my palm?"

He folded her fingers inward, his eyes intent upon her face. "Yes," he hissed, a flash of anger in his eyes. He stood "I also saw where you placed your bag. Come, I'll help you."

She swallowed heavily and allowed him to help her to her feet. He saw everything? "How far back can you see? My birth?"

He wrapped an arm around her shoulders, making her stomach flip. He nodded, curt. "If given enough time. Reading palms helps to focus my mind on the landscape of a life."

Weak, she leaned against him as they picked their way through the snow. Her breathing came fast and shallow. Her head swam.

"Stay with me. We're not far."

"Keep talking. It helps."

He gave her shoulders a squeeze in response. "Well, actions, good and bad, paint one's soul in vibrant tones. A life poorly lived, for example, is sometimes so overwhelmed with shadows and corners, that the good they've done can be lost."

"You see an entire life in one picture?"

"Think of it as an ongoing, narrative mural. It begins at your birth and depicts important events and choices. It's ever changing because your choices lead you down varying paths."

"How does this help you find my bag, again?"

He laughed lightly. "Well, for starters, looking at your palm, helps me retrace your steps. Thankfully I didn't have to look too far. Ah, I think must be your stump."

It was. She waited as he pulled the bag free, besmirched with bits of rotting wood. He slung it over his shoulder as spots formed before her eyes. Before she knew it, the world went dark.

Later, she awoke. She knew the passage of time only from the changing light. The purpled horizon told her the lateness of the hour. Early, rather. The rising sun chased away the clinging dark. She blinked, her body slow to rouse to her mind's requests. She *was moving*, though not under her own power. The leafless branches in her purview passed by slowly.

Lord, she was so tired, her head heavy and sluggish. She inhaled the scent she'd begun to associate with Arawn: subtle pine with the barest hints of smoke. There was something else, something like bergamot or sandalwood, she couldn't decide. She turned her nose toward the aroma and only then realized that Arawn cradled her in his arms. She immediately ceased her questing nose and sank into him, knowing she was safe.

"We're nearly there," he said, his voice thrumming through her side. His tone didn't betray he'd noticed her sniffing, thank goodness.

He wasn't carrying her, they were *riding*. She lifted her head with monumental effort. They were riding the...the *bones* of a horse. She gasped. "Tell me you didn't just resurrect a dead horse."

Arawn's chuckle moved the hairs on top of her head. "Such censure from someone only recently deceased. But no, not resurrected, merely repurposed."

"Where did you find it?" She stared at the swaying sheets of scapula just in front of her, dirt and *other* stuff still clinging to its surface.

"You'd be surprised how many dead things lay hidden under your feet at any given time," he said airily.

Maryn didn't have the energy to shudder. "I don't want to think about it."

The horse's bones clunked together with each step, reminding her of the bamboo chimes her Lolly hung in the garden. "Where are we going?"

"Home. To Annwn," he said, pulling the braided reeds that formed the steed's reins to the right. "Quiet now, I don't want to announce our location to any nearby living souls."

Good idea. The sight of Death and a resurrected Maryn riding a dead horse would cause no small amount of panic. She didn't fancy being stabbed again any time soon.

Maryn's rear end, unfortunately, started to take notice of the knobby vertebrae with each clop of a hoof. "Are we going to the boat?" she asked.

"We won't go by the sea. I can travel quite easily and take you with me through any of the usual doorways."

A light sensation—like a soft tapping—pulsed against her shoulder, where her body was pressed against Arawn. "You have a heart?" she asked, unable to hide her surprise. "But I thought you were dead."

"Some might say I lack a heart, but no. All gods can die, so therefore, we all live."

Maryn absorbed the information, so tired her brain seemed to have trouble keeping up. She lacked the energy to form coherent questions let alone stoke the fires of propriety that presently lay dormant. Later she would find time for embarrassment at her lounging against the god of death. Now, she could only exert enough energy to keep her eyes open.

"I'm sorry, Arawn," she mumbled into his chest. "I don't mean to lean into you. I can't seem to find the energy to sit up."

She felt his chin brush the top of her head as he looked down at her. "You needn't apologize to me."

They crested a small rise and Arawn pulled their summoned ride to a stop. "Do you think you can stand or shall I carry you?"

If anything could motivate the lame to walk, it would be a reanimated corpse. "I'd like to try."

Arawn swung down, a leg sweeping behind the steed to accommodate Maryn, and lifted his hands in invitation to her. She didn't hesitate and fell forward.

Just as before, his touch ignited something in Maryn, causing her blood to thrum through her veins at a rapid pace. Despite her basically lounging in his lap seconds before, something about his long-fingered hands spanning her ribcage sent her heart racing.

The immediacy of her body pressed against his as she swayed made her blush. *It can't be helped.* She chased away any thoughts that developed in her mind toward Arawn. *He's the god of death for heaven sakes. Get ahold of yourself, Ferguson.*

He held her steady as her head swam, her nose as good as pressed into his sternum. She couldn't even feel her feet. "What's wrong with me?" she asked. Yes, she'd just died, but come on. Not feeling her feet seemed extreme.

The fingers of his right hand brushed her side as he moved to lift her chin. Butterflies erupted violently in her middle and scattered to her extremities. Oh, she did have feet after all. He studied her face, looking into her eyes as if he could read her like a book. "Hmm," he muttered. "Your pupils are blown wide. Let's try and get you moving."

His arms fell away from her, though a hand hovered at her elbow.

"I'm ok," she promised. "My heart." She pressed a hand to her chest as if doing so could force it to calm. "I'm just tired, I think."

He frowned, his gaze sweeping over her face. "You've got a headache too," he said, smoothing her scrunched forehead with a thumb. His cool fingers brushed against her flushed skin. "You'll feel better after you've eaten a proper meal and had a long rest."

With a wave of his hand, the waiting bone horse crumpled to the ground in a heap. Another wave and the jumble sank into the ground as if the soil were made of quicksand, instead of rocky earth. "This way," he said, taking her elbow in a gentle hold.

Maryn lingered, staring at the spot that had swallowed their steed. "Er, thanks," she muttered to it. Despite her ardent desire to dig up the past, using the dead in such a manner felt wrong. On many levels. At least she'd never used any of the dead she'd studied or uncovered for anything more than the acquisition of knowledge.

Arawn, patient as ever, slowed further as they navigated the brushy slope. Emerging from the vegetation, Maryn stared, open mouthed, at the wide, stony circle carefully created in the bowl of the surrounding hills. Thousands of stones were nestled neatly together like the cobblestones of a street, forming a circle. In the center stood a three-sided doorway, like a miniature Stonehenge, marking an entrance.

"A cairn." Maryn barely breathed. "It's got to be at least forty feet across." She turned her stare to Arawn, who didn't share her awe. And no wonder. A grave would be commonplace for him. "This is the door you spoke of?"

"For me, every grave is a doorway. I couldn't send you and Durvan this way because I wasn't with you."

"But you're here now," Maryn said, her mouth gone dry. She'd studied cairns, of course. They were an archaeologist's dream come true, but any of the carefully constructed tombs had long since been emptied and examined by the time she'd come along. She'd only seen artifacts at the university or in museums.

Entering one now, witnessing in real time how the Celts prepared and kept their dead, to see unspoiled artifacts and offerings, to witness the tomb, unsullied by years of wear and graffiti was a dream come true. Or it might be for someone not terrified of dark, enclosed spaces.

Maryn's trembling had nothing to do with the cold or fatigue. She stalled, staring into the shadow the standing stones created.

The sky lightened further, the purple twilight turning grey. She swallowed her fear as best she could. Arawn was right. She needed a bed.

"Are you well?" he asked.

She found him staring at her wound site and followed his gaze. Her shirt, ripped and stiff with dried blood, made her stomach turn. "I'll be better once I get a hot bath."

He helped her up the revetment wall, leading her over the lumpy forecourt, holding her steady. Maryn squinted into the dark, watching her feet as they drew closer to the center stones.

"I'll light our way once inside. I don't wish to draw any unnecessary attention." He looked about them, as if searching out prying eyes in the meadow beyond the stones. His eyes darkened to a rich amber in the limited light.

The shadows waiting under the eave of the limestone orthostat entrance hid the stairs that would bring them in with the dead. The little foyer entrance was close. Maryn's breath quickened and her hands grew clammy.

Worse yet, the stone steps were not quite deep enough for Maryn's full booted foot to fit the tread. *Dry boots,* she noticed, no doubt thanks to Arawn. The sensation that she'd tumble into the awaiting abyss with the slightest misstep overwhelmed her. She stretched out her hands, fingers streaking along the cold walls, swaying on her feet.

Arawn stood at her back, a step above. His hand settled on her shoulder, keeping her on her feet. She held her breath, staring into the clinging pitch, her heart beating a wild tattoo against her ribs. It ached. Everything ached.

"I'm afraid," she confessed. She closed her eyes, tears gathering in the corners. She didn't want to cry. If she started now, she'd never stop.

"I know." There was no censure in his voice. No pity. Just a statement of fact. He squeezed her shoulders, sending a shock of sensation through her arms. They tingled slightly, like a whispering current of electricity.

Her awareness of him, his closeness, his touch that pulled her senses like iron shavings to a magnet, distracted her from her cycling thoughts. Her fear, though not abated, withdrew, allowing her to catch her breath.

The step just ahead of her blurred into focus, a mere whisper beckoning the next footfall. She couldn't make herself take it.

"When I was in the throes of the puka's attack, you told me that the darkness should be afraid of me." She shook her head, searching for words. "I can't see how that's possible."

"But you've already taken the first steps into the darkness. That's the hardest part."

Maryn pressed her lips together, as if doing so would dam the flow of her warring emotions.

"You doubt me?" he asked. "No journey is ever complete so long as you remain. Stepping off a path, into the darkness, is the *only* way to finish this voyage you set your feet upon." He gave her shoulders another squeeze. "Go, and see for yourself, and you'll find this fear you hold is only made of shadow. It cannot hurt you."

She turned her head to look up into his face, searching for his eyes in the dim. "But there are things that could harm me. The pukas…."

She felt him nod more than saw it, so dark was the enclosed space. "And in the end, you overcame them. Darkness cannot linger for long. You may have to live within it for a time, but you don't have to let it overwhelm you. Take the next step, Maryn, and find your strength. You'll find light on the other side."

Maryn licked her lips, her eyes stinging. She blinked rapidly, forcing the tears away. She *would not cry*. He was right. Face her fears and all that. "You—" She swallowed heavily and took a deep breath. "You won't leave me?"

"Never."

"What's in there? More pukas?"

She felt his shrug. "Bodies. Perhaps the odd ghost. Nothing that can harm you."

Maryn stalled. "Ghosts, huh," she repeated, a smile in her voice. "Losing your grip on your souls, are you? Letting the dead walk free, willy nilly now?"

He laughed lightly. "Not quite." She could almost hear the humor in his tone. "You might recall that I must hunt down souls from time to time. Those on errand might come to visit their body, while others are too involved with what they're leaving behind to move forward." He paused here and she knew he was trying to make a point.

Maryn took a steadying breath and stared hard at the grim line of the stair only just visible below. She extended a shaky leg. Her toe found the next tread without incident. She took a breath, then moved to the next, her hands trailing along the smooth stone.

The next three steps plunged her into complete darkness. The solid stone on either side of them gave way to rectangular pieces fitted tightly together. Her fingers brushed against something soft and she recoiled.

Arawn's teasing tone seemed to open up the tight space, stealing away some of Maryn's trepidation, "Yes, I can see how moss might frighten the hardiest of warriors."

Maryn laughed at herself and thrust an elbow into his middle.

He grunted and chuckled. "Careful, Little Mortal."

The cold damp settled around them. "How deep does this go, anyway?"

She felt his hand move through the air, disturbing whisps of hair at her temple. The soft glow of golden light he produced nearly matched his eyes. She blinked against the sudden flare until the world came into focus.

They stood at the bottom of the stairs in a circular antechamber. The stones were dark with weeping moisture, the air heavy with damp. A battened oak door blocked the entrance just ahead of them, replete with Pictish runes etched along the lintel.

"You made it." His smile was so genuine that Maryn couldn't help but return it.

"At least this far. Thank you."

"Don't thank me yet," he said, his tone light. He walked around her for the door with a purposeful stride. "Not until you're safe in Annwn, in any case."

"What does it say?" she asked, stalling. He probably knew it, but he answered her all the same.

He pointed to the bottom right of the door. "We are nothing," he said, lifting his hand to follow the script up the lintel. She followed his finger as he swept it down the left side. "Without those who proceed us."

Maryn stared at the script, all curved lines and intersected circles. "It's rather beautiful," she said. "A nice sentiment that those we love and interact with shape us."

Arawn glanced at her. "Are you ready?" He must have sensed her fear. "I'll be with you the entire time."

She nodded, unable to speak, as he lifted the bar from the door with a wave of his hand. It lifted effortlessly and deposited itself against the wall. The door itself was several inches thick and held together with iron bands. As one would expect, it creaked ominously. *Great.*

Arawn's fairy light floated in first, bringing streaming cobwebs into sharp relief. "Of course there's spiders," she muttered. Arawn stepped in first and she followed closely after, unwilling to have any significant distance between them. She grabbed a handful of his strange cloak, not even caring that curling smoke wound its way up her wrist and forearm.

The carefully fitted stone walls closed in on Maryn, making her apprehension grow. She shuffled closer to Arawn, both afraid to see and unwilling to close her eyes. The walls were unadorned unless one counted the weeping moisture that discolored the stone.

"Say something," she whispered into Death's back. "Anything to distract me."

She thought he might refuse or at least scoff, but he did neither. After a moment he cleared his throat and said, "When I was a child, I nearly drowned. It was winter and the ice too thin for crossing, but when another child declared that I wasn't brave enough to try, I had to."

Maryn tried to imagine him as a youth. She'd never considered that he'd had a childhood. Somehow it seemed quite plausible that he'd simply sprouted from the ground, fully formed and functioning as a god.

With a little effort, she could picture a dark haired, freckle-faced boy. She envisioned him as small and quiet...perhaps picked on by others, but maybe she was merely projecting her own childhood onto him.

"Did you have many friends?"

She could hear the censure in his voice. "I thought everyone was my enemy. Arrogant and peevish, I found insults where none were meant." He shrugged. "One of my many failings."

Maryn had nothing to say to that. "How is a god made? I just thought that, well, I guess I've never really considered that gods really existed, and yet here you are." She paused, her mind whirring. "Who are your parents?"

Arawn slowed, pausing at a causeway, the fairy light bobbing over their heads. Maryn eyed the gloom with distaste.

"This way," he said, turning to the left. As they turned the corner, the light illuminated the path not chosen. A dim outline formed from the forward chamber. The white shroud-wrapped bodies carefully laid within the stone walls winked into view, and then were gone. Maryn pressed herself closer into Arawn's back. "I am different than other gods in that I was born to mortal parents. Cailleach and other seasonal gods were formed from the All Father's Cauldon."

Maryn's brow scrunched as she tried to recall what she knew about the All Father. "Dagda? Is that right?"

"The very same," he said. "But 'god' is merely a title. Just as I was once a mortal man, others, so too, can be Made like me."

"Made?" asked Maryn. Her feet collided with his and Arawn, apparently having enough of their strange arrangement, paused long enough to pull her around to his side. She held onto his forearm as they followed the narrow passage. Still, she pressed close, unwilling to touch the weeping walls.

"Made," he affirmed with a nod. "Once the mantle of Death was placed upon me, I became the god of the underworld."

Maryn fell silent, taking in the new information. Her fears lessened as she reordered her thoughts. "What happened, Arawn?" she asked. "What is your story?"

She noticed a sudden change in him at the question. He did not appear upset, but she could still sense his reluctance to speak of it in the set of his shoulders and the firm line of his mouth. "Perhaps one day I will tell you. For now, let's get you through to Annwn."

Maryn felt her face heat from her forwardness.

After a short walk and another turn, stoneware urns appeared. They lined the path, sealed with pine tar, if the smell was any indication. A few swords and round, wooden shields leaned against some of the more sizeable pieces, catching her gaze. Grateful for the distraction, she slowed and peered at them, the fairy light hovering over one, as if knowing what she wished.

The shield, covered in embossed leather, depicted the shape of a three-legged triskele. Anything pulled from the earth during modern eras showed the ravages of time and the elements, but this was perfect and breathtakingly beautiful. She itched to touch it.

She leaned in to take in the sword next. The cross guard winked gold from the orb. "Steel," she muttered. "Most likely resulting from a bloomery furnace. Am I right?"

Arawn nodded. "Quite right."

"Different from Roman swords." Maryn leaned closer. Cobwebs clung to the weapon, and she wiped them away before picking it up. It was heavy, the leather-wrapped hilt too large for her hand. "Nothing we have from this time survived all that well."

She peered at the curved, ornate blade, muttering to herself. "The mass-produced Roman swords didn't hold this much character." She glanced at Arawn. "I suppose I should have asked to pick this up. Am I going to be haunted by its owner now?"

Arawn's mouth twitched with a budding smile, the discomfort she'd imagined between them melting to nothing. "Men are rather fond of their swords," he agreed, "but I doubt he'll come for you. Not unless you damage it."

Maryn returned the weapon, carefully placing it behind the urn from which she'd plucked it. "I take it these are his remains?" She gestured to the sealed urn.

"Ælfflæd of Dál Riata."

She gaped at him. "You remember every person that's died?"

He shrugged. "It comes with the territory. Godly mantle, remember?"

"So, who was he then? What do you remember?"

Arawn shook his head, his tone grave. "Mmm . . . some would say he was too often in his cups. His wife and child suffered greatly at his expense, unfortunately."

She raised a brow. "A real piece of work, huh? Who's this?" she asked, indicating the next urn.

"His mistress, both killed at the hands of Ælfflæd's wife."

Maryn grimaced. "Yikes."

"We're almost there," he said motioning toward the end of the hallway. The orb bobbed forward, illuminating a stone coffin, set on end. The lid leaned heavily against the empty stone box, flat and devoid of adornment.

"Tell me we're not getting inside that thing." Maryn's heart rate increased just thinking about it.

"It's just a doorway, Maryn. You only need walk through."

She frowned. "If you say so." She didn't bother pointing out how mortals might find some difficulty walking through solid objects.

With a wave of a hand the heavy lid of the sarcophagus moved to the side, giving them full access to the supposed doorway into Annwn.

"Stand here," he said, indicating that she should go first. She moved to stand just before the tomb, swaying slightly with fatigue. She really needed to lie down, and soon. She closed her eyes and took a deep breath, trying to force calm.

The air stirred around her and she opened her eyes, but could see no change in the portal. The solid stone bottom of the coffin was still there.

"You need only walk through, Maryn. I'll be right behind you."

She lifted a brow and cast a look over her shoulder. He looked different, like he was outlined in chalk, his face dark. *Weird.*

She turned back to the door, lifting a hand to stop herself from plowing into anything. Beyond all belief, her hand met, then went through the barrier. She jerked it back, staring at her fingers. They were all there, at least.

"Didn't believe me?" he asked, so close to her back she could feel the heat of him. A part of her wanted to lean into him, while another wanted to move away. She chose the latter, stepping purposefully into the unknown.

Bright light assaulted her. She squinted against it, and then moved hastily out of the way as Arawn followed behind. The same strange stirring of air came again, throwing the room into relief. Whatever magic he'd done, the colors now seemed more vibrant.

They stood in a wide hallway, their feet on a red runner she realized she'd seen before. She frowned at her feet, trying to recall where she'd seen it and then realized, quite suddenly, that she knew exactly where they stood. They were in Arawn's castle. She'd walked this very carpet once before.

"Welcome home, Unmaker," said a familiar voice from behind. Arawn's captain.

They turned around and, to Maryn's surprise, the cairn they'd just left was no longer there. Instead, they stood before the open twin doors of the great hall. The lady selkie that had first brought Maryn down this very carpet stood in the arched doorway and bowed neatly at the waist. Her leather armor squeaked with her movement.

"Forgive the interruption, but there are some matters that require your attention." The selkie's black gaze flitted over Maryn, snagging on the bloodied hole in her bodice.

Arawn nodded, giving Maryn a once-over. Their intense scrutiny made Maryn want to fidget.

"Mistress Ferguson is in need of some care. See to it that food is brought to her rooms."

The captain nodded, a question written in her eyes. "Of course."

Arawn reached a hand toward Maryn's elbow, then, apparently thinking better of it, let it drop. "You'll have everything you need in your rooms above." He gestured her down the hallway. They walked in silence, a strained, living thing.

His demeanor was so far removed from his recent easy-going nature that Maryn didn't know what to think. Was he ashamed of his association with her? Is that why he acted so stiff and proper in front of his subject? Or maybe it was her. Was she reading too much into every little thing?

So what that he'd cradled her in his arms atop the horse? What did it matter that he'd touched her in a familiar way all through the cairn. Who cared that their easy banter and familiar way of speaking was suddenly at an end? She didn't. They weren't *friends*. He was a god, for heaven's sake. Gods didn't have mates, she was sure. And if they did, they wouldn't associate with mere *mortals*.

Maryn's fatigue doubled as her thoughts tangled.

They turned a corner that led to the stairs leading to her wing. She scoffed to herself. Listen to her! *Her* wing, as if she had a place here. The treads loomed before her and she slowed. How could she ever make it up? Her head swam, her heart hurt. She felt like crying. She needed to get alone, and fast.

"You have things to do," she said in what she hoped was an offhand way. "I know the way. You go. I'll be fine."

Was that disappointment she saw flash in his eyes? No doubt just concern. He probably didn't want to have to put her back in her body if she fell and broke her neck. "Really," she assured, forcing more energy in her words than they probably warranted. "Go. I'll see you later."

Arawn's wide mouth turned down as he considered her. Finally, after a stretched silence, he nodded once. "As you wish," he said, and turned to go. "Dinner will be at seven, should you wish to join us," he added, his gaze raking over her form as if he wasn't quite sure she was still in one piece.

She shooed him away. Couldn't a girl cry in peace?

Maryn waited for him to leave before slumping down onto the bottommost step. She scrubbed her face. What was wrong with her?

"I'm just tired," she told herself. Weariness pierced her to the bone. She stared at the polished marble floor, black with ivory veins running through it. She'd *died* today. She'd looked down upon her remade body, at her grimy hands and stiff tunic. The scent of iron filled her nose. Dirt and soot painted her nails a dingy black.

She'd lost Brigid's blade. She'd abandoned Durvan. She hadn't intended to, of course, but guilt still gripped her. Arawn had said Durvan still lived, or he'd been at the time Arawn sent the selkie to fetch him. Was he still?

Tears sprang to her eyes, hot and immediate. She could not stop their flow. Maybe Arawn would put Durvan back in his body if she asked.

She did not know how long she sat there, weeping into her hands. Eventually, the same toothy servant she'd first met in the great hall found her, tutting softly at the pathetic sight she presented.

"I've just come from Himself," he said. "Asked me tae look in on you, and no wonder."

Maryn sniffed and observed him through watery eyes. "I can't get up the stairs," she said thickly.

As he sat down next to her, she saw he carried her bag.

She sat straighter. "Is the hammer still in th-there?" she hiccupped.

He offered it to her. The familiar weight of Cailleach's totem calmed her worries. Still, she peeked inside to ensure her satchel hadn't somehow been filled with stones instead.

"Thank you. I couldn't stay awake after—" She trailed off.

The servant's kind expression increased her urge to cry. "Rough day?"

Maryn's watery laugh echoed in the stairwell. "You could say that."

He made a commiserating noise in his throat and said, "We've all had such days, Mistress. There's nothing a hot bath and a meal won't do to cure what ails you, I say."

She hiccupped softly and asked, "What's your name?"

"Fionn, Milady."

"It's just Maryn." She cast him a small smile. "Thank you, Fionn."

He stood, offering his spindly hand. Together, they made the trek up the stairs. Maryn had never been more grateful.

Chapter Thirty-One

Brigid's Lamentation

After a bath, a light snack, and a visit to Durvan, Maryn found a waiting note slipped under her door. Curling black script on a stiff, white notecard invited her to Arawn's study to discuss "today's events, et cetera."

She tapped the card against her opposite hand. She had many questions. Maybe she should write them all down to ensure she didn't accidentally omit one.

She sighed. The previous day's misadventures now behind her, calm determination settled within her. She had the hammer. Durvan had been healed. But what now?

Durvan, for his part, looked far better than the last time she'd seen him. Witnessing the dwarf sitting up in bed, his color restored, she'd been overcome with relief. His rebuff at her forced hug hadn't bothered her at all, nor his refusal to let her see his injured leg. In fact, to her mind, his refusal solidified his mending.

Dinner at seven turned out to be a rather private affair. A selkie came to escort her to Arawn's private study, where a small, prepared table awaited her, laden with platters of food. She brought Cailleach's hammer along with her, nestled in her bag, now slung over her shoulder. After losing Brigid's blade, Maryn didn't want Cailleach's totem out of her sight.

Arawn sat at his desk, back to them, as they entered. The room itself shone brightly with magical light. Silver and gold orbs swirled lazily across the intricate board and batten ceiling, casting wavering light throughout. The way the diffracted light moved over the floor and walls gave the impression of being submerged underwater. Books lined one side of the room, near Arawn's desk. A rectangular frame, covered with black velvet, sat on the right side.

In the opposite corner of the room hung a large ornate bird cage; little buntings flitted from perch to perch, their colorful bodies drawing her eye. She'd always loved birds. She moved toward them, peering into their shining black eyes. She didn't know what to do with herself, couldn't explain her sudden shyness. Was it borne of embarrassment? Did Grosh tell Arawn about her weeping on the stairs?

"I'll be just a moment," called Arawn from where he sat. He looked to be writing something in a book. "Please, make yourself comfortable."

The selkie bowed herself out as Maryn cooed to the birds, poking a finger through the thin bars. One of the birds fluttered to her finger, its little talons light against her skin. Arawn's lingering gaze felt like a weight on her back.

"Did you rest well?" asked Arawn.

"Yes. I visited Durvan," she said, her voice small. "I'm afraid I slept the rest of the afternoon away." Seeing that Maryn had nothing to offer the little bird, it hopped away, gliding to a perch.

Maryn made her way over to the table and sluffed off her bag, placing it against the table leg. The food provided for her in her room seemed a very long time ago. The smell of roast fowl filled her senses, making her stomach growl.

"I'm glad to hear it." He stood, apparently finished with his work, and joined her at the table. Without his cloak, Maryn could assess him properly for the first time. In fact, she'd never seen him in such a relaxed state. His billowy white shirt, untucked from his black trousers, lent him an air of composed casualness that she rather enjoyed. It made her abandon the need to be so formal, in any case.

"Writing to your pen pal?" she asked, only half teasing. She chased the awkwardness pervading her away with questions, a nervous habit of hers.

He gestured to the leatherbound tomes lining the wall in dark colors. "Keeping a record. Each Death before me has done so."

Maryn stared at the shelves. There had to be a thousand books at least. "And they're filled with, what? Day to day musings of the underworld?"

Arawn smiled, following her eyes to the rows of book spines, gilt lettering sparking. "Not quite. Most of these deal with the law, actually. Very boring business, that."

Maryn frowned, surprised. "Law?"

He met her eye from across the table. "Oh yes, you'll remember that we gods are bound by laws, just as mortals are. Many of these tomes list human rules and explain different cultures around the globe."

"But why?"

Arawn leaned forward, plucking a bottle of wine from the table. He filled her glass, the silence pressing in on her.

"How could I judge a soul fairly without knowing the laws by with they lived? Some laws are universal. Treating others how you'd like to be treated, for instance. What do you call that?"

"The Golden Rule."

"Ah, yes," he said, filling his own glass. The red liquid swirled around the belly of his goblet, reminding her of blood—her blood, so recently spilt.

"Can you tell me more about the connection between Brigid and me?"

Arawn replaced the bottle and gestured for her to fill her plate.

"That's one of the reasons I thought we should meet privately. I knew you'd have questions and likely wouldn't want others listening in." He chose food for himself, a buttery roll and dark pheasant meat, among other things.

"Cailleach said something once about taking a lover—or not doing so, rather," said Maryn. "She made it sound . . . distasteful. Beneath her."

Arawn cast her a knowing look. "Cailleach has a history, as we all do, that causes her to spurn the idea of anything that might do her harm." He paused, considering Maryn for a moment. "Her sister, Brigid, however, tends to be less cautious in the art of love. It's in her nature, you see. The spring goddess is a master in creation: life, smithing, and healing. Cailleach's call is different."

"I see," said Maryn, sipping her wine. Currants, sharp and sweet rolled across her tongue. It was quite good. "So Brigid took a lover—a human, am I right? Was that the sin, then? Getting pregnant with a half mortal child?"

"Not at all. There is nothing more natural than the goddess of love and fertility bearing fruits. The sin, as you say, occurred when she broke Dagda's law by bringing her lover to the Eternal Waters without consent. She snuck him into Dagda's realm and bade him drink so that he could live with her forever."

He looked rather sad.

"Seems natural to me, to wish never to be parted from the one you love. Especially with a child on the way."

His eyes, dark in the swirling, low light, lifted from his glass to her face. "Yes, I quite agree, but she broke the law. If she'd, perhaps, gone about it differently, things would have ended up more favorably."

"So where did she mess up?"

Arawn pressed his lips together in thought, as if searching for the right words. "It's sometimes easier to live with the consequences of your actions and get what you want, rather than to live without."

Maryn lifted her glass only to find it empty. She blinked at it. When had she drunk it all? Arawn refilled it without comment. Maryn took a bite of bread, hoping the drink hadn't gone to her head. She felt pleasantly warm and her head only slightly fuzzy. Any awkwardness she'd felt upon first entering his study was now gone. Better if she ate something, in any case.

"She bore the child, a son called Ruadán," said Arawn, "whom she loved. The child, only half god, lived a long life. Like his mother, he fell in love with a mortal woman, and Brigid, who did not wish the same heartache upon her offspring, released him from her court. The two lived quite happily in the mortal world, creating life in many ways. But soon, as all mortals do, Ruadán's wife and children grew old. Death claimed them."

"What happened to Ruadán? Where is he now?"

Arawn's sad eyes lingered on the edge of his wine glass. "He threw himself upon a spelled spear. He took his own life for the loss that pervaded him."

Maryn blinked away emotion. "What a terribly sad story."

Arawn agreed. "Oh yes, and so you see, Brigid has lost everything she's ever really loved, including the respect of her peers."

"But why? You should feel sorry for her, not belittle her."

"I do no such thing," he said. "I can well understand her grief. So can others. It's not her choice to love a mortal, nor her grief that other gods hold against her. It's that once she broke the law, Dagda no longer allowed freedom of movement between our worlds. Before, seasonal gods mingled with their worshippers. They knew them and cared for them in person. After her transgression, the gods were relegated to leaving only on the feast days, when the rites must be performed."

Maryn exhaled, her mind touching upon her own grief. God and mortal alike, it didn't matter. They all grieved for love lost in one way or another.

"And I'm a descendant of Brigid—after a long line of any number of great grandchildren to have come from Ruadán's line."

Arawn nodded. "Quite right."

"Why me, then? There's got to be more of us around. Why did Cailleach choose me?"

"Why indeed?" he asked. "Do you think it's a coincidence that you happened upon the blade, Maryn?"

She frowned in thought. Had her life been predestined—planned—to bring her here and now? Had she been led to the study of the past or had it been a natural part of her? What else would bring her to the lost temple of her ancestor? All of her loved ones were deceased and on this side of the veil. How neat and tidy it all was, with none left to worry over or mourn her sudden disappearance.

"Do I even have a choice?" she asked, deflated. "If this has all been predetermined, how can you say I have a choice?"

Arawn leaned forward, looking intently into her eyes. "There is always a choice. You decided when you took upon yourself the mantle of Winter's Handmaiden. You chose again when you reentered your body. You can still choose to walk away."

Maryn disagreed, pulling her gaze away. "It doesn't feel that way. If I hadn't agreed to help Cailleach, there would be no returning home. If I didn't go back in my body, the world would suffer along with Cailleach and Brigid until the end. And what if I decide to walk away now? I can't go home. I can't get what I truly want."

"You're quite right; we're not permitted to choose the consequences of our actions. In agreeing to become Winter's Handmaiden, you set off a chain reaction of aftereffects. Some doors closed, others opened."

Maryn didn't like his answer. Her eyes fell to the starched white tablecloth.

"I don't like the choices left to me. I—" she swallowed budding emotion away. "When I agreed to take the hammer, I didn't think I had any other choice."

Arawn made a sound of regret in his throat. "I understand your dissatisfaction." He leaned forward, resting his elbows on the table, piercing her through with his absorbing gaze. "Do you think just anyone would choose as you have? Do you think another, as broken and tormented as we all are, could take on another's burdens—the world's burdens—with such determination?" He shook his head. "You forget, Little Mortal, that I am in the business of souls. You cannot count the number I've reaped nor the sheer vastness of Annwn's judged. You do not know yourself, but I can see you clearly."

He reached for her hand; she did not stop him, couldn't decide if she enjoyed his touch or if it only fascinated her. He turned her hand over, palm up, exposing the etched lines of her life.

"You chose differently," he said, voice low. "You opted for selflessness and goodness, to restoring the balance of the seasons, for every dimension and in every time. You returned to your body, despite your fear." He lifted her hand, pulling it close and traced a finger over her lifeline. "You've chosen the more difficult path, the selfless route, where others would not."

She didn't feel selfless. Her motivation from the start had been to return home. The sooner she found Brigid, the sooner she could go back to her time, to her life. She'd failed, of course. She was no closer to finding Brigid than when she'd first tumbled through time into the heart of the North Mountain.

"You said 'we'. You said, 'as broken and tormented as we all are.'" Maryn licked her lips, sweet with wine. It made her bold. "What torments you, Arawn?"

Arawn's eyes had gone dark, his pupils wide. "Once, I was human. Long ago. I must say, you've made far better choices than I ever had. You are singular, Little Mortal. Do not doubt it." He folded her fingers into her palm and released her.

Warmth that had nothing to do with the wine spread through her body at his words, a blossom of emotion Maryn could not name.

"How does it end?" she asked, her hand moving to clutch her wineglass. "Do my choices bring happiness?"

He reached for his own glass with a slight shrug. "I cannot say," he said, somber. "There are still choices left unmade."

Maryn stared at the pinkness of her hand, at the branching and intersecting lines running over the surface. "You can't see if I go home?"

Arawn smiled at her, his eyes lingering on her face. "I have no doubt you'll make the choice that will lead you right where you belong."

Maryn didn't feel like eating any longer. She stared at the birds in their cage, wondering if she opened the door what choice they would make because suddenly, Maryn didn't quite know herself. She didn't know where she belonged, or if she had the strength to flee her own cage.

She looked over the table laden with food. "There is so much suffering in the world. In the village, the healer was taking apart a shoe to boil the leather so they could eat." She shook her head, feeling ashamed of herself. She'd been so lost in her own problems that she lost sight of what truly mattered. "Can't we do something?" she asked, meeting his gaze.

Arawn's mouth twisted with regret. "The Unmaker does not involve themselves with the living world. We do not interfere—"

"But their suffering is not a consequence of a choice they made," she interrupted. "This has everything to do with whomever stole Brigid. And, by they way," she added, leveling him with a significant look, "you do interfere with the living. I'm proof of it." She placed a hand over her heart, where he'd remade her.

Arawn considered her, looking slightly uncomfortable.

She continued: "Cailleach is diminishing, people are dying—starving—and here we sit drinking wine while our food goes cold." Maryn shook her head. "I'm ashamed," she admitted, the set of her shoulders deflating. "I know the best way to help is to find Spring, but I'm no closer to finding her than when I left. If fact, I've lost ground. That druid, Ciaran, took Brigid's blade." She pressed her lips together as emotion welled within her. Swallowing heavily, she said, "I don't know what to do or where to go at this point."

"Cailleach is sustained through me, so you needn't worry on that account. As for the missing blade—" He lifted a hand in a helpless gesture. "It's true that her totem could be used against her. I appreciate your willingness to help those suffering from the enduring winter, but you mustn't run headlong into danger. Going to the Spring Court is pointless at this point—" He held up a hand forestalling her conjecture. "Now that we know there are people actively seeking you out, we must devise a new plan."

"But they think I'm dead. I could go quite easily, now I know to avoid villages."

He shook his head, saying, "I will call a council with the other two seasonal gods, which will take some time. Be patient. As you said, the best way to help is to find Brigid."

Maryn sighed heavily, disliking exercises in patience. Yes, but where was she to go from here? "Ciaran said he had a new mistress giving him power. Does that sound like something the goddess of war would do? Share knowledge and power with a human?"

Arawn stared into the middle distance, thinking. "It's possible. I doubt she'd turn away potential followers, in any case, but I've never heard of her gifting magic to mortals."

Maryn paused, processing his words. "Maybe she's making promises she doesn't intend to keep."

"That sounds much more like the Morrigan I know."

Chapter Thirty-Two

A Greedy Choice

Maryn was halfway to her room when she realized she'd left her bag. She hurried back through the hallways. Despite knowing the hammer would be perfectly safe with Araw, Maryn didn't like being without it.

The door to his study stood ajar, an inch of space inviting her in. She paused, listening hard, but heard nothing. Perhaps he'd gone? She'd just slip in and nab the hammer. No harm done.

The door opened silently, revealing the cozy room in full. Arawn hadn't left after all. He stood, back to her, facing his desk. She opened her mouth to speak, to alert him of her presence, but she stopped short. Light notes of laughter, distinctly feminine, tinkled through the air.

Maryn scanned the room. Who laughed? But only she and Arawn occupied the space, unless some invisible entity had joined him.

Arawn shifted on his feet, exposing the corner of the rectangular frame she'd seen before, though now the draped fabric had been removed. She gaped. A screen or a mirror. *A magic mirror.* Indiscernible shapes passed across the surface.

The woman's cheerful laughter rang out again. Maryn had clearly interrupted something. Could she tiptoe to the table and retrieve her bag without notice? No way. He'd see her. Better if she announced herself.

She cleared her throat softly. "I'm sorry to intrude. I don't mean to be rude—I left my bag and I thought I'd pop in and grab it."

Arawn, who'd turned at her throat clearing, looked just as shocked as she felt, but for probably different reasons. His amazement, no doubt, centered around the mannerless drop-in now occupying his private study.

Nice, Ferguson. Classy.

Maryn's gaze strayed to the mirror. She couldn't help herself. The foggy edges, framed in an ornate onyx border, gave way to the clear image of a beautiful young woman. Her blonde hair and soulful, large brown eyes drew Maryn in.

The subject in the glass sat at a table, her full mouth curved into a warm smile. Her eyes danced with some unheard, unseen delight. Shadows of other souls moved beside her, behind her, and the woman in the reflection followed them with a turn of her head. Joy lived in her eyes, a spark of life.

Maryn stared, rapt, as an older man draped an arm across the woman's shoulders, giving her a brief kiss on the cheek.

Questions ricocheted through her brain. Who did he watch? Did he love her? Something pinched Maryn's heart at the thought.

Maryn's questions fell to pieces as she registered the glistening of unshed tears in his eyes. The pressure in her chest increased. She'd barged in on him doing . . . something. A private moment she'd interrupted. "Arwan, I'm so sorry. I'll just—" She whirled to the right and stooped to grab her bag. In her haste to stand, she hit the back of her head on the underside of the table. China rattled. Her face erupted in flames. Her bag clutched to her middle, she raced for the door.

"Maryn . . . don't." The whispered words stopped her in her tracks.

She turned in time to see him drape the mirror once more with velvet. Solemn longing hung on him as heavy as a stone. Maryn wanted to both retreat and comfort him at the same time. She did neither.

Sarcasm and quips she could handle. Quiet introspection? She was a pro. Moodiness? Bring it on. But this? *A weeping god*? Maryn fumbled for something to say. For what could Death possibly mourn? But Maryn's heart knew the answer. She'd sensed his melancholy before.

"Why do you show me this?"

He paused, staring at his hands. "You asked me about my torment." He gestured to the covered mirror, his eyes dark. "And now you see."

Of course. Love lost. He'd understood Brigid's grief, for he'd lost a lover, too. Something sharp scraped against her heart and she winced away from it. She swallowed heavily. What could she say? She gripped her bag tighter. "Do you—do you want to talk about it?"

A pause. He shuffled on his feet, looking just as uncomfortable as she felt. "You asked me why I refused to reap your soul."

She scrunched her eyebrows, confused. What did reaping her soul have to do with the girl in the mirror? "You said I couldn't die because I had a job to fulfill."

"I did say that." He paused and licked his lips, his hand fluttering to his chin. The rasp of his hand against his stubble filled the silence. She'd never seen him in such a state. She held her breath, both afraid and ready for what he was about to say.

Her understanding of gods was comprised solely of their roles. She had no idea they wept, healed, *loved*.

Maryn's time with Cailleach, though brief, had filled her with trepidation and uneasiness. Where Winter was strange and otherworldly, Death was affable and so *normal* that she often forgot what he was. She rather *liked* him, as absurd as such a notion was.

She had to stay and hear him, no matter how out of her depth or inexperienced she may be. He drew in a long breath, his uncertain gaze pinning her to the spot. "That woman you saw in the mirror is my foster daughter." He paused for a moment, no doubt letting Maryn wrap her head around his words.

Maryn barely breathed. *Foster daughter?*

"I lived long ago, but it wasn't a good life. The choices I—" He paused, as if searching for words "—I hurt people for a living. I was a mercenary with a heart so black, I had no qualms in spilling the blood of children right before their parents' eyes." He shook his head, unwilling to meet Maryn's shocked gaze.

She held her breath.

"Anything for money. Anything to make people pay."

The pain in his voice broke something in Maryn. Tears pricked her eyes.

"My atrocities and love of coin secured my judgement. Soon after my death, I was given a choice: join the other souls in The Deep, or return and endure the same suffering I inflicted upon others." He gave her a quick, wry smile before continuing. "I've never been one for the sea." He shrugged as if to dismiss the details.

"The girl . . . her name is Lilah. She was mine for a time during this second life. An orphan I found. And while she was not my daughter by blood, she was the daughter of my heart. She . . . she died in my arms, killed because I was *afraid*."

Regret laced his words. Maryn's heart ached. His features softened, his eyes full of remorse.

"I was afraid to pick up my sword, you see, after the life I'd lived." He closed his fist, as if it held a sword there, his gaze as distant as the stars. "I feared that the bloodlust would return and I'd unlearn everything I'd endeavored to change."

His gaze seemed to plead with Maryn to understand. "I'd already been through so much, reforging myself, that when the thieves came, I didn't grab my sword and cut them down. I hid Lilah in the stable and went back to the house in an effort to draw them away."

Maryn held back, despite the innate desire to reach for the suffering man in front of her, to comfort him with soothing words and a warm embrace. To do so might break him from whatever spell had overcome him, but such intimacies might not be welcomed. Instead, she swallowed words and hugged her lumpy canvas bag to her breast.

His voice low, his eyes stared at some unseen place, lost in memory. "But what sort of thieves only search a poor man's hovel when the prize was in stock and a beautiful daughter?"

Overcome, a sound of regret fell from her. Tears spilled from her eyes.

"When I found her, it was too late." His Adam's apple bobbed as he swallowed, his eyes glassy with emotion. "In loving and losing her, I learned what it meant to lose a child. Like the countless children I'd stolen from other parents."

Maryn had no words. Any she might have said had been swept away by the rough waters of his memory.

His mouth tugged into a sad smile. He motioned to the covered mirror. "But, as you saw, she is happy with her real parents. She has a sibling. She laughs in the comfort of her hearth and home. At peace."

She could hold back no longer. Where words failed, human touch triumphed. Maryn dropped her bag with a loud *thunk*, and moved the step that separated them to wrap her arms around him. Her face pressed into his chest; his heart beat wildly against her cheek.

He'd stiffened at her abrupt touch, but then softened. Tentatively, he returned her embrace, a heavy hand falling into her hair. Gooseflesh erupted along her neck.

"I'm so sorry, Arawn." "Sorry" fell woefully short for what he'd lost, but Maryn knew something of such pain.

"I don't want another subject, Maryn," he said, his voice vibrating through her. "I need you alive. I need my . . . my friend."

Maryn's mind caught hold of the word, snatched it from the air and held it close. Warmth bloomed in her chest. *A god* considered her a friend. Not just any god. Arawn. More absurd yet, she returned the sentiment.

"Keeping you alive was a greedy choice," he continued. "Even now, after so long, I still cannot choose as unselfishly as you."

What could she possibly say to comfort him? After all this time—centuries, if she had to guess—and he still mourned the loss of Lilah. She pulled away, wiping her tears, and promised him the only thing she could. "I'll always be your friend, Arawn. Even after I return home."

Chapter Thirty-Three

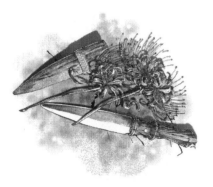

Soul Hunting

Apparently, her affirmation of friendship hadn't lifted his spirits much. In fact, his frown deepened at her promise to always consider her his friend. Had she said something wrong? Her arms fell away from him.

Wishing to distract him and lift the mood, she suggested they get out of the castle. "As you said, we have a bit of time to kill now, until you can arrange a meeting with the other seasonal gods. What are your plans for tomorrow?"

Arawn's dubious look didn't dissuade her. "Why?"

She shrugged, smiling. "Distraction is the key to avoiding emotions. This is beginner level stuff, Arawn. Welcome to Trauma 101."

He laughed lightly. "Distraction? How will that solve anything?"

Maryn's smile grew. "I never said anything about *solving* problems. Now, what are we doing tomorrow?" she pressed.

"*I'm* going hunting," he said, one brow raised.

Ah, of course. He was rumored to be very talented. Watching a master at work would be interesting, even if she had nothing to contribute. "Great," she said without false cheer. "I'm coming. What time do we leave?"

Arawn raised a brow. "You want to come hunting with me? Have you ever hunted anything in your life?"

Maryn shrugged, a smile pulling at the corner of her mouth. "Socks, lost keys . . . nothing so dramatic as venison, I can assure you."

Arawn matched her smile. "What about souls?"

Maryn faltered but did her best to hide it. No wonder Durvan called him a great hunter. He wasn't looking for meat—he hunted lost souls. "I . . . I'm a quick study," she affirmed.

His lengthy pause spurred her on to press her advantage. "It's just the sort of things friends do. Go on a hunt together, boast of their surpassing skills and mock each other. I might even be better than you."

Triumph lanced through Maryn at his bark of laughter. "How long has it been since you've done that?" she asked.

His smile changed as he considered her. "What? Laugh? Far too long, I'm sure." He filled his lungs and shook his head as if he couldn't account for her. "I suppose I do tend to be rather serious. It comes with the job."

Maryn lifted her chin, her hands clasped behind her back. "All the more reason to let me come. You can laugh at my attempts to hunt."

Arawn narrowed his eyes.

"Please?" she begged. She batted her lashes. As far as last lines of offense went, beguiling a god with ones eyes wasn't a strong choice, but she still held out hope.

"Oh, all right. You can come," he said after a moment of consideration, "but only if you follow my instructions. You can do that, can't you?"

Maryn shot him an affronted look. "I listen," she insisted.

He surveyed her with some skepticism, but she could see the soft smile he battled against. "We'll see about that."

She smiled, triumphant.

"Don't get too excited. Hunting souls isn't always easy. There are formalities that need to be addressed. Laws to be obeyed."

Maryn restrained herself from rolling her eyes. "I'm a scientist," she reminded him. "Rules are my bread and butter."

"Mmmph." Arawn held her gaze, his mouth pressed tight.

If she stayed any longer, he would probably change his mind. She ignored the impulse to touch him, to take his hand in a last-ditch effort at comfort. "Thank you, Arawn," she said, all teasing gone. She motioned to the covered mirror behind him with her chin. "For sharing."

Arawn's hand grazed the back of his neck. The weight of his eyes followed her out of the room.

The next morning Arawn waited for her outside of her chamber, his grey cloak effervescing as usual. "What's that thing do for you, anyway?" she asked, shutting her door behind her. "Aside from add to your overall, menacing charm."

Arawn looked askance at his shoulder, where a curling tendril of smoke met the air. "You don't like it? I find it rather dashing."

They walked down the hall, Maryn unable to account for her good mood. They were going hunting for a lost soul. A normal person might have misgivings over such an endeavor, but she could only feel the hum of anticipation. Then again, she'd never put much stock in normalcy.

"Oh, it's dashing in its own way, I suppose," she conceded. "When I first saw you, I found it terrifying." She made a show of looking him up and down. "But I suppose that has its own reward."

Arawn scoffed and pulled his cloak more securely around him. "I'll have you know that this shields me from the purview of others I wish to avoid. A handy tool when confronting wandering souls."

"And yet you wear it constantly. Avoiding people, are you?"

He smirked, his eyes glinting. "I'll never tell?"

She rolled her eyes. "Please," she drawled. "This is exactly why I'm coming along today, to add some life into your daily chores. Get it? *Life*. Because I'm *alive*."

He shook his head. "That's terrible."

"What? That was funny."

Arawn's answering look only made her more determined to make him laugh. "So where exactly are we going?" she asked, patting the pocket of Cailleach's skirts, to ensure she still carried her room key. He'd asked her to wear them for their outing, though he didn't say why.

She'd left the hammer in her bag, hidden behind the mountain of pillows on her bed. The totem should be safe enough, but she couldn't help checking her pocket every few minutes.

He made a show of looking her over. "I suppose you're dressed appropriately enough for where we're going. We're headed to the thirteenth century. Not far from here. A little village called Perthshire."

"Are we travelling via cairn again?"

"It's the surest and quickest way," he said.

Having descended the stairs, they walked the hallway that led to the great hall. The rich runner muffled their footfalls on the wide planks. "Tell me about this soul? How did you learn of them?"

Arawn nodded at a passing selkie, who, upon seeing them, stopped to bow. "He wasn't of a good sort. They usually avoid the call to the underworld. I sensed his passing and when he didn't come—" He trailed off.

Maryn frowned as she thought back to her own death. "I don't remember any pulling sensation after I died."

"You were dead for mere moments, Little Mortal," said Arawn. "Had you lingered much longer, you would have felt the lure of Annwn, I assure you. Some see the passage as a bright light or a tunnel. Others see nothing at all and merely find themselves outside of the black gate. This man, however, this soul we hunt is so full of rage and vengeance that I'm not surprised he ignored the call."

"Vengeance? Was he murdered?"

"Yes. And no," he said cryptically. "His death could be best described as a consequence for his ill deeds. A fitting end for such a one."

Maryn recalled the patient mercy she'd witnessed of Arawn at the feast her first night in Annwn. Arawn had been so calm and fair. Patient and forgiving. Her curiosity grew. He didn't seem annoyed at having to go hunt down this wandering soul as he'd previously hinted.

"So you enjoy hunting souls?"

Arawn bobbed his head from side to side in a very ungodlike way. Something about it endeared him to Maryn. The gesture seemed so *human*. "I enjoy getting out of the keep," he admitted. "I enjoy entering the human realm, but there are drawbacks. These souls are often rebellious and seek to evade justice." He cast her a look, his golden gaze touching lightly on her features as if to gauge her understanding. "All of the universe is governed by laws. If the wayward soul rejects the order of life and death and does not comply, I must act for them."

"How will we catch him?" asked Maryn.

A smile played upon his mouth. "Have you ever seen a fox chase down a rabbit, Little Mortal?"

She shook her head. "No, but I can't imagine it ever turns out well for the rabbit."

His smile grew. "No, it doesn't. I never fail in finding lost souls."

She didn't doubt it. "Am I in any danger?"

They neared the elaborate doors to the great hall. Even in the day, with the light streaming in from the windows lining the gallery, the floor sconces erupted to life. The mirrored, embossed tree glinted orange, the underworld sun and moon flashing.

"No, Maryn. As I've said. Others, living or dead, can hold no power over you save what you allow. Do not make agreements with the dead and you'll be fine." He gestured to the door. "You recall this, I assume?"

How could she forget? She'd been terrified the first time she'd been brought to this spot, not knowing what awaited her beyond. "I do."

"There is only one thing remaining," he said. Maryn met his eyes, expectant. Her stomach squirmed uncomfortably. Looking into his eyes, standing so close, seemed rather intimate, though she couldn't say why. "Close your eyes." His soft voice whispered across her, as reverent as a prayer.

Her eyes fluttered closed of their own accord. "I told you I could listen," she muttered, smiling.

She stilled as his breath fanned over her cheeks. Her blood began to surge as she sensed his nearness, far closer than what was customary or needful. His mouth pressed gently against her left eye, then her right. Shocked, still she held perfectly still, like a deer caught in headlights. Her sharp intake of breath was the only sound save for the guttering sconces.

He moved away and, after a beat, she opened her eyes, awash in the strange sensations he'd caused. Her face flushed and she stared back at him, thinking that he looked just as discombobulated as she felt. The dark stubble shading his cheeks and peppering the sharp line of his jaw couldn't hide the flush of his own skin.

"So you will see the dead in the other realm," he explained, not meeting her eye. His baritone vibrated through her. She suppressed a shiver. And then the spell was broken. Death knocked once upon the door, a crack of sound that jolted her. He looked at Maryn, his hand resting on the door handle. "Ready?"

Was she ready? Did it matter? "As ready as I'll ever be."

"Grab hold of my arm," he instructed, "and whatever you do, do not let go."

Could he feel her fingers tremble?

He pushed the door open, but it wasn't the great, glittering hall full of stained glass she'd seen before. Darkness pooled beyond the lintel, the air heavy with damp. She blinked as her eyes adjusted to the dim. Light from their side—Annwn's side—spilled into a room cluttered with stone and wood sarcophagi. Maryn gasped at the change.

"It's a portal," she said, her voice full of awe. "Can it take you anywhere at all?"

"Wherever there is a grave."

He drew a fairy light from thin air, the golden globe bobbing through the door and into the resting place of so many ancient people, whomever they were.

Maryn, no longer afraid after her first cairn experience, walked into the space, leaning close to the nearest of the carved likeness of a deceased person. She'd seen similar tombs, of course. Examples of these exact coffins littered parts of Europe, displayed in grand cathedrals. Here, though, the colors appeared vibrant and intact. No cracks veined through the paint and the gilding sparked bright under Arawn's light.

These would be nobles. No peasant would be buried in such a way. Maryn peered closely at the closest coffin. A woman: her boxy headdress correctly showed the time period of the high Middle Ages. Her hair, painted a dark shade of brown—maybe black in this light—shone the same color as her eyes. Her elaborate dress, full of folds of bright red and gold, fell from her pressed palms.

"It's beautiful," she remarked, looking about her for more details.

"You'll have to get under my cloak," said Arawn, distracting her.

Maryn froze. Under his cloak? She turned just as he lifted his hood to cover his head. She blinked at the sudden change his action produced. One moment Arawn was solid and immediate and the next he'd turned to mere vapor, melding into shadow.

"Woah!" She moved closer, though it did nothing to aid her seeing him. "How shall I—" she began, unsure how go about entering the very intimate confines of his cloak, when his hand, nothing more than haze, latched around her wrist. She flinched, staring at where she felt the unseen contact.

Her wrist was almost normal. Where he touched her, her skin looked slightly *off*, as if that part of her were underwater. He pulled her closer. The air stirred as he lifted the folds of material and, before she knew it, she was pressed against his side. The fabric, as light as smoke yet still tangible, settled over her. *Like stepping through a spider web. A lot of them.*

His scent surrounded her, rich and spiced. She took it in, a heady sensation fogging her thoughts. She shook her head and leaned away from his frame. Was sharing the cloak necessary? Couldn't she have her own so she wouldn't have to feel every part of his side?

"I'll shorten my stride to accommodate you."

"Er, thanks," she muttered, blinking at the change in the room. Everything from under the cloak appeared in tones of white, grey, and black. The sort orb light he'd created burned as a brilliant ball of flame, the tombs the color of an iron-grey sky, and the path between the coffins black as pitch.

"We are under a church," he informed her. "You mustn't speak. While the cloak is able to shield us from view of both the living and from the dead, it cannot hide your voice. There is no one above that I can sense, but there are people without."

His voice, low and intimate, thrummed through her. She lifted her hand to her face and waved it around. The breeze the movement cause rippled the draping cloak, but she couldn't see her hand. "This is brilliant," she said, smiling up at him.

Wide steps, most likely to accommodate the easy transport of sarcophagi, lead up to the chapel. The doors at the top of the stairs were shut but luckily well oiled, for they opened without a squeak.

As he'd said, no worshipers lingered in the church proper. The high, buttressed ceiling drew her eye. Benches lined the chapel on either side with an aisle between them. Sun shone brightly into the space, spotlighting the gilt instruments of the priests and the paintings along the walls. It was beautiful.

"Can we stay a bit and observe?" she whispered.

Just then the door at the back of the church opened and a priest appeared, speaking quietly to an older woman who took the stairs into the nave at a slower pace. Arawn's arm wound around Maryn's shoulders, giving her a start.

He cocked his head toward the door. *Now's our chance*, he seemed to say, and steered her toward the priest still standing at the opening, waiting patiently for his parishioner to amble up the stairs.

Moving together under the cloak became easier with practice. They walked in step, elbows and hips bumping.

The yard bustled with activity. A blacksmith's pounding reverberated across the space. Pigs squealed. A man with a wheelbarrow full of manure shuffled past. Maryn stared, transfixed at the surroundings—a working castle, complete with manned battlements. Knights dressed in armor walked the catwalks, laden with spears and bows.

Arawn leaned close to her ear. "Our man is outside the walls."

She nodded, lifting her mouth close so that she could not be heard between the rhythmic pounding of a hammer on steel. "Is he with his body?" Despite never hunting anything in her life, Maryn was curious about Arawn's responsibilities.

Arawn paused, as if searching for some sort of inward compass and shook his head. "No. His body lies in the forest beyond the wall. His spirit is somewhere in the village below."

Maryn loved the village. She stopped Arawn several times to simply watch people as they went about their day. They crossed a stone bridge spanning a swift river, banked with snow. On the other side, nestled amongst the trees, a quaint village waited.

A heavily wrinkled fish monger threaded silver-scaled herring over a fire, his fingers just as red as his nose. Young women took turns drawing water from a nearby well, wrapped against the winter chill in their arisaids. Maryn listened intently as they gossiped, giggling behind their hands.

A goat bleated, presumably wishing to be milked if the sight of its distended utter was any indication. "Quit yer havering, ye auld nan," said a lad of about ten. He tied the rope dangling from her neck to a post near the well and filled a waiting patron's pail for a coin.

Maryn could have listened and watched all day, taking in the homely tasks of a time gone by but Arawn nudged her with an elbow. "He's near," he whispered into her hair.

They found the errant soul in the tavern, just a stone's throw from the busy well. The building was two storied but small. The smell of unwashed bodies and spilled ale sullied the air. Maryn covered her nose with her hand, waiting for her eyes to adjust.

The low ceiling intensified the dim confines. Flames danced in fat, tallow candles atop each table. Benches lined each trestle, upon which patrons sat, scattered about. A cat dozed in the only window, grimy and unpolished.

Spotting the errant spirit wasn't difficult. He paced just beyond a table of soldiers drinking ale and playing a game of chance. The spirit in question was a large man with bowed legs and a protruding middle. His bald head shone dully in the torchlight as he passed back and forth.

Frothing with anger, he turned sharply as he came to the aisle running down the center of the room and sneered at the drinking men. He swore colorfully, his face mottled red with emotion, and glared into the closest soldier's face. "Imbecile," he hissed, a mere inch from his face. "Avenge me," he commanded, pounding one beefy fist on the table. "My body rots in the wood while my assassin lives free. Kill her, damn you!"

His words—and his strike against the table—went unnoticed. He pulled a fist back, ready to strike the soldier he'd verbally abused. His knotted hand sailed straight through the soldier's head. Maryn stared at the interaction and took a step closer to Arawn. Something about this man frightened Maryn, despite Arawn's assurances that the spirit could not harm her.

The soldier looked about him, muttering about a cold draft, then returned to his game.

Maryn followed Arawn's quarry with growing distaste. He'd said this soul was not of the good sort. Whatever this man had done, she knew it must have been horrific. To be killed by a woman in this time.... Maryn didn't have to think too hard on what sort of debase hobbies the rebellious spirit enjoyed.

Apparently realizing he would not get help here, the spirit moved through the wall, disappearing beyond her view.

Arawn's hand fell to her back again, a light pressure indicating they should follow. A shiver ran up her spine that she barely suppressed. Arawn escorted her toward the same wall the spirit had disappeared through. Did he mean to walk through the solid wood planks of the tavern? She stiffened as he ushered her forward. He didn't slow. Maryn tensed and screwed her eyes shut.

She would bruise her nose on the wall. Arawn still propelled them forward.

Cool air. Sunlight filtered in through her eyelids, painting the world red. She opened one eye. They were suddenly, miraculously outside. The weak sun shone down upon them. A breathless laugh tumbled from her. "How is this possible?"

The smug tone of his reply made her smile. "You did ask what my cloak could do."

"Can I borrow this?" she teased. Maryn rubbed the silken fabric between her finger and thumb. "You don't need it every day, surely."

"You'd have to be a very good girl to warrant using this, Little Mortal."

She felt the weight of his eyes but, coward that she was, could not meet them.

He made a motion with his hand to quieten her, though she'd said nothing, and gestured toward the street where two men made their way to the tavern. "This way," he whispered.

They followed the spirit easily enough, as he was still spitting curses and pulling at his clothes as if he'd like nothing more than to tear them from his form. They followed him some distance, the winter air sharp and cutting. They walked along the river and into the woods near the curtain wall of the castle. The spirit muttered to himself, making plans, promising pain and eventual death for his enemy by his hand.

Arawn slowed, laying a light hand on her wrist. Could he feel her heartbeat there?

Energy sparked between them, electric and alive. This was it. She could feel it. The spirit, too engrossed in his own turmoil, did not notice the change in the air. Arawn lifted his hands and removed his hood, exposing himself to the spirit. Maryn trembled against Arawn's side, her gaze fixed on his prey.

"It's past time for your judgement," said Arawn, his voice flat and without emotion. "Come willingly now into Annwn and accept the reward you've sown."

The spirit's wild, enraged eyes widened, then narrowed. "Who are you, to command me?" he growled

Arawn, patient as ever, said, "You know well who I am. I am the Unmaker, come to deliver you into Annwn for judgement."

"I will not, Unmaker. I have unfinished business here," hissed the spirit. He pointed at the stone wall, indicating that whatever or whomever he wanted was just beyond. "And I will have my vengeance."

Arawn shook his head. "No, Baldwin. Your business is with me, in Annwn. Do you come willingly?"

The ugly sneer changed, intensified, distorting his ruddy face. Maryn did not like this man, knowing in her marrow that his judgement would be severe. She hoped it would be over soon. She didn't know how Arawn could enjoy this. But no, he'd said he enjoyed leaving Annwn, not hustling rebellious spirits.

"Not until that *filthy bint* gets what's coming to her," he spat. "If I must be consigned to death, she'll be coming with. *I will have my revenge.*"

"You have no authority to make such demands," said Arawn, patient as ever. Maryn marveled at his forbearance.

Maryn couldn't take her eyes off the spirit. He looked as if he'd like nothing better than to run Arawn through.

"Refusing Annwn's justice will not go favorably, Baldwin," said Arawn. "Do not destroy your hereafter in the same way you damaged your life."

"What do you know of my life?" spat Baldwin.

Arawn knew everything, of course, even which tea Maryn preferred. She pressed her lips together, her breath shallow, wishing, despite the spirit's vileness, that he would listen.

"You will be *destroyed*, Baldwin. Do not do this. Come with me."

Baldwin sneered, his lip curling, and told Arawn just what he could do with his afterlife.

Arawn's sigh showed his regret. "So be it," he said.

Arawn turned his hand upward and folded his fingers toward his palm. A rushing wind filled her ears and then, quite suddenly, the ground heaved. The spirit and Maryn both stared in alarm at the rising, oblong shapes that pushed up against the snow, as if Arawn commanded the earth's crust.

The snow-encrusted heaps took on a familiar shape as green replaced the white. Snow sluffed away, revealing the mossy coat of Arawn's hell hounds.

"Go," said Arawn. "He chooses oblivion."

The two *cù sìth* rose from their crouches, twin growls reverberating through Maryn's body, their lips revealing needle-like teeth. The coarse hairs along their backs, reminiscent of spring grasses, rose stiffly.

The rage absorbing the spirit receded. His mottled face drained of all color, his eyes wide. Maryn felt something very similar, though she imagined it was all the worse for Baldwin, who held the monster's full attention.

He turned to run but didn't even make it a foot before the hell hounds leapt upon him, snarling and tearing. They took hold of the spirit, one on his arm, the other on a leg. They thrashed their heads, pulling him apart. Maryn couldn't look away.

The spirit's howls of pain died as he fell, the hounds tearing into him with abandon. Ethereal pieces of the hunted spirit flitted in the air like confetti before smoldering and turning to ash.

The *cù sìth* bayed and snapped at the few floating bits of Baldwin that remained until nothing lingered. The resulting silence was a heavy, living thing. With a start, she realized her hands were clenched around Arawn's bicep, her nails digging into his tunic. She forced herself to loosen her grip and swallowed.

"What did he do to deserve that?"

Arawn ran a hand through his hair. "He took from women what they did not offer, used unnecessary force, gloried the pain of others, and used his position of power to manipulate and abuse." He met her eyes, regret written there. "In short, no less than I."

Maryn wetted her lips, placing a hand on his arm. "But you chose differently, Arawn. In the end, you chose to make amends."

Arawn's gaze flitted away. "I'm sorry you witnessed that. They don't—this is a rare thing, eternal death."

Maryn took a stuttering breath. She wasn't necessarily sorry she'd witnessed the ordeal—she wanted to know everything about the afterlife—but she did regret the man's choice. *Choices*, she amended. In life and in death, he'd chosen poorly.

"What happened to him is permanent?"

"Once a soul refuses justice, there is no place for them. Their life is forfeit and their essence is returned to the world."

Maryn considered this new information, her brows raised. "Essence? I don't understand."

"Their make up. Their energy. In your time, you call it the first law of thermodynamics. Mortals in this time call it magic."

She raised her brows. *Energy is neither created nor destroyed, just changed from one form to another.* "So there is something worse than The Deep."

"Oh yes." He lifted a hand and the questing hounds trotted merrily to him. They sat on their haunches, purple tongues lolling. "Not much of a hunt, but still eventful." It sounded like an apology.

Maryn stared at him. *Not much of a hunt?*

"They like the chase," he explained. "If I have need of them, they tend to send the spirit on quite the chase." He shrugged slightly, as if to banish an uncomfortable thought. "This soul, however, would not see reason."

She'd only ever read about such people, those who would watch the world burn for pride's sake. "I didn't know. I didn't realize we were even given a choice in the end."

"Choice is everything, Maryn," said Arawn softly, "the instrument of life in both worlds."

She shook her head slightly, as if doing so could order her thoughts. She motioned toward the monstrous hounds. "Er, what now?"

Arawn removed the fold of cloth covering her, exposing her to the world. She missed his warmth immediately. He then lifted a hand, flat palmed, and the beasts rose, obedient to the slightest command. The hounds closed the short distance between them.

The closest *cù sìth* sniffed curiously at Maryn's limp hand, a cold, wet nose nudging her. She jerked her hand away.

"You needn't be afraid," said Arawn. "They're quite harmless."

"Harmless," Maryn deadpanned, her voice dripping with skepticism. "I just watched them tear apart a man. And, if you'll recall, one of these attacked Durvan and me in your borderlands."

Arawn made a sound of regret with his tongue, scratching under a *cù sìth's* chin. It groaned in pleasure, its eyes closing blissfully. "Not these. These are well trained."

"I see that," she said, grimacing. She lifted a trembling hand and let the questing *cù sìth* sniff her fingers again. The beast pushed itself under her palm, begging for affection. The green coat stood stiff in places, like the dry stalks of summer grasses. Underneath these, though, the downy sponge of moss met her fingertips. Maryn dug her fingers into it, scratching its massive head.

"See," said Arawn, smiling. "Nothing to be afraid of."

Maryn lifted a brow. "So says their master."

After a few minutes of doting, Arawn returned the hell hounds to the earth. They circled their resting places before lying down. Their green coats faded to a dull grey, then to white, as they sank back into the earth, leaving a smooth expanse of undisturbed snow behind.

Arawn turned toward her, pensive. A light glinted in his eyes she hadn't seen before as he surveyed her. "What do you want to see?" he asked. "We don't have to get back right away and I know how much you enjoy the history of your world."

Maryn stared.

"I know you're still curious. Or we could visit another time. Ask, and it's yours."

Maryn's heart skipped a beat. Clearly, as Death, he could visit any time in history if their present circumstances were any indication. "You mean it?"

He scoffed playfully. "Would I lie?"

How could she possibly decide? It would be like choosing a favorite star in the sky. Should she go back to the Ptolemaic dynasty to see the making of the Rosetta Stone? Observe the construction and purpose of Stonehenge? Or see the hands that painted images in the Spanish Altamira cave? Each possibility excited her, but she discarded each idea almost as soon as they surfaced.

The time and place she longed to see had nothing to do with world history or archeological discoveries and everything to do with the missing pieces in her heart.

Maryn found his eyes, knowing he would see the long hurt buried within her and, somehow, she was okay with it. He would understand her feelings, because she'd witnessed the same longing ache in him only last night as he'd watched his foster daughter in the glass.

"I want to go back to when I was five," she said, her voice soft. "To before my mum was sick." Her soft voice sounded frail even to her own ears. "Please."

Arawn's cast her a look that garnered his understanding. He didn't pause to consider or try and talk her out of it. He held out his hand, palm upturned, as he offered her the world.

Chapter Thirty-Four

Old Wounds

T HE STREET OF HER childhood home was not as she remembered, and not because she viewed it from under Arawn's strange cloak. Smaller and far dingier, she stared a long moment at the little pieces of litter that collected under the boxwoods that lined the walk. She'd forgotten how the tape covering Mr. Gutherson's cracked window peeled away and fluttered in the breeze as if waving.

She might interpret it as a friendly gesture, if not for her memory of the old man. His perpetual frown came easily to her mind. As an adult, she could make excuses for him. As a child, though, he'd terrified her.

"Are you sure?" whispered Arawn. "Sometimes the thing we wish for most only hurts us."

Maryn swallowed. She felt as though she were floating outside of herself. Surreal yet hopeful. *Was* she sure? Now that she was here, seeing this world view from a different perspective, she wasn't so certain. What if, after entering their little flat, she'd find that the colorful memory her brain had constructed was actually false?

Maryn stared at the yellow door, faded from the weather. She and her mum lived just beyond. Could she turn away now that Arawn brought her here? Should she?

"The choice is yours," he said.

Choice is everything. Yes, quite right. Her decision would hurt, no matter how she chose. Go in, and she would ache with longing. Leave, and regret would weigh her down. Either way, she was bound to go away with a splinter in her heart.

The wind picked up then, but Arawn's cloak didn't stir. The smell of spring poplars found her nose and her longing increased. She'd forgotten that detail of her childhood as well. "We'll be baking biscuits today," said Maryn. "Mum and I walked to the market. She must have spent the last of her pay on the ingredients." Maryn glanced up at him. "Of course, things like budgets are lost on five-year-olds." She laughed lightly. "Mum . . . she let me lick the bowl clean. I had dough all through my fringe."

Tears already close to the surface, Maryn wrapped her arms around her middle. "I want to see," she said, her voice barely loud enough to be heard over the wind in the trees. "I want to go inside."

Arawn nodded and held out a hand, gesturing for her to move first, allowing her to choose.

"I helped plant these," she said, pointing at cheery yellow tulips bobbing their heavy heads. "I loved the buzz of bumblebees when they went inside for pollen." She smiled, her eyes stinging, and blinked the emotion away. "Still do, in fact."

Arawn said nothing, his face a mask. Patient as ever, he waited for her to get up the nerve to press them through the door. She took a steadying breath and stepped into the solid plank of fiberglass, her breath held.

Immediately the sound of a spoon clanking against a glass bowl met them. A soft murmuration, a laugh.

Maryn inhaled slowly through her nose, trying to control her emotions. A blue loveseat sat under the picture window. Her favored stuffy—a cat called

Bonkers—lay discarded, next to her library book. They'd read from it earlier that day. A story about a frog if she recalled aright. She faltered, not ready to enter the kitchen just yet.

Her mum's red cardigan lay draped over the arm rest. Maryn picked it up through the folds of Arawn's cloak and brought it to her nose. She inhaled her mother's scent: strawberry shampoo and spritzed vanilla perfume.

She closed her eyes, soaking in her childhood home.

"Lovie, you're supposed to be stirring in the chocolate, not eating it all!"

Her mother's laugh broke the dam holding back Maryn's tears. They rolled down her cheeks, hot and quick. She returned the sweater and wiped at her tears with the heels of her hands.

Arawn placed a hand on her forearm, a silent question. She found his concerned gaze. *Are you well*, he asked without words.

Yes. And no. Her mother was alive. She smelled just as Maryn remembered. Maryn heard her laugh again. Everything should have been perfect at that moment, but the ache in her heart warned of impending pain. If she'd hoped to spare her feelings it was far too late for that.

And yet, she couldn't stop now. She might never forgive herself. Years from now—or even days—Maryn might regret running from the overwhelming emotion that clawed at her throat. She straightened her shoulders and cast Arawn a sideways look and nodded once. She was as ready as she ever could be.

The kitchen was more cramped than in her memories. The wood laminate countertop stretched only five feet from the sink. Five-year-old Maryn sat there, industriously picking out chocolate chips from the batter as her mother dug in the drawer for a spoon.

Even then, years before Maeve's death, she was ill. Thin and wan, with dark circles under her eyes from her medication, she still smiled, happy and fierce and brave. Bravery had come easier when she'd believed the doctors could help.

Five-year-old Maryn's favorite white socks with pink hearts peeked out from her jeans as she sat, cross legged, the bowl in her lap, perfectly oblivious to future hurts. Adult Maryn envied her. Her world was complete. Perfect in the most imperfect way.

Adult Maryn's watery smile nearly became a laugh as her mother turned, brandishing the spoon like a sword. "Thief!" her mother cried. "I will have my revenge!" Mum took a fencing stance, one hand on her hip. Maryn giggled and pulled the dough-covered spoon from the bowl. They crossed "swords," pieces of batter flying.

"Have at you!" cried her mother.

Oh, Mum's smile—there was nothing quite like it in the world. Maryn barely breathed as she drank in the scene, thirstily taking her mother in, committing to memory all the little things she'd forgotten. She was more petite than Maryn remembered; her dark hair shorter than memory served. Her green eyes, though, fitted well with Maryn's recollection. So much like her own, they sparked with promise as she forgot their spoon fight and started a new war.

Her mum swooped Maryn into a bear hug and pecked her face with kisses. "Nom nom nom," she said with each peck. "You taste like biscuits! So delicious!"

Maryn's squeal of laughter filled the small space. "Not the cookie monster!" her younger self cried, halfheartedly trying to escape.

Maryn's heart filled with such longing that it nearly choked her. She should leave before she broke down in sobs and alerted their past selves of their presence. Still, she lingered, unable to walk away.

You're past this already. But it was a lie. Maryn hadn't moved on. Could she ever?

Arawn's gentle hand at her elbow pulled her from her thoughts. Her mother directed the younger Maryn in spooning out the dough onto a baking sheet.

The time to go had come. If only she could bottle the smell, the feel, of this space, the love showered on her as a child.

She wrapped her arms around herself as Arawn's arm cocooned her against his side. They left the place as silently as they'd come. Arawn brought her to the empty park down the street, sat her down on the bench, and held her while she fell to pieces.

Some time later, as her tears slowed and his conjured handkerchief could hold no more, she croaked her gratitude. Maryn realized then, that the love she'd held for her mother—and her mother for her—had not been buried with her. It lived in Maryn's beating heart.

In her mother as well, in Annwn.

"You will meet again one day, Maryn, and the love you bear for one another will only grow."

Chapter Thirty-Five

Just Rewards

Ciaran wiped his sticky hand against his woolen robe, soiled with the woman's blood. It did little good as it was mostly dry now. He huffed in disgust, seeing the streaks of evidence all down his front. He hadn't noticed before in the commotion.

He didn't care for killing people, but the woman's'—Maryn's—wicked plans to harm Brigid could not be tolerated. She'd already done irreparable harm to Cailleach, if the weather was any indication.

Yes, he'd done right. The stolen blade would be returned to its place, keeping Brigid safe until they could locate her trapped soul.

To the woman's credit, despite his best efforts to loosen her tongue, he still didn't know the full truth. He grimaced, recalling her fervent cries. If The Morrigan had not warned him against her, he might have believed the woman in the end. He shivered and quickened his pace up the winding stair, thinking instead of what reward The Morrigan would bestow upon him or his faithfulness.

The blade in question thumped softly against his thigh with each step, a reassuring beat, as he walked the long corridor that would lead to Morrigan's council room. She was not expecting him yet, Ciaran returning at least two weeks early.

He knocked on the door. The motion filled his nose with the sharp copper scent of spilled blood. He wished for a basin of water to cleanse his hands.

A shuffling of feet, a muffled order—no doubt to one of her many attendants—and then the heavy door opened. A puka stood before him in a goblin-ish form, short and wide, with skin as brown and as warty as a toad's. Two canines protruded from an exaggerated underbite, as white as ivory.

It grunted, much like a pig, and turned, leaving the door open for Ciaran to follow.

"A magic seeker, My Lady," croaked the guard. "Come unannounced."

Morrigan appeared from around a purple velvet curtain, her brow scrunched in confusion, a short sword dangling from one hand. She wore a black gown, as light as gossamer, a bell-sleeved robe drooping from her shoulders. Ciaran diverted his gaze to the vicinity of her knees, to the glint of metal on the edge of her weapon.

In retrospect, Ciaran realized that he should have waited for an audience instead of barging in, but no one had stopped him. In fact, the keep seemed rather quiet and desolate. Ciaran followed the edge of the blade with his eyes. It curved wickedly; the wide, bejeweled haft was worth more than his life.

"What business brings you here, so informally, to my door, Druid?" She scrutinized him with black eyes, her confusion softening to one of understanding as she took notice of his bloodied attire. "Ah, I see you've been hard at work. Leave us, Grekel. It appears that our guest brings important news."

The puka changed shape, morphing taller. Its dark, bumpy skin smoothed out to a human's. It shuffled into the hallway, its heavy breathing overloud, and shut them in together. Alone. He was *alone* with the goddess of war. He might ask for any number of favors without witnesses. She'd be more willing to give indiscriminately.

Ciaran bowed, licking his lips, tasting iron and salt. "Mistress Morrigan," he said, rather breathless. He straightened and met her gaze. "I do, indeed, bring glad tidings." He pulled the knife from his pocket, holding it out on two flat palms.

Her eyes glinted with delight, a spark of excitement he well understood. He alone had fulfilled her wishes and well she knew it.

She approached slowly, her hungry gaze fixed upon the Blade of Somnolence. "Well done, faithful Druid."

The Morrigan removed the blade with her free hand, her avid expression never leaving the totem. "You're quite sure she's dead?"

"By my own hand," he said, straightening his shoulders.

The weight of her gaze settled onto him, one slight brow arched. "As I see." She placed the blade in the black bodice of her gown, her eyes never leaving his person. The green tinted hilt protruded from between her small breasts.

Ciaran suppressed the urge to fidget under her scrutiny. He bowed, his hands clenched. The Morrigan would not tolerate hidden truths. It would be better to confess all than to receive unworthy praise. Any gifts bestowed by the goddess might be revoked, and worse, should she feel lied to.

"I regret that I could not pull from her the location of the beloved Brigid. The girl . . . she died with the knowledge still within her."

Morrigan canted her head to the side, her face unreadable. "Tell me your name, noble druid."

His heart fluttered in anticipation. What further magical knowledge would she share with him? "I am called Ciaran, Mistress."

"Ciaran," she repeated, her smile soft. "A good name." She took a breath, her chest rising, and with it, the blade nestled in the fabric of her bodice.

His eye caught hold of it. He'd felt the power in it as he'd handled it, a magical hum of potential energy.

"Settle your mind. Tell me, have you told any of your brothers and sisters you found the knife?"

He shook his head. "No, Mistress. I came straight here."

She nodded, a pleased smile gracing her beautiful mouth. "Very good of you, Master Druid." She paced before him, then paused after a few steps. She lifted her black gaze to settle onto him once more. "Have the others in your order located Brigid's body yet?"

"I—yes, Mistress," he said, confusion coloring his features. What use did she have of Spring's body? "We have a long-standing friendship with Brigid and her court, so it took little effort for her subjects to accept our invitation of help."

The Morrigan's smile grew. "Perfect. Kneel, if you please, so that I might bestow my gift upon you."

Ciaran's heart raced as he settled onto his knees. He bowed his head, eager. He stared at the goddess's slippers, gold with shimmering gems of all colors.

"For your obedience," she whispered, just before the whistle of a sword cut through the air.

Ciaran did not feel pain, per se. The bite of steel came and then left just as quickly as his spirit rose from his body. His eyes followed the roll of his head as it settled a few feet away, vacant expression, mouth agape.

His life's blood surged toward Morrigan's slippered feet and dragging hemline. She stepped away, careful to avoid besmirching herself and called for her guard. "Grekel! I've need of you, Dearest."

The puka, apparently just outside in the hall, reentered. If he was surprised to find Ciaran dead, he didn't show it. "I need this"—she waved a hand at Ciaran as if he were spilled wine—"cleaned up." She handed the blood-smeared weapon off to her minion. "And this, if you please."

Grekel took the offering and bowed.

"A shame, really," The Morrigan muttered, "but it couldn't be helped. The other druids cannot know the knife has been found. Spring Court will want it returned."

"When will you kill the spring goddess?" asked Grekel. "Shall I rouse the army?"

Ciaran's spirit form stared between the two speakers, horror growing within him. He'd been tricked. Lied to. They all had.

"Hmmm," said The Morrigan. She moved to the velvet curtain she'd first emerged from and pulled it back. Hidden within the shadows was an iron cage, set atop a narrow table. Ciaran followed, the movement effortless. He only needed to *think* of moving and he found himself by the goddess's side.

A mountain hare turned snowy white sat within. He looked between the goddess and the hare. This was no ordinary rodent.

"No army just yet," said The Morrigan. "Spring Court will be mine, but I would not dominate them through show of force." She bent at the waist and peered into the cage. "Soon, Brigid. Soon I will free you from this form." She pulled the bone knife from the confines of her bodice. "All I lack is your body."

"What of the hammer?" asked Grekel, who busily wiped the soiled blade upon Ciaran's robes.

The Morrigan sighed and straightened. "We will find it in time. Cailleach's days are numbered. She will die with or without our claiming it." She shrugged. "We need only let nature take its course and be watchful."

Ciaran's mind raced as he processed the information. She held Brigid against her will. She, The Morrigan, prolonged winter, not the mortal woman he'd killed. The Morrigan, thanks to his help, now held the weapon that could end Brigid's life. But for what? Why did she want Spring Court—and from the sound of it, Winter Court, too—when she had her own kingdom to rule?

"When will we preform the rite?" asked Grekel. He placed the cleaned sword on a nearby table and considered Ciaran's body, as if trying to find the best way to dispose of him.

"Beltane, I think," said The Morrigan. "It's not far away, but it gives us enough time to further infiltrate Spring Court."

"Very poetic, Your Highness," said Grekel. "Will you rally your army, then?"

The goddess pursed her lips in thought. "Yes, perhaps it would be wise. Send half to the North Kingdom to prepare for my coming. The other half will remain behind."

She lifted the Blade of Somnolence into the torchlight, besmirched with dried blood. "I would be prepared should any other gods have grown suspicious."

Ciaran could not make out the puka's reply. A sound like the rushing of wind filled the room and a light appeared behind him. Neither the Morrigan nor her servant seemed to notice the glaring illumination. Engrossed, Ciaran stared into the golden orb, its beauty and warmth beyond anything he'd ever seen. What strange magic was this? And then it took him in, pulled him forward until he merged with the light. It filled him with such joy that he wept.

Chapter Thirty-Six

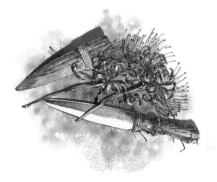

Verdicts

Maryn didn't think she could ever get used to a judgement day, no matter how long she stayed in the underworld. Once again, the recently departed gathered in the hall with little fanfare, brought to the hall by selkies and banshees alike.

Maryn walked to the hall, her mind heavy on Durvan and recent events, and stopped short at the sight laid before her. The usual dining table was gone, replaced by Arawn's imposing throne, white bone stark in the candlelight. A smattering of souls lingered at one end of the spacious room, opposite their judge.

Selkies and a few other servants loitered along the walls, silent witnesses to the event soon to transpire. While accountably interested in the goings on after death, she couldn't help but feel like an unwelcome voyeur. Maryn hesitated at the door then sidled to the left, wishing to go unnoticed.

One of Arawn's servants, Frenrick, approached the gathered departed with a tightly wound scroll. He opened the roll and called out the first name. A very young child—Maryn guessed five years old—stepped forward, shy and accountably nervous. The girl eyed Arawn with no small amount of distrust but instead of insisting or forcing, Arawn removed the skull headdress and stood, leaving it behind on his seat.

He approached the child soul with a smile in his eyes, his hand outstretched. "Come, Fanny, I won't hurt you."

The child looked about herself, as if searching for a friendly face to come and save her. After a beat, a banshee came forward from the sidelines and took her little hand. She spoke softly to the child and then, after some deliberation on the child's part, walked her to Arawn.

He sat on the floor, his legs folded, and beckoned the child closer. "Do you want to see a magic trick?" he asked.

Apparently, Fanny liked the idea of magic enough to release the grip she held on her escort and inched forward to stand before Death. He waved a hand to show it was empty, then turned his palm upward, blowing softly. A flame appeared, a dancing flicker of fire that grew legs and arms. The child's eyes, wide with delight, leaned closer. Twin flames bowed and rolled in her dark eyes as she watched, rapt.

"Again!" she cried, bouncing on her toes. Arawn took her hand, helping her to form a cup, and slipped the flame into her palm, which she promptly dropped. The flame hit the polished planks at her feet and dissolved into smoke. Her precious frown could have softened even the hardest of hearts.

Arawn smiled and waved a hand, whispering under his breath. An orange tabby kitten appeared at her feet. "Albie!" she cried, scooping it up. She kissed its fur, tears in her eyes. "My wee kitty, how I've missed ye so."

Arawn looked quite relaxed, even happy. "You've been a right good lassie, Frances Maragret. I'm proud of you."

Fanny nodded, agreeing that she was a very good girl, indeed. Maryn found herself smiling despite the circumstances. Somewhere a mother and father mourned the loss of their sweet daughter. Or maybe they didn't. Maybe she came from a broken home. Either way, Fanny would find happiness on the other side of life.

Maryn watched as the banshee that had escorted the child walked her back to the group. Another name was called, then another. One by one, souls stood before Death, reseated on his throne with his mask replaced. Sometime through half of the score of souls Maryn recognized him. She stiffened in shock, fear seizing her. *Ciaran.*

Maryn pressed a hand to her chest, rubbing where the druid had stabbed her. The site of the injury didn't hurt any longer, but the bite of the blade as it sank into her flesh, the agony of breaking bone and torn muscle, lived vibrantly in her mind. Her hand grew cold with the memory. They'd gone cold then, too, as her life's blood poured out of her with each beat of her heart.

Maryn wanted to melt into the wall, to flee to where fear did not grip her, but if she left now, he'd be sure to notice her.

The selkie called his name and he stepped forward eagerly, swiftly approaching Arawn's throne. For someone with murder on his hands, he certainly approached Death with confidence. The black eye sockets of the deer skull settled on Maryn like a weight. She knew what he'd tell her, were she close enough to hear him. *Be still. He cannot harm you.*

Maryn did her best to swallow her fear.

Ciaran fell to one knee, his head bent low. "Master of Death, Unmaker," he said. "I bring pressing news of a plot against Brigid."

Arawn stood and stepped from his throne. He circled the druid priest; the smoke curling from his cloak turned to flame where it touched the floor. What had ignited his robes? Was he angry?

Having walked full circle around Ciaran, Arawn stopped in front of the druid. "Tell me of this plot, druid, and quickly."

"The Morrigan deceived me and others within my order. She told us of a plan, perpetuated by a mortal woman, to undermine the seasonal goddesses. She claimed that this mortal woman stole Winter's hammer and took hold of Spring's blade." His hands trembled, his voice wavering. "To my everlasting shame, I believed this lie and took the woman's life, all in the name of saving

Brigid." He took a calming breath, his voice thick. "The Morrigan killed me and took the blade I won from the mortal woman."

Maryn's fear and anger changed shape. He'd been lied to and, as a result, murdered her to prevent Brigid's demise. Was he at fault? *Yes.* And no.

"The Morrigan," he continued, "she plans to kill Brigid on Imbolic, at the spring temple. I heard her speaking to her servant after . . . after she took my life."

Arawn didn't speak for several long seconds, his head canted toward the kneeling priest.

"You willingly took an innocent's life," said Arawn.

"I was deceived," complained Ciaran. "I only wished to save my mistress, Brigid."

"Ah," said Arawn, "but you have a new mistress now, do you not? The goddess of war does not value life so well as Spring, it would seem. How does a druid of the seasons align themselves with The Morrigan?"

Ciaran seemed reluctant to say. He didn't need to, Arawn spoke for him. "What did she promise you in return for spilling innocent blood?"

Ciaran's shoulders shook.

"It's a hard thing to see your life in the balance and find it wanting," whispered Arawn. Yet, his voice carried across the cavernous room. "Still, I know what it means to give your life blindly to the wrong cause. I would hear what your victim has to say on your behalf, if anything."

Arawn held out a hand, waiting for Maryn to respond. She swallowed her uneasiness and forced herself forward. The weight of fifty pairs of eyes followed her across the expanse, her footfalls echoing through the room.

She did not look at the man who'd taken her life. She couldn't. Not yet. Arawn took her hand, lending her strength. "This is your murderer, is it not?"

Maryn's eyes lifted from the polished floorboards to Ciaran's feet, up his body, to rest on his shocked expression. "Yes," she said. "That's him.

Ciaran crumpled to the floor and crawled to her feet, his fingers brushing the toes of her boots. He bathed the floor with his tears. "Mercy, Lady. I didn't know. I didn't know you were innocent. Forgive me."

Maryn's stomach tied itself into a knot. She took a step back. Ciaran's pleading turned to sobs.

"I understand that he felt he had no choice," said Maryn, squeezing Arawn's hand. Did Ciaran deserve to live out eternity as a lesser being, as a whisp of light? If she'd been deceived, would she want to be held accountable for what she didn't know?

There is always choice," supplied Arawn, his tone unfriendly.

Maryn expelled a shaky breath. Quite true, but how was she to choose? No matter Ciaran's violence against her, she had no wish to retaliate. "Let him serve penance as you will it." She released Arawn, her hands trembling.

"You prove your worth yet again," praised Arawn. He lifted the deer skull mask from his shoulders, his eyes flinty, and set it atop his throne. "Druid," he said, his deep voice commanding. "Arise and receive your judgement."

Ciaran stood, swaying slightly on his feet, his eyes pleading.

"You have a choice," said Arawn evenly. "You, whose greed overcame compassion, will live as a lesser being, a dark creature who knows no rest. You will die a thousand violent deaths, hunted and slain, only to be reborn. Once this penance is complete, you will return to me so that I might weigh your soul in the balance."

Ciaran's eyes flashed. He clenched his jaw. "What is my other choice?"

"You will live endlessly in The Deep with no hope of rest."

Ciaran's mouth twisted in anger. "That's no choice! I am a holy man, a druid. I've given my life to the service of the gods. Where is your mercy?"

Arwan took a threatening step toward Ciaran, who cowered away, his teeth bared. "I have shown more mercy than you deserve," he growled. "Make your choice."

Ciaran looked about him, as if searching for someone to come to his aid, to speak for him. "I—I don't understand." Ciaran addressed Maryn then, "Help me," he pleaded, staggering forward to grasp her hand.

Arawn stepped between them. Ciaran, in his haste, ploughed into Arawn then promptly fell backward onto his rear end.

"*Do not touch her*," commanded Arawn. My judgement is made. Which do you choose?"

"I—I will die a thousand deaths!" sobbed Ciaran. "I choose violence over endless Deep."

Arwan whipped around, the flames at the hem of his cloak spreading to his knees. "The judgement is finished. Leave me," commanded Arawn.

Selkies rushed forward, grasping a weeping Ciaran and lifted him bodily, half-dragging him from the room. Other souls scattered, frightened faces peering over shoulders as they pushed and jostled each other in their haste to exit.

Maryn alone remained, at a loss for words. What had just happened?

She moved to where Arawn stood, head bowed, a white-knuckled hand gripping his throne.

Tentatively, she placed a hand on his forearm. A tremor ran through him. "Why, Arawn? Ciaran wasn't half as bad as that soul we hunted. A thousand deaths?"

"No?" he asked, turning to meet her eyes, his brows raised. "You pity your butcher?"

"The Morrigan swiftly repaid his violence against me, in case you hadn't noticed. Besides, I've chosen to forgive him. Why the heavy-handed sentence?"

He sighed, the hard line of his shoulders deflating. He ran a hand over his face. "It's been a long day. The council I've called will meet tonight. I . . . I must go and refresh myself. Will you inform Durvan, please? Excuse me."

Maryn stared after him, at a loss for words. She stood in the middle of the vast space alone for some time, her mind full of questions.

Chapter Thirty-Seven

A Council of Gods

Maryn and Durvan entered the hall to a handful of Arawn's gathered servants, some of who had sailed on the boat and some from around the castle. A Dullahan, dressed in a black cape drifting in an absent breeze, stood at Arawn's right. The eyes in its detached head, held neatly in the crook of his elbow, followed she and Durvan as they entered. They stood in a wide semicircle around the throne, quiet and grave.

Arawn sat there, his gaze stormy. With an uplifted hand, he directed them to stand on the left side of his throne. Why must they stand so close? She'd much rather slink into the back and go unnoticed. She grimaced at the thought that he might wish for her to speak.

She trailed after Durvan, who walked with renewed strength and vigor, healed and whole. His return to health pleased her just as much as his oiled and braided beard.

Maryn stared at the throne's armrest, made up of what looked like actual radius and ulna bones of some giant. What sort of creature did these come from?

With a wave of a hand, the wooden planks between Arawn's throne and gathered selkies parted ways. A gap appeared, splitting the space in two. The selkies did not move; they did not need to, having carefully stood at the edge of the growing pit, roughly ten feet square.

Maryn gawked at the black mirror that lived just under the floor. Or was it water? A shimmer raced across the inky surface, like the flash of some fallen comet, there and gone again in a blink.

"We counsel with Brigid's and Cailleach's sisters," explained Arawn. "They cannot travel outside of their respective kingdoms aside from feast days, as you might be aware, so we must use the obsidian mirrors to communicate."

Maryn barely glanced his way, her attention focused on the glassy surface at the foot of the throne. "Why didn't we use this to try and communicate with Spring when I first arrived?" she asked, pulling her eyes away from the spectacle.

"Ah," he said. "The mirrors can only be accessed and controlled by the gods who own them. Without Brigid there to control her mirror, we wouldn't have been unable to make contact."

Smoke gathered over the obsidian mirror, a billow of roiling cloud obscuring the square space.

"Somone has accessed their own mirror," whispered Durvan.

From the mist rose a figure, life-sized and three dimensional, but semi-transparent. Like a hologram. The woman in the center of the mirror, curtseyed before Arawn, fog clinging to her, swirling around her knees.

Maryn stared, spellbound, at the goddess's beauty. From her looks, the goddess of autumn. A wave of auburn hair fell in loose curls around her shoulders. A crown of ripened wheat circled her head. Freckles peppered her cheeks. Plump and full ripe with life, Maryn thought her the most beautiful creature she'd ever beheld.

"Kerridwen, most wise goddess of autumn," said Arawn, his deep voice filling the room. "Welcome. Thank you for agreeing to meet this day."

Kerridwen's dark eyes took Arawn in, then Maryn. As unexpected as a mortal's presence surely was, still the goddess did not betray any feeling.

Next came another figure—no doubt Summer—rising from the swirling mist as soundlessly as a specter.

"Welcome, Áine, industrious goddess of summer," said Arawn.

Her olive skin, unblemished—*of course*—shone like the very sun radiated from within her. Maryn stared at her wild, wheat-toned hair, which fell in magnificent waves over her shoulders and down her torso. Her crown, a golden array of gorse heather, fanned skyward.

Maryn stared in rude fashion, amazed at the brilliance of these women—gods, rather. Of course they'd be beautiful. What would Cailleach would look like once restored to her full glory? No doubt just as radiant.

"It is not often we are called to converse with Death," said Kerridwen, her voice as soft as leaves drifting in a breeze. "By what honor do we meet?"

Arawn lifted a hand in Maryn's direction. "May I present Winter's Handmaiden, Lady Maryn Ferguson."

Lady. Maryn refrained from correcting him. She would not speak until asked to do so.

The goddesses barely spared her a glance as Arawn summarized the purpose for Maryn's presence. The women exchanged dark looks as Arawn told them of The Morrigan's crimes.

"Most contemptible," said Autumn.

Áine raised haughty brows. "But how can The Morrigan think to take the running of two seasons upon herself without retaliation?"

"I doubt she understands the toll of ruling even one season, Sister. Two would be nigh on impossible," said Autumn.

Arawn shifted on his throne. "I doubt she intends to control only two seasons," he said ominously. "Imbolc would call you, Áine, to the spring temple to perform the rites, would it not?" He didn't wait for Summer to answer. "I believe she will endeavor to strike you down as well. With Brigid dead, Cailleach will soon succumb. That leaves only you, dear Áine, who will conveniently arrive to the Spring temple as is your duty."

Áine scoffed. "She could not dare to dream up such a scheme and it go unanswered."

Arawn exhaled through his nose, no doubt striving for patience. "How else could she hope to resolve this plot of capturing Brigid? She must destroy all of you if she hopes to get away with her crime."

Maryn suppressed the desire to fidget and folded her hands behind her back. "What of Dagda? Shouldn't he stop her?"

Kerridwen scoffed at Maryn's question. She flushed hotly at the derisive sound. "The All Father does not insert himself into our lives. He appointed us to oversee the world and leaves us to it."

"Even if he knows of Morrigan's plot, he cannot intervene," explained Áine, sparing a glance for Maryn. She paused, pensive. After a beat she asked, "What do you propose, Unmaker?"

He sat back in his chair, his large hands draped over the skull armrests. "She would not risk such a bold scheme without the might of her army behind her," said Arawn. "Which means we must show up in kind."

The gravity of the situation fell over the occupants in room, a solemn burden to be sure. Maryn could have heard a pin drop in the silence that followed.

Finally, Áine stirred. "We have not warred for millennia. Nor counseled since Brigid's illicit dealings with her mortal lover."

"Shame, really," said Kerridwen with a pout, "that we only meet when trouble arises."

"If you agree,," Arawn said, pulling them back on track, "we will march into the Spring Borderlands and meet the war goddess as she prepares for the rite."

He paused. Maryn turned and met his gaze, finding concern in the tight press of his lips.

"And with our presence," he continued, "Winter's Handmaiden can then complete the task she set out to perform."

Was it regret she heard in his voice or only concern? Perhaps she merely projected her own fears onto him, but she rather thought Arawn sounded worried.

"You'll leave Brigid's rescue to a mortal, Unmaker?" said Áine. Even diffracted as she appeared in the scrying mirror, Maryn still found the goddess imposing.

Despite standing below the throne, Àine seemed to stare down her nose, first at Arawn, then Maryn, her strong arms crossed over her chest. Maryn didn't take offense; she had her own misgivings. She'd like nothing better than to stand by while someone else rescued Brigid from the war-loving Morrigan.

Arawn nodded, his gaze lingering on Maryn for a moment before sliding back to Áine. "She is Winter's Handmaiden, is she not? She will steal away Brigid's soul before The Morrigan can force Brigid back into her body. And you, Áine, who will come to perform the rite to usher in your season, must stay alive."

Well, that seemed simple enough. Nab the hare, with Brigid's spirit still inside, while Áine avoided certain death.

Maryn's trepidation grew. In her experience, straightforward theories rarely unfolded as planned. What if she couldn't find the cage? Or perhaps she did locate it, only to find it empty? What if they were too late? She could think of a hundred undesirable scenarios, never mind that she was likely to be the root of anything going awry.

If all went to plan, however, with Brigid's soul free from the iron, she could return to her own body and face The Morrigan herself—along with Áine and Kerridwen. And Arawn, of course. Brigid would reign, as she was meant to, and Áine would usher in her season. Cailleach, the poor woman, could finally rest. And, best of all, Maryn could go home.

She would miss this strange world, full of the bizarre and beautiful. She'd even miss Durvan's surly attitude. Maryn's gaze flitted to Arawn as he listened to the autumnal goddess's suggested plan of attack. He leaned heavily on the arm of his throne, his gaze intent upon the woman. Maryn would miss him, too.

"The Morrigan willnae let the opportunity to wet her blade with our blood go so easily," grumbled Durvan, pulling Maryn out of her thoughts. "She willnae simply concede, no matter how many of ye show up." He tapped the side of his nose with a blunt finger. "Mark my words, The Morrigan will meet our blades, and happily so. I only wish there was time to rouse Cailleach's warriors."

Maryn shook her head. Cailleach had quite enough to be getting on with at this point. Rallying troops ranked rather low on the list.

"Go to Cailleach," instructed Arawn. "Rouse her subjects to defend the mountain, should plans go awry."

Durvan bowed. He would not waste time obeying.

Arawn steepled his fingers, his mind working behind his eyes. "Let us meet The Morrigan at Brigid's temple. Áine's subjects will be responsible for mingling with the humans and protecting them while Kerridwen and I surround our unwitting hostess."

The summer goddess pursed her lips. She curtseyed, however, her heavy gaze lingering on Maryn. She fought the urge to fidget.

Kerridwen bowed, a soft smile pulling at the corners of her pouting lips. "A suitable distraction for Winter's Handmaiden, Unmaker."

Chapter Thirty-Eight

Confessions

THE NEXT FEW DAYS were filled with preparations, less so on Maryn's part—she tried to distract herself with books and when that didn't work, she walked around aimlessly, her stomach in knots.

While touring the hallways, selkies raced by, carrying weapons or armor, all industriously engaged like a hive of bees. Arawn had brought Durvan back to Cailleach via cairn, so he might watch over her mountain should Morrigan attack. Maryn missed the dwarf already, her mind lingering on Cailleach's wellbeing.

Maryn found her way to the great hall, focused on what the sun would bring with its rising. She played possible scenarios and outcomes in her mind over and over again, most of which ended tragically.

Her only hope lay with the other gods. With Arawn on her side, she had a chance, and with the additions of Summer and Autumn, they were sure to win. Even against such a formidable foe as a war goddess. *Weren't they?*

Tomorrow her adventure would come to an end, one way or another. With Brigid restored and winter finally concluded, Maryn could go back to her life.

Why then, did her heart feel so heavy?

The great hall stood empty save for Arawn, his eyes cast upon the stained glass windows. Maryn hesitated at the open door, not wanting to interrupt him.

"Feeling nervous?" asked Arawn, still not looking at her.

He half turned and met her eyes, a lingering sadness laced on his features.

"Of course I'm nervous," she said, moving toward him. Her boots rang on the wide planks, the only sound in the room.

She stood beside him, her mind full of questions and of half-formed thoughts better left unsaid. She'd come to say goodbye but couldn't find the words. The warmth of him radiated into her as she took in the beautiful glass. Her gaze lingered on the last image of the father cradling the dead young woman. It brought the imminent business of tomorrow into sharp relief. Who would Arawn lose? Thanks to the errant spirit, Baldwin, she knew the dead could suffer a second death.

And there was the very real and terrifying possibility that she would fail. Death itself didn't worry her after witnessing the wonders that came in Annwn, but the promise of pain certainly did. She rubbed the remade wound near her heart, the ghost of pain lingering in her mind.

"You'll play your part well," he said faithfully, with assurance. "You're Winter's Handmaiden, after all." He cast her a soft smile, though it didn't quite reach his eyes.

Maryn didn't bother to disagree. She lifted a shoulder in a half-hearted shrug. "I wish Cailleach had chosen a better candidate than me."

The wrinkles between his brows deepened.

"Or, if it had to be me, I wish that Durvan and I hadn't tumbled into Annwn. You'd be spared going to war tomorrow at least."

"I do not regret your coming," he said, turning to frown down at her. "The Morrigan's plans ultimately involve every one of us, god and mortal alike. This is not your doing." He looked away, drawing in a long breath. "Besides, I've grown rather fond of you, I'm afraid."

His confession sent her heart skittering. She didn't breathe for one long moment. She felt the same, of course. He'd become a wonderful friend. She'd miss him most of all, but she couldn't bring herself to say it. Her throat tightened at the thought of not seeing him again, or, at least, for as many years as she had left to live.

"Are you looking forward to returning home?" he asked, filling the strained silence.

She blew out a careful breath, casting him a wavering smile. "Yes, she said automatically. "And no," she added, unable to hold his gaze. She stared at a spot in the stained glass, as the weight of his stare bore into her. "We've had a bit of adventure together, haven't we?" she said, rubbing her arms absently. "Are you nervous, then? About tomorrow?" She dared to look at him. "You seem as jittery as me."

His gaze roved over her face. "Not nervous, though I admit I find no glory in war. Not any longer."

"Then what is it? Worried for Brigid and your subjects?"

Arawn didn't speak for long seconds, his features introspective. "The castle will be changed once you leave."

She gave Arawn an assessing glance.

"Who will tease me when you're gone?" he asked, his smile somber. He took a long breath, as if searching for words. "There are times I feel I could break beneath the weight of my solitude," he confessed, his voice soft, low, as if ashamed. "I fear that with your absence, the return to solitude will overwhelm me."

Her mind raced, trying to decipher some hidden meaning behind his words. Despite herself, hope swelled in her breast, then quickly deflated. The god of death does not form attachments to errant, mortal women. The sooner she left, the better off she'd be, for her heart teetered precariously on the cusp of spilling the truth the lay buried within her.

She followed his gaze to the last image painted in glass. His words came back to her in a rush. *This subject you see here so artfully illustrated, is burdened still, even in death.*

Still burdened in death.

That night, in his study, as he looked in his magic mirror, his torment had been made clear. She turned sharply toward him, her hand falling to his forearm. "Arawn," she said, her voice laced with the force of her discovery. "Tell me, is this—" she gestured to the wall of glass with her other hand, "—is this story yours? Is this *you*?"

Of course it was. How stupid of her not to realize it sooner. Maryn's heart ached for him. "This is your foster daughter."

How cruel. He lived with this devastating memorial to his sins, this monument to agonizing grief.

And she'd thought it beautiful.

"I wish I had a stone," she said, a tremor in her voice. "I would shatter it into a million pieces."

He huffed a laugh, a dark and fragmented jape at his own expense. "We cannot undo our past. Only learn from it. I made this. I alone fitted these pieces together. It is both my shame and my redemption."

She wanted to hold him, to comfort him, but she refrained, afraid of herself. Instead, she asked, "How long have you been alone, Arawn?"

"I try not to think of it," he admitted. "Counting the years only seems to hone the sharp edge of eternity. If I'm not careful, it can cut me."

Something broke within Maryn's heart, a neat snap of destruction that brought tears to her eyes.

"So you see, I cannot regret your coming and I fear your leaving. With you here, I—" He swallowed and reached out a hand to brush a lock of her hair behind her ear. "The burden of time has abated."

Her belly erupted in butterflies at his caress. *Just a friendly touch.* Despite her mind's insistence that he could only regard her as a friend, a seed of hope sprouted in her breast. It quivered, reaching for nourishing light.

But friends did not say such things to one another in her experience. Maryn pushed the budding hope away, burying it deeply amongst other dangerous thoughts. No matter how she'd brightened his life, and he, hers, the goal—Cailleach's goal—remained the same. Return Brigid to her throne and she would send Maryn home. Maryn *wanted* to return to her old life. Didn't she?

Despite her mind's insistence that home is where she belonged, a thorn pricked her heart.

His fingers lingered at the shell of her ear. Such a simple thing, this innocuous touch, but it burned her. "I could never regret your coming," he said.

Her heart stuttered, flooding her with longing. Her mind grasped for logic, where her heart would be safest. These words—these touches that melted the walls of her heart—stemmed from their mutual loneliness. Nothing more.

Against all odds and, just as notable, against all *logic*, they'd stepped cleanly over the invisible boundary of king to subject—god to mortal—and formed an improbable bond. She should celebrate it. It wouldn't end. She'd go home and live a full life and when she eventually died, she'd come back to Annwn to . . . .

An image unfurled in her mind of a mourning Arawn gazing longingly into his magic mirror as he watched his foster daughter. A daughter he loved and craved but could not have. Maryn's chest tightened.

When her death eventually came, she'd enter Annwn and happily rejoin her loved ones, separated from Arawn, who could only ever be a king and she, his subject.

After tomorrow, she would go home, and the tether of their friendship would be severed. The tender seedling within her breast withered and died.

She clenched her jaw, choking back disappointed tears. She'd mourn the loss of him, as she had her family, all her days.

She stared at him, wide-eyed, as the truth she'd hidden from herself, buried in her heart, surfaced. She didn't want Arawn for a season. She didn't wish to breeze in and out of his life. She wanted more. She wanted *him*.

The realization, like a bandage pulled roughly from a half-healed wound, bled freely. Her heart stuttered from the pain of him. How could she have not recognized her feelings before?

After ignoring all of her intuition and side-stepping caution, she had no one to blame but herself.

"What did I say?" His hand brushed under her forearm, searching out her hand.

She jerked away, reminding herself that her heart stood guarded for a reason.

"Are you . . . hurt?" The concerned look in his eyes only made it worse.

Had he hurt her?

Yes.

No.

She drew in a tremulous breath, tears far too close to the surface. "No, Arawn. You didn't hurt me." The words tasted like a lie.

He moved closer, his hands hovering, the uncertain concern in his eyes making her chest ache anew.

She turned away and placed a fist against her sternum, forcing the torrent of emotion swelling within her away. She didn't want him to see her shame. She couldn't do this, couldn't stay here, where he would witness her unraveling, but her head swam drunkenly.

She sat heavily on the bone throne, her face slack. *Fool, fool, fool,* the thumping in her chest echoed.

"I'm sorry," she said, running her clammy palms down her thighs. "I'm just . . . I'm a little anxious about tomorrow, I think." She drew in a breath and blinked rapidly, unwilling to meet his searching gaze.

Arawn crouched beneath her, his hands on the armrests of his throne, trapping her in his judgment seat. He peered into her face. Stupid man—god—whatever he was. He was too observant, too aware. Too *Arawn*.

"We have so few hours left, do not sully them with lies."

She tried to laugh, as if she didn't know what he meant, but the sound that escaped her was far too reminiscent of a sob.

He placed a warm hand over her bunched fist where it rested on her knee. "Do you think it's any different for me?"

Maryn inhaled sharply through her nose, her chin lifted.

Arawn shook his head, his tone softening to a mere whisper. "You can deceive yourself all you want, Maryn, but you can't lie to me."

Far too close, his scent surrounded her.

"Look at me."

Her breath hitched in her throat. Her heart tripped, a frantic staccato of warning. *This will hurt. You will never recover.*

"I love you," he said, his eyes intent on her face.

Maryn grasped his hand, his words a balm to the broken pieces of her heart.

"I'd forgotten, you see," he said, his eyes hungrily taking her in, "forgotten what it meant, what it felt like, to hope." His hand rose to touch her face, his thumb hovering over the swell of her cheek. He didn't touch her, but she still felt the call, the pull of him. She fought the urge to lean forward and press her face into his hand.

"I thought it was enough," he whispered, "the reaping and the judging. Ruling was enough. I was needed, wasn't I? But then you came." He faltered, swallowing his words. He shook his head as if to clear it. "When you came that night, into the great hall, and I touched you, I felt something." Fingertips grazed her cheek, her jaw. She pulled in a careful breath, her heart hammering.

His gaze swept over her features and lingered at her mouth. "But you weren't afraid of me," he said, astonished. "Do you know how long it's been since a soul has looked at me without fear or expectation or disappointment? Since someone dared to touch me? I can scarcely recall."

His words gave the hope living in her breast new life. Desperate longing surged upward, choking her.

He wiped a tear from her cheek. He stared at his thumb, glistening with her heart's fears. Something akin to awe entered his eyes. "You came and you awoke something within me. It was both terrifying and restorative, as if I were a flower who forgot I craved the sun."

More tears fell. Arawn swept them away. He stared into her eyes, intent and so full of feeling she found it hard to breathe. "It will hurt," she said, bringing a hand to her chest. Anxious energy coursed through her. She wanted to run, to stay, to fall into his arms. Nothing made sense.

"Love doesn't have to hurt, Maryn."

"Liar," she said, the word losing its sting for the tremor in her voice. She dared to meet his eyes. Of course, love hurts. He, more than anyone else, should know that.

"No," he answered, his mouth hovering mere inches away from her own. "Love sustains. Whenever you're near, eternity doesn't feel so heavy." His breath fanned across her skin, making her shiver. "I would give up my charge and diminish to nothing if it meant that I could have you for just one day. One day, Maryn, in all of eternity. Just one."

If a day was all they had, then she would savor it. Unable to suppress the urge to touch him any longer, she leaned into him, pressing her forehead against his. Immediately her blood raced, her spirit reaching for him. She drew in the scent of him, the heady sensation his nearness caused flooding through her.

She'd pitied him once because he'd shouldered his duties utterly and devastatingly alone for so long. She realized now, however, that she hadn't pitied him, but empathized with him. She saw her selfsame scars written upon his tender heart.

He stood, pulling her to her feet, and cupped her cheek. His other hand, warm against her waist, pulled her far too close. The wide expanse of his chest met hers, firm and immediate. Euphoric joy cascaded through her.

"Tell me you feel the same, Maryn. Tell me you love me as I love you. I could live forever happily hearing the words."

She swallowed her fear. "I do love you, Arawn." The declaration unraveled the tight knot around her middle. She smiled tearfully, trembling. A lightness filled her heart and mind. "I do. I think I've loved you for some time, but I was too afraid to admit it, even to myself."

In answer, Arawn closed the scant distance between them, his mouth pressing against her own, warm and tender.

A riot of sensation erupted within her. He deepened the kiss, the heat of his hands seeping into her back. Heady with disbelief and longing, Maryn wrapped her arms around his neck, pressing her body more fully against his.

"Again," he said, peppering kisses along her jaw, "tell me again."

Her fingers traced the swell and hollow of his cheek. "I love you, Arawn."

A glimpse of a smile. He stroked her bottom lip with a long finger, the barest of brushes, but warmth spread throughout her body, pooling in her belly.

Only one day, but a gift all the same.

Chapter Thirty-Nine

Hand Fasting

Some moments later, breathless from his kisses, Maryn's brain resurfaced. The great hall, vast and empty, felt suddenly far too public. "Let's go somewhere," she said. She ran her hands up the swell of his arms. "Take me to your favorite place. In all the world, where do you love to go?"

He thought about it for a second before casting her a mischievous grin. "You're sure? It's rather smelly, I'm afraid."

Maryn lifted a brow. "Of all the places in the world and in time that you can go, you prefer to spend time covering your nose?"

He laughed and gave her a squeeze. "Well, yes. Once you get past the body odor and the tasteless fare, it really is rather lovely."

Maryn laughed and shrugged. "When in Rome," she muttered.

Arawn's smile grew. With a snap of his fingers her tunic and trousers changed, glamouring her into a gown reminiscent of something from the sixteenth century, a great gold and wine-colored affair, her hair pulled up under a boxy headdress.

She lifted an eyebrow. "I didn't think there'd be costumes involved."

He wore red hose and a black doublet, unadorned save for a garnet studded belt. His velvet hat, a rather floppy affair, replaced his knotted crown. She held back her laugh. Barely.

"What?" he asked, looking mildly affronted.

Maryn gave his legs a pointed look. "I never thought to see you in tights is all. I think you pull them off better than I could."

He cast her a smug look. "They do show off my calves rather nicely, I think." He turned out one leg, pivoting on his toe to give her a better view.

She rather agreed with him. He did have lovely legs.

"Shall we?" he asked, holding out his hand.

He led her to the twin arced doors of the hall. They stood in the hall without, the curious-yet-beautiful tree sparking gold. "Ready?" he asked, smiling down on her. At her nod, he knocked five times then threw open the door. He led her through, into another church crypt, passing inert bodies wrapped in cloth and coffins.

Maryn barely paid them any mind, having grown accustomed to Arawn's manner of travel. The setting sun cut orange and pink across the horizon as they exited. She looked about them, taking in a hamlet of Tudor style buildings. People filled the lane, bustling to and fro. Despite the chatter and the rumble of a wagon that passed, the faint sound of music—a lute and a harp—reached her ears.

Arawn pulled her out of the way of a boy shepherding a gaggle of geese, tapping the ground with a long stick. "Where are we going?" she asked over the noise. She slipped her hand into his, reveling in the freedom to touch him.

He leaned close to her ear and pointed a short distance down the road. "To the tavern. Just there."

She laughed. "Of all the places you could go, you choose a tavern?"

He shrugged, unapologetic. "You'll see."

As they made their way down the lane, people tipped their hats in their direction. Because of the grandness of their clothes, Maryn had initially assumed she and Arawn to be dressed as nobility, but everyone else on the lane looked much the same as they did.

When Arawn pushed open the door to the *Sword and Scabbard*, the lilting music from the street grew louder. A person at the door greeted Arawn with a ready smile. "How blest we are tae see you again, Master Arawn," said the toothless man.

Maryn shot Arawn a look. *They knew his name?*

The patron's bow gave Maryn the perfect view of his shining skull, poorly disguised with a bad combover. Arawn spoke to the man genially, looking just as pleased to be there as the elderly host. "What brings ye tae our parts again? Got another shipment at the docks, eh?" asked the old man.

Arawn smiled. "Something like that."

"And 'oo is this fine leddy ye've got on yer arm?" He lifted his bushy brows. "I ain't n'er seen such a beauty in all my days, tae be sure."

"Arthur, please meet my lady, Mistress Maryn."

My lady. A nameless thrill raced through her.

"Ooh, and as fine a lady as I ever saw. And no wonder! What a beautiful couple the twa o' ye make."

Maryn couldn't help her smile at the mention of she and Arawn as a couple. For today they would be. She'd cherish every moment.

"What'll it be then, sir—uh, and madam," Arthur added, tipping a non-existent hat, his fingers to his wrinkled brow. "The usual table for ye this fine e'en?"

"Please," said Arawn. Maryn glanced at him, gratified to see him so at ease.

Arawn passed him a coin and asked for ale then escorted her to a wobbly table near the wall. Only half of the room was occupied with places for patrons, the other half cleared away. Where the tables and chairs had been removed, several stains from spilled drink marred the wide planks.

A young woman with blond curls escaping a kerchief brought them tankards in short order, smiling at them both, her blue eyes lingering on

Arawn's profile. Maryn couldn't blame her. Even in his usual garb, he was the most handsome man in existence.

More people piled into the room, some stopping to greet them, others with the singular purpose of finding a seat. The atmosphere beckoned her own sense of celebration, though she had no idea what was soon to happen. Soon, just as Arawn had warned, as more patrons entered, the odor of so many unwashed bodies made her eyes mist.

He pulled a handkerchief from his sleeve, magically perfumed; Maryn pressed it against her nose. "Thanks," she muttered.

Despite the smell, the festive ambience explained Arawn's desire to come to such a place, where he could be among common folk, who knew nothing of him save for his name and a pretend occupation. They would not ask about his comings and goings, only be glad for his coin and his company. He'd craved human interaction for so long and here, as fleeting as it might be, he got a taste of his old life.

A man in elaborate makeup and dressed in a flimsy dress entered the room from some unseen place. He swept in, batting his lashes. Another man followed, this one dressed in the extravagant vestments of a clergyman.

The room quieted immediately, a hush of expectation in the air. The first actor bowed.

A play. He'd brought her to a play.

"Welcome patrons. I am Lady Helena," said the man in the dress. "Drink plenty and toss your coin. Enjoy our play: All's Well That Ends Well."

Amidst a smattering of applause, the actors bowed and took their places. More players entered the scene.

"O, were that all!" exclaimed the fair Helena. "I think not on my father; and these great tears grace his remembrance more than I shed for him!"

Maryn leaned in close to Arawn, whispering. "This isn't . . . it's not Shakespeare, is it?"

Arawn's flash of teeth was answer enough. He smiled down at her. "Like it, do you?"

Maryn stared at the actors, absorbed. How amazing that she could witness such history. While she'd never really drooled over the famous playwright—she'd been far more interested in the sciences—she appreciated the significance of the event.

"I do like it," she said.

"The author is not performing, but I can take you to another time to see him in action, if you'd like."

Eventually someone brought a basket of bread but when Maryn reached for it, Arawn discreetly shook his head. He leaned in close, his breath stirring her hair. Her stomach somersaulted. "People in the sixteenth century aren't known for washing their hands."

Enough said.

After the play—a rather raucous affair where the patrons shouted throughout—the players bowed, then joined the audience. They drank together, laughing, some moving on to quiet corners, others starting games of chance.

"There's one other place I'd like to visit, if you're willing," said Arawn, his hand moving to take hers under the table.

I'll go anywhere you lead me. "Sure, let's go," she said.

Arawn bowed his exit, leaving a smattering of silver coins on the table for the owner, saying his goodbyes to those who called out to him.

They didn't return to the church crypt. Instead, they walked down the wide lane, hand in hand, the odd torch painting the way for them.

"How often do you come here?" she asked. "The people in the tavern knew your name."

He shrugged. "Not often. Only when I feel I must or be overwhelmed with my circumstances. My name is all they really know that's true about me. I haven't been in some time."

Maryn gave his hand a squeeze. "How nice for you to hear your name instead of a title. I can see why you come."

He gestured for them to leave the lane where a smaller path cut between two leaning buildings. The structures looked to Maryn as if bending close to eavesdrop. The narrow pathway opened to a meadow just past a stable and a chicken yard. A bell clanked from some barnyard animal, a doleful, homely sound.

They walked some way into the meadow, the cool night breeze lifting the fine hairs at the back of her neck. The village appeared as a distant smudge of the edge of a grey canvas. She shivered as the wind picked up, billowing her skirt.

"Look," he said, pointing up to the where the clouds drifted. They rolled away like a curtain, exposing the velvet night sky, studded with countless stars.

Maryn pulled off her hat. The Milky Way glowed pearlescent, a breathtaking smear of white light. With a wave, Arawn drew into existence a blanket and laid it in the swaying grass. They lay upon it, side by side, staring at the beautiful scene.

"This is the sky of my childhood," he said softly. "Before I left home, I would go on hunts with my father, brothers, and other men from our village." He drew in a breath, lifting an arm as if he could brush his fingers against the fabric of the night's canvas. "My father would tell us stories as we camped. Long after, even as a blackhearted mercenary, I couldn't look at the stars without a pang in my heart. They remind me of where I came from. Of my family. Of whom I once was."

Maryn said nothing. Turning to him, she propped herself up on one elbow. Despite his beauty, she could hardly believe him a god, not here, when he spoke in such a way. He was simply Arawn, her friend. *She loved him.* Her acceptance of the fact, so newly acknowledged, sent her heart to racing. She dared to reach out and twine a lock of his hair around her forefinger.

"I don't want tomorrow to come," she whispered. "I'm afraid."

Arawn's gaze locked on hers. "What is there to fear? You will not be harmed; I'll make sure of it, and if I'm struck down, then I will welcome the end of my reign and meet Dagda happily."

She frowned. She didn't like this way of speaking. "Cailleach said that if she died at the hand of another god, she wouldn't go to *Brú na Bóinne*. She said her soul would return to the ether, like that spirit your hounds destroyed."

All too easily the image of the ravaged Baldwin surfaced in her mind. She repressed a shudder. The idea of him falling in battle against The Morrigan seized her with fear. Clearly, he was prepared for such an event—an end to his rule—but what about her? What did that mean for *them*? Didn't their confessions of love for one another mean something?

Suddenly, Maryn's nose pricked with unshed tears. Confessions or no, nothing had really changed. Either way, no matter how the battle ended, Maryn would lose. Once Brigid returned—rightfully restored to her throne—Maryn would go home, but how could she live a full life with her heart still in Annwn?

Dying would bring her no relief, either. Once dead, she'd be his subject, and he, her ruler. She would have no place at his side, as a peer, a friend or lover. She would go to her family and live out her existence there, and as wonderous as seeing and living with her family would certainly be, it wasn't enough.

Panic gripped her heart. If Arawn died, she would have even less. There would be no promised reunion with him at her own passing. As fleeting as the event might be, it was her only solace, her only chance to be near him again. With his death, she would be judged by another.

If, by some miracle, she found a place in his service, working like one of his selkies in the afterlife, perhaps then she could be closer to him. The thought brought no comfort, however. How could she live so agonizingly close to him and yet never have him for herself?

Still, she could not regret loving him. She leaned in and kissed him, holding him close. He rolled to his side, cradling her face in his hands. Her legs tangled with his, her blood thrumming through her. A heady awareness prickled through her, a response to the hard line of his body against hers.

"My darling friend," he whispered, emotion heavy in his voice. "How well we fit together. Your heart and mine."

"Yes," she whispered, her voice full of feeling. Despite herself, tears gathered in her eyes once more. "Like I am a lock, and you are the key."

Arawn brushed hair from her cheek, their breaths mingling. "If I am the key, you are the treasure, Maryn. Every part of you."

He closed what little distance separated them, his hand finding the curve of her waist, the swell of her hip. Warmth erupted through her. "Arawn," she whispered against his lips. "How can I bear to be parted from you?"

He stilled, a quiet tension pervading his bearing. She could feel the breath held hostage in his lungs. "Then don't," he said on an exhale. "Stay. Be my equal. Be my queen."

A similar paralysis took hold of her. "But how? You said when Brigid took her lover to drink from—"

He shook his head. "I would not sneak you to Dagda's Cauldron like some thief. I would make you my companion, my wife. I would you bring you to the All Father and together we would make our declaration."

Maryn stared, her mind reeling. "You'd take me to Dagda?" she asked, awed. "And he'd, what? Just let me drink his magical brew?"

Arawn smiled at her description. "He would honor our choice and make you a goddess of Annwn, a twin ruler. Should this be your wish, you'd drink from the cauldron, just as I did, when I was made Death."

Maryn balked. *A ruler*. True, she'd pitied Arawn's perpetual duties, had bemoaned how unfair it all was for him to shoulder so much on his own, but she, a goddess? Laughable.

He stroked her arm. "It's not a matter of allowing, Maryn. What concerns the All Father is our choices—our *will*. If our desire aligns with the law, there is nothing to stop us."

Maryn licked her lips, her breath shallow. "But Brigid's lover—"

"Brigid broke Dadga's decree. She snuck her human lover into *Brú na Bóinne* and attempted to steal the Eternal Waters. Her lover did not wish to be immortal, never desired to share Brigid's throne. He couldn't bear to leave his home or his family. He didn't want what Brigid offered."

"So she lured him there under false pretenses?"

"Yes. Dagda could not allow it. He grew angry, of course, that Brigid would dare to deceive another in such a way and punished her. Punished all seasonal gods, really, since the new law forbade them from intermingling."

Silence settled between them as her mind filled with remembrances of her life's work, of what awaited her in Annwn.

"What of my family? Will I be separated from them forever like you are? You never see your daughter. What of your family?"

A shadow fell over his countenance. "My rule has not prevented me from interacting with them," he admitted. He faltered, glancing at Maryn then away. "Long ago, when I first became Death, I went to my father. I found him on the bank of a distant mountain lake. He fished there, with my younger brother, Amal." He found her eyes, a spark of shame lingering within. "He looked so peaceful and happy...but I remembered something he told me while living."

He took a careful breath, his eyes full of pain. "I came back, you see, at one point when my travels brought me near. When I came, I learned that my mother had died. My father told me not to seek him out again. He said that...he said I'd caused her death. I'd broken my mother's heart. I feared that he would not wish to look upon me, even in death."

Arawn's disgrace shone in every feature. He rolled onto his back, staring at the sky, his hands clenched atop his middle. "Why should any of my family wish to see me after causing them so much suffering? I can never go home to them, not even now."

Maryn's heart broke for him. All this time she'd thought him bound by some eternal law, some godly rule that separated himself from those he loved. Instead, he'd made his own prison, unable to forgive himself. "You never sought her out? You never...you never spoke to your family?"

He shook his head, his eyes screwed shut. "How could I? I was supposed to stay and take care of my family. I, the oldest, was meant to ensure my family did not starve. My absence caused much suffering. I failed them. I would not add to their pain now, when they are finally at rest."

Maryn scooted closer, her hand covering one of his fists. "Arawn," she whispered. "You are loved. Your mother and Lilah, they love you. Even your father," she added. "People say cruel things when hurt, especially to themselves."

Arawn's sorrow pained her. "How can they love me?" he whispered. "My life's choices sent my mother to an early grave and my cowardice took Lilah. They're happy without me. I've seen it."

Maryn licked her lips, searching for words. She placed her palm over his heart. "A mother that dies from the pain of losing a son will not reject him in the afterlife. You think she's forgotten about you? I assure you she hasn't."

A tear slid from his eye, rolling down his temple to be absorbed in his dark hair. His throat worked as he tried to hold his emotions under a tight rein. "What if she can't forgive me?" he asked, his voice tight.

"She already has," she said, her voice soft. "Forgive yourself, Arawn."

He turned his head away, hiding his face from her view. She laid herself against his quaking side, this weeping god, who punished himself. "You've been remade," she reminded him. "You're a new creature entirely. What greater gift could a parent hope for than a restored child?"

She felt his effort to hold his emotions in check. Maryn held him tighter. "You judge yourself too harshly, Arawn, so I will be your assessor." She pulled his face toward hers and wiped the wetness from his cheeks. His glassy eyes searched her own, both hopeful and wary.

"If you can read my soul, then I can read your heart," she said, her palms soaking up the heat of his face. "You're good and fair and patient. You're disciplined and considerate, and humble, and above all, Arawn, you are *worthy* of love."

He pressed his lips tightly together and he fell into her, crying softly against her neck. After a time, his quaking stilled, and his breath evened out. He lifted his head, the evidence of his spent tears coloring his face. She wished she could conjure a handkerchief like he'd done for her in the past. Instead, she offered him her squashed hat. He took it with a breathy laugh and shook it out, transforming into a tissue. He wiped his face, looking rather bashful.

"Don't you dare apologize," she told him. "We're all broken in one way or another. Besides, it's your turn, anyway; you've gathered me up enough times after having gone to pieces. The least I can do is return the favor."

He muttered into the handkerchief. She thought he said something like, "that's my job."

"Nonsense," she said, giving him an assessing look. "Being kind isn't a job. It's who you are, and I rather love you for it."

He stilled at the word. "I don't know if I'll ever grow used to hearing that."

He sighed and stared into her eyes, flexing his fingers where they rested at her waist. His lingering touch seemed to lay claim to her. Her body warmed, a pervading heat that found all the soft places in her heart. Her breathing shallow, she pressed her lips to his, tasting the salt from his tears. "I do love you, Arawn. You can expect me to tell you as long as I'm near."

"Then stay," he whispered. "I meant what I said. Be my queen."

Maryn's mind went to her lonely flat, filled with vacant distractions of work. She realized with a small jolt that it had been some days since she'd thought of home with any sort of longing. "Yes, Arawn," she said on a breath. "Yes, I'll marry you."

He laced his fingers through hers, his eyes gone soft with affection.

"Do we need to go Dagda or—or have some sort of ceremony?" she asked, a nervous serration running through her middle.

He kissed her softly, lingering, his hands tracing the long line of her arm and waist. "This is all the ceremony we need," he said. He sat up, legs crossed. Maryn followed suit, eyes intent on the small knife he pulled from his boot. He cut the fatty part of his hand, a line of dark blood appearing.

He held out the knife to her, waiting, his eyes lifted in a question. *Will you?* he seemed to ask.

Yes, she would.

She took the knife, biting her lip, her hand trembling slightly from the weight of her choice so recently made. The sharpness of the knife prevented serious pain. A lance of heat, a pinch, and her own blood welled to the surface.

He produced a golden cord, a gleaming, silken rope and took her hand in his, their blood mingling. Her skin heated as the cord wrapped around hands and wrists so that they were bound together, a spiral of light against their skin.

Handfasting.

She looked into Arawn's eyes, her smile growing. She loved him. And he loved her. She could think of no better way to bind herself to such a man, for Arawn was not *god* to her, not her judge nor her king. He was her heart's desire. Her best friend. Her equal.

"I bind myself to you, Maryn," Arawn said, his low voice curling her toes. "Your path is my path; your joy is my joy. I willingly take your sorrows, your burdens, your desires as my own. All that I have, I give to you in love and loyalty."

Some foreign energy surged through Maryn, an overwhelming sensation of warmth almost like static electricity that spiraled through her. She swayed, her head swimming. "What's happening?" she asked.

Arawn's eyes sparked with promise. "You are made my queen."

Maryn's breath stuttered from her. She repeated Arawn's words, the surge of energy peaking as her voice died away. Maryn thought she could run all the way to the spring temple for how euphoric she felt.

Arawn's breaths came fast. He pulled her to him their clasped hands pinned between their chests. His heart thundered against the back of her hand, a gallop of emotion she shared.

He unbound their wrists with a twitch, the cord slackening and falling away. Maryn pocketed it, the silken fibers slippery in her fingers. She'd treasure it all her days.

He kissed her, his lips soft yet possessive all at once. *Mine,* he seemed to say. She kissed him back, her head spinning.

Some hidden, unknown part of Maryn melted as he deepened the kiss, turning her to water. Her heart pounded, echoing through her body. The gentle press of Arawn's body brought them to the blanket, his chest's solid weight a comfort, a joyous exhilaration.

Maryn's hands mapped the hills and valleys of his arms and his shoulders, gasping as Arawn's mouth found her throat. Her fingers delved into his hair, an unexpected softness that matched his tongue on her skin.

Her breaths came short, her chest rising and falling rapidly as his hands charted the swell of her hip, the curve of her waist. He tugged at the laces along her ribcage as he found her mouth, loosening the ties that held her together. Undone. He'd undone her, body and soul.

When first they'd touched, that day in the great hall, the spark of his skin on her own lighted the flame in her belly. Such a simple thing, the graze of a foreigner along her palm. She couldn't have predicted then, how her body would react to his kiss, to the sensation of his breath against her skin. To the intimate press of his body.

Cool night air pebbled her skin, only to be calmed by his heated hands and mouth. With each caress, Maryn realized she'd been wrong. Before, she'd thought Death called her spirit to him, some accidental consequence he could not help. He didn't pull at her soul, as if he wished to collect it. No, her spirit reached for *him*, tinder searching for a flame.

Maryn, drunk on Arawn's touch and love for her, gazed at the sea of stars as she caught fire. They burned together, desperate and tender by turns, praying the sun wouldn't rise and tomorrow would not come.

Some time later, as the stars began to wink out of view as the eastern horizon's hue turned from black to grey, they stirred. Maryn lay over Arawn, her head resting on his chest, savoring the feel and sound of his heart. The night had passed so quickly. Today they marched to battle. Today either one of them might die.

Arawn ran a hand over her bare shoulder, warm under the cover of conjured furs. "I'm afraid we've run out of time."

Maryn pushed terrible thoughts away, unwilling to ruin the experience they'd just shared. "Let's run away," she said, only half joking. "But I suppose you're not type to run away from a bully."

"Neither are you," he said simply.

He wasn't wrong. With great reluctance they dressed. He banished her gown and gave, instead, simple clothes to be covered with lavish armor. He bucked the ties of her breastplate, tugging on the straps until her body swayed. Next came leather armguards lightweight and studded with polished steel studs. He knelt before her, securing protection over her shins.

He would dress for war once back in Annwn. Once finished with her armor he stood, his forehead pressed to her own, his hand cool on her cheek. "You'll do as we discussed," he said, though the words felt more of a question.

"I promise," she said.

"Be careful." He paused, the press of his mouth hinting at his worry. "Don't take any unnecessary risks."

"I'm too terrified to do anything outside of what we discussed," she admitted. Her hand went to his heart. "You promise me the same. Be careful."

He kissed her. "I will. I would do nothing that might separate us."

He pulled his cloak around them both, plunging the world into strangeness. They walked through the village, the windows dark and the road empty. She hugged his middle, soaking in the solid warmth of him, committing every part of him to memory.

Chapter Forty

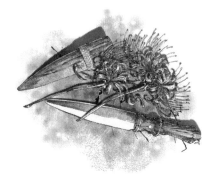

Spring Temple

If the war depended on which god possessed the more terrifying army, Maryn had no doubt Arawn would win. Maryn stood on the stairs just outside the great front doors, both shocked and amazed. *And a little scared, if she were honest.*

Two Dullahan commanders, set atop their fierce black steeds, commanded a battalion of six hundred creatures apiece, all set in neat rows in the field beyond the bridge. They controlled the cavalry, which Maryn was astonished to see included armored centaurs and shape-shifting pukas that couldn't seem to decide on what monster they preferred. Double headed dragons morphed into amalgamations of lions, wolves, and bears, parts intermixed.

Maryn barely breathed as she took in their strangeness. Other companies of fierce creatures marched past the stairs and over the bridge. Brownies, boggarts, red caps, dwarves, and even an ogress that towered over everyone. A smattering of humans, both men and women, painted with woad marched passed, much to her astonishment.

Some creatures covered themselves in what looked like plates of bone, lined with glittering silver. Their helms sported curling horns of sheep and sharp antlers of stags. Some creatures held flaming swords, others onyx bows. Maryn gaped as a line of selkies passed the stairs, their features changed. Gone were their human faces, black eyes notwithstanding; blunted teeth altered to conical points, perfect for shredding muscle from bone, their noses elongated to a muzzle.

They carried harpoons and great hooks, spears and serrated blades, all winking in the sun.

Arawn came after, speaking to one of his selkie captains. His armor, tightly fitted like the scales of a fish, did not reflect the light at all. Instead, it seemed to absorb the sun, like individual black holes, beautiful and formidable at once. They pulled her gaze, just as they did the daylight. He made a formidable general. Maryn thought him the most handsome man she'd ever seen.

The last of the marching warriors filed past the steps. Arawn separated from his captain, his gaze steady upon Maryn as he mounted the stairs.

"All is prepared. They only await my word upon the field."

Up close, the overlapping scales of armor, a swirling black in their centers, were ringed with orange light, like the embers of a fire, ready to be stoked and burst into bloom. He held a mask in his left hand, a replica of a skull, open under the nose and cheeks.

He bent his head, kissing her. She leaned into him, wishing for more time. Exhausted as they both were, she could happily return to the castle and spend the day holed away in his bed, sleeping and *not*.

"Come and meet your subjects," he said, an eager gleam in his eye. Something told Maryn that the announcement excited him.

He held her hand as they descended the few stairs to the oyster shell walkway and lifted Maryn into the saddle, his hands lingering on her waist, trailing to her thigh. His smile fell away with the weight of what was to come settled over them. "Stay close to me," he instructed. "And once we cross the border and arrive at Brigid's temple, I want you to wear this."

He opened her saddle bag, exposing the smoking folds of his cloak. "You'll be able to hide yourself from everyone. Even me." The hard line of his mouth told her he didn't much care for that detail, but she knew why he asked it of her. With his cloak, she'd be able to sneak into the temple and, if everything went according to plan, free the captured Brigid and—if possible, nick the Blade of Somnolence before The Morrigan could use it against Brigid.

"You've not yet tasted Dagda's eternal waters. Queen of Annwn you might be, but a god, you are not. Do not take unnecessary risks, Maryn."

If he died at Morrigan's hand, he'd turn to ether, absorbed into the world. If she died, she'd come to Annwn, a bodyless subject. Either scenario terrified her. She nodded and bent at the waist, pulling him in for one last kiss. "I love you," she said. "Don't do anything reckless."

"I am not so easy to kill as you might think," he said, and mounted his own horse, its great hooves stamping. And just like that, with a flick of the reins, they were off.

The horse's hooves chimed on the stones of the bridge. A horn blew as they crested the rise of the grassy field.

Maryn followed behind, scanning the gathered souls, a sea of helms and weapons, winking in the sunlight. They stopped midfield. Arawn's horse pranced sideways as he raised his fist into the air.

"Salute your queen!" he shouted.

Cheers erupted, a cacophony of sound that shook her bones. Thousands of weapons lifted into the air.

Speechless, Maryn bowed her head in humble acknowledgement. These were her people now. And while she knew nothing about co-ruling a kingdom, she felt a keen sense of duty settle onto her shoulders at the sight before her.

"This day," Arawn cried, "you serve your queen. This day you help to fulfill her duty to the goddesses Cailleach and to Brigid."

Another bone-shaking cheer filled the air. Arawn placed the mask over his face and he...*transformed*.

Every scale of his armor burst into a furious blaze, the smoke rising from the flames draping over him like a hooded cloak. His face...his face embodied the death of her nightmares. A gleaming skull with staring, terrible eyes. He surveyed the gathered warriors and drew his sword, a flaming double edged brand nearly three feet long.

"Justice!" he cried, his horse rearing, forelegs churning the air.

Arawn's vast army loaded onto boats. The Deep itself churned as if frenzied sharks swam just under the surface instead of countless damned souls. Their faces surfaced here and there, their mouths pulled into grotesque shapes, an unearthly howl escaping them before fading away.

Maryn dismounted her steed with Arawn's help, his gauntleted hands spanning her waist. She stared into his fiery gaze, both awed and frightened. This version of Arawn, this avenging god, fit so poorly with what she knew of him, Maryn couldn't think of what to say or do. She followed him onto the boat, her eyes fixed upon the disturbed water, her hand tight on the railing. She understood then, the danger of falling in.

"Why are they so agitated?" she asked Arawn, speaking up to be heard over their wailing.

He removed his mask and the conjured hood and fire instantly fell away. "They are bloodthirsty souls; they would fight if I allowed it."

Maryn blanched. She could just imagine a horde of shrieking, murderous spirits descending upon mankind and shivered. Were the other souls boarding the boats any better than the damned?

"An awful, bloody business it would be, too. They're undiscerning; they would kill whomever they came upon, or worse. They had no honor in life and have none now."

"Worse?" asked Maryn. She felt suddenly lightheaded and reached out for Arawn's hand.

"Death would be a mercy comparatively," he said. He gestured to the water. "The selkies are off." Hundreds of sleek seals swam, cresting through the black surface only to disappear once more, undisturbed by the spirits inhabiting the water.

Crossing The Deep took no time at all, what with the unsettled damned pushing them on, eerie wails making Maryn's skin pebble to life. Arawn's cloak slithered through her fingers as she prepared to disembark, her mind replaying her role. She wished she could stay with Arawn, but knew she'd be safer sneaking under his cloak, skirting around the battle, while The Morrigan was distracted.

Cailleach's hammer, safely secured on her belt, gave her added comfort. With Arawn's cloak and Winter's hammer, she could easily break Brigid free, or so Arawn told her. "The iron cannot withstand Cailleach's magic," he'd said when they'd gone over the plan again that morning.

Maryn remounted her horse and followed at a quick pace through the throngs of souls. Her horse, apparently accustomed to the strangeness of Annwn, did not balk as the warriors wound their way up the banks and into the forest beyond.

Once they crossed through the doorway—the same great tree she and Durvan used—the souls changed. Even her horse.

In Annwn, their forms were distinct as individuals, but in the world of the living, they resembled a roiling black mass of mist that churned and lurched across the snowy landscape. Maryn's white mount turned opaquely transparent, like a window misted over with fog. She could feel the animal move, sense its solid body under her, but she could also see the ground through it. A surreal experience, to say the least.

Watching the ground through her steed made her queasy so Maryn focused on the roiling cloud of souls instead. Parts of creatures, suggestions of horses, shapes of spears and swords within the great mass rose and fell away again, a strange fog spreading over the landscape. If looked upon from her periphery, Maryn could see them far more clearly, but even without a clear view of the warriors, her stomach clenched uncomfortably.

They were marching to battle, to meet the goddess of war head on. Summer and Autumn goddesses would come from behind, sandwiching The Morrigan's troops together. With any luck, The Morrigan would surrender. Maryn hoped so, though Arawn thought it unlikely. Apparently, submission didn't suit the goddess.

Arawn led the charge, Maryn following close behind. The ride was effortless, as smooth as if riding a cloud. They passed the small hollow where she'd died, skirted the village, quiet and empty of smoke. *Were its inhabitants at the Imbolc ceremony?* Maryn hoped not. Despite their mistrust and intended violence against her, she knew they'd been lied to. She didn't want them to be caught up in a god's war.

Ciaran had spoken true: Brigid's temple was a mere three miles from the village, and beyond it another span, lay the lake in which the water horse lived. Spring's doorway.

She and Arawn crested the hill first, the Army behind so as not to be seen. The temple itself appeared simple enough: an open-air rectangular structure made of stone, the roof held aloft by eight wooden beams, square and carved with runic symbols Maryn could not understand. From the hill upon which she and Arawn sat, Maryn could barely make out what looked like an altar within.

"Is...is there a body on the slab?" asked Maryn.

Arawn nodded. "Yes," he said, giving her a significant look. "It will be Brigid. Let's hope her spirit still inhabits the hare. She'll be easier to remove that way."

Worse than Brigid's prone form on the altar stone, however, was the mass of warriors and humans surrounding the temple itself. The amount of people reminded Maryn of a modern-day concert in a park. Bodies fitted close together surrounding a stage, difficult to disperse and nearly impossible to walk through.

Arawn's brow drew together, his eyes a cold a steel as he surveyed the people. "Áine is not here."

Maryn whipped her head in his direction. "What do you mean? She *has* to be here!"

They'd been spotted from afar. A rider galloped toward them, some sort of ghoul that Maryn could not name, skirting around the mass of the crowd.

Arawn swore softly under his breath, casting Maryn a dark look. "Cover yourself. Quickly now. We'll have to carry on without her."

"But—"

"You know what to do," he interrupted. "Perhaps she will still come. She and Kerridwen." The worry lines between his eyes told her another story.

Maryn's words turned to ash in her mouth. *Why hadn't they come?* Had The Morrigan preemptively captured them?

The time for goodbyes and last-minute kisses—for reassessment and deliberation—had gone. She slid off her horse and twirled the silken fabric of Arawn's robe around her shoulders with shaking hands. She gripped the hood in cold fingers, her eyes intent upon Arawn. What could she say?

He spoke first. "Go, Maryn. I will see you again soon."

She lifted the hood, her hands shaking, and the world changed from full color to grey, outlined in chalk. Maryn dashed away, one hand holding the folds of the cloak closed, the other pressing the bouncing hammer against her hip.

A selkie took up her horse as Maryn silently drifted away, the thunder of approaching hooves as fast as her tripping heart.

Chapter Forty-One

A Fallen God

Morrigan's army, even split in half, made up the majority of the inhabitants in the field. Maryn knew they belonged to The Morrigan solely by their armor. Overlapping bronze cuirasses adorned their shoulders, seamlessly intersecting with a sculpted breastplate. Black feather plumes erupted from the ridges of polished helms, some held wicked-sharp blades in gauntleted fists.

Amid the soldiers stood the surrounding human populace, laden with furs and blankets, giving the mingling soldiers wary glances. The snowy meadow surrounding the temple teemed with people, spilling into the surrounding forest. Maryn crept along, careful not to give herself up by breaking branches or sending snow flying in her haste. The wells in the snow from her feet could not be helped so she picked her way around the gathered crowd, giving everyone a wide berth.

The gathered humans, either come to celebrate the peak of spring or forced here by The Morrigan's soldiers, hunkered together against the cold. Maryn wondered about them. What did they believe was about to happen?

Were they confused by the spring goddess's body laying upon her own altar stone?

Maryn's eyes roved past the crowd back up to the hill where Arawn spoke with Morrigan's emissary. She wished she could hear. She wished the summer and autumn goddesses would keep up their end of the bargain. Maryn took a steadying breath, pulling the hammer from its leather loop.

The weight of Cailleach's totem comforted her. "Looks like it's just you and me," she whispered to the hammer. "Cut me some slack, eh? Words might not come so easy to me right now."

Maryn squeezed the handle tightly in her fist to keep it from quaking and pushed to the right.

A group of villagers, none that Maryn recognized, whispered together as she passed their small circle.

"It is as the druid claimed, The Morrigan heard our prayers and has come to deliver us."

"Deliver us?" said another of their party. "Look at all these soldiers. Who's to say the war-loving goddess is not the cause of Brigid's death?"

The last word seemed to echo in Maryn's mind. *She's not dead*, she told herself, and pushed on.

The going became more difficult the closer she got to the temple itself. She waited there, nestled in the trees, her breaths stilted. Maryn's inward view of the temple, while obscured by the pillars and the milling crowd, was still sufficient enough to see the goddess of war, surrounded by her agents, spears and bows in hand.

The Morrigan was fearsome, indeed. Even viewing the world from Arawn's cloak in greyscale, Maryn caught sight of long dark hair, braided and coiled atop her head. Her bronzed skin glistened in the weak sun. Her eyes shone bright, like twin fairy lights. She raised her hands over her head, thankfully empty of weapons. For now.

Maryn crept closer, hiding behind a haystack of gathered tree limbs and logs. "Hear me!" cried The Morrigan. "Death has come to claim Brigid!

Look!" She pointed to the crest of the hill, where Arawn's formidable black shape waited, a terrible silhouette against the grey sky. Morrigan's messenger galloped back, the crowd hastily parting for the horse.

The ghoul emissary dismounted at the base of the temple. Tall with abnormally long limbs and a protruding underbite, the creature loped up the steps with surprising grace. The humans shied away in fear, jostling others in their attempts to distance themselves. A baby cried, splitting the quiet tension that filled the air. Maryn forced a breath into her lungs. Where would Brigid's cage be stored? She strained her eyes, looking for any sign of it amid the columns and people of the temple, but could see nothing.

She couldn't hear, couldn't even make out what the creature reported by studying its strange, wide mouth. Maryn dared to creep closer, nearly tripping over a half-buried stump. A gasp escaped her, and she fumbled to catch herself. A man standing a mere five feet away turned around, his eyes swiveling from tree to tree to identify the source of the sound, no doubt. Maryn held very still and dared not breathe.

The man, distracted by the goings on in the temple, gave it up in short order. *Thank the stars for small favors.* Maryn kept her gaze on The Morrigan's face, searching for any sign of what she might do next.

The goddess's mouth pulled into a brief frown. She spoke to the servant, who then backed away, retrieving his horse.

"My beloved subjects," cried The Morrigan, moving from behind the altar to face the gathered crowd on the steps. "I hear your cries for winter's end! I am here to relieve your suffering!"

The messy pile of wood Maryn had just left burst into flame. She jumped, her heart in her throat. Seconds passed as she stared at the pyre. If she hadn't moved, she'd be badly hurt or dead. The intense heat of the blaze sent people scrambling.

Dozens of similar fires dotted the temple grounds. Maryn hadn't even noticed them before, so intent she'd been on the war goddess. Cheers erupted. Maryn used the distraction to edge into the throng, mindful of not getting too close.

If Brigid's cage wasn't in the temple, she'd have to search elsewhere.

Maryn dared wind her way through the celebration. The temple, simple yet large and imposing, loomed before her. The Morrigan's triumphant smile worried Maryn. She skirted around the foundation, waiting for a drunken man to unsteadily move away from the corner of the structure.

The creatures loitering around the back of the temple no doubt belonged to the goddess of war. They huddled close together, weapons drawn. One of the greyer beings, a horned, piggish monstrosity Maryn couldn't begin to name, moved aside, revealing a cage. An iron cage with no door, and inside sat a snow-white mountain hare, its fuzzy nose twitching as fast as her own heart.

A horn blared from the hill. *Arawn*.

People screamed and Maryn, forgetting caution, hurried around the corner of the temple base, intent to know what transpired. Where were Áine and Kerridwen? People would be slaughtered!

The sight of Arawn's charging army stole her breath. She watched in abject terror as the roiling, black cloud ate up the ground, war cries renting the air. Gooseflesh erupted all over her body.

An eruption of chaos followed upon the expansive field, a cacophony of noise that echoed in Maryn's belly. She thought she might be sick and pulled air in through her nose, forcing calm.

"He means to stop me," The Morrigan said from somewhere above Maryn, disbelief coloring her tone. "Oh, this is too much," she cried in delight. "Bring me my bow, Grekel."

Startled out of her anxious condition, Maryn turned back around, limbs quaking with adrenaline, and fumbled toward the cage. Only one grotesque guard remained, the others no doubt leaving to join or watch the battle.

Maryn crept closer, her eyes scanning the area for any hidden dangers. As she neared the creature and the cage, icy fear erupted within her heart.

What chance did they have against the goddess of war? If they did not bend the knee to their new mistress, they would die. Maryn's limbs trembled and her feet slowed.

The guard standing over Brigid's cage turned his head in her direction, yellow eyes, so much like a goat's, searching in her direction. Thankfully the snow, trodden as it was, hid her footprints. Still, the chill creeping up her spine told her she wasn't so well hidden as she'd hoped.

The creature sniffed the air, his piggish nose shining wet in the weak sun, eyes squinting in her direction.

The creature flickered, morphing into a dark shadow figure, humanoid in shape, save for its obscenely long limbs and jagged eyes. It reminded Maryn of a paper doll, holes for mouth and sockets torn away instead of neatly cut. The image came quickly, there and gone again. If she'd blinked, she would have missed it. The eruption of fear made sense now.

Puka.

She *hated* pukas.

The chill clinging to her bones increased as the creature loped in her direction. The closer the distance, the worse her fear became. Everything Arawn taught her about the creatures seemed to vanish from her thoughts, slipping away into fog. The fear of death—or Arawn's death, of Brigid's, her own—froze her in place. What could she possibly do against The Morrigan? Against her vicious creatures, one of which seemed to know exactly where she stood.

Screams from the field pierced through her thoughts, spiking her panic.

The goblin sneered. It licked its bulbous lips, its vicious smile exposing sharp teeth, perfect for shredding.

The hammer hummed to life in her frozen fingers, a tether to grounded thought. Arawn had taught her how to deal with Pukas. They fed off of fear.

The puka, nose lifted in the air, sniffed closer. "Come out, come out," it croaked, yellow eyes shifting over where she stood.

The hare—Brigid—sensed the chaos surrounding them and thumped warnings, brown eyes wide and staring. Brigid hopped around the bottom of her prison. *Thump. Thump.*

Maryn's heart echoed Brigid's warning, her blood pounding through her. Maryn lifted the hammer, thinking of what words she might use. If she opened the earth, the cage might fall in, right along with the puka. If she called down lightning, the iron would act as a conduit.

Pukas fear the light. Arawn had told her to shine. But here, in the sun, there was no literal darkness to dispel, only that which lingered in her mind.

"I'm going to tear your skin away from your body piece by piece," it promised, stalking forward. It pulled a dagger from its waist, horny hands flexing over the hilt.

It meant to scare her, to drive her fear. She couldn't let him. She saw when he would strike in the coiling of his muscles, in the bend of his knees.

The hammer sang in her hand, a current of electric energy that raced through her veins. "You can try," she whispered.

Static sparked, popping in her ears as she neatly sidestepped the puka, just as it thrust forward, stabbing the air. Maryn swung the hammer with all her might. The cudgel hit the side of the puka's face, splitting thick, rubbery skin with a sickening crack. Bone glistened white in black-green blood. It fanned over the snow, melting it with a hiss as it hit the ground. The creature quaked as if hit with a taser. It gave a guttural stutter of pain and then silence as it lay quite still.

Maryn pulled in a shaky breath, her skin a mass of gooseflesh. She stared for one long second at what she'd done and then surged into motion. She ran for the cage, not even trying to quieten her steps. She took it up, the iron cold in her hand. The rabbit thumped, turning in a circle, making the cage rock to one side. Maryn nearly dropped it.

"I'm a friend," Maryn whispered. "Cailleach sent me." Maryn hastened to pull the folds of Arawn's cloak around the cage so that it wouldn't be seen.

So close to the temple and surrounded by madness, it wouldn't be safe to open the cage here. Lockless and doorless, Maryn had no idea how to even go about doing so. Best to take it into the woods. There she could work it out with less likelihood of being caught.

Holding the burdensome cage made walking difficult, but she held on tightly, her fingers aching against the icy iron. The hammer bounced against her thigh with each step. As she left the back of the temple, the full panorama of destruction came into view.

People screamed, pukas fed on cowering humans, black shapes tearing at them as if trying to get *inside* their hosts. Pity for what terrible fears overcame them pricked at her heart. Arawn's soldiers battled against The Morrigan's forces, blades and bodies moving so fast they seemed only a blur.

As Maryn's gaze roved over the field of churning warriors, she saw Morrigan atop the temple steps, pulling a black-tipped arrow from a quiver at her hip, an ugly sneer upon her face.

Time seemed to slow as the goddess of war nocked her arrow and drew back the string, her eye trained across the field. Maryn followed the trajectory of the arrow with her eye. It was not difficult to spot him, a flaming god, skull mask gleaming as he cut through Morrigan's forces. His horse kicked and fought along with him, fiery eyes wild.

All the breath left Maryn as Morrigan relaxed her fingers and the arrow shot through the air, straight toward its target. It hit Arawn with such force that it knocked him from his steed. Maryn cried out as he tumbled backward, the flames of his armor winking out.

No. No, no, no, no! He can't be dead.

She waited, breathless, the edge of the cage biting into her middle. She searched for a sign of movement. He would stand any moment, injured, maybe, but not *dead*. His horse bucked and kicked and ran from the chaos, its scream renting the air.

Arawn didn't stand. She couldn't see him.

Maryn's frantic gaze whipped back to The Morrigan, a smug smile on her face. She said something to one of her lackeys, a boast no doubt. Rage filled Maryn, a surge of wrath so intense sparks sputtered from the hammer at her side.

She'd kill the goddess herself.

Without thought, without casting for the right words, Maryn set the cage down at her feet, the cloak hiding it from view, and pulled the hammer free from its leather loop. Thunder rumbled close, a bellow of her own outrage from the roiling clouds. They formed with a mere thought, a bruise upon the sky.

The players on the field stalled, everyone looking heavenward. Even The Morrigan faltered, a look of alarm entering her eyes.

"Cailleach has come!" shouted one of Morrigan's soldiers. Attacking pukas slipped free of their prey, morphing back into ghoulish warriors. Humans ran from the field, screaming, some holding children to their chests as they escaped the terror.

The wind picked up, pushing the cowl from Maryn's head, exposing her to the world.

Maryn pointed the hammer at The Morrigan, a mere thirty yards away, her teeth bared.

Lightning split the heavens; a spark of ozone permeated the air. The earth groaned and cracked, splitting apart like fresh ice over a pond. The seam in the earth raced from Maryn's feet to the temple, a jagged breach in the frozen soil that hit the steps with a resounding *boom*. The temple slid off its foundation, like a ship tossed by an errant wave. Those standing within cried out and fell as the structure settled its corner into the broken earth. Pillars cracked and fell, dust billowed up, obscuring the scene.

Had it worked? Was Morrigan dead?

Maryn forced breath back into her lungs. The chaos on the field died away, all eyes turned toward the temple.

Maryn couldn't see her. The temple steps, cracked and broken as they were, were empty. Maryn took a step, ready to investigate, to go find Arawn, but stopped short.

A raven cawed, fluttering from somewhere inside the temple, a ripple of green-black wings. It landed upon the stairs, now a tumble of crumbling stone. The bird's squawking increased, an incessant screech that grated on Maryn's ears.

Was this one of Morrigan's precious spies?

In a blink, the bird shifted and grew, forming a laughing war goddess. Her laugh resounded in Maryn's ears.

Hope drained from Maryn as fast as the clouds dispersed overhead. Morrigan, perfect and powerful, walked down the broken stairs, carefully navigating the cracked earth. She t*sked*, sparing a pitying look for Maryn.

Before Maryn could act, she felt hands grip her arms, pinning them in place as Cailleach's hammer was wrested from her grip. She'd been so busy staring at her failure, she hadn't noticed the goddess's minions sneaking up on her.

Another soldier pulled the folds of her cloak open, revealing the imprisoned Brigid. It plucked the cage from the snow, a smug look on its impish face, before obediently bringing the hare toward its end, to the temple with The Morrigan.

Maryn's captor pushed her toward the temple steps. She stumbled and ground her teeth, her mind whirring. She craned her neck, searching for any sign of Arawn. She couldn't see his forces. Perhaps they couldn't linger with him . . . gone. She, alone, stood between The Morrigan and the world. Cold dread filled her.

Maryn stopped at a narrow crevasse that had splintered sideways, a scant handful of feet from the steps.

"I can see your mind working. Don't bother, Little Mortal," said Morrigan.

"Don't call me that," spat Maryn.

"Winter's Handmaiden, then," she said, dipping into a mocking curtsey. She smirked. "I've won. Soon Áine and Kerridwen will meet their fates, but first, I have business with Brigid." She curled her fingers invitingly to the soldier bearing the cage, who dutifully hastened forward.

Together they climbed the fractured stairs. Maryn followed him with her eyes, desperation overcoming her. She eyed the hammer in the soldier's fist. Could she take him by surprise and win it back?

She paused at the topmost stair and addressed Maryn. "None of this—" The Morrigan waved a hand over the field of soldiers and the remaining humans, many of whom lay dead or dying "—could have happened without you, Handmaiden. Thanks to you and your lover's efforts, I have stolen away not only Winter and Spring, but now Death as well."

Despair filled her. Arawn was gone.

The Morrigan pouted mockingly. "Oh, I know how tempting he can be." She filled her lungs, a wistful turn to her mouth. "Delicious as he is—*was*—I can't blame you." Her eyes sharpened, the teasing leaving her. "I admit, I've never seen anyone spur him to such lengths as open war. Big on self-restraint, Arawn. I've never had the knack for it, myself."

She moved toward the intact altar, her black skirts billowing behind. The shrouded body—Brigid's body—still waited there, vulnerable. The angle of the tilting temple foundation forced her body to slide toward the declining corner, the edge of the shroud tucked tightly against her frame where she'd drifted.

"You, however," Morrigan called over her shoulder, casting Maryn an ugly look, "were the key. Not even I would have dreamed of winning Annwn. Who knew he had a weakness for plain, weak mortal women?"

The Morrigan stood behind the altar; she lifted her hand, addressing the crowd at large. "Beloved," she bellowed. "Hear me! I am The Morrigan, goddess of war, of death, of winter, spring—and soon—summer and autumn."

Maryn's stomach dropped.

The Morrigan's eyes flashed with triumph before settling on Maryn once more. "My other forces, whom I'd first thought to send north, changed directions. They hold Áine and Kerridwen hostage for me, even as we speak. No more must you squabble over which gods to serve. No more will you suffer the whims of the seasons. Now you will worship me alone, your benevolent goddess of life *and death*."

Chapter Forty-Two

Brigid's Blood

Time slowed for Maryn as she watched The Morrigan pull the snowy white hare from its cage. She held it by the ears in one hand. The hare's feet kicked, ineffectual.

"No," whispered Maryn. Her eyes darted from Morrigan to the hare, to the prone form on the altar. Maryn struggled against her captor, fighting and bucking. She got one arm free and struck some part of him with her fist. He grunted but his hold did not slacken.

"I wouldn't, if I were you," said The Morrigan, her black eyes narrowing on Maryn. "Not if you value your life."

Cold steel touched Maryn's neck. She stiffened, eyes wide. She breathed rapidly through her nose, a whistle of air that filled her ears. The knife pressed lightly against her skin, a delicate yet effective warning to keep her feet.

Despite Maryn's pervious death, and her reluctance at that time to reenter her body, Maryn had no desire to repeat the process, especially now that Arawn was dead. *He would not be there.*

Maryn didn't—couldn't—fight. She stared, horrified, as the goddess of war placed the hare upon the platform, just at Brigid's feet.

The animal housing Brigid's spirit kicked and fought valiantly. The Morrigan barely kept it in her hands, but finally managed to do so with one hand clamped around its delicate neck. "I could break you into a hundred pieces if you'd rather," hissed Morrigan, a wicked smile pulled at her lips. The hare ceased its wild behavior.

The Morrigan's soulless gaze settled once again on Maryn. "Pain is a powerful motivator, for men and gods alike." With her free hand, the goddess pulled a knife from her bodice.

The Blade of Somnolence.

"Do you know what this is, Little Mortal?"

Maryn curled her lip.

"I'll enlighten you, shall I?"

The hare twisted its head and thumped its feet. The war goddess *tsked* in a patronizing way and applied more force to the hare's neck. "Very brave of you, Sister, to try, but I'm afraid it's quite useless." She smiled apologetically at Maryn, as if to excuse Spring's rude interruption.

"Now, where was I? Oh, yes, this blade, as you might have discovered from using Cailleach's hammer, focuses Spring's power. Just as Cailleach can use her little tool to make and break the world, Spring can use this knife to sow life and healing. *I* will use it," she added, "to restore my dear sister to her body." She lifted twin, arched brows as if in expectation of applause.

Maryn glared then hissed as the knife at her throat twitched. Whether on purpose or not, the sting of a cut blossomed to life an inch above her clavicle.

"Careful, Dearest," crooned The Morrigan. "I'd hate for you to miss this. Enough talk, I think. It'd be better just to show you."

The stained bone blade Maryn had pulled from the earth so long ago hovered over the hare's body. Maryn's heart beat so hard she could feel it in her ears.

She'd failed.

Cailleach's hope in her had been for naught. Spring would die, then Winter. The Morrigan would control all the seasons and, despite only just meeting her, it didn't take a genius to work out that she'd be a tyrant.

Maryn forgot to breathe as The Morrigan brought the tip of the blade to the curve of Brigid's animal back. Maryn cringed at the same instant the hare did, just as the blade punctured the its delicate skin.

A breath fell from Maryn as she realized that Morrigan hadn't intended to run the animal through. The relief was short-lived, however, as Morrigan turned the blade this way and that, so as to keep the droplet of blood from falling and brought the knife to Brigid's still form.

A strained sound escaped Maryn's throat as one of The Morrigan's druids rushed forward to pull back the cover. Another took the hare and set it free. It ran, frantic, around the floor of the temple, then disappeared over the side.

Brigid was, in a word, magnificent, and not at all what Maryn had expected from the goddess of spring. Maryn had anticipated golden, flowing hair and skin as smooth as cream, something akin to drawings depicting Grecian goddesses. She'd assumed Spring as someone wreathed in golden light and surrounded by butterflies, someone so beautiful it almost hurt to look upon them.

Brigid was not at all like she'd pictured. Beautiful, yes, but she was also *plain*. Naturally lovely, like an unspoiled brook, bubbling over rocks or the first apple blossom opening to a watery sun.

Brigid's long hair, a rich brown, framed a heart shaped face. A crown of ferns adorned her head, and her face... it was *painted*. Maryn couldn't stop staring, as if trying to memorize every part of her.

In what looked like ash was drawn the shape of a leafless tree. The smudgy charcoal trunk started just under her lower lip and continued over her slightly hooked nose, the bump in its bridge only seeming to add to the artful adornment. Fusain branches sprang forth around her eyes and eyebrows, where they disappeared under the leafy ferns encircling her head. *The tree of life.*

Maryn had met Brigid once before, in a different time and in what felt like a world away. Brigid's skin had been well preserved then, but it had been free of whatever ritualistic drawing now graced her features. Still, she recognized the body she'd discovered, and it was with some shock that Maryn realized Brigid would die. The hope that, somehow, this goddess could overcome The Morrigan, died and fell away as quickly as ashes in the wind.

So much she saw, before the Morrigan held the bloodied tip of the knife to Brigid's inner forearm. "Blood is power, Handmaiden."

There was no twitch of pain, or outward indication that Brigid had felt the cut, no indication that the ritual had worked at all, save for Morrigan's triumphant expression. Her gleeful smile fueled Maryn's desperation.

The change happened in an instant. Where Brigid had been lifeless—breathing but unmoving—she was inert no longer. She opened brilliant green eyes then came up fighting, trying and failing to snatch the blade from The Morrigan's grasp.

"Treacherous snake," hissed Brigid, her voice a rasp, no doubt from long dormancy.

Her fingers in claws, Brigid raked her nails down The Morrigan's face and neck, eliciting a grunt of pain from her enemy. "Aye, blood *is* power, Morrigan," cried Brigid.

They grappled together, the two goddesses, both falling to the floor of the temple.

The hands around Maryn had grown slack, her captor engrossed in the scene before them. Maryn, eyes on the hammer, went limp, the full weight of her body pulling her from the creature's hands. Her fingers slid down the shaft of the totem and caught hold of the heavy cudgel. She wrapped her cold fingers around it, fisting it like a rock.

Maryn twisted and swung with all her might, straight at the ghoul's head. Pain from the impact juddered up her arm. It buckled with a cry. More of Morrigan's soldiers moved toward her.

Maryn's breathing came rapidly, her throat burning as she righted the hammer and swung. Her would-be captors shrank away from the sparking power that emanated from its head. A jolt of lightning connected with a soldier; he crumpled like a puppet without strings. The ground vibrated under her feet, the split in the earth widening. Some fell into the crevice, others fled from it.

A great *crack* rent the air as the temple's foundation shifted further over the growing chasm. It would swallow the temple whole soon, taking both Morrigan and Brigid with it.

"Drop it or I'll slit her throat!"

Brigid's green eyes registered no fear as The Morrigan held the stolen blade to her throat. Everyone froze, staring between the mortal woman and the goddess.

Maryn faltered, the hammer's vibration lessening. She didn't know how to win. Brigid was restored but held captive still. Arawn . . . her heart ached at the thought of him. Even he had failed against The Morrigan. How could she overcome such a foe?

Despair threatened to overcome her, but Maryn fought against it. She would die, but she wouldn't go easily. She refused.

She'd have her mum at least, and her grandparents.

She gazed at the spring goddess, so calm and serene before her death. Brigid was a part of her. Somehow, the goddess was the only living family she had left. It was preposterous, and yet she knew it to be true. Tears blurred her vision at the reminder of him. She blinked them away. She'd seen the flowers, borne from her own blood with her own two eyes.

She was a descendant of this god. She was Winter's Handmaiden. Arawn had told her so.

Maryn's chest rose and fell as she met Brigid's viridian gaze. The goddess blinked slowly, her lashes falling to meet her freckled cheeks, as if in acceptance.

"No," said Maryn, though it came out as a whisper. She recalled Cailleach's blackberry canes, twisted into useful objects and the flowers that had sprouted from her spilled blood. Could she, with the power of her inherited magic, coupled with Cailleach's hammer, defeat The Morrigan? She had to try.

Hands numb, the hammer slipped from her cold fingers to the ground. It thudded dully, like a death knell.

Morrigan's sneer widened. "Stupid Mortal. Now you've got no chance."

Maryn crouched and pulled Durvan's gifted knife from her boot. In one swift motion, she sliced open her palm and fisted her fingers. Blood drip-dripped onto the snow.

Brigid smiled. The Morrigan laughed.

Maryn swept up the hammer, her bloody hand slipping over the bone handle. "Grow!" she commanded.

Blackberry canes twined from the ground, supple and green, an unfurling of life, but it was not enough. They grew too slow.

Morrigan's shocked gaze hardened as she realized just who Maryn was. In one swift motion, Morrigan swept her blade across Brigid's neck.

Blood poured from Brigid in a pulsing river as she fell onto the steps. It pooled on the stone and ran over the edge into the snow.

A cry rent Maryn's throat. "No!"

Spring sputtered and gasped, her eyes still focused on Maryn. It was all too terrible to watch, yet she couldn't look away, wouldn't look away, as her life's blood soaked the earth.

Dark, twisting brambles and clutching vines sprang from the ground where Brigid's blood pooled. A noise like thunder filled Maryn's ears and the ground trembled under her feet at the force of the vine's eruption.

They twined and snaked into the sky, partially obscuring Brigid and Morrigan. Maryn peered through the brambles.

"No!" screamed Morrigan, as a prickly vine wound itself around her wrist. She slashed at a questing bramble as it climbed her leg with the ritual blade. It cut through the bramble but did not wither and fall away. From its lower leaves, a new stalk emerged, undulating toward Morrigan's face.

She screamed and slashed and kicked, but her movements slowed as the vines overtook her. Her lower half was nothing but vicious, writhing creepers, like hundreds of constricting snakes. Another vine wreathed her neck and tightened.

"Curse you," Morrigan spat, lifting her chin as though to escape the runners from entering her mouth and nose. She gasped, her eyes wide and feral. She looked at Maryn, staring open mouthed a short distance away.

The sight horrified Maryn.

Morrigan's face twisted in hatred. She jerked and pulled, but her hands were held tightly by Brigid's plants, outstretched as if in welcome. "Curse you!" she repeated, venom on her tongue. "Kill her!" she demanded, but her subjects did not come closer. They stared, as Maryn did, at the end of the goddess of war.

Maryn looked away as tendrils of creepers entered the goddess's open mouth and up her nose. Maryn closed her eyes and covered her ears to block out Morrigan's muffled, gagging scream. It didn't help. She could still hear her dying howl and the crack of bone as the vines crushed her.

She glanced back, just in time to see the blade fall free from Morrigan's lily-white hand, the only part of her not covered in writhing plant life.

A rumble filled the air as the temple, unable to withstand gravity, fell into the earth. The steps were all that remained.

Chapter Forty-Three

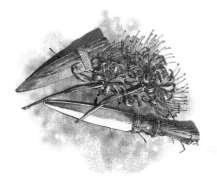

Dagda

The resounding silence hung in the air like a living thing, pressing in on Maryn's ears.

She sank to her knees, her strength borne from adrenalin spent. She spared no thought for her own life. Any of the remaining soldiers could easily capture her and she would not care.

She didn't know how long she sat there in the snow, shivering, staring at the crumpled temple. Again and again her gaze traced the jagged line of the rent she'd formed with Cailleach's hammer, stopping just short of Morrigan's suspended body.

Her own little blackberry cane withered in the cold, the green of its leaves curling black at the edges. How long before the world froze over? With Spring gone, Cailleach had no hope at all of recovery.

A crunch of feet in the snow from behind pulled her from her thoughts. The fight gone in her, she welcomed the blade of whomever approached. She was ready.

The sharp sting of a blade did not come. The snow stirred around her and then a man sat beside her, cross legged. A big man, much larger than any she'd ever seen, with thick red hair and a braided beard. A gnarled and battered club rested across his knees, the grip bound with leather. Where had he come from? She hadn't seen him in the thick of the battle, not that she'd had much attention to spare.

He stared at the hole in the ground, at the crumpled temple, and the dead goddesses. The wet tracks of tears tracing his cheeks awoke some human part of her. She patted the man's arm.

"I couldn't stop her," she said. "I tried."

The man wiped at his nose with the back of his hand and nodded. "I know it. I tried, too." He shook his head. "Not easy to influence, The Morrigan."

His words pricked alarm. Maryn eyed him warily. Was he one of her druids? Another puka, tricking her with a human form?

"Be at ease," said the man with a dismissive wave. "I'm neither of those things."

Maryn stood, finding that she could still find strength in caution. If he could read her mind, then he must be a god. "Who are you?" she demanded.

The man's gaze lifted to her eyes, brown and somber. "I am Dagda, the All Father. I've come to send you home."

Maryn's fear deflated. The All Father himself. She didn't have the energy to be awestruck. She stared down at him, anger bubbling up from the recesses of her exhausted self.

"You don't want to go home?"

"I have no home, thanks to you," she said, bitterness lacing her words.

He lifted ginger brows.

Maryn unclenched her jaw and blinked tears away. "Why didn't you stop her?" she asked, thrusting a finger in The Morrigan's direction. "If you knew about her plans, about Brigid's capture, about *me*, why didn't you do a damn thing to stop it? Don't you care that they're dead, that Arawn—" Maryn's voice cut off as emotion filled her throat, a knot of misery she couldn't swallow away.

Dagda looked away, staring at the goddess's ruined bodies. "Of course I care," he said. "I made them and loved them. I watched them grow." His gaze found her once more, grief written in his eyes. "But I do not control my creations, Maryn."

She scoffed. "More laws."

Dagda sighed. "I am bound by them. I cannot stop anyone, no matter how terrible their choices. I can only inspire. Influence."

"Well, it didn't work," she said, sitting heavily beside him. Her fatigue made holding her anger impossible. It leaked from her like water through a sieve.

They were silent for long seconds, Maryn's knees gathered up to her chest.

"If you don't wish to return to your time, what of Annwn? You've a family there. Life goes on."

Grief weighed her down. She saw, in her mind, the arrow striking Arawn with such violent force that it threw him from his horse. "Yes," she agreed thickly. "Life has a way of doing that." The whole of her life was one great lesson on how little the world pitied the broken. Life continued, even when there was nothing left worth living for.

The wind picked up. It lifted Arawn's cloak away from her body, making her shiver. She pulled it tighter and pressed her nose to the cloth, breathing in the familiar scent of him. It only made her heart ache all the more.

"I've got a bit of a problem," said Dagda.

Maryn suppressed a hollow laugh. *He had problems?*

"I've lost two of my daughters here." He shook his head as he gazed upon their broken bodies, gruesome and bloody. "Worse, I've a son, who tells me he wishes to relinquish his godhood to live with a mortal woman."

Maryn lifted her head, her heart lurching. "What did you say?"

Dagda gave her a significant look. "He's claims he's declared you his queen."

"You've spoken to him? He's . . . he's okay?"

Dagda laughed. "He's full of fire and making demands. Hasty, fools, men in love."

"You mean he—he's *alive*?"

"Oh, quite alive, I assure you, and eager to return to you. I thought it best to come speak to you myself first. Get all this mess settled."

Maryn forgot to breathe, her mind whirring. Arawn lived. He wanted to give up his godhood for her. Joyous relief flooded her heart. "But how? I saw him fall."

"Only paralyzed for a time by Morrigan's poisoned arrow. His subjects took him away against his will. Once able, he came to me."

Maryn's relief softened the joints of her body. Her breath clouded in front of her. "Where is he? Can I see him?"

Dagda frowned and rubbed one long finger across his chin. "I can't bring you to my halls as you are." He shot her a sideways glance. "The problem," Dagda continued, "is *you*, Maryn." He pointed to the wilting blackberry her blood conjured, flitting in the wind. "As descendant of Brigid, you are an excellent choice to govern Spring."

Maryn laughed. "Me?" She stared at him. "You're serious."

"Who else could have conjured this plant in the dead of winter?"

Her mouth worked like a fish. "Well, the hammer lent me some strength—" She trailed off, flexing her hand where the cut still smarted across her palm. She'd purposefully used her blood to try and save Brigid. Her gaze lifted to the crumpled form of the goddess, at the strength of the plants that had sprouted with such force from her blood. In the end, Brigid had saved Maryn and the rest of the world.

Maryn stared at her struggling sprig. "I don't know how to rule and," he met his gaze, "and wouldn't ruling restrict me from seeing Arawn and my family? According to your edict after Brigid's sin, I would be stuck in Spring Court until the feast days."

Dagda lifted a brow. "Do you think Arawn knew anything about ruling a kingdom when he became Death? Governing comes with time and practice. Besides, you'll not be without support. You'll have help from me."

She might have smiled at the idea of New Employee Orientation from the All Father but her mind was too intently focused on the matter of separation. "And my other concern?"

Dagda sighed, gazing at the fallen goddesses. "It might be time to relax my decree."

Maryn's heart leapt with hope. If she agreed, she could have it all. Well, except the career she'd loved.

"You'd be the first of your kind," Dagda said. "A co-ruler of Annwn, and the goddess of spring at once."

Maryn blinked at him. "Wait, what?"

"You're the queen on Annwn, so says Arawn. Do you wish to relinquish your place by his side?"

Maryn shook her head. *No, never.*

Dagda smiled. "Once your duties as Spring are fulfilled, I don't see why you cannot return to Annwn."

Hope and relief spiraled through her. "You'll teach me about my powers?"

Dagda smiled. "Of course. But don't take too long to decide. Cailleach is growing impatient."

Maryn's heart pounded. Spring goddess *and* queen of Annwn. How could she ever pull it off? Even as she questioned herself, something within her, some hidden primal part of her blossomed to life. Brigid's blood flowed through her veins. Magic sparked in her belly, a turn of excitement that raced along her limbs. She reached out a trembling finger toward her blackberry sprout, which seemed to stretch toward her, eager to meet her touch.

Maryn stroked a curled edge. Golden light radiated from her fingertip, much like sunlight. The little sprig shivered with some keen delight and grew another inch, the brittle leaf turning supple.

Such a small thing, her touch, yet in its aftermath, the earth groaned awake. It stretched beneath her, a curious movement of spirit rather than body.

She'd always considered spring a gentle thing: soft rain and sleepy apple blossoms, the subtle turn of dormant things going green.

She'd been wrong. Spring embodied the violence of stored life bursting from a seed, of desperate strength, struggling to break free of the earth's crust. Spring expressed itself through the agonizing labor of a child's first breath and a mother's sigh of relief. Spring was *power* and it pulsed through her veins. It surged through her frame, making her shake with the sensation.

She pulled away from the plant with a gasp, her wide eyes going to Dagda's.

"You see," he said. "Magic lives in your blood. You *are* Spring. What do you say?"

Maryn pretended to consider. "Mmph, I accept on one condition," she said.

"Oh? What's that?"

"I get to bring my cat, Darcy along."

Dagda's booming laugh echoed through the meadow.

Chapter Forty-Four

Spring

Dagda buried Brigid in her temple, deep beneath the surface, her bone blade nestled in her folded hands. Just as Maryn had found her weeks ago.

Brigid's vengeance, borne of her blood, devoured what was left of The Morrigan. The vines, writhing and curling around the goddess's body, fell still only after nothing remained of her. Dagda wiped the destruction away with a wave of a hand, his eyes full of sorrow.

"You'll need your own totem," said Dagda. "Something representing you."

Maryn could not think of what she might use. The tools of her trade ruled her old life. She thought of Arawn, of his flaming sword, of Cailleach's hammer, of Morrigan's bow. Even Brigid's totem, the blade, was a weapon.

"Must it be destructive?" she asked.

The All Father considered. "It must draw blood. Your own and that of your sisters," he added, seeing her disappointment. "There's power in blood."

The Morrigan had said as much as she prepared to murder Brigid.

Maryn frowned. "Uncovering lost history ruled my life. What can I do with a brush or a trowel?"

He smiled. "Much," he said and pulled from the very air, an ivory spade, delicate yet strong. It gleamed in his hands, etched with runic symbols that curved along the sharp edge.

"What does it say?" she asked, her eyes wide.

"It says, 'If lost, please return to Maryn.'"

She laughed. She couldn't help it. "No really. What does it mean?"

He pointed to the curling, strange images. "It says, 'Blood is wordless memory.'"

It seemed like a profound statement, but Maryn hardly possessed the capacity to ruminate on it right then. "What now?" she asked, taking hold of the trowel. It sang in her hands, a vibration of energy twanging through her body. Her skin erupted in gooseflesh. This totem felt differently than Brigid's blade or Cailleach's hammer. The trowel, made just for her, seemed to speak some secret language only she understood.

Build, it said. *Awaken. Heal.* She ached to trust it in the soil, to plant and grow things long in slumber.

"'What now?' you asked. Now we make you a god."

He drew a circle in the air with a long forefinger. The center of his doorway fell away, dissolving like wet rice paper. The rim of the hole sparked with life, a crackling filling her ears. Bright sunlight poured through the tear in the world. He gestured to it in a "after you" gesture.

Maryn, trowel in hand, hammer at her waist, climbed through the portal, her breath held. A few weeks ago, she never would have so brazenly stepped into the unknown. The time for uncertainty was far past, however. Her future lay before her, a shining beacon of happiness ripe for the picking.

A green field met her, spicy with the aroma of flowers. A white circular building sat across the expanse of the field, a glittering dome ceiling topping it. She turned her face to the sun. It seemed a lifetime since she'd known its warmth.

She felt rather than saw the All Father's arrival. The portal shrunk, then closed with a sound like rushing wind.

"Arawn is just there, probably wearing a thin spot in my rug with his pacing. Come, let's put him out of his misery."

Maryn placed her totem carefully in Arawn's cloak pocket and followed Dagda through the grassy meadow, rife with the scents of summer.

The inside of the structure surprised Maryn, making her wonder when she'd stop finding herself astonished. She'd expected a throne and doting subjects. Instead, and beyond all reason, a large tree with silver and gold leaves filled the vertical space. The floor, a white marble with an inlaid mosaic design encircled the wide, rough trunk. A runner, a deep blue trimmed in gold, cut through the stone.

Rapid footfalls sounded from the opposite side of the tree and then Arawn was there, pulling her roughly against him. He squeezed her so tightly she lost all her breath, but she held on, desperate relief coursing through her.

He loosened his hold, allowing her to spy his wound. The Morrigan's arrow had expertly and against all odds, found a weak spot under his arm. Dried blood soaked his exposed tunic and caked the crevices of his armor where it ran down his ribs.

"She hit me right as I lifted my sword," he explained, looking Maryn over carefully. "No holes in you, I hope."

"No holes," she said, shaking her head, joyous tears stinging her eyes. "When I saw you fall from your horse—"

He did not let her finish her sentence. He kissed her soundly, wrapping his arms around her waist. She forgot what she'd meant to say after that.

Dagda cleared his throat. "I hate to rush you, but I'm sure Cailleach would welcome respite, not to mention the rest of the world."

They reluctantly pulled apart. Dagda busied himself pulling leaves from the tree, three glittering, veined verdure that caught the light. He held them out, palm flat. Arawn selected one and placed it into his mouth. Dagda did the same. Maryn, eyeing them both, took the last and copied them.

The leaf melted on her tongue, tasting like sun-ripened pears. The tree and the columned walls grew hazy, as if viewed through a heat mirage. She turned in a circle, watching their surroundings dissolve. The blue rug under her feet gave way to an obsidian glass dais. White walls became rough, natural rock, close and dark.

Light poured in from the ceiling. Maryn looked up, astonished to find that instead of a glass ceiling, an open circle of sky met them. A bowl of a dormant volcano.

"The fires of my forge have long since died away," informed Dagda. He motioned with his arm around the space, to the uneven, sloped walls. A large bellows, as big as a Volkswagen, waited alongside one wall, a giant anvil adjacent. A table laden with tools, covered in ashes and a century's dust, sat not far away.

So much Maryn saw before her attention turned to the cauldron set before her. Half full of black liquid, the circle of light from above reflected in its surface, Dagda's Eternal Waters seemed to whisper to Maryn. It called to her in an unheard language.

A fire sprang to life under it with a whoosh that made Maryn start.

"What is this place?" asked Maryn, blinking away the spell she'd been under.

"This is the womb of the world and all that lives upon it," said Dagda. "Stand here, if you please," he said, motioning her closer to the black mouth of the large pot. It rose to mid-thigh and was large enough to fit all three of them inside.

"I don't have to get in there, do I?" she asked warily.

Dagda laughed and shook his head. "No, my dear. You need only drink from it. Doing so will make you a god." Dagda pulled a horn cup from his side, capped with gold, and offered it to her.

Maryn took it carefully, afraid to drop it. Polished to a sheen, the curved horn cup weighed her down, like a paperweight for a soul.

"And I just—" she mimicked scooping the horn into the water.

"Yes," said Dagda. "If that is your will."

Maryn instantly found Arawn's eyes. His gaze, soft and sure, told her everything she needed to know.

She dipped the edge of the cup into the water, breaking the surface into dozens of ripples. The whispering grew louder; the water steamed as if boiling, but Maryn barely felt its warmth.

She lifted it to her lips, sniffing. A hint of sulfur—normal for a volcano she supposed—and tossed her head back. The liquid effervesced, popping and sparking on her tongue and then it was gone. She'd swallowed the Eternal Waters.

"I don't feel any—" she said, then stopped short. Warmth spread through her middle, building and growing until it spilled into her arms and legs. Heat bloomed into her toes, her fingers, and her scalp. She stared at her hands, thinking that her eyes deceived her. They must be tricking her. The scar on her thumb joint from an accident in the kitchen long ago disappeared. It faded away as if it had never been.

Her hair, short and jagged as it had been, grew long, falling in a cascade over her shoulders, rich and full. Her insides felt different, too. Somehow, the knot of anxiety she'd lived with for so long and hardly noticed ceased to exist. A lightness pervaded Maryn so that she thought it a wonder she hadn't floated through the ceiling yet.

She stared at Arawn, then Dagda, eyes wide. She patted herself down, feeling both herself and decidedly *not*. "What's happened?" Her questing hands found her face. She wished for a mirror.

"You're still you, Maryn, just perfected," said Dagda.

"She was already perfect," quipped Arawn as he pulled her in to a hug. He kissed her softly. "My lovely queen," he whispered. "How do you feel?"

Maryn couldn't find the words. *Amazing* seemed woefully short. She settled on, "Weird."

Arawn brought her to the North Mountain temple, where a sleeping Cailleach waited, bundled in a bear rug. Durvan greeted her with a harumph, full of quiet agitation. She'd expected nothing less.

He seemed completely unphased at her change from mortal to Goddess of Spring, his sole interest being the ritual that would end his mistress's season so she could finally rest.

"Took yer time in coming, I see," said Durvan, though she thought she saw his mustache twitch with a budding smile.

Arawn carried the shrunken frame of Cailleach, furs and all, to the cavity in the rock. The temple guardians, the wulvers, greeted Maryn with excited yips and hops. She rubbed their thick coats, scratching behind their ears. "I'm happy to see you, too."

Arawn laid Cailleach upon the ice altar at the mouth of the cave and motioned for Maryn. She removed the hammer from her belt, placing it in the crook of the goddess's left arm. "This belongs to you," she whispered, stroking hair from Cailleach's papery forehead. "I'm Winter's Handmaiden no longer, as you can see."

Maryn pulled her own totem from her pocket, liking the surge of connection that came with it. Her trowel, while not sentient, certainly gifted her with a sense of relief whenever she held it. Dagda had instructed her briefly on the simple ceremony.

"Crone, mother, sleep now. Rest. Be the maiden when you awaken. Spring is come." Maryn lifted her trowel and held tightly to Cailleach's bony thumb with the other. "Sorry," she muttered, carefully slicing the meaty part of Winter's palm. Cailleach didn't even flinch. Bright red blood marred her withered hand, coalescing into a fat line. She stretched out Cailleach's arm so that the drops would fall into the snow at Maryn's feet. Beads of her life's blood dripped, pattering onto the ground.

Maryn then sprinkled mallow sweet seeds into the snow over Cailleach's sacrifice, her breath held. The tip of the trowel burned her skin as she pressed it to her palm, an icy scald borne from Winter's blood marring its surface. She pushed the tip until the sharp point of the totem broke skin.

Maryn's Magic erupted through her, an unseen trembling of power that raced to her self-inflicted wound. She smeared the pearl of blood across Cailleach's lips, staining them crimson. The stark contrast between her wan face and her painted lips startled Maryn. She'd grown so frail, like a corpse.

Cailleach's eyes fluttered under heavy lids, her lips parting on a sigh. And then she laid still. Maryn stared. *Is that it?* She pressed her ear to Cailleach's chest, searching for a heartbeat. None came.

"She's at rest," said Arawn softly beside her. "We'll return her to her chambers, but first you must awaken the earth."

Maryn bit her lip, replaying in her mind the instructions Dagda had given her. She left Cailleach and ducked into the cave, seeing there the pool of lamentation. She dipped her thumb in the icy water, watching as tendrils of blood spiraled into the clear liquid. She next grabbed the nearby creel and scooped up her offering. Miraculously, as it had done before, it held water.

Without the cave, basket in hand, Maryn tipped it so that the water dribbled into the snow. "Awaken," she commanded.

Setting the vessel aside, she retrieved her trowel and broke through the crusted ice and snow. Below, the waiting earth rejoiced as Maryn worked the blade of her totem into the soil.

A bird fluttered overhead, sending a cascade of snow from a branch.

Maryn smiled. "Spring begins."

Epilogue

The two-story, white-washed cottage nestled against the green hills reminded Maryn of the childhood home she'd shared with her grandparents. The front garden, lush with colorful foxglove and cheery chamomile beckoned to her.

She smiled at Arawn, anticipation filling her. "It's perfect. Just what I'd imagined."

He squeezed her hand, his gaze sweeping over the cobblestone walkway. "Very quaint."

"Lolly and Pop's house wasn't quite so idyllic, of course" Maryn chattered, "what with the mole holes that were likely to turn your ankle."

A shaggy dog trotted down the steps, greeting them with a wagging tail. Maryn gasped and knelt, throwing her arms around its grey neck. "Duff!" she exclaimed. It licked her face, making her laugh.

The red door swung open and her grandmother appeared there, younger than Maryn recalled ever seeing her in life. Grey hair gone, Lolly's dark curls fell to her shoulders, full and rich.

"What's the stramash—och, is that you, Mare?" Lolly said with a gasp. "Gerald, Maeve, come quick! Maryn's come at last!"

Lolly exited, wiping her hands on her apron, followed closely by her grandfather. Even Pop's eyes smiled. Maryn swallowed happy tears and fell into Lolly's embrace. She even smelled the same, like freshly baked bread and rose water.

Maryn pulled her grandfather into their embrace. Pieces of herself, bits she'd thought long lost to her, resurfaced, and knitted themselves back together. Joyous relief filled her frame, so much so, that she didn't know if she could contain it all.

The soft exhalation from the stoop pulled Maryn's eyes.

Mum.

Lolly and Pop's arms loosened their hold. Maeve stared at Maryn, confusion giving way to shocked delight.

Perfect and whole, unencumbered by illness, Maeve seemed to shine from within. Her mother rushed to her, pulling Maryn into a tight embrace. Maryn could hardly recall the last time they'd hugged, but the familiar hold of her mother overwhelmed her senses. Her mum, the only person in the world entire who could love Maryn so well, trembled in her arms.

She broke down in sobs, clinging to her mother's neck. They stood there in the yard for long minutes, both weeping, before they pulled away.

Her mother wiped Maryn's tears with the pads of her thumbs and lifted onto her toes to kiss Maryn's forehead. "My sweet darlin', come at last."

"Oh, how we've pined for you," said Lolly, similarly glassy-eyed. "We've been waiting as patiently as we could."

Maeve stroked Maryn's hair, her eyes lingering over her features. "You've grown up so beautifully." The soft look in her eye filled Maryn with such love she thought she might burst.

"We're all so proud of you," said Lolly, contentedly watching their reunion.

Pop, recognizing that Maryn didn't come alone, went to shake Arawn's hand. He offered him tea and cake inside. Lolly and Maeve beamed at Maryn, then Arawn. "Yes, do come in," said Lolly. "We have ever so much to catch up on."

Arawn graciously agreed, smiling softly at Maryn as he followed Pop toward the stairs. Lolly took Maryn's left arm while her mother took her right. Sandwiched between them, Maryn thought she could never be happier. The relationships she'd longed for had not been lost. They'd picked up, right where they'd left off, as if no time had come between them.

Lolly nudged Maryn, pointedly looking at Arawn's retreating form. "I can see ye've no' been faffing about in our time apart."

"Aye, very braw," agreed Maeve, her eyes dancing.

"I suppose he'll do," said Lolly, winking.

Maryn laughed. She agreed. *Yes, he'd do quite nicely.*

"I'm so glad you've come," said Maeve. "I've missed my girl. You'll have to catch us up on all that's happened since we last saw each other."

Maryn couldn't help but laugh. Where to start? "Well, keep the kettle warm, then. There's lots to share."

"Och, we've time, Lassie!" said gran as they climbed the steps. "We've all the time in the world."

The End.

Also By

Other books by J.C. Wade include:

The Fate of Our Sorrows: a prequel novella
Carlisle, England
-1287-

Join Edyth in this prequel novella to its companion piece, The White Witch's Daughter, as she navigates the complexities of self-discovery, only nine short years before her life takes a most devastating turn.

Nine-year-old Edyth DeVries does not know she's different. She does not yet understand what fate has in store for her. But after a terrifying nightmare becomes a reality, she questions who she is, and what her visions could mean.

A Conjuring of Valor: Book Two
1296 Scotland:

In the village of Perthshire, Edyth Ruthven finds that life as the new mistress of the household is not as comfortable as she'd hoped. Rejected by her husband's people as an outsider with a dangerous reputation, Edyth struggles to make a place for herself amid the rampant rumors of her past.

What's more, Edyth struggles to make sense of her nightmares, forewarning of a deadly event fast approaching. When her only friend and good sister Caitriona is forced into an arranged marriage, the full weight of a divided and prejudiced people falls upon her shoulders.

Ewan, meanwhile, walks along the edge of a twin blade, forced to choose between loyalty to his own people or to embrace the English King. When a nefarious sheriff is appointed to their lands, the life the Ruthvens had hoped for unravels before their very eyes, leaving them in a tangle of wicked machinations set forth by the wicked sheriff.

A Storm Summoned: Book Three

From twice nominated Whitney Award finalist, J.C. Wade, the thrilling true history of Scotland's first fight for independence comes to life in this, the final installment of The White Witch's Daughter trilogy.

1297

Scotland

A Storm is coming.

While England's king conscripts Scotland's sons for a war not of their making and his sheriffs tax and repress a burdened people, the seer Edyth Ruthven foretells of an uneasy future. Even as King Edward's fist tightens around Scotland's nobles, a whisper of rebellion spreads.

The world holds its breath as the very fabric of a divided kingdom is held together by conspiring men. Men who know well at what cost freedom is won. For Ewan and Edyth, life has taken a difficult and uncertain turn. But political machinations would be nothing if Edyth was not also navigating a difficult pregnancy.

Iain, meanwhile, is thrust into the midst of a treasonous act all while traversing a new and unwanted relationship. As Iain and his betrothed, Alice

Stewart, work toward mutual compromise, their burgeoning relationship is put to the test.

Last, Cait, who has always craved action, learns that getting what you wish for is not always so sweet. With the escaped fugitive, Andrew Moray, in her new home, Cait no longer must listen at doors, but is she ready for what is surely to come?

With new alliances comes unfamiliar territory, thrusting the Ruthvens into treacherous waters. Can Ewan navigate his scattered family through the clashing swords and scheming hearts that pervade the political landscape? Can Edyth's efforts keep her men alive and free?

If you'd like updates on current works, sneak peeks, and free books, you can join J.C. Wade's monthly newsletter here, or by contacting her via email at: contact@authorjcwade.com

About the Author

Jalyn C. Wade is an American author who currently lives in northern Virginia with her husband, three sons, and two cats. Married to a military man, she has had the great opportunity to move often and fall in love with people of all walks of life. Her works merge multiple genres, featuring elements of historical fiction, romance, fantasy, and adventure. She has been a public educator—specifically a teacher of the deaf and hard of hearing—for most of her career but has dabbled in creative writing her entire life. Outside of writing, Jalyn also enjoys gardening, painting, kayaking, and spending quality time with her family.

Acknowledgements

Winter's Handmaiden could not have come into existence without my dear friend, Kristal Winsor. On a visit in June of 2023, we sat down together and came up with a wild writing experiment (We're crazy like that, partying in a way only book nerds can understand.). The plan: using the outline we created, we'd return to our separate holes and write the book. Once complete, we'd compare how wildly different (or strangely similar) our manuscripts had become. It didn't take long before our mutual outline was thrown out the window.

The experiment reiterated a lesson for me that I learned years ago; Kristal is my person. She talks me off ledges, gives me frank, useful advice, and has my back, no matter what. I should also thank Rob, her husband, for reading parts of the manuscript and for sharing his wife's time with me.

Many others helped to make this book what it is, namely my lovely beta team: Tresha Beard, Heidi Dyre, Jessica Blackwood, Kathryn Schultz, Vereen Kennelly, Michelle House, Laura Carver, and Debbie Calderwood. Thank you for your feedback, your pointed questions, your praise (because we all need that from time to time), and for your willingness to wade through the unpolished version of Winter's Handmaiden.

Thank you to the women in my ANWA critique group, Paige Edwards, Kyla Beecroft, Cindy Hale, and Ellie Whitney. You've helped to shape me into a better writer.

I also need to thank my three editors (yes, three, so if you find any mistakes, kindly ignore them and remember we're all human here.). Christina

Richins, Kelly Horn, and Ellie Whitney, thank you for your insights, your keen eyes, and for putting your talents to use on my book.

Thank you to my husband, who takes over the bulk of parenting while I'm holed away in my office, tapping away. Thanks for your reassurances, for your belief in me, and for holding space for me when I'm overwhelmed. I love you. I'm one lucky girl.

Author Notes

The wulver legend cannot be discussed without first talking about its origins. In Shetland in the 1890's, a man name Jakob Jakobsen (how about that for a name?) collected place names in the area, many of which began with "Wol-/Wul-" (being Old Norse in origin). Jakobsen, who knew his stuff, said these names meant "fairy", and so places were then given such charming names as "Fairy Hill" or "The Fairy Knowe" by the locals.

Fast forward a bit to the time of Jessie Saxby, a folklorist with a vivid imagination with no qualms about embellishing a story. Not feeling that the origins of these colorful place names derived from boring Old Norse, she invented a story she felt worthy of a fairy tale. Claiming that he was rather fond of fishing, she said he was known to "sit fishing sillaks and piltaks for hour after hour." Thankfully, he was a benevolent creature, as she'd seen him frequently leave fish on window sills of those less fortunate. Saxby's wulver, unlike my own, had the body of man, all covered in hair, with a wolf's head. And there you have it: Saxby the wulver.

The song, "Donald Where's Your Troosers" was written and performed by Scotsman Andy Stewart. Sources say he wrote the song in about ten minutes while he sat in the bathroom of a recording studio. It's entertaining and catchy so it's no wonder that it was ranked 17th in a poll of the UK's favorite comic songs in 2009. Check it out online.

Made in the USA
Middletown, DE
08 April 2024

52680619R00241